# Praise for This Is How It Begins

WINNER OF THE 2017 MAUREEN EGEN WRITERS EXCHANGE
AWARD FROM POETS AND WRITERS

"A gripping and sensitive portrait of ordinary people wrestling with ideological passions."

—KIRKUS

"In this remarkable novel, Joan Dempsey brings together contemporary America and Holocaust-era Warsaw to tell a riveting tale of family secrets, civil rights, and the persistence of memory. Here are pastors and politicians, teachers and activists, historians and spies— all of them, on every side of the cultural divide, imbued with genuine humanity. *This Is How It Begins* is an essential story for our time."

—Matthew Goodman, *New York Times* bestselling author of *Eighty Days: Nellie Bly and Elisabeth Bisland's History-Making Race Around the World*

"Joan Dempsey's debut novel explores the limits of empathy and the unpredictability of violence. Thoughtful people who reach opposing conclusions are at the all-too-human center of *This Is How It Begins*, a prescient road map for our times."

—Mary Rechner, Author of *Nine Simple Patterns for Complicated Women"*

"Joan Dempsey's spellbinding novel illuminates how the tides of history repeat themselves with different characters. When a group is targeted for discrimination there will be resisters and rescuers, but mostly bystanders. *This is How It Begins* superbly demonstrates the clandestine nature of rescue, and the irony that those who ought to be rewarded for their conscience and courage remain hidden, and live in fear. Reading this moving adventure compels us to bear witness to the past and present and think about our own complacency to everyday discrimination in our midst."

—Eva Fogelman, Ph.D., Author of the Pulitzer Prize nominee *Conscience and Courage: Rescuers of Jews During the Holocaust*

"Dempsey brings her characters to life with equal parts empathy and tough-mindedness, from the three generations of the Zeilonka family—refugees, artists, politicians, teachers—to the pastor and radio host striving together to remake the United States into a Christian nation. A riveting story of the clash between LGBT and fundamentalist Christian cultures, and the way its violence reawakens historical trauma, this striking debut is essential reading for our times."

—Judith Frank, Author of *All I Love and Know*,
a Lambda Literary Award Finalist

"Into these tumultuous and politically polarized times comes a beautifully wrought novel that plumbs the roots of bigotry, hatred and intolerance. *This Is How It Begins* makes it clear that we have been down this road before and we ignore the lessons of history at our own peril. A riveting, immensely satisfying read."

—Bill Lundgren, co-author of *Becoming (Other)wise:
Enhancing Critical Reading Perspectives*

"Joan Dempsey's debut novel is a compelling story that seems to rise out of the rancor of current national headlines—about hate, bigotry, and intolerance. The story has deep roots in the darkness of the horrific persecution and betrayal of Jews during World War II. Twin story lines—then and now—illuminate how close we yet remain to the hellish cauldron that fear enflames."

—Frank O. Smith, Author of *Dream Singer*,
a Bellwether Prize finalist

"This exquisitely drawn and timely novel will remind you why we have freedom of expression, ideas, sexuality and religion, and leave you wondering why we're so quick to forget the lessons of the past."

—Paddy Murphy, Material Pictures

# This Is How It Begins

# This Is How It Begins

## A Novel

### Joan Dempsey

SHE WRITES PRESS

Published 2017
Printed in the United States of America
ISBN: 978-1-63152-308-3 pbk
ISBN: 978-1-63152-309-0 ebk
Library of Congress Control Number: 2017939857

For information, address:
She Writes Press
1563 Solano Ave #546
Berkeley, CA 94707

She Writes Press is a division of SparkPoint Studio, LLC.

*For Bert*

*It's long been a point of mine that the freedom of religion, which this country alleges to support, works two ways. We're not only free to practice the religion of our choice, we should be free from having someone else's religion practiced on us.*

—John Irving, *Keene Sentinel*, March 26, 2007

*If we take the capsulation of minorities within the nation-state as a given condition, the implication of the Holocaust is that the life and liberties of minorities depend primarily upon whether the dominant group includes them within its universe of obligation; these are the bonds that hold or the bonds that break.*

—Helen Fein, *Accounting for Genocide*

*Danny would have thought it comical if it had come from any other source, on any other day, in any other country. But Curtis had come to the table with something they'd never expected, something they would have thought outmoded and outlived in the modern age: a kind of fundamental righteousness that only the fundamental possessed. Unfettered by doubt, it achieved the appearance of moral intelligence and a resolute consciousness. The terrible thing was how small it made you feel, how weaponless. How could you fight righteous rage if the only arms you bore were logic and sanity?*

—Dennis Lehane, *The Given Day*

# Part I

# 1
# The Roslan

In her favorite gallery of the Baldwin Museum in Hampshire, Massachusetts, Ludka Zeilonka spun around to face her honors class, fast enough that one of the young men gasped. She staggered backward and flung out an arm, ostensibly to make a sweeping introduction to Alexander Roslan's most famous painting—*Prelude, 1939*—but in truth to brace a hand against the wall to avoid falling. Ludka was keenly aware of how she appeared to others, not because she was vain or insecure, but because she was long accustomed to the consequences of casting particular impressions. In this case—a dazzling and hip, if ancient and somewhat tough professor.

In a stage whisper too loud for the museum, she demanded that they tell her what they see. This was unfair. She wanted them to see what *wasn't* in the painting: legible signage, playful children, well-stocked grocers' bins, churches, and eye contact among the ordinary people going about their lives. On loan from the National Museum of Warsaw, the canvas was as long as a train car, as tall as an average-sized man, and the street scene painted on it covered two city blocks, one of which was dominated by a synagogue.

The Roslan depicted what could have been any European city, but Ludka knew it was Warsaw, not only because Roslan had still lived there in '39, but because Ludka had, too. Without the title you could miss the point altogether, but that was part of Roslan's genius, part of what made him a master; the prelude was the true invasion, incremental and insidious, possible anywhere.

Ludka still felt a bit off, and in the guise of stepping back to get distance from the painting, she moved past the students and sat carefully on a tufted black leather bench. Will, a tall and talented junior who'd been exceptional enough as a painter to get into her graduate class, and who'd made himself known to her on the first day by pumping her hand as if she were a wrestling coach—a welcome if somewhat jolting occurrence after so many years of assumed fragility—stepped up to the painting and squinted at the adjacent title mounted on the wall. His jeans were tight and too short, very Eastern European and a refreshing break, Ludka thought, from the hanging bulks of denim slouching around campus. He absentmindedly flicked a finger back and forth along the half-dozen silver rings that cuffed his left ear as he ambled along the length of the painting.

"I see Will in the way," someone said. A few students laughed.

"The color is something," said Will. "It doesn't fit the mood."

Ludka nodded, then glared around at the rest of them. They said the usual: the light and shadows, the realism—*it could be a photograph*—the way you could almost hear the violin from the street busker, although they didn't use that word. The young busker looked so eerily familiar that Ludka often wondered if she'd seen him in Warsaw back in '39, playing near the merchants' stalls in Rynek Starego or by the central fountain among picnicking families in Ogród Saski, or if he was simply another manifestation of Roslan's genius, a sort of everyman who touched those who cared to see him.

Although they tried so hard to sound erudite, none of her students saw beyond what was obvious, and she just kept asking until every one of them stopped trying to impress her and finally fell silent. One painfully quiet, solitary young woman—Sophie, who dressed more plainly than the others—gave Ludka hope; Sophie hadn't stopped staring at the Roslan and hadn't reacted to her classmates. The girl seemed a bit stricken, and that was appropriate.

"Yes," Ludka whispered in her direction. Sophie appeared startled.

To the rest of the class Ludka said, "Now that you have stopped the guessing of what I might like to hear . . . *see*."

Because this was an honors class, and because her frank approach made them think they were finally getting what they signed up for, they shuffled closer to the Roslan, squinted and strained. Annika, a skinny young woman wearing only a T-shirt and jeans, who always underdressed for the cold to showcase the tattoo sleeves on both arms, followed Will's lead and slowly walked the length of the painting, getting alternately closer and farther away. Sophie clutched her purse strap and closed her eyes. Ludka wanted to press her, to get her to tell these *dzieci* a thing or two, but for all Ludka's blustering she was not a teacher who put students on the spot. Sophie's hand strayed up to her throat and touched her buttoned cardigan as if she were toying with a necklace, which was, in fact, what she was doing. The gold cross was a new addition in the past year. She tucked it away only on campus.

Annika crossed her arms, cradling her elbows in her cupped hands. "Nobody's smiling," she said. "Not one person."

"And no one's carrying a book!" said Will. "What's up with that? In 1939 there should be at least one book, no?"

Ludka was shocked she'd never noticed the absence of books. Thus, she felt a fondness toward Will and immediately began to ponder Roslan's possible intention—clearly something to do with the imminent murders of the Polish intelligentsia, to which her parents had belonged. Ludka closed her eyes against the sudden pulsing of the cavernous room's pale walls. Even as a young woman she'd felt light-headed in museums, and she'd fallen in love with many a painting after latching on to it, a visual horizon from her unsteady boat. At the start of today's class she'd had to latch on to the Roslan to avoid alarming the students, an alarm she'd seen on the faces of those who'd beckoned her back from the dissociative episodes she and her husband, Izaac, were optimistically calling her reveries. The first time she'd had one, sitting in the garden at home last summer, Izaac had summoned her, his face inches from her own, and when she surfaced, he sank into his rocker, breathing as if he'd climbed the stairs to the attic. It had taken her a moment to realize he'd been calling to her in Polish, a rare departure from their decades-old covenant to speak English in America.

"Was I muttering?" she asked. Izaac shook his head.

"Again I was fifteen," she said. "Like yesterday."

They'd sat side by side, looking at the morning glories and the field and wetlands beyond, he wondering how much his heart could take should she precede him, she wondering if this was how her mind would go, if one day she'd no longer hear the summons.

Now Ludka praised Will for noticing what wasn't on the canvas, and then the murmuring began as the students finally started to talk about what Roslan had left out.

"Always," she said, "I imagined Roslan had two studios, one for all his omissions."

"What if he painted it all," said Will, "and then covered it?"

"Ah! Now here is idea!"

She stood abruptly, remembering caution too late, and swayed for a moment, thin calves pressed into the edge of the bench, wool shawl clutched against her throat, gaze tethered to the Roslan. These were some of the teaching moments that made her happiest, when someone like Will shook her out of her own limited vision. She couldn't fathom that she'd missed this in her research, but imagine if it were true, if one could tease off the outer layer and read the signs and see the books and fill the empty grocers' bins! She could see why Roslan might go that route. Carefully she stepped away from the bench, and suddenly Will was beside her, commandeering her by the elbow, hustling her forward. Had he been anyone else, she would have tossed him off with a hiss, but she could sense his actions were more pragmatic than decorous, fueled by his desire for quick companionship to scrutinize the work. A not unpleasant aroma of warm wool arose from his threadbare peacoat, along with a hint of stale sweat. Once in front of the painting, he released her so gradually she knew he'd let go only when he stepped away and bent down to inspect the street busker's violin case. She searched for evidence that the missing books had been covered, and while she found none, she did marvel that she'd never noticed their now obvious absence, there in the cocked arms of the stooped old rabbi, for instance, or in the idling hand of the fey young man she'd always thought of as a poet; he reminded her of her father, a sculptor who'd been stronger than this young man, but possessed of a similar other-worldly sensibility.

"No evidence of covering," said Will. "Let's go with the two studios theory."

"There's a synagogue . . ." Sophie seemed surprised she had spoken aloud, and glanced at Ludka, who nodded at her to go on. "But there isn't a church?"

"Why do you think synagogue and not church?"

"Because it's a Jewish neighborhood," said Will.

"Or maybe," said Sophie, tentatively, "Mr. Roslan was anti-Christian? It's not uncommon."

"I can see that," said Ashley, a chunky girl who excelled at oil portraits.

"I know, right?" said Sophie. "I don't really see any evidence of God, do you?" Her hand strayed again to her neck. Ashley gravely shook her head.

"God?" said Will. "Seriously?"

"Well, there's no joy. Anywhere."

"What's joy got to do with God?" said Will. "So they're not joyful, so what? Would you be? It was 1939. They were about to get the crap bombed out of them. It's got to be about the church's collusion with the Nazis. That Rome turned away from the Jewish people, and, by the way, from the gypsies and Poles and mentally ill and disabled and"—here Will drew quotes in the air—"homosexuals. So, no church. But not *no God*."

*Bravo*, thought Ludka.

"But not all Christians colluded, right?" said Sophie. "So it's got to be more about Mr. Roslan's perspective? I think maybe we should consider that he might have wanted to paint a city without Christians. He was a Jew, right? And the Jews did kill Jesus."

"Seriously!" said Will.

Ludka felt a quickening near her heart, the flush of a once too-familiar adrenaline. She pulled the wool shawl farther down onto her shoulders and thought about returning to the bench. Why had she worn quarter-length sleeves on such a cold February day?

"And there are homosexuals," said Sophie, lifting her chin toward the painting. She said "homosexuals" as if the word tasted bad.

"Meaning?" said Will. He considered the painting. "Those two guys? Seriously? I would have said scholars, but as you like it."

"I don't like it. I just noticed it."

Ludka pulled the shawl more tightly around her.

"Who has something else to notice? From the rest of you, I'd like to hear."

She hurried back to sit on the bench. She fruitlessly tugged her sleeves down past her elbows, marveling again that these were her forearms, with brown and reddish splotches daubed along the length of her papery skin. Only the pale underbelly, with parallel aqua veins running from her wrist to the crook of her elbow, was a ghost of the color of the fair skin she thought of as her own.

Ashley sidled over toward Sophie, the scuffing of her boots resounding in the cavernous space. She smiled shyly, and laid her hand for a long moment on Sophie's shoulder, an unusually intimate and uncommon gesture for two strangers this early in the semester. This didn't raise Ludka's suspicions at the time, overshadowed as it was by Sophie's distasteful tone when she spat out "homosexuals," but later she would remember how easily and instinctively they'd joined forces and cite it as the moment in which she began to have concerns about them both.

What Ludka admired most about *Prelude, 1939* was that it

captured the insularity of the people, the way they had so clearly huddled into themselves, individually or with one or two loved ones. There was no eye contact among any of them, not one glance, with one notable exception—the poor busker searched the faces of the passersby, pleading for even the briefest of connections. He got nowhere, and to Ludka's mind his raised bow, jaunty with hope and forever suspended above his tilted, empty case, was the epicenter of the whole tragic painting.

Will asked if he could escort Ludka back to her office, and when they arrived, the art department's administrative assistant flagged Ludka down as she unlocked her door.

"Message."

Ludka pushed open the door, circled her desk, where she dropped her keys and soft leather satchel, and began to unfasten her black wool cape. Will tossed his backpack on some papers piled on a chair and turned his attention to her bookshelves.

"Stanley Brozek," said the assistant. "Doing research on Polish artists from the World War II era. Looking for information on someone named Apolonia?"

Ludka froze. *Attention, Ludka, uwaga!* She fought the sudden gravity that threatened her bowels, that demanded she collapse into her chair. Unbidden, a dormant instinct honed to an art form nearly seventy years ago arose and assumed command, demanding she carefully compose her expression and glance as if nonchalantly out the window. No one in the quad seemed out of place.

"Take this, young man." She cleared her throat. "Hang it there."

Will took her cape and hung it behind the door. Ludka sat abruptly, betrayed by her old knees. She thought furiously, scanning her memory for a Stanley Brozek, hands anchored on her desk, fingers splayed and immobile, an old trick to steady herself, to curb instinctual rash action, to disguise anxiety. Sixty-three years since she'd been addressed as Apolonia, even by Izaac, who, like her, had shrouded certain pieces of their history in silence. The assistant handed her the note. Ludka didn't trust her hands not to shake, so she flapped them impatiently at her in-box and cemented them again on her desk, a sudden damp sweat apparent in her palms. Will eagerly scanned the spines of her books. The assistant laid down the message and inched out the door, clearly anxious to be on her way.

"Specifically, he inquired for me by name?"

Ludka could hear the alarm in her voice, and when the assistant nodded, she rushed to cover it up, saying she would phone him on Monday. The assistant walked off, wishing them both a good weekend.

Will pulled a book off the shelf and leafed through it. "Can I borrow this?" He showed her the book, an introduction to abstract art in America, and suddenly she wondered who, exactly, he was. She searched his eyes, dark blue behind the narrow rectangles of his wire-framed glasses, and gave him a fierce look. He shifted his attention to the window behind her, then back to the book in his hands.

"There is library. From here, books disappear."

He didn't shy away, just smiled and slid the book back into its place. Unlike a lot of young men his age he stood to his full height, just over six feet, shoulders back, head high, an open and confident young man.

"Who's Apolonia?"

"Please, I must work!"

He seemed puzzled, and tugged the rings on his ear. She softened. He was a boy who liked art, nothing more. This was 2009, she must remember. A lifetime had passed. He knew nothing.

"I'm looking forward to seeing your collection," he said. "When is that, next week? You have a lot of abstract art, right?"

"From today, five weeks. The thirteenth of March."

He smiled and shouldered his backpack. "Want me to close the door?"

Ludka nodded. As soon as he was gone, she hurried to lock the door, then took hold of the cord on the venetian window blinds. After another scan of the quad she tugged to release the brake. She didn't hold tightly enough, and the slats came clattering down onto the sill, and this was when she began to shake. She twisted the clear plastic rod, and the slats pivoted in lockstep, obscuring the last of the day's sun. Ludka lowered herself carefully into her chair and took hold of the message. A California number, which of course meant nothing. He could be a continent away or outside in a car with his cell phone. Either way, he was too close.

# 2
# Apolonia

In front of a wide fireplace, built by hand more than two centuries ago with stones extracted and hauled by horses from the nearby Adams River, Izaac was turning a page of the *New York Times* when he heard a car coming swiftly down the driveway.

More than forty-eight years ago, late one winter night when they'd been living in this house only a week, and their first son, Lolek, was an infant, Izaac had woken in a panic. Ludka had heard a truck coming down the driveway and was shaking him, calling him Krzysztof Wincenty, the Polish name she had assigned him in 1940 when she'd spirited him out of the Warsaw ghetto to keep him hidden in her family's apartment from the Nazis. They were to use this name at all times, memorized with the fictitious life story of a Catholic cousin from Krakow. Izaac's real name had been forbidden, but Izaac chanted it, silently and incessantly, knowing even at ten years old that a person could willfully disappear. He'd never stopped incanting his name, even after reclaiming it in blotchy ink on the immigration papers on New York harbor's tarry dock, even after influential journals had given him countless bylines that had catapulted his civil rights career, even after he'd been elected attorney general. At eighty years of age, Izaac murmured it still—the way a more religious man might murmur his prayers: *My name is Izaac Szymon Rosenberg, Izaac Szymon Rosenberg.* But that first week in this house, hearing "Krzysztof Wincenty" in the dark bedroom, Izaac had sprung to attention and, like Ludka, had heard the rumble of a Nazi truck before he remembered where they were: America, postwar. It had snowed. The neighbor with his plow had kindly come to open up their driveway.

Now, all these years later, he still started when cars approached the house at unusual hours. He deftly closed the paper and folded it into quarters, leaned well forward and pushed off the arms of his chair to get himself up. His stature had collapsed with age and he slumped a bit, not burdened with a full-blown dowager's hump, but pitched enough to sling back his elbows for balance as he shuffled in his slippers to the back entrance hall. He eased aside the curtain covering the narrow window that flanked the door, just enough to peek out: Ludka, home unexpectedly early. He pulled open the door and waited behind the storm door, frigid air emanating from the glass. He held the paper in both hands behind his back. Ludka parked the car so it was facing back up the long driveway. Izaac frowned; it was customary to pull into the garage.

Ludka got out of the car, her spiked black galoshes clomping one at a time onto the dirty ice, her subsequent steps slow and cautious, left arm clutching her satchel's shoulder strap, the other cocked and held out to the side, as if reaching for a handrail. When she got to the door, he pushed it open. The cold air felt fine after the heat of the fireplace, and in it he detected the smell of oncoming snow.

"What's wrong?" He scrutinized her face. "What is it?"

"Let me in, Izaac."

His shoulders tensed. He stepped aside. Ludka unfastened her cape and hung it on one of the brass hooks they used in lieu of the coat closet, which they'd converted to storage for their paintings. Her eyes darted past him. She rapped her fist on his chest and gave him a little shove.

"Right, right." He gave her some space. She sat down in a straight-backed chair next to the door and bent over to unzip her galoshes.

"You're driving me to drink, here, *kochanie*. What is it?"

"No drinking! I need your wits. Someone has come looking for Apolonia."

He would have expected an icy dread to descend at this exact moment. He had, in fact, in the early years, conjured that very feeling countless times by imagining such a scene as this, preparing for its inevitability. Now that it had arrived, he realized that the dreadful weight of anticipation that had burdened him all these years had been a misplaced concern, a habitual, unexamined holdover from another lifetime that should have been laid down the minute he stepped onto American soil in 1950. In this country, nothing could touch his Ludka, not back then, not now.

"Stanley Brozek. I'm wracking brain, Izaac. Who is he? This name is ringing a bell, but I cannot place it."

Izaac tapped the paper lightly against his thigh. "I don't know. Come."

He tossed the newspaper on top of her galoshes to offer Ludka his arthritic hands, which were still good enough for leverage.

"Take a breath, kochanie, and come with me into the kitchen.

I'm going to have a little drink and I suggest you do, too. One drink won't shatter our wits. Come now."

In the kitchen, while Ludka related the story of Brozek's phone call, Izaac took a bottle of Belvedere out of the freezer and poured two small measures into crystal shot glasses. Ludka stooped to see out the pass-through from kitchen to dining area, scanning the view out the three-paneled French doors into the yard and field and wetland beyond, all of which were only palely illuminated by the mild light reflected from the snow. She had a vague sense that she was being overly alarmist, but she'd wound herself up tightly enough that she couldn't begin to tease loose her more sensible mind. When she straightened up, the kitchen cabinets above the pass-through obscured her view and she hit the closest cabinet once with the side of her fist, rattling the dishes inside.

"Already we should have torn these down. I've told you years and years and still you haven't done this. How can I see? I break my neck, craning."

Izaac gently took her hand, and put a shot glass into it.

"Look at me. Tell me what's troubling you about this Stanley Brozek. Do you think he is some grudge-bearing Polish partisan or communist anti-Semite come all the way to Hampshire, Massachusetts, to persecute an old Jew-lover like you? This is not postwar Poland. The Ministry of Public Security has not found you out and come to shoot you. Who cares anymore about an old woman who rescued some Jews? This is decades beyond, this is America. Be reasonable. Even with the Nazis they just extradited—I read it in today's *Times*—the Germans want to move on. 'Whispers of enough,' the paper says, and they're talking about Demjanjuk! If no one wants to prosecute Demjanjuk for what he did at Treblinka and Sobibor, no one's going to care about you defying the Nazis. Brozek's probably a scholar, studying Polish art. He must have come across your sketches. He's not skulking around in our garden, ready to break down our door. It's a ridiculous notion."

"Is that it? Is lecture over?"

Immediately she regretted her acerbic tone. Those sketches were the last she'd ever done, and she didn't want to think about that. She did sound ridiculous, she knew, but Izaac did not know everything. She took a drink of the vodka, and the spreading warmth brought the promise of calm. Izaac leaned against the counter and closed his eyes, and Ludka felt her muscles begin to drain of the adrenaline that had propelled her for the last hour.

"No one will ever know I did sketches."

"I'm not so sure about that. They found the archives shortly after the war."

"I know this, Izaac, but it makes no difference. I did not sign them, only I tagged them with an *A*. Who would even know to trace them to Apolonia, much less to me?"

"Maybe Brozek is finally the excellent scholar who's putting two and two together."

She hadn't considered this. If Brozek were to ask her outright if she was the artist, what would she say? She drank her vodka too fast; it hurt going down. Her greater concern, though, was that Brozek might suspect what else she had done. But even if he did suspect—and she hadn't yet thought of a way this would be possible—he was far more likely to visit her at the office than he was to invade her home.

"I am ridiculous old woman, Izaac, you know this. This Brozek will want to stir the pot."

"Maybe it's time the pot got stirred. Maybe it's time. And if it isn't, if you really don't want Brozek to know you're Apolonia, don't let him. It's simple: tell him you know nothing and he'll go away."

He tossed up his hands as if dispatching a carrier pigeon. It amused her that she hadn't thought of this simple solution, and then with a sudden and immediate clarity she knew why—she was wildly eager to learn what Brozek knew. She smiled at Izaac and thumped him on the forearm, not yet aware of the next thought that was pushing its way forward, that wouldn't manifest until later tonight when they were in bed, lights off, Izaac lightly asleep: Stanley Brozek could be Oskar.

# 3
# At St. Hedwig's

If Oskar had even survived the war, he would be eighty-six by now, and he certainly wouldn't be at St. Hedwig's for Sunday morning service. Nonetheless, as Ludka slowly walked the length of the nave, she checked each pew, studying all the unfamiliar old men, trying to reverse the years to see who might emerge as her former comrade. All day yesterday she had berated herself for leaving the phone number sitting in her in-box, and told herself that one more day after all these years wouldn't matter. And while it was certainly possible that Stanley Brozek was Oskar's given name, the name Ludka had never known, it was far more likely Stanley Brozek was a perfect stranger.

She took her usual seat three-quarters of the way into the third pew on the left, as always leaving room at the end for her older son, Lolek. He was the most powerful state senator in Massachusetts and came home from Boston to the district each weekend to attend church with his mother and Marta, his wife. In earlier years, their two children had come, too. Lolek and Marta always came in through the east entrance, and Lolek led them straight through the transept up to the crossing, so it would appear as if they were trying to slip in unnoticed, which of course never happened. Ludka herself didn't use the more convenient east entrance because she liked to walk all the way down the center aisle; Professor Zeilonka wasn't too high and mighty to attend mass, even if she never volunteered in the kitchen. At St. Hedwig's, as in every other Polish church, this was akin to sacrilege, and the other women gossiped about her, making things up in the absence of information, something about which Ludka was aware but stubbornly shoved from her mind. They complained to each other that she could do more to preserve their heritage than decorate her traditional *pisanki* Easter eggs each year, a serious accusation given Poland's history of being repeatedly butchered by invading armies, the pieces divvied up among the occupiers like so many cuts of lamb. It was critical Poles stick together, and for these women the best way to persevere was through simmering pots of *bigos* or boiling *pierogis* or baking a pan of *klopsiki*. They had only a vague idea that Ludka had already accomplished far more in the eyes of historians for the preservation of Polish culture than centuries of church bazaars. Ludka was also, of course, married to a Jew, and not just any Jew, but the first Jewish attorney general in Massachusetts, something most people, including Izaac himself, could hardly believe had come to pass. But Izaac's predecessor had not been an honest man, which opened an unexpected midterm vacancy. Izaac's prominence, then, coupled with their influential son, put Ludka in a league of her own.

There was a stir from the people nearby, and Ludka knew that Lolek and Marta had arrived. She felt a little start of excitement to see that Tommy, her grandson, was with them. He was thirty-six, an English teacher at Adams River High School, but Ludka still saw him as an overgrown boy, with soft skin and his father's large ears and misbehaving hair. When he saw Ludka, he lifted his chin in acknowledgement and moved past his parents. Lolek was shaking hands, with Marta tight-lipped beside him, looking as if she'd rather be anywhere else. Tommy genuflected and slid into the pew next to Ludka, put an arm around her, and kissed her cheek.

"*Babcia!*" he said.

Ludka regarded him quizzically. Tommy only ever came to church at Christmas and Easter. He withdrew his arm from her shoulders.

"I could stand to pray." He avoided eye contact. "Miss me? How's *Dziadzio?*"

"Dziadzio is Dziadzio, happy at home with his *New York Times.*"

Tommy smiled like this was the best news he'd heard in a long time.

"I'd love to wear a cape like this," he said, fingering Ludka's sleeve. "Wouldn't that be so dashing? I'd have to move to London or Paris. Or maybe New York. They'd drum me out of Hampshire in a heartbeat."

He sounded sullen, and his right leg bounced up and down. Ludka laid her hand on it and he stopped, sighed, and lowered his head as if in prayer.

"What's trouble?"

Tommy pushed his fingers under his round, wire-rimmed glasses and rubbed his eyes.

"After mass you will come back to house. Tell me and Dziadzio." Tommy nodded.

The congregation had filled in behind and around them, and the church resonated with rustles and murmurs, the cadences of English and Polish all blending together. St. Hedwig's was a glorious church, classified as a minor basilica, in deference to St. Peter's in Rome. Ludka had chosen it not only for its Polish congregation and its beauty, but because it reminded her so much of the church in which she'd grown up: Bazylika Archikatedralna święty Jana—St. John's. Gray marble columns flanked St. Hedwig's nave and held aloft the intricately carved arches—sky blue and gilt-edged—that crowned the clerestory and framed its stained glass. In the sanctuary, just above the priest's chair, rose a large painting of the famous Black Madonna of Częstochowa, and when the sun hit it just right, at this time of year usually toward the end of the Eucharist, the Virgin Mary and her holy son shone as if a brilliant sun had risen before them. The church had weathered a lot since its erection in 1889, including a near schism during the Second World War that almost closed its doors, and a fire in 1991 that destroyed enough to make the renovation more like a rebuilding. The fire wasn't caused by ancient wiring as everyone suspected, but by an arsonist who hit more than one church in the area and was disappointed when he saw mostly thick black smoke billowing from St. Hedwig's, not the flames he had imagined licking at the feet of Christ on the Cross. In fact, once the damage was assessed, Ludka and Izaac's younger son, Frank, who had been a volunteer firefighter at the time and was now the fire chief in the nearby city of Huntsfield, wondered if perhaps it was a miracle that Jesus was untouched despite the char and ash all around him. Then his mother told him the legend of the painting of the Black Madonna of Częstochowa, how back in the twelfth century, in its first home in Jerusalem, its holy presence was said to have saved the church from fire. Frank had momentarily considered returning to his mother's church, the church of his childhood, but quickly caught himself—the shadow of his brother had already been too heavily cast at St. Hedwig's. Ludka had long since given up on bringing Frank back, although she still missed his weekly presence in what she thought of as the family pew.

Now the organ increased in volume, and the people quieted. Ordinarily this was the time Ludka would close her eyes, working to keep in check her deepest yearnings for her home country, yearnings that inevitably arose from the familiar ancient mass and the murmurings in Polish. But today Ludka kept her eyes open. She craned her neck, searching in every direction until Tommy gave her an inquiring look, at which point Ludka methodically studied the backs and sides of every old man's face she could see without turning around.

Marta settled into the pew and leaned across Tommy to smile at Ludka. Lolek genuflected and crossed himself, groaning inwardly as his hips and thighs pushed too tightly against the fabric of his pants, as his waistband pressed into his gut. He took off his overcoat, draped it over the end of the pew, and then reached out a hand toward Ludka, palm down. He flapped his fingers.

"*Dzień dobry, Matka.*"

"*Dzień dobry,* Lolek."

And then Father Skurski was there at the altar, and everyone stood and made the sign of the cross.

"In the name of the Father, and of the Son, and of the Holy Spirit."

After murmuring *Amen,* the congregants were meant to turn inward to reflect on their own relationships with God, as channeled through the ages-old liturgy and the presence of the priest. Some of them still missed the lyricism of the Latin and wished the sign of peace that interrupted their reflections had never been instituted, but Ludka was not one of those. She believed strongly in offering her hand to others, because despite personal experience littered with examples to the contrary, despite the pessimism of history, she was still at heart an optimist who wanted to believe that even a small connection like a proffered handshake could make a difference should push come to shove.

For Lolek, mass was the one hour in his week when he could retreat into himself and cease to be a senator, and for most of the service, except when he prayed, he took in only the church itself, not the faces of the people, not even Father Skurski. He had trained himself to relax into the cadence of the mass, the scent of the incense, and the beauty of the basilica. Today, though, because of his foul mood, he had trouble letting go. His son had just angrily dismissed him in the parking lot, and Marta had been utterly silent on the drive over. He felt too heavy inside his suit, his armpits stuffed tight with three layers of fabric from his undershirt, Oxford, and jacket. Next to him, Marta's eyes were closed, head tipped up, hands resting on the back of the pew in front of them. She wore her wedding band, engagement ring, and mother's ring with two birthstones all on the same finger, a bit crowded, Lolek thought. And what in God's name was his mother doing, glowering around at the crowd? He was startled to find Tommy eyeing him warily. Tommy quickly averted his gaze and faced Father Skurski.

"Lord have mercy," said the priest.

When it came time for communion, the organ music escalated and the whole family rose and moved in a line along the pew toward the center aisle. As Ludka stepped out into the aisle before Tommy, a man from the end of the pew behind them took hold of Tommy's jacket sleeve and held him fast.

"Don't you dare take communion," said the man, loud enough to compete with the organ.

*Brozek*, thought Ludka insensibly, and turned just in time to see Tommy pulling back against the man's grasp, trying to extricate himself, a panicked look on his face. Without thinking, Ludka reached out and smacked the man's forearm.

"Desist!"

"No need to make a scene," the man said to Ludka. And then to Tommy, almost conspiratorially, he said, "I heard all about you, son. Just sit back down."

People were peering around now for the source of the disturbance, and Lolek and Marta had crowded out into the aisle.

"Mr. Kulek," said Lolek. "What's this about? Is there a problem?" The man seemed surprised that Lolek knew his name.

"No problem, Senator." He let go of Tommy's sleeve, and the release catapulted Tommy's arm back across his own chest in an angry-looking gesture. Kulek circled around them and hustled forward to join the dwindling communion line. Ludka glared at him.

"And so it begins," murmured Tommy.

"What begins?" said Lolek.

Ludka gestured toward the altar, but Tommy shook his head. At first it seemed like he'd go back into the pew, but then he turned away and strode down the center aisle, trying—and failing—to walk as naturally as if the service had come to an end. The people were polite and tried not to stare, but most cast sidelong glances as he passed. Those who'd somehow missed the commotion admired the cut of his Gibson London jacket. One of his students pressed her hand over her mouth to suppress a giggle and elbowed her friend, who looked him over with obvious appreciation. Still others perceived it was all he could do not to break into a run. Tommy finally made it to the foyer. He ignored the holy water in its marble font, pushed through the enormous wooden door, and stepped out into the cold February morning.

The chill of the air outside felt almost warm compared to the stillness inside the church, and Tommy breathed it in, trying to calm himself. Less than a block away, a raucous group of people burst out of the wide entrance of the old Regent Theatre that five years ago had become home to the Hampshire Redeemer Fellowship. As if they were heeding a fire drill, the people quickly burgeoned into a thick and steady stream flowing out onto the sidewalk. Tommy squinted through the direct sunlight at the crowd, certain the superintendent of schools would be among them, the one person he wanted to avoid. He started down the stairs, but behind him the door opened and Ludka emerged, the spikes of her galoshes click-clacking on the granite. She detoured over to the black iron handrail to make her way down, and Tommy retraced his steps and offered her his arm.

"What the hell are the fundamentalists putting in their sacramental wine?" Tommy inclined his head toward the crowd. "I didn't think the old Regent could hold that many."

Ludka gave the crowd a passing glance, then peered intently at Tommy, who was surveying the crowd as if they might attack.

"What's trouble?" She gave his arm a little shake. "Tell Babcia."

Tommy sighed, closed his eyes, and lifted his face to the sun. After a moment, he glanced behind him at the doors to the church and said, "He's not coming, is he."

Ludka shook her head. "But your mother already is right behind, after communion. We will wait here for her."

"The devout senator."

Ludka winced at his bitter tone but knew enough to keep silent.

Most of the fellowship's congregation were gathered in groups in front of the old theater or out on the sidewalk, and many others walked past St. Hedwig's, heading for the municipal parking lot less than a block away. Thigh-high piles of freshly shoveled snow bordered the sidewalks, and in the parking lot a group of kids clambered up a huge snow pile and pushed each other down, jockeying to be the next King of the Mountain. Ludka realized with some surprise that she didn't know anyone who belonged to the Regent—as she thought of it—although just then someone called hello, and there were Sophie and Ashley from class. Ludka gave them a little wave and they walked on, their heads nearly touching as they conversed.

Hampshire wasn't a small town, but it also wasn't so large that people didn't know each other, especially people affiliated with the university who'd been around as long as Ludka had, and she wondered where all these people had suddenly come from, and when. It seemed the old cinema was a hive full of strangers, disgorging its congregants into animated clusters; it unsettled her. Still, like America herself, Hampshire had a history of welcoming immigrants—most notably the Poles—and Ludka supposed that just like the Poles, the new people had fallen in love with the town and encouraged a surge of their friends to join them. Nothing wrong with that. The Poles, though, no matter which century, had come to America largely to escape something: unemployment, foreign occupation, Communist oppression, and ethnic discrimination. Ludka and Izaac were no exception. They'd looked with hope to America for safe harbor, and they'd found it. But what was the story with these people? They were not foreigners, but Americans. She pulled the edges of her shawl out of the neck of her cape and snugged them up against her chin.

"Will you come see Dziadzio, Tommy?"

"I've been fired, Babcia." Tommy spoke calmly, but she could feel him trembling. "I need to talk to all of you, back at the house. You'll need to be prepared."

# 4
# God's Warriors

Inside the recording booth in the old projectionist's room at the Regent, Warren Meck plucked a thumb drive out of the console and flipped off the final switches. He would upload the recorded sermon to his website as soon as he got home. The numbers of people who streamed Pastor Royce Leonard's sermons had swelled by the tens of thousands in the last five years, and sharing the videos on Meck's website had been instrumental in marshalling support for their campaign, as well as providing a fivefold increase in Meck's radio listenership.

Out in the hallway, he buttoned his navy sports jacket and pulled on his camel hair overcoat as he trotted happily down the broad staircase to the gold-leaf-festooned lobby. Even after five years, Meck could still feel the initial excitement from when Pastor Royce had recruited him to lead the statewide effort of the national campaign to restore America to its Christian roots. Sitting at the right hand of one of the most important Christian leaders in the country while leading an educational campaign of this magnitude had been the greatest challenge and honor of

Meck's life. So far the effort to unburden the Christian kids from the homosexual agenda that pervaded the public schools had progressed exactly as they had envisioned, and to win Massachusetts under Pastor Royce would mean Meck could move his mission— and his radio program—to the national stage. It also meant he could continue working with Pastor Royce, and Meck could think of nothing he'd rather do more. Soon they would head into the campaign's final phase, and Meck's confidence was high.

He scanned the crowd for his wife and boys but didn't immediately see them. Whit Hammond, the man Meck had five years ago considered a capable colleague and who was now his dearest friend, saw Meck coming, smiled broadly, and swept his arm in a wide arc to encompass the size of the milling crowd, which slowly moved its way toward the exits.

"We'll need a stadium before too long," said Whit, when Meck reached him. "Getting to be a fire hazard in here, all those people standing in the back."

Whit was an imposing man, especially next to the unusually diminutive Meck, who stood only five foot four and about whom everything was small except his uncommonly large voice. He'd never quite gotten used to people's shocked expressions when they heard him for the first time, the way they'd snap back their heads, then awkwardly try to recover. It wasn't until he'd found his place in radio that he learned of the power inherent in modulation.

Whit leaned down and whispered.

"We need to talk. Immediately."

Meck felt a flutter of anxiety, and asked Whit what was up.

"Not here. Green room."

Meck looked again for his family and found them—most of them—at the refreshment table. Jill, even smaller than Meck but just as fair-haired, was pouring a cup of juice for their middle boy, John, who bounced up and down on his toes like an eager terrier about to be fed. He hadn't stopped moving since the day he was born eight years ago. Andrew, the five-year-old and their youngest, stood with his back to the table, chewing studiously on a plain donut as if it were the most important meal of his life, seemingly oblivious to the crowd around him. Ben, as usual, was nowhere to be seen. Meck felt a sudden and profound sense of well-being, and wished he could join them for their usual Sunday brunch instead of hearing Whit's news. Jill smiled when she caught his eye. Meck gestured to Whit and mouthed for her to go ahead home, he wouldn't be long. She nodded.

Whit and Meck made their way back toward the theater. Three senior boys from the high school basketball team, all standing tall in shirts and ties, stood between them and the theater doors. A gangly boy, Brandon Braddock, stepped forward and looked down at Meck.

"Sorry to bother you, Mr. Meck, but we were wondering. Would you say it for us? You know."

Meck could feel Whit's tension, but smiled up at the boys, squinted, and cocked his head, pretending to consider. The boys exchanged glances. Then, as if he were their coach, Meck beckoned them to lean down into a small huddle. In a slow, wavelike cadence, he said in a deep and gravelly voice, "You are on the air with Warren Meck." And then, in a lighter, almost whispered staccato: "Tell-it-like-it-is."

"Yes!" Brandon stepped back and pumped his fist. "Tell-it-like-it-is!"

Meck awkwardly mimicked Brandon's fist pump to cover an unexpected rush of emotion. That he meant something to these boys had been a surprise, and an ongoing source of joy.

"Are you ready for this one?" said Brandon.

He lifted his hands as if poised to play a piano.

"Come on now, Brandon," said Whit. "Even Mr. Meck needs a day off. It's Sunday."

"He's fine, Whit, we'll only be a minute. Go ahead, Brandon, give it your best shot."

One of the other boys whispered to Brandon, who nodded, repositioned his hands, and sang in a high, breathy voice:

"Even when the rain falls, even when the flood starts rising, even when the storm comes, I am washed by the water."

"Needtobreathe, from *The Heat*. 2007. Track thirteen."

"Encyclopedic! I told you guys. He's invincible."

"Easy one, though," said Meck. "Give me something more challenging next time; we'll see how I fare."

Inside the theater, Whit clapped a hand on Meck's shoulder. "They adore you, Warren."

"I don't know about that. I know they like the music."

"There's some false modesty if I ever heard it. Anyone who can make a call-in program that appeals to both adults and high school kids clearly has a gift. Take the compliment: they adore you."

Meck smiled. At the old green room's door, he unlocked the deadbolt and door handle. Meck and Whit both loved this room—the seat of power, as they thought of it. Meck loved it not only because of the incredible strategy they'd put together over the past five years from within its confines, but because other than the radio station it was here he felt most at home, which for him meant most competent. In front of one wall stood a mobile whiteboard on which was drawn a complicated flowchart with accompanying timeline. On another wall they'd fastened an enormous corkboard. Across the top of it stretched a red, white, and blue plastic banner: *Imagine America— Restoring Our Christian Nation*. Below it was a large group photograph taken about four years ago on the Regent's stage. Someone had written *God's Warriors* on a piece of scrap paper and tacked it up on the lower left corner of the photo. Another scrap said *Acts 29*, a metaphorical shorthand for their ongoing missionary work, which carried on beyond the 28th and final chapter of *Acts of the Apostles*. Meck's favorite Bible passage was one among many tacked on the bulletin board: "Train up a child in the way he should go, and when he is old he will not depart from it (Proverbs 22:6)." There were two desks, shoved face-to-face under the corkboard, both gunmetal gray with dented drawers and tidy surfaces, and a long dining table that seated twelve on the other side of the room in the area that used to house racks of costumes. They'd kept the old couch that came with the theater but cleaned it up with a new slipcover, on which Meck had insisted.

Whit closed the door behind them.

"You're going to want to sit down for this one, Warren."

Whit himself sat in one of the desk chairs, closed his eyes, pressed his large hands together as if in prayer, and lowered his face against them. Again, Meck felt a stir of alarm. He carefully folded his overcoat and laid it on the arm of the couch. He hiked himself up onto the dining table, tucked his hands under his thighs, and leaned forward. His yellow bangs fell over one eye. Whit bumped his head against his hands.

"They fired the Adams River teachers. Friday."

Abruptly Meck's energy fell away. Had he been standing he would have needed to sit. He gaped at Whit.

"Pastor Royce gave them the green light. He told me just before the start of the service. He's supposed to join us shortly."

Meck closed his eyes and shook his head, dumbfounded, the list of consequences racing through his mind like a line of cascading dominoes. He frowned and ran his flattened fingers across his forehead, drawing his bangs to the side. With his fingertips, he pressed them several times against his temple, as if he might make them stick. They fell back over his forehead. He sat again on his hands, breathing slowly to calm himself.

"Apparently, Arnie and Ed were both insistent," said Whit. "Pastor Royce said he didn't want to hold them off any longer. Ed's been getting increasing pressure from the parents, so he turned to Arnie. And you know Arnie—he thinks as superintendent of schools he's sitting at the right hand of God. They felt a responsibility to act sooner rather than later. Pastor Royce said they couldn't take the moral corruption one more day; he couldn't stop them."

"But he knows as well as we do the importance of the sequence! It was his responsibility to convince them otherwise. This is a serious problem, Whit. We're not ready, you know that. Besides, by law they're supposed to give ten days' notice before firing anyone. The teachers could be reinstated on that fact alone."

Meck's voice assaulted the room, banged off the metal desks. He dropped his head and closed his eyes. His fingers began to feel squashed, his wrists strained. Five years in the making, this campaign, and Pastor Royce had allowed a serious misstep to threaten everything, a misstep that could destabilize every one of their careful calibrations. He studied the whiteboard.

"I assume that was the only school?"

Whit shook his head. "Unfortunately, word began to spread, so a couple others immediately followed suit. I spent the entire service in here on the phone, trying to rein in everyone else. I think all told we're looking at up to eleven teachers."

Meck blew out a long breath, his smooth cheeks ballooning and deflating. "This undermines our entire strategy. Now they're going to argue discrimination, which dilutes our focus on the kids."

"Let's be honest, Warren—we've known all along they'd argue discrimination."

"Of course, which is precisely why the sequence was crucial, to minimize their opportunities for succeeding with that defense. It's one thing to argue against discrimination for one teacher, quite another for a whole group of them. Too many red flags. We were supposed to stagger the dismissals to attract less notice, he knew that."

The door opened and Pastor Royce walked in. Despite Meck's anger, his instinct was to stand by way of greeting, but he reminded himself to stay seated. Despite their years of working and worshipping together, and despite the pastor's deliberately strategic informality, Meck still leaned toward formality in the great pastor's presence, as if he were royalty, a holdover from Meck's childhood in Pastor Royce's first church. Meck had been a boy when his mother had gone to work for the pastor, and because Meck had never known his father, the pastor had quickly become a paternal figure; often, Meck still felt childlike in his presence. But Pastor Royce had convinced Meck that formality didn't belong in a relationship with as much history as theirs, and Meck had tried to acclimate to the idea of the pastor as a peer. Even so, no matter how many times Pastor Royce had encouraged Meck to call him "just Royce," Meck couldn't bring himself to do it. Now

Pastor Royce closed the door behind him, leaned heavily against it, and swept back his white mane of hair with both meaty hands. He left his hands on his head as he shook it.

"Warren, my friend, you are absolutely correct. I did know about staggering the dismissals."

He dropped his hands, pushed himself off the door, and trundled into the room. With a heavy sigh, he lowered his bulk into the desk chair opposite Whit. Last year, at age sixty-four, Pastor Royce had begun to put on significant weight. Now he wore loose-fitting, untucked shirts that draped over his jeans, but which did nothing to hide his ample stomach. He'd always made it a point to preach in comfortable clothing, believing it put the younger generation at ease.

Meck, now too warm, and still not trusting himself to temper his tone, hopped off the table and stripped off his sports coat. He threw it onto the couch and then, regretting the disarray, methodically folded back his pressed shirtsleeves to just below the elbow, exposing ropey forearms.

"I told Whit earlier, Warren, that I prayed on this all through the weekend, asking the Lord how I could have allowed myself to cave in to those men, knowing what I know. I feel deep contrition; I will say that. Deep, deep contrition."

He inclined his head and said each of their names, an indication that he was about to offer a private sermon, something Meck usually treasured. Today, he had to work to overcome his impatience. He rubbed hard at the back of his neck and quietly blew out a long breath.

"You know when you're a believer how you have two natures?" said the pastor, lifting his hands as if holding an accordion. "There's the believer, and then there's the prebelieving you, the one who wants to do what's easiest, what's most convenient, what will cast you in the best possible light, whether it's good for you or not. That was me, fellas, when facing Arnie and Ed."

He dropped his hands to the desk and briefly drummed his fingers.

"I felt the pressure they were under and I wanted to ease it, not— if I'm being honest—for them, but in order that they would feel grateful for my blessing, that they would see me in the best possible light. I'm reminded of Paul, in Romans, chapter seven, who doesn't understand why he acts the way he does, who doesn't do what he knows is right. I did wrong when I told Arnie and Ed to go ahead and dismiss those teachers. I know I did wrong. I am terribly, terribly sorry."

He held out his hands in supplication and shook his head, berating himself. Even when Pastor Royce sermonized, there was always an authenticity and humanity in his voice that never ceased to move Meck, as he was moved now. The pastor never shied away from admitting his all-too-human failings, and Meck found this made him all the more holy. Meck had long ago learned that emulating Pastor Royce in this regard made life a lot less complicated, and far more virtuous. Honest confession disarmed people, and also served to cleanse the confessor. Meck softened, and forgave him on the spot.

"What's done is done," said Whit.

Meck crossed over to the whiteboard, grabbed a red marker out of the tray, and smacked it into his palm. He repeatedly snapped the cap off and then on. He was nothing if not political, and despite his frustration he could feel the kick of gearing up for a new challenge. He reviewed the strategy map, and after a few moments brandished the marker at Whit and the pastor.

"Okay then. Game on."

"Atta boy," said Pastor Royce.

"Even when the flood starts rising," said Meck. "How many were dismissed from Adams River?"

"Three," said Pastor Royce, "including Senator Zeilonka's son."

"This changes everything, of course," said Meck. "No flying under the radar, no easy scores on Beacon Hill, no further inroads. Here's where the past five years get put to the test. Here's where we find out how committed these people truly are, how willing they are to become effective advocates."

"We've got a strong core," said the pastor. "Probably forty percent of the congregation, don't you think?"

"Sounds about right," said Meck. "But we're going to get pummeled by Zeilonka, and not only on the legislative front. He'll help his son—and his son's colleagues—when they appeal their dismissals and demand arbitration. We can't wait now on getting those students and their parents ready for the arbitration hearings. They'll need to be coached on two fronts: harassment leading to unequal educational opportunity, and threats to their right to free speech. We also need to fast-track at least one of those bills to the governor's desk, preferably 1298."

"I'll alert the parents," said Whit.

Whit rose and joined Meck at the whiteboard, towering over him. Pastor Royce pushed himself out of the chair and, like every great leader, Meck thought, stood out of their way and watched with gratitude as his best people worked through the problem. Before Pastor Royce, Meck had never experienced the empowering freedom of working for an utterly trusting supervisor. He prayed that when they won Massachusetts, the three of them would move together to the national stage.

"Here's what we do," said Meck. "We approach the ACLU, get the families to talk with them. We'll focus on having them testify at Zeilonka's arbitration hearing, for maximum publicity."

"You really think the ACLU will back us," said Whit, "when they could be defending the homosexuals?"

"You'd be surprised. Remember West Virginia State Board of Ed. v. Barnette? Supreme Court, 1943?"

Whit and the pastor both shook their heads. Meck wrote ACLU on the whiteboard.

"Barnette was the Supreme Court's first important freedom of religion ruling. The ACLU filed an amicus brief for Gathie and Marie Barnette. Jehovah's Witnesses, sisters. They refused to pledge allegiance to the flag, which was required by law for all public school kids. Their argument? 'It's against our sincere religious beliefs.' The vote was six to three in favor of the Witnesses."

"So they set the stage," said Pastor Royce.

"That's exactly right. The ACLU will be all over it. They've actually got a track record of supporting the rights of Christian kids in public schools. To wear T-shirts with religious or pro-life messages, to use Christian themes when they're assigned to choose their own topics, that sort of thing. One poor second grader in New Jersey was told she couldn't sing 'Awesome God' at a talent show; thanks to the ACLU, the federal district court told her she could. The ACLU of Missouri even spoke up for Shirley Phelps. Not a school case, but still."

"Phelps?" said Pastor Royce. "From the Westboro Baptist Church?"

"One and the same."

"How they can picket at soldiers' funerals and still call themselves Christian is beyond me," said Whit.

"Even so," said Meck, "the Constitution's on their side. The ACLU will think we're a walk in the park compared to Phelps."

Pastor Royce moved behind and between them and laid his heavy hands on their shoulders.

"Well then, fellas, it sounds like you've put together the start of a new plan. Let's work it now, shall we?"

Meck's earlier frustration was gone. Under the warmth of Pastor Royce's confident hand, and with Whit by his side, he felt renewed determination; there wasn't a thing the three of them together couldn't accomplish.

# 5

# The First Volley

Deep beneath the golden-domed majesty of the brick-clad State House, bearing the weight of more than two centuries, lay the land on which John Hancock had once grazed his cows, cows who routinely wandered down the brow of Boston's highest hill to the shores of the Charles River. One might wonder if they were uneasy one morning in 1795 about the unforeseen appearance of fifteen white horses who paraded up the hill and into the pasture, hauling a slab of granite to Governor Sam Adams and Grand Master of the Masons, Paul Revere, who ceremoniously secured it in place—the cornerstone of an august building that would bury the pasture and transform the city into the permanent seat of the commonwealth's government.

Inside the State House, sitting at the wide oak desk in the President of the Senate's cavernous inner office, Lolek massaged his forehead. Tommy's news had precluded any rest last night, and he'd finally gotten up at two-thirty to drive back to Boston. The early morning darkness still pressed in through the tall windows of nineteenth-century wavy glass, and he wished he could justify building a fire in the marble-faced fireplace, but they used it only occasionally for meetings and ceremonies. He could hardly call an ordinary Monday morning ceremonial, although he suspected the situation demanded a press conference before the end of the day and, given what was going on, it might not be a bad idea to host it here. The oak boiserie that anchored the walls with its precisely carved panels and scalloped decoration, the embossed paper ceiling, and the elaborate winged clock above the mantel tended to convey an aura of gravity that seemed to tame the media and elevate whatever Lolek said to State of the Commonwealth status. He'd been surprised by how immediately at home he'd felt within the grandeur of these Victorian sur-roundings. He loved the steep of history, the feeling that he was continuing the legacy of the eighty-six presidents who had served before him, some of whom gazed sternly from small portraits embedded in the oak mantel. The gothic desk, circa 1850, was broad and solid and practical, his favorite piece in the room, and sometimes, as now, early in the morning or late at night when few others were around, he would sit with his hands on its surface and study the portraits of the men who'd also touched it. He'd scrutinize their faces until he'd peeled off the veneer of history and reputation and myth, and seen them as the mere men they were, no different from Lolek, who felt the winter chill, whose hip ached, who faced a desk covered in bills that needed his immedi-ate attention.

It was far too early, but he could hear Aggie Roth, his chief of staff and favorite person in the building, already coming through the door of the outside office, making the usual noises that announced the start of the day: her bag thumping to the floor next to her desk, the *thunk* of her boots as she removed them one at a time, the soft vacuum sigh of the mini fridge door, the scrape of the coffee pot. He called to her to come in.

"Pretend I'm not here yet, Mr. President. Daily briefing's not for another two hours."

When he didn't respond with something witty as usual, Aggie poked her head into his office.

"Now that's the definition of a hangdog expression, right there." She stepped into the room.

Lolek had loosened his tie but still wore his wool scarf looped around his neck, his sense of decorum relinquished only outside of normal working hours and only in this private setting with Aggie, who'd been with him since the beginning and had seen it all. His hair, still jet black and thick at fifty-eight, stood up like the bent bristles of an old bottlebrush. His face was slightly doughy—more so this morning from lack of sleep—and his sideburns were a bit wider and longer than was advisable, which drew attention to the protrusion of his ears. He did not waste a moment of his time wishing he were more handsome.

"Good morning to you, too, Aggs. Sit down a minute, yes?"

From long habit, Aggie pulled out the chair across the desk that was closer to Lolek's left side. The hearing in his right ear wasn't the greatest, a result of some kind of allergy that intermittently flooded his eustachian tube. He tended to orient himself in the other direction, and a chronic ache in his left hip was the result.

Aggie leaned over the desk to inspect the bills. "Education Committee?"

"We've got ourselves a Trojan horse, Aggs. Take a look. Gauch filed it. Senate Bill 79."

Aggie felt a stir of excitement. She'd not heard Lolek call out a

Trojan horse for many years. Back then they'd coined the term to indicate the most worrisome bills, the ones that concealed possible hidden agendas, strategically buried "unintended" consequences should the bill become law. As a joke, Aggie had purchased a custom-made rubber stamp of an intricately carved Trojan horse and used it to mark such bills, but after a senior representative caught on to their code and made a bit of a stink, it was relegated to a place of honor on Aggie's desk, and eventually tossed into a drawer where it had languished ever since.

Aggie read the bill. "It's kind of genius, really, isn't it? Is this the only one?"

"I don't know yet; I didn't get very far. There's something else, though, Aggie. Tommy was fired on Friday. 'Conduct unbecoming,' they told him. He was one of three teachers at his school. Apparently, though, there were others in the district, I don't know how many. Looks like they've been laying the groundwork for some time."

"Oh god, Senator. Here we go."

She stood and scanned the bills, quickly deciphering Lolek's categorization. She collected them into one pile and began to page through them. "They can't have filed just one. I must say I'm a little surprised they'd be ballsy enough to target your son. Although I suppose it would have been obvious if they'd singled Tommy out by not giving him a pink slip. Plus, he's a guaranteed media platform."

As if on cue, the phone began to ring. Lolek and Aggie stared at each other until it went to voice mail. Aggie checked her watch and shook her head. "This is going to be huge."

"Call the rest of the staff," said Lolek. "Get them in here early."

Aggie nodded. "How's Tommy taking it?"

"Hard to say. He told me he's ready to contest it, that he and Robert talked it over and are prepared to do what it takes, but I truly don't think they have the first clue how much this could disrupt their lives. He laughed when I told him to install a security system."

What Tommy had actually said was, "You might think we're just a couple of helpless pooftahs, Dad, but now you'll be forced to take a second look."

Lolek didn't know at exactly what point Tommy had begun to resent him; he couldn't recall the last time they'd had an easy conversation. "I'm going over to Education to see if anyone's in yet. No doubt Gauch has lined up his troops. Let's find out who we're dealing with here. When you find the other bills, draft up a statement and some talking points, and I'll review them in fifteen. Oh, and call my son. Tell him not to answer the phone until he hears from me. In the meantime"—the phone rang again—"don't answer that."

He buttoned his double-breasted suit coat and headed out into the wide and empty hallway. Every heavy step resounded on the ancient marble floors and ricocheted off the iron balustrades lining the balcony above the Grand Staircase. Each massive stone stair had been sculpted over the centuries by an endless tide of parading statesmen who had given more of themselves than the average person could truly fathom. Few people understood what it truly meant to serve in public office. They saw the power and assumed it was glamorous, almost an aphrodisiac. They didn't know about the endless list of obscure bills, the constant dickering over small things, and how often you felt at sea because you had to be a generalist who knew just enough to converse with some semblance of intelligence after being briefed by your more knowledgeable staff. They didn't know about the brutal schedule—that there was no such thing as off duty, except for the wee hours of the morning when you rose in the darkness and drove alone in a state-owned car for a few blessed hours, radio off. "Thankless" was the word most often used by those who had done the job, and they complained continually about having no life and swapped stories of family strife and swore they'd finish out the term and quit, and then when it came time, there they were, making their families pose for photographs, running again in the next election.

Lolek passed the top of the Grand Staircase and walked up a set of narrow marble steps to the fourth floor, his energy increasing with each step. Tommy had not seemed scared, exactly, but bewildered; he'd always possessed an abiding faith in people's innate goodness, a faith Lolek himself had instilled and encouraged in his children and still, for the most part, believed. Tommy, however, had finally run headlong into someone else's differing definition of *good*, someone else's unwavering faith, and it pained Lolek that Tommy would soon discover what Lolek had learned his first year in office: a person's faith—however defined—could be as entrenched and unmovable as the granite cornerstone anchoring the State House itself; reason was powerless to budge it.

For Lolek, however, entrenched simply meant a greater challenge, and he loved a good challenge, particularly at this time in the legislative cycle, when a slew of them cropped up in every bill, each one needing a decisive strategy that fell into two general camps: kill or champion. Some bills he'd arrange to kill immediately, while others he'd have to tirelessly combat; some would die a natural death for lack of interest; and some he'd push into study committees where they'd languish forever, essentially dead.

The few bills he'd choose to champion he would shepherd along on their lengthy journey, nurturing small victories at each successive stage until he stood next to the governor, who signed them into law, when at long last they could finally begin their real work of transforming people's lives which was, after all, the point. Despite the often thankless nature of the job, there was nothing Lolek would rather do. It was true what people assumed about the power—it was fantastic.

In the Education Committee's modern, darkened suite, no one was at the reception desk, but beyond it Chairman Gauch's door stood ajar, light on, and Lolek called out so as not to startle him.

"Early to rise, then, Mr. Chairman?"

A chair scraped, and then Representative Gauch appeared in the doorway, a mug of coffee in his hand, silver-rimmed reading glasses anchored high on the bridge of his nose, which was long and thin, like everything else about him. He lowered his head and raised his eyes to peer over the top of his glasses, but they were on too securely and he squinted through them, not able to see Lolek clearly. He stripped them off and tossed them back into his office where they skidded across his desk. He strode out to meet Lolek.

"President Zeilonka! To what do I owe the honor?"

"Senate Bill 79, Steven. What have you got on file?"

"Why, yes, Lolek, I did have a nice weekend. How about you?"

Lolek smiled and offered his hand. Gauch had always been a worthy opponent, and even though they saw eye to eye on almost nothing, Lolek admired his political acumen and respected his work, which had always been evenhanded and ethical. Gauch shook Lolek's hand and turned on the receptionist's desk lamp, setting his coffee mug beside it.

"Unless Lori's reorganized again, the files should be just here."

He opened a drawer.

"You can't truly think SB 79 has a chance," said Lolek.

"Not ordinarily, no. But . . ."

He pulled out two accordion files, both thick with written testimony, and set them on the desk in front of Lolek.

"You've been busy," said Lolek.

"Not me. 79 is by request, a constituent of yours, actually. Warren Meck, you know him?"

"The radio host?"

"My son and I love his show. He's a legislator's dream. Well, *this* legislator's dream, anyway. He's pretty determined. Have your people get these back here before eight if you can. Nothing leaves Lori's suite. Get me in a heap of trouble."

Lolek lifted the heavy files, pressing them against his chest, an awkward bundle.

"Did you know my son got fired?"

"Not until it was over, Lolek. I'm sorry."

Lolek's feet felt too tight inside his shoes. Gauch met Lolek's gaze. Lolek hiked the files a bit higher up on his chest.

"A courtesy call would have been appreciated."

Gauch straightened his back, as if he were about to protest, but then he sighed and stared at his coffee. He knew he should share the testimony for the related bills. A goodwill gesture, the right thing to do. It was only a matter of time before some staffer of Lolek's would come to retrieve it.

"This one could get ugly, Mr. President. I want you to know in advance it's not personal."

Lolek gave a short laugh. "Listen to yourself. Even you don't believe that. This one's as personal as it gets."

Lolek had a fleeting thought of keeping the files in his office until noon, making Gauch sweat, but even as a freshman representative he'd known enough not to succumb to those juvenile urges. Still, the thought gave him a moment of mean-spirited pleasure. He stepped toward the door just as it flew open, nearly hitting him.

"Hey, whoa, sorry, Mr. President," said Carey Best, Gauch's top aide. "How goes the battle? Hey, Chief, good morning."

"Carey," said Gauch.

Best unzipped his black parka and looked eagerly at his boss, trying to gauge what he might have missed.

"Right. I'm out of your way then. Carry on. I'm in my office if you need me."

Lolek had never understood what Gauch valued in this guy, a shiny-faced, erect young man who thought compromise was something for "sissies." Best disappeared, and Gauch shrugged, knowing what Lolek was thinking.

"What can I say? He's always three strategic steps ahead. A little reining in now and then—small price to pay."

They appraised each other for a moment, as if awaiting a bell to send them back to their corners. Then Lolek thanked him for the files and walked out.

# 6
# The Chopin

It had been Oskar's encouragement that ultimately convinced Ludka to "liberate"—as she preferred to think of it—the world famous Mieroszewski portrait of Chopin from the Ciechomska's vacated Warsaw apartment after the Nazi occupation. Today the priceless portrait of Poland's most celebrated composer—the earliest known portrait—was officially classified as missing, just another of the innumerable confiscated artworks evaporated into a Nazi-riddled history. In reality it hung just there, above Ludka's dresser in Ludka and Izaac's bedroom. The painting, oil on a canvas not much bigger than an American-sized sheet of paper, was carefully hidden—even from Izaac—in a museum-quality frame, tucked behind another portrait by an unknown artist of a young woman glancing back over her shoulder. Affixed to the back of the frame was a folded note containing the precise location in Warsaw of the buried provenance papers. Oskar had gone back to the Ciechomska's weeks later to locate them. They were thorough, he told Ludka, a short list detailing each owner since the painting had left Mieroszewski's studio in 1829, ending with the listing for Laura Ciechomska. Oskar had carefully sealed them inside a glass vodka bottle, which he thickly wrapped in burlap, laid in a tin box, and buried one night in Ogród Saski, deep at the base of the oldest tree, one of the few in the park that had weathered the initial bombing. He had drawn her a detailed map, and only the two of them had known the location. At the end of the war, however, when Oskar had been missing more than a year, there'd been no possibility for Ludka to find them; the city had been razed. Nevertheless, Ludka had always imagined someone happening upon the box, a construction worker during the rebuilding, or a city gas worker or park gardener, someone with enough intelligence and initiative to recognize the papers' importance, who would do the right thing and turn them over to museum officials, who would understand, perhaps with a moment of joy, that the Nazis had not succeeded in stealing the Chopin, that someone else had rushed in to protect it. And then, of course, there was the prospect that Oskar himself had survived the war and unearthed the papers.

Only when Izaac went away—which he hadn't done for some time now—would Ludka take down the painting, open the frame, scrub her hands, don her white cotton gloves, scrutinize the condition of the varnish, check for dust and insects, and clean the painting when necessary. Over time she had built a small ritual around this act, and every time it brought her a calm and uncommon sense of security. Still, she often felt a vague uneasiness about the compulsive quality of this secretive ritual—and each time she became aware of the uneasiness, she suppressed it. Izaac regularly complained about her constant fussing with the dehumidifier and thermostat— "it's just a bedroom, kochanie," he'd say—but she'd shoo him away, pretending she wanted to keep the room allergen-free, and claiming credit for their good health. For all these years, and even though Ludka had been an advisor and contributor to the Commission for Art Recovery, which sought justice for victims of Nazi art theft, she had continued to tell herself she was doing what was right—keeping the painting safe. The Ciechomska family would have wanted her to save it, of that she was certain, and so her original notion of liberation continued to serve as a comfortable justification, a justification that should have become null and void the minute the war was over. She had always intended to return it to Poland, to hand it over with pride to some authority who would immediately appreciate the care she had taken, who would tell her what she'd always believed herself—that no one could have done a better job. But somehow, for reasons she didn't fully understand and didn't push herself to examine, she had allowed the days to pass, and then the years, and there it hung, a lifetime and a reputation later.

"Do you need me to zip up a dress, kochanie, or are you having a reverie up there? You're going to be late."

Ludka was surprised to find she was sitting on the bed in only her silk tank top, slip, and tights.

"Hold the horses, Izaac. And don't shout! Deaf I am not."

She put on her favorite black turtleneck, head first, then each arm. She fastened the hammered silver necklace Izaac had given her for their twenty-fifth anniversary, then sat on the edge of the bed to step into an ankle-length gray skirt, her customary winter attire. Another wardrobe standard: solid black ankle boots. She always kept her boots next to the bed, easy to step into the way Izaac stepped into his wool-lined slippers every morning, because you never knew when you'd have to flee, you never knew when those boots were the last pair you'd have for many years. It had gotten so habitual, the buying of sensible boots, their place on the old pine floor, that Ludka had long ago lost sight of her habit's origins, which had become like the floor's dark stain, so deeply ingrained as to seem its natural color.

Downstairs, Izaac stood in front of the French doors, newspaper clasped behind his back, watching three deer standing in the morning light beyond the garden at the edge of the field abutting the vast wetland waters, now covered with ice and snow.

"They love the salt lick, you see?"

Ludka stood next to him and felt the chill off the glass. The deer were beautiful. Healthy. When Lolek and Frank were toddlers, there had been only forest and field out there, and then one day a pair of beavers had arrived and resurrected the dormant wetland, drowning the forest in the process. Ludka loved the water but had never gotten used to the way the dead trees jutted up like so many standing chimneys in a bombed-out city. She rapped sharply on the glass. The deer lifted their heads and bounded off, white tails flashing. Izaac frowned, and Ludka shrugged.

"Too much trust."

He shook the paper at her.

"But they can trust us!"

She hurried into the kitchen to put something together to take for her lunch, and Izaac followed.

"You lure them, Izaac. How can they differentiate? They'll venture into one of our neighbor's yards and get heads blown off."

"*Niech to szlag trafi!* You underestimate their intelligence. This Brozek character has you all stirred up."

"Don't swear at me, old man." Ludka patted his hand. "Don't worry. I won't disrupt your salt lick. Deer will be back."

"You drive me to drink, I'm telling you. Here. Here's your

travel mug. And call Brozek this morning, will you? Clear up this mystery."

Ludka lifted the mug's lid, took a tentative sip.

"Already again with the ice cube?"

"You'll scald yourself. Cause an accident."

She gave him a little harrumph. She wondered when, exactly, Izaac's eyebrows had grown as white and bristly as his hair. They gave him a fierce expression that would have served him well when he'd been working. She secured the lid. Drinking tepid tea was simple enough, a tiny accommodation she could manage. She took a plate of sausage and some cheese out of the refrigerator.

"I'm worried, kochanie. I was up in the night, thinking about *conduct unbecoming*, which of course is a smoke screen. We know this. But the people don't know this, the parents; they'll quickly believe any accusations. We have to pay attention, not be too naive."

"It is misunderstanding, that is all. Abe will do the favor, take care of it."

"Oh, I'm sure Abe will do us the favor, it isn't that. It's just . . ."

He pushed a hand roughly through his hair. Ludka tried to wedge a couple of sausages and a large piece of cheese into a Tupperware container shaped like a slice of pie. She had to cut them into pieces and even then it was a tight fit. She used both hands to try to secure the lid but wasn't strong enough: ludicrous, but nonetheless true. Old age had proven to be an irritating exercise in curbing impatience. She handed it resignedly to Izaac, who muttered as he pressed hard around the edges without success, his arthritic fingers sharply painful. He still hadn't finished his thought, and Ludka glared at him impatiently.

"Tommy's trouble, Izaac, is far from decree. I know you are

thinking this, that this is like the decree, is like your father all over again."

Izaac frowned. He'd been nine when his father had been fired, had come home from the university in tears, not just the quiet, constricted tears of a man but the mucous-wracked weeping of a terrified child. Izaac hadn't yet understood what his father already knew: the Nazi decree that destroyed his livelihood was only the beginning.

With a savage push of both thumbs, Izaac finally snapped the last corner of the Tupperware lid into place. The center of the lid bulged. He rubbed at his thumbs.

"*Jezu*! Next time just admit you need a bigger container. I know it's not a decree, Ludka. Don't be ridiculous. I wouldn't be as concerned if Tommy's was an isolated case. But two other teachers from his school were fired, too. That changes the landscape significantly."

She flapped a hand dismissively and retrieved an apple from a basket on the counter.

"You and Abe will fix."

She put her lunch into a well-used paper bag and swiped a cloth back and forth across the kitchen counter. She didn't want to worry about the fact that there were others.

"I suppose you're right." Izaac spoke quietly, as if trying to convince himself. "I've already written up a request for the review. By law the principal and superintendent must review Tommy's case within ten days, but I expect that will be pro forma. Then we'll petition the commissioner for an arbitration hearing, which they also must grant and hold within thirty days. I suppose any arbiter worth anything will see what's going on."

"You see?"

She flapped the towel against his arm. The wall phone next to the refrigerator rang, and Izaac moved to answer it.

"Do not answer! Lolek advised."

Izaac gave her a look and picked up the receiver.

"Izaac Rosenberg."

He held the phone away from his ear.

"*Mój Boże*, man, don't shout! I can't make out a word you're saying!"

Izaac listened. He grew very still. Tightened his jaw. Ludka felt a stir of something she realized with surprise was not only a growing foreboding, but also a creeping doubt: What if *conduct unbecoming* wasn't a smokescreen? What did she really know about Tommy's private life? The voice continued its tinny harangue as Izaac carefully placed the receiver back in the cradle. His hand was trembling, but he regarded Ludka with determined eyes.

"I'm calling Abe."

"Who was it? What did he say?"

Izaac shook his head and dialed the phone.

"Do not attempt protecting me, Izaac. Nothing surprises. Nothing!"

He closed his eyes. She started to speak again and he held up a hand to silence her.

"Judy, good morning. It's Izaac Rosenberg. Is he in?"

# 7

# Stanley Brozek

Ludka stepped off the elevator, clumped out into the carpeted hallway of the art department's suite, and headed toward her office. She'd left Izaac in the midst of an animated conversation with Abe. Even in his baggy cardigan and wool-lined slippers, Izaac had sounded every bit the competent attorney general he'd been, and the creeping worry she'd begun to feel had subsided.

She stripped off her gloves and shoved them into her bag. Up ahead, the door to her office stood open. She frowned. Behind her in the open area of the suite, the assistant's desk was unoccupied, lights off. No one else but the cleaners had a key, and their rounds were long over. It happened, she supposed, that they sometimes forgot to lock up. As she got closer, she heard a soft cough from her office. She stopped, then crept forward as quietly as she could, her spiked galoshes making tiny tearing noises each time she lifted them from the carpet. She stepped boldly into the doorway and there stood a man, looking out her window, and as he turned, she experienced a terrible moment of disorientation, a floating sensation as if she had discarded the husk of her old body and was standing in another doorway in another time altogether, peering into the attic studio where she and Oskar had always met, because here before her was Oskar as she'd known him, here was Oskar at twenty-two. She closed her eyes to reset her mind, but when she opened them, he was still there, as solid as the desk between them.

"Oskar." Her voice was reedy, broken.

The man took a step toward her.

"So you *are* Apolonia! I'm Stanley Brozek. You have no idea how hard you were to track down. Oh, Christ, I'm sorry, are you passing out on me?"

He rushed around the desk and threw one arm around her back, just under her shoulder blade, the other under her elbow. He guided her into the desk chair, keeping a light hand on her shoulder. Ludka's vision cleared and she stared at him, unabashedly looking him up and down.

"Dear God."

She reached up and grasped his wrist, then took his warm hand in both of her own. Had he been closer, she would have laid a hand on his cheek. He was older than twenty-two, she could see that now, probably closer to forty, a faint tinge of gray in his beard stubble and spiked through his chestnut hair. And heavier, of course, softer, because at twenty-two Oskar had been starving, like everyone else. But this man standing before her was the proof she'd never stopped hoping she would find: Oskar had survived the war.

"They say I look like him, but I don't know. 'Oskar,' as you call him, was my grandfather, Pawel Brozek."

He slowly pulled his hand from hers. He reached behind her and retrieved a large cup of Dunkin' Donuts coffee from the windowsill, then moved away to make himself at home in the other chair. A scarred, tan briefcase stood on the floor at his feet. He regarded her in much the way she was regarding him. Ludka, dizzy, realized she'd been holding her breath. She inhaled slowly through her nose, felt the air expand her lungs and belly, then slowly released it. She slumped a little in her chair, heavy with the sudden gravity of inevitability; despite impossible odds, she'd never stopped expecting to see Oskar again, and here now was a young man who had given her hope, a man who could dash that hope with a few simple words.

"Should I come back at a better time?"

"You don't just resemble, Mr. Brozek. You are spitting image. Like a ghost. Like time evaporates."

Stanley passed a hand over his mouth and chin, glanced out the window, then back at Ludka. He began to say something, and stopped. "Please, call me Stanley. And I'm afraid I don't know how to address you. Professor? Apolonia?"

"Forgive old woman, Stanley. You are a bit of a shock. I am Ludka."

Her heart was not calming down. *Was*, he'd said. Was my grandfather. She was grateful she'd not yet taken off her cape. The radiator under the window was just beginning to clank to life. Maybe she had misheard him, maybe he had said *is*.

"Is Oskar . . ."

She couldn't go on. Sixty-four years she'd been wondering. If Oskar was alive, this young man was about to tell her where she might find him. If Oskar was . . . She closed her eyes. Her heart thudded in her ears.

"I was hoping you might tell me," said Stanley. "He disappeared two years ago. Left all his stuff behind. We're pretty sure he's gone back to Poland, but we haven't been able to track him down. Maybe you've heard from him?"

Ludka felt buoyed—he had lived a long life after all! Perhaps he was living it still, at eighty-six. She didn't bother to ask how it was they hadn't found him. Oskar knew how to disappear.

"Oskar I have not seen since 1945."

Had he searched for her, too, then, as they had promised? It had been impossible, with nothing but code names. How many times had she berated herself for not having asked his given name, or shared her own when she'd had the chance? Of course he wouldn't have told her, and thank God for that. What they'd done to him in Pawiak Prison . . . she never could have held out.

"Pawel Brozek," she whispered. "Pawel."

For years she'd sought out works by every sculptor she could find, in an array of countries where Oskar might have landed: Poland, of course, and America, but also France, Holland, Switzerland, Israel, Australia, even Germany and Italy. In 1960 she'd been grateful to join the newly founded International Sculpture Center, and each month she scoured every last page of their magazine, including the classifieds, the same with their newsletter. Every so often she'd see a sculpture Oskar might have conceived and then she'd spend some thrilling moments, sometimes hours and sometimes even days, before the advent of the Internet, doing research in a highly agitated state until she discovered the inevitable artist's photograph that dashed her back to square one.

"I kept searching for his work. I am anxious to see."

Stanley cocked his head and frowned.

"His work?"

"His sculpture, his drawings." She was suddenly wild with impatience to hear everything and she gestured to him to hurry up.

"But he wasn't an artist. He built people's kitchens. Home Depot. I'm the one who's into art. A dealer. Nothing major at all, just working my way with a small gallery. I only recently came across you—your book on collectors of Polish art in America—and that's when I suspected you were her. It was in his things I found out about you. I can't believe I'm sitting here with Apolonia! I thought for sure you'd be . . . well, it's just wild that I'm here. And what luck that you're there."

He gestured toward her with his coffee cup, then took a long drink. He slipped lower in the chair, rested the cup against his stomach, and in this posture his resemblance to Oskar began to diminish.

"His things?"

"Papers, drawings, diaries . . . you know."

Had Oskar written of her sketches, then, or of . . . ? Her stomach tightened. Did Stanley know about the Chopin?

"Last we saw him was at his place in San Francisco. We thought maybe he'd gone back to New York. He lived there until my grandmother died."

Ludka had lived in New York for three years before Izaac arrived on the boat in 1950, and then they'd lived there together until Lolek was born. Imagine if she'd seen Oskar on the street! She worried at her scarf, tugging it this way and that, and still it sat uncomfortably on her neck.

"God, he must have been seventy-five or more when he finally retired. He did want to take up sculpting—stone, of all things— which was a surprise to everyone, but of course he couldn't manage the materials and he wouldn't hire any help, so he dubbed around with wood, but he couldn't handle that, either. Finally, he did a bunch of drawings, but he was so weird about them, refused to use anything other than vine charcoal. My father gave him a great set of compressed charcoals along with sticks and chunks of graphite and a bunch of other tools, and they're all still sitting in their boxes. What a waste. Poor bastard, made no sense at all. As for me, I've decided to branch out into Polish art, learn something about my heritage, all that jazz. Would have pleased him no end. I don't suppose you're about to teach a class I could sit in on?"

Ludka started and checked the clock behind his head. She thought of Izaac hollering that she'd be late and told Stanley he was welcome to sit in, yes, she'd like that. To Ludka, Oskar's choice made complete sense. He'd been limiting himself, building a structured frame within which to work, like a poet confined to villanelles. Vine most closely resembled the charred wood they'd used in Warsaw, abundant when the fire-stormed buildings were still smoking, but rare when the fire was out, since people scavenged whatever wood they could find, even the char, which they used as fuel and burned to fine ash in whatever makeshift stove they had fashioned.

Oskar building kitchens for Home Depot . . . Ludka shook off the thought.

"What kind of paper?"

"Paper? Oh, that my grandfather used? Nothing but newsprint, the trimmings he collected from the local rag after their weekly run. Crazy old man. Did reams and reams of them. Wait! I almost forgot. I brought one along that seems to be of you. It says *Polly*, but I suppose that's short for Apolonia?"

Ludka grew instantly warm. She unfastened her cape and

loosened her scarf. Oskar had always called her Polly, always with a dreadful attempt at an American accent. Like Humphrey Bogart, he would insist, pretending to be stricken by her dismissive laugh before he threw his arms around her and, in early times, before persistent hunger necessitated focused energy, lifted her off the floor. Stanley retrieved his briefcase and, holding the edge of the Styrofoam cup in his teeth, set the case on his lap, opened it, and retrieved a rolled paper, secured with a rubber band. Ludka wanted to leap across the desk, so long did it take him to close the case, futz with his coffee, and, with tiny twanging sounds, roll off the rubber band and unfurl the drawing. He considered it, peered skeptically at Ludka, and shook his head.

"Like I said. Keep it, it's yours."

He turned it around. Ludka groaned involuntarily and laid a hand on her collarbone, the chill of her silver necklace cutting the heat of her palm. No doubt it was Ludka. But not as she had been when she'd known Oskar. Rather it was Ludka as she was now, as perfectly rendered as if she had posed. She imagined him imagining her, adding up the years, taking into consideration gravity and foolishness and wisdom, sketching away in some spartan studio. Brozek handed it across the desk. The paper seemed to retreat from her tremulous hands, tried to curl back into its accustomed shape. She anchored it on her desk, one hand pinning each side. In the bottom left corner was written, simply, *Polly,* and in the bottom right it was signed with only the letter *O.*

Maybe Oskar hadn't imagined. Maybe he had found her.

Brozek was talking when she came to.

". . . but he got me turned on to war-influenced works, so I have him to thank for that. There seems to be a growing market, and I'm sick of seascapes if you want to know the truth, although that's steady money. That's really why I'm here, to get some advice. Well, in addition to asking about my grandfather. I understand you know a little something about the war era—Seksztajn, Roslan, Mieroszewski, those guys."

*Mieroszewski?* For a moment, she couldn't make sense of what he had said, and then she realized why—he had situated Mieroszewski in the wrong century. Either her fear was founded that he'd learned she was harboring Mieroszewski's Chopin, and he was deliberately baiting her, or he didn't know the first thing about war-influenced Polish art. Ludka gave herself some time to think by making room for Oskar's drawing in her top desk drawer. She snuck a peek at Stanley and found him glancing around, looking as if he'd misplaced something, and then he stepped over to the wastebasket and dropped in his cup.

"Mieroszewski was early nineteenth century. You can cross him off list."

Stanley frowned and asked if she was sure. When she nodded, he smoothed his hand over his mouth and chin and shook his head.

"Exactly why I need to attend your class. You see?"

He seemed a bit lost, then, like an insecure man in a new profession who'd applied bravado where knowledge was lacking. When she told him to come along, they were going to be late, he smiled gratefully, and once again she was beholding Oskar.

"Oskar's grandson." She shook her head in disbelief. "So many questions for you I have."

# 8

# All These Trojan Horses

When Lolek arrived back at his office with the accordion files, Aggie was operating in high gear and started to talk before he'd even had a chance to get through the door.

"Not only is there more than one, there are at least ten that could be related, all of them having to do with hiring and firing teachers. The good news is they didn't try to mess with the anti-discrimination statute. They probably knew they wouldn't stand a chance trying to reverse that one."

She followed him into his office and, more forcefully than was necessary, slapped the bills down one by one on the conference table adjacent to his desk. Lolek dumped the folders next to them.

"Find out everything you can about Warren Meck. He got Gauch to file SB 79, maybe the rest of these, too."

"Meck's enormously influential," said Aggie, "and not just around here. He could be the next Rush Limbaugh. No, really, I'm not joking. A broad demographic listens to him, but all Christian, of course. This guy's a whole lot scarier than Limbaugh, though—he's totally likable, gentle in his delivery. If Warren Meck is behind these bills—and based on what I just saw on my first pass through them—we shouldn't underestimate this campaign. Case in point."

She smacked a hand on top of each accordion file.

"None of these bills are explicit, I'll tell you; they're very clever. Here, look at this."

Lolek moved to her side and leaned over the table.

"Forget about SB 79," said Aggie. "We can easily kill that one in committee. But check out House Bill 1298, also from Gauch, also filed by request: *An Act Further Protecting Our Schoolchildren.* This is the one to watch. They're mucking with Chapter 71 Section 38G. They've added a paragraph that allows the board of education to define *sound moral character*, which basically means that whatever characteristics the current board likes in their teachers—or, maybe more importantly, doesn't like—the board gets. They just write it into their policies and guidelines. In other words, a tabula rasa for their agenda. It's classic, because the public will see through their own lens what the board might do and of course trusts that the board will be fair, so the definition could easily fly under the political radar. Or, let's face it, how many voters are even paying attention to the board? A select few with vested interests. In other words, this is the perfect Trojan horse. Whoever wrote these bills knew what they were doing. Lesson learned, I imagine, from the '78 Briggs Initiative defeat in California. They're not coming right out and saying 'get the homos out of the classroom' like Briggs did; they're just setting the stage to make it possible. Way more strategic than going straight to the ballot."

Lolek smiled inwardly. A riled Aggie Roth was a sight to see. In general, she tended to mess with her already unruly hair, and when she was wound up, it got downright wild, like the hackles on an attacking dog.

"Here's another one. They want to strike Chapter 71 Section 39 in its entirety, meaning people applying for teaching jobs could once again be asked about their religious beliefs and political affiliations. And this one here is a doozy. It dusts off Section 30, which nobody has thought about since John Hancock was governor. At first glance this law seems to be specifically about Harvard, but really it's a broad brush that demands all teachers 'impress upon' the kids the 'principles of piety and chastity and temperance' and all that rubbish. All they've done here is add two words—*administrators* and *and*—which effectively means that in addition to teachers, anyone on the board of ed, school boards, superintendents, principals, you name it, has to uphold this totally vague law which also, by the way, says they need to point out the flip side of the good principles or, as it says in the law, the 'evil tendency of the opposite vices.' Now that's going to be a fun one at the public hearing, if it gets that far."

Lolek walked over to the window. The sky was getting lighter and commuters were hustling to and fro on Bowdoin Street, chins tucked into collars and scarves.

"But why fire them?" he said.

"What's that?"

"I mean, why fire them now? That's more of a Briggs-type move. With all these clever Trojan horses, they might have been able to stay off our radar right up until the morning of the public hearing, and it's certainly possible no one would have considered that people getting fired, or not being hired in the first place, could be a consequence if these became law. But now we're on alert. It doesn't make any sense. Unless one hand doesn't know what the other is doing."

"That would be good. Or maybe it's just bad strategy? Rogue elements? Could be fishing for sacrificial lambs, too. Give the public some juicy, real-life case studies."

Lolek turned his back on the window and strode over to his desk to erase the image he'd just had of Tommy in some easily misconstrued situation, his photograph on the front page of *The Boston Globe*, or on the Channel 7 news. The phone rang. Before it could complete a second ring they heard someone answering in the outer office.

"Shit," said Aggie. "Eric."

She threw Lolek an apologetic glance and rushed out.

"We will absolutely let you know as soon as we know anything further," said Eric. He smiled at Aggie as she mouthed "hang up." He nodded as if to say he was already on it, jotted down a name and phone number, thanked the caller, and hung up.

"No worries. I didn't reveal any state secrets."

He lifted a DeLuca's Market bag off her desk, offered it to her, and asked her where things stood. Aggie took the bag and dug around inside.

"Did you bring me a chocolate croissant?"

"What do you think?"

"I think you'll go far in this business." She smiled and took a bite of the croissant. "Come on in so I can put you to work. Thanks for getting here so quickly."

Lolek was paging through the testimony and took the DeLuca's bag from Aggie. Probably not the best idea, but he chose a ham and cheese croissant and smiled at Eric as he took a bite. Eric Barton had been with them only since the end of the summer break but already he was indispensable, cheerfully willing to do everything from scut work to drafting legislation. He'd be an elected colleague before too long, Lolek was sure of it, but in the meantime, they'd reap the benefits of his ambition. His black wool overcoat hadn't a speck on it, his pale blue scarf was tucked in just so, enhancing his blue eyes, and Lolek knew that his suit would also be top of the line. He suspected the kid had gone into debt to look the part, but that sort of investment was advisable; look the part, act the part, the part's yours.

"I hate to tell you, but teachers were fired in other districts, too," said Eric.

Aggie froze in midchew. Lolek felt a prickling sensation between his shoulder blades; he shuddered involuntarily.

"My friend Peter texted when I was on my way over. His colleague got an early morning call telling him not to come in to school. He's down in Fall River. He checked with some other teachers he knows around the state and they had similar stories. There could be as many as a dozen."

"Oh my god," said Aggie. "This is a full-frontal attack."

"And an entirely new ballgame," said Lolek. "Eric, I'm going to have you run off copies of every last page in these files, and get them back to Education before eight. Aggie, where are you with talking points?"

Aggie tapped her temple. Eric left with the files. Lolek strode around his desk and took a fresh legal pad out of a drawer. Aggie started to pace and counted off on her fingers.

"One. You talk directly about Tommy, say you support him, that this is very personal, that you can relate to what other families are going through. Two. We immediately frame the argument: civil rights. This was a deliberate attack on a targeted minority. Use an example from civil rights days to stimulate people's sense of fairness and put this issue into a context that connotes politically incorrect, passé. Three. We put on a second frame that will appeal to the conservatives: this is an attack on civil liberties. Don't forget Ronald Reagan himself came out against the Briggs Initiative based on a libertarian argument: kids could accuse any teacher of being gay, for any reason, and bam!—there goes his career, based solely on allegations. Basic violation of privacy. Use Reagan. And four, stress that we're just learning about it now and are gathering the facts about who's behind it. We'll have more to say later today.

"They'll ask you about your father, of course, if he's going to be involved, and I imagine the answer to that is yes? Good, that will help tremendously. They're also going to ask you some pointed questions about Tommy. I hate to ask, but do you know anything about Tommy's private life? About his . . . ? We really shouldn't have any surprises."

She hesitated a moment, and when Lolek didn't answer, she went on.

"Right. You'll need to find out from him if you can, or you're going to be finding out on tonight's news, and that puts us behind the eight ball, which we need to avoid at all costs."

Lolek tossed down his pen on his pad. "Get me phone meetings before noon with the usual crew on the Education Committee and bring that testimony as soon as Eric's done. Tell him to get anything else from Education on the other bills, too; tell him to ask Gauch personally so Gauch knows I don't appreciate being kept in the dark. Alert Mary over at GLAAD and Cyril at MassEquality; make sure to ask them about gay teens and suicide. And put somebody on discovery for the latest research about the pedophilia connection—we know that one's going to get trotted out. And get me a meeting with Warren Meck, even if it's in the district. I want to talk with him directly. I'll need to be fully briefed, so give yourself time to do the research. And Aggie? Don't delegate that one—I want you on Meck."

Aggie nodded and closed the door behind her. Lolek reached into his bag and slipped out his slim silver laptop, alien on the antique oak. He opened his browser. It was time he learned something about his son.

# 9

# The Praying Indians

At the State House on Monday afternoon, more than a week after the dismissals, Warren Meck stood alone in the narrow marble balcony high above Memorial Hall, girding himself for his meeting with the senator. He'd climbed there to take inspiration from Henry Walker's mural of John Eliot preaching to the Nipmuc tribe in the mid-1600s. Eliot was one of Meck's heroes. By learning to speak the Nipmuc language, Eliot had created fourteen theocratic towns. He'd even translated the Bible for the newly converted "praying Indians." He also wrote the first American book on politics, *The Christian Commonwealth: or, The Civil Policy of the Rising Kingdom of Jesus Christ*. Of course, the General Court had finally banned the book and demanded every copy be destroyed, all because Eliot had had the courage to say what he believed: that Christ alone was the true heir to the Crown of England and should govern not only England, but the world, including the new England. Meck smiled; despite the banishment, here was Eliot's portrait, towering above Memorial Hall, holding court in the most important building in the state. Eliot, in casual tunic and knee breeches, legs grounded in a wide stance, arms outstretched and chest thrust forward, offered salvation to the Nipmuc, the same salvation, Meck realized with a profound sense of destiny, that he himself had accepted into his life when Pastor Royce had offered it.

"Tell-it-like-it-is," he whispered. He checked his watch. It was time. He smoothed his bangs across his forehead, glanced once more at Eliot, and set out. His clipped steps echoed around the rotunda, and every visitor in the hall below looked up, surprised to discover the balcony wasn't off limits.

In the senator's office, Aggie welcomed Meck with a firm handshake and ushered him straight into the inner office, where he didn't waste any time marveling at the room but strode right up to the senator, hand outstretched. He didn't temper his volume, but allowed his voice to fill the regal space.

"Mr. President, it's a delight to finally meet you in person. I hear you've been of stalwart service to this community for some time."

"And I hear you've spent some time in Washington, Mr. Meck. Special campaign advisor to Colorado's Youst, if I'm not mistaken?"

"Those were brilliant days on the hill, yes. And it's Warren, please."

Meck smiled, a handsome smile that transformed him entirely, making him seem taller, more expansive, the kind of smile Lolek could imagine wanting to elicit, it was so much like a gift. Lolek warmed to him. Eric came in with a tray of coffee and walked past them to set it down on the low marble table between the rococo couches. They'd decided earlier that the meeting should be both special and casual, a friendly chat by the fireplace, just to get a read on the man.

"This is Eric Barton, our intern," said Lolek.

"Well hello, Eric! We've met, actually. Nice to see you again."

Aggie and Lolek exchanged a look of surprise, and Eric frowned fleetingly, something only Meck noticed as they shook hands.

"Representative Youst?" said Meck. "Remember?"

"So *that's* why your name was familiar." Eric considered Lolek and Aggie in turn. "I was a page in Congress then. Seems so long ago. I'd completely forgotten."

"Glad to see you're still climbing the political ladder, Eric. I'm not at all surprised."

"The senator's given me a great opportunity here, no question."

He smiled at Lolek, and excused himself, citing a busy schedule.

"So, Warren." Lolek gestured for him to sit down. "I truly appreciate you coming all this way. We won't take a lot of your time."

Lolek and Aggie claimed one couch. Meck unbuttoned his slate blue suit jacket, gave a little tug to the knees of his slacks, sat on the edge of the opposite couch, and helped himself to coffee. After stirring in a scant teaspoon of sugar, he settled back, trying to appear as comfortable as if he wore an old pair of jeans and a beloved sweater. It was only then that he gazed with appreciation around the room.

"If I had a desk like that, I'd never leave the office. Exquisite."

He could tell by the senator's expression he'd hit home. Meck and Whit had agreed that there was one primary goal for this meeting: to humanize Meck in the eyes of the senator, to demonstrate that he was a reasonable, likable fellow with whom deals could be done. And, if possible, to get through the meeting without mentioning the senator's son.

"But of course you have far more on today's schedule, Senator, than chatting with me. What can I do for you?"

Aggie fanned out the series of bills on the coffee table.

"We don't like to beat around the bush," she said. "We'd like all of these to go away. It's as simple as that. We thought we'd come straight to the source to see what it would take to make that happen."

Meck smiled and sipped his coffee, looked from Aggie to the senator, and back.

"I appreciate your candor. We all know it's not quite as simple as that."

He leaned forward, placed his cup on the coffee table, and rested his forearms on his knees.

"I have my own constituency, I'm sure you understand, and they are energized and determined. Their goal is to put every one of these bills on the governor's desk, and as many times as I've told them this isn't quite reasonable, they're raring to go. You and I both know they're being naive, but they need to take their own journey. I, however, am on a slightly different journey and am more than happy to work for half the loaf. There's always room right here for reasonable accommodation." He patted his chest with an open hand. "That's democracy at her best."

"I do want to be clear," said Lolek. "I don't like these bills. And I don't agree with the opinions behind them, nor can I imagine what half a loaf would look like. But we do work hard in this office to understand every facet of every issue, and we do value educated dialogue, which is why I wanted to meet you from the outset, rather than later in a heated debate, once lines have been drawn. You'll find that our office likes to learn so we can make informed decisions. You are welcome to be in touch with Aggie directly, and she'll do her best to be as responsive as her schedule allows. Does that sound amenable?"

"Better than amenable. Thank you, Mr. President."

Meck moved forward on the couch as if to get up, but Lolek held up a hand to stop him.

"Tell me, Warren. In a nutshell, what is it you want to accomplish?"

Meck stayed perched on the edge of the couch. He'd have to tread carefully here—what he said today would set the tone for the whole legislative fight. He turned his attention to Aggie, stalling for time.

"I trust you've already received copies of the testimony? Those folks pretty much spell things out. I can ask for future testimony to be copied directly to your office, to your attention, Miss Roth. Save you some work."

Aggie nodded. She and Lolek waited in silence. Meck rubbed his hands on his knees. He pictured the second hand on his studio clock ticking up to the top of the hour, the red *on the air* sign alighting, the microphone less than an inch from his mouth. He thought of John Eliot.

"Here's the story. It's pretty simple. School has become unwelcoming and unsafe for our kids. Starting as early as kindergarten, they're bombarded with curriculum designed to indoctrinate them into the idea that their Christian faith is wrong. When they try to express their own deeply held moral opinions, they're silenced, ironically in the name of tolerance and inclusion. We tried for a long time to convince the schools that our kids' beliefs matter just as much as other kids', that they're protected by law, but we got nowhere."

He gestured to the fan of bills on the coffee table.

"This is the result. We just care about our kids. My wife and I finally decided to homeschool our own children; we'd love to have them in public schools, but not in this climate."

"Well done, Mr. Meck," said Aggie. She reached forward and straightened the stack of bills into a neat pile. "No mention at all of the elephant in the room. Very impressive."

Lolek suppressed a smile. When Aggie decided to put on her bad cop hat, she clamped it down tight. Meck covered his frown by smoothing his hair. Aggie Roth might pose a real problem. He took his coffee cup and held it in both hands.

A quick knock sounded on the door, and Eric stuck his head in and apologized for the interruption.

"It's Governor Patrick, Senator. Wants to see you as soon as you're able."

Lolek nodded curtly, then turned back to Meck.

"If I understand you, then," said Lolek, "your people just want your kids to have equal time and consideration in the classroom?"

"That's right. And we'd like the option to exempt our kids from certain curricula and discussions." He paused and took a sip of his coffee. His palms had gotten damp. He hoped the governor's request would truncate the meeting, but the senator was regarding him expectantly. "We believe—to address the elephant directly, Miss Roth—that issues pertaining to human sexuality, procreation, sexual intimacy, and the holy basis of matrimony should remain private, within families. Our parents want to be the ones to introduce these issues to our kids. As I'm sure I don't have to spell out for you, we believe homosexual behavior is immoral. It violates the laws of the God of Abraham."

"Luckily for us," said Aggie, "we're not ruled by the laws of the God of Abraham."

"Not at present, we're not."

"You're joking, right?"

Meck forced himself to speak in what he hoped would emerge as a gentle tone.

"You may not be aware of this, Miss Roth, but this great commonwealth was founded on deeply held Christian beliefs. We believe it's beyond time to excavate those foundations and stand upon them proudly."

He'd sounded terser than he'd intended. He could imagine Pastor Royce laying a restraining hand on his arm, telling him to tone it down, ratchet back the talk of God. "It closes people's minds if you're too forthright about this stuff," he always said. "They need to tiptoe into the idea of faith."

Aggie put a hand to the back of her head and thrust her fingers repeatedly into her hair. "Our great commonwealth was founded on the idea of religious freedom, not religious prescription; our constitution is explicit about that."

"Our constitution also explicitly praises 'the great Legislator of the universe' and states that it is 'the duty of all men to worship the Supreme Being, the great Creator and Preserver of the universe.' Article II. *The duty.* It was John Adams himself who said 'Our constitution was made only for a moral and religious people. It is wholly inadequate to the government of any other.' And as I'm sure you know, the original Article III demanded that the state ensure there be 'public teachers of piety, religion, and morality' and that 'all the subjects must attend to their instruction.' Why? 'To promote the happiness of a people and the good order and preservation of a civil government.' No small matters."

"*Original* Article III. That article was replaced a long time ago, with good reason. Those provisions were not about public schoolteachers as we think of them today, but about instructors of religious societies."

"Ah, but it doesn't negate the provision that religious believers 'shall be equally under the protection of the law.' That's all we're trying to preserve."

Meck unconsciously raised a tense forefinger as he spoke, using it to punctuate his words. When he realized what he was doing, he blushed and lowered his hand.

Lolek stood abruptly and buttoned his jacket. Meck followed his lead, feeling relieved; he'd waded into waters best avoided this early on.

"You know the state's constitutional history, Warren. I'm impressed," said Lolek. "But let's save the debate for a public hearing, if things progress that far. I appreciate you coming in today. Please feel free to get in touch with me through Aggie." He handed Meck a business card.

"If she'll take my calls, Senator." Meck smiled at Aggie and for a moment she thought he might wink. She grudgingly gave him credit when he didn't. He retrieved two business cards from his inside breast pocket and passed one to each of them. He buttoned his jacket and offered a hand to Aggie, who shook it with a stronger grip than she usually applied. They made their way to the door.

"I do like a reasoned debate, Miss Roth. I look forward to some friendly sparring as things unfold."

Meck made a little bow toward each of them and walked out. Aggie closed the door behind him and turned to Lolek.

"What's the governor want?"

"He's annoyed I appointed Doug Sullivan chair of Third Reading. He can wait. What did you think of our Warren Meck?"

"Weirdo," said Aggie. She bowed. "It's like he's from another era, trapped in a twenty-first-century body. What guy in his thirties talks like that? I mean, come on. Friendly sparring? I do like a reasoned debate? Stalwart service?"

She'd deepened her voice in a poor attempt at imitation, and Lolek couldn't help but laugh, even as he shook his head in a pointless gesture of reproval. He worked hard to walk the high road when it came to mockery and gossip, but he wasn't immune to their appeal and could always count on Aggie for some rousing vicarious pleasure. He tossed Meck's business card into a tray of other cards in the top drawer of his desk.

"Only problem, Aggs? He's very, very good. They're going to frame it as a civil rights issue, too: freedom of speech, religious tolerance, parents' rights. We've got our work cut out for us."

She picked up the stack of bills from the coffee table.

"But he also tipped his hand about their bigger agenda. The laws of the God of Abraham? That'll land him in the whacko category with the vast majority of people."

"Except for those who've infiltrated school boards all over the state," said Lolek.

Saying it out loud caused a visceral reaction; the hair on his arms stood on end. He could tell Aggie felt it, too, because she pulled the bills to her chest, stood uncharacteristically still, and stared into the fire.

"You were right from the outset, Aggs. We can't underestimate him."

She nodded slowly, her cheeks flushed. He checked his watch.

"Whoever called in the last fifteen minutes, get Eric to call them back and tell them I'm with the governor. I need my day as freed up as possible. Clear my schedule as best you can."

# 10

# Leaves of Grass

When Tommy arrived at the high school that evening, Abe Goodman was waiting for him outside the brightly lit main entrance, talking on his cell phone. The glassed-in rafters of the gym were also lit up, and as Tommy emerged from the parking lot, he could hear echoey banging basketballs in the thin winter air, a coach's muffled whistle, and muted shouts from the boys' team as they began their practice. In the past these sounds would have loosed all kinds of demons from his own tenure as a student in this very building, but the job of teaching here for ten years had stripped them of their power. A trio of girls burst out of the main doors and, as if they'd left their dexterity behind them on the basketball court, they awkwardly bumped into each other as they tried to choose a direction for getting around Abe. Despite the frigid temperature, their hair was wet and their parkas unzipped, slung back off their shoulders by the pull of fake fur-trimmed hoods. Bulky gym bags bumped against their thighs as they headed to the parking lot.

"Hey, Mr. Zeilonka," called the tallest one. All three gave him a wave as they walked off to their car, and that was that—exactly what they would have done had the past week never happened. Tommy felt a surge of gratitude, and for the first time since this hearing was scheduled, he allowed himself a moment of hope. He shifted his grip on his new Kenneth Cole briefcase—leather glove on leather handle—and swung it slightly with what felt like courage; Robert had presented it to him last night, a soft leather case, rich acorn color with brushed metal hardware, more casual than the one Robert carried to his law firm each day. Inside were two crisp pads of lined yellow legal paper, a black and silver Schaeffer ballpoint pen, and a bag of Werther's hard caramels. In the public library's reading room on a Saturday afternoon more than six years ago, Robert had unwrapped a Werther's, the crackling plastic too loud for the quiet space, fashioned the wrapper into a sort of vessel, laid the candy inside, and pushed it across the table to Tommy, who'd been trying to stifle a cough. This was how they'd met.

Abe had advised that for now it was best if Robert stayed out of view, and worked on the case behind the scenes; the focus should be on Tommy the English teacher, not Tommy the gay man. Robert, whose legal expertise was in consumer protection, had at first been furious, but had finally acquiesced, deferring to Abe's seniority and experience. Now, in front of the high school, Abe acknowledged Tommy with a small lift of his head, said something else into the phone, ended the call, and reached out to shake Tommy's hand.

"Guess we kept it under wraps after all. Is this the first time you've been out without the press?"

"We prefer *paparazzi*."

"Ah yes, I'll be wanting your autograph before this is over."

Abe broke into a smile, warm and direct and reassuring. Then his expression turned serious.

"Anything I need to know, Tommy, before we walk in there? You know the drill, right?"

Tommy gave him a wry smile. "The hearing's pro forma. Don't expect a thing, just get through it. Be polite, professional, say as little as possible, see what we can learn. That's it."

"Perfect."

Principal Ed Shaw's office, bright with fluorescent light, was overly warm. Superintendent Arnie Dengler's large face was pink and damp, his hand clammy. Shaw made introductions all around and showed them to a bright blue pedestal table, barely big enough around for the four of them and the same table where Tommy had sat for his annual reviews, all of which had been exceptional. Shaw had only been principal for the last two, and his knowledge of Tommy's work had been poor at best, but still he'd given Tommy highest praise.

Tommy sat, lifted his briefcase onto his lap, and took out pen and paper, enjoying the pleasing smell of the expensive, dyed leather. Dengler took the chair next to him and had to work to get his hefty legs under the table; he rammed Tommy's knee.

"Pardon me," said Dengler. "Feels like we've been relegated to the kids' table here."

He smiled around at all of them. Shaw began to sit down, but halfway into his chair he hesitated and looked around the room as if he were expecting someone else.

"Do we need drinks? Coffee? Soda?"

Tommy shook his head, but Abe, who was draping his overcoat

on the back of his chair, requested water for both of them, and Tommy understood why when Shaw seemed a bit put out.

"Get me a Diet Coke then," said Dengler. "Thank you, Ed."

Shaw stepped out of the room, and Dengler leaned forward to retrieve a handkerchief from the back pocket of his slacks. He dabbed it over his broad forehead and well back to the edge of his receding hairline, then set it on the table. He noticed Tommy staring at it and put it back in his pocket. He folded his hands and perched them on the edge of the table. Shaw came back with two bottles of water and two Diet Cokes.

Abe thanked him and took a silver handheld tape recorder from his overcoat, slid it to the center of the table, and pressed record. Shaw started to say something, but Abe interrupted and directed his comments toward the recorder.

"Gentlemen, we are four of us here at Adams River Regional High School in Hampshire, Massachusetts, on Monday, February 16, 2009—Principal Edward Shaw and School Superintendent Arnold Dengler along with English teacher Thomas Zeilonka and myself, Mr. Zeilonka's counsel, Abe Goodman—for a review of Mr. Zeilonka's dismissal on Friday, February 6. This meeting is being recorded."

"Is that really necessary?"

"Just a formality, Ed; I'm sure you understand. Shall we begin?"

And just like that Abe commandeered the meeting. Tommy suppressed a smile; this was only the beginning, he knew, but Abe's confidence infused him with a sudden and determined energy he felt could propel him all the way to the Supreme Court, should it come to that. Tommy lifted his round wire-rimmed glasses higher up on the bridge of his nose. He jotted down the date and all four of their names. He glanced expectantly at Abe. Dengler twisted around in his seat and cast about in a pile of papers on the bookcase behind him. He turned back and fanned a thin pamphlet in front of his face.

"Judas Priest, Eddie, can't we turn down that heat?" He retrieved his handkerchief and mopped his neck. Shaw shook his head.

"It's tied into the whole system, I'm afraid. Nothing I can do."

"Let me open a window, at least. Sorry. Please, Abe, carry on."

Dengler pushed up and out of his chair, squeezed behind Shaw, and opened the large window behind Shaw's desk. He bent over to breathe in the cold air. Abe leaned back in his chair and directed his comments toward Dengler.

"Actually, Arnie, I'd like to hear from you. This dismissal is without merit. What, exactly, was your rationale? And don't tell me conduct unbecoming."

Dengler turned to them and leaned against the windowsill, his ample stomach pooching out. "But conduct unbecoming is the reason." Dengler considered Tommy with a soft expression.

"I know you're a good teacher, son. You've given this school district ten years. But we simply couldn't ignore the complaints any longer. I'm sure you understand that your lifestyle is a cause for concern for many of our students and their parents. Your classroom had become unsafe for a large number of kids. They felt targeted by your agenda."

Tommy winced. He sat back in his chair and propped the pad of paper on the edge of the table. *Unsafe*, he wrote. *Lifestyle. Agenda.* A trickle of sweat inched down the small of his back.

"Please don't be obtuse, Arnie," said Abe. "What specific complaints did you receive about my client? What behavior are you talking about?"

Dengler came back to the table and sat down. He carefully

twisted the plastic cap on his Diet Coke, which released the constricted air with a long, slow hiss. He seemed to think a moment, then turned to Shaw and held out an open hand, indicating Shaw should answer. Shaw shifted in his seat and tugged at the knot of his green necktie. The skin under his eyes was loose, bluish, and he rubbed at it with both hands, then sighed and addressed Tommy directly.

"I'm afraid many of our parents feel you've promoted what they call—and I'm quoting here—your 'homosexual agenda.' You've not allowed their kids to express their sincerely held Christian beliefs that homosexuality is a sin."

"And it is a sin, son, make no mistake about that," said Dengler. He leaned closer and Tommy could smell the Coke on his breath. His eyes were kind. "We know you've gotten trapped in homosexual behavior, and I'm very sorry about that. We can help you, you know. I'd be more than happy to facilitate a process to that effect."

"Arnie." Shaw frowned and shook his head.

Tommy looked at Dengler in disbelief and opened his mouth to speak, but Abe put a hand on the back of Tommy's chair and tapped him just once: *say as little as possible.* Tommy clenched his jaw and drew a box around Dengler's name.

"And at what point did you seek out my client to talk with him about this issue? Was he informed about the complaints, given a warning, given an opportunity to address any concerns as, by the way, is required not only by law but also by the rules in your own school handbook?"

Shaw exchanged a look with Dengler and pulled at the knot of his tie.

"Shame on you," said Abe. "Ten years of exemplary reviews and not even the courtesy of a conversation? Does he have that chance tonight, gentlemen, or are we just going through the motions here?"

"Please, Abe," said Shaw. "We're as concerned as you are."

For a moment Tommy felt sorry for the principal, who was again rubbing his eyes. He'd not been a bad head of school, just a tired one, a man who'd been around the block one too many times, a man counting the days until retirement. Shaw looked beseechingly at Tommy.

"There was too much pressure, Tommy. I'm afraid the school board's vote was unanimous."

Abe held out both palms and raised his eyebrows, asking for further explanation, and Shaw sighed and ticked off the reasons on his fingers.

"Whitman's *Leaves of Grass*, Ginsberg's *Howl*, Carson's *Billy Boy*, Anderson's *Find Me*—all of which were protested by parents."

He turned around and retrieved a manila file folder from his desk and opened it on the table in front of him. He leafed through the contents and began to read in a tired monotone.

"Mr. Zeilonka held my daughter after class and berated her for expressing herself. Mr. Zeilonka told my son to shut up, that his Christian beliefs were hurtful to other students. I won't have my son reading that filth. My kids have the right to opt out of his peculiar curriculum."

Shaw looked up. "Shall I go on?"

"I'll need copies," said Abe. "I assume you've noted the specific parties who made these complaints?" Shaw nodded.

"I'd never tell a student to shut up," said Tommy.

"I'm just quoting," said Shaw.

"Tell me something, Ed," said Abe. "How long have you been getting these complaints?"

"I'd say the last couple of months?"

"And that didn't strike you as strange, that after ten exemplary years there were complaints coming in, all of them similar in nature?"

Shaw threw a glance at Dengler.

"I just assumed they were new classes of kids, with different experiences than earlier classes. It happens. What I know is that these kids and their parents were distraught."

Dengler briefly laid a hand on Tommy's forearm.

"It's all about fairness, son." He spoke quietly, confidentially. "That's all. Our kids don't want to be told their beliefs are wrong, and their parents don't want their kids indoctrinated into something they believe is sinful. Public school, by law, is supposed to offer a tolerant, open learning environment—for everyone. I'm sure you can understand that. We had no choice but to let you go. Our kids were at risk."

Dengler's sincerity surprised Tommy. He'd been prepared for animosity, disdain, even disgust. All he felt was compassion. He was suddenly aware of the sweat in his armpits. He drew his arms more tightly against his sides. *At risk*, he wrote.

"You do understand, gentlemen," said Abe, "that everything you've said here is suspect under the Fair Employment Practice Law? That what you're doing here is discrimination, pure and simple?"

Shaw and Dengler exchanged a look.

"It's clear to me you might have worked something out with my client had you come to him, but here we are. I've heard nothing that leads me to believe you'd reconsider your decision. Am I wrong?"

Shaw lowered his head.

"I'm sorry, Abe, but our decision stands," said Dengler.

"I expect those copies in my office by close of business tomorrow, Ed, along with Tommy's performance reviews and anything else that's in his personnel file. Now, since I rather suspected this meeting would conclude as it has, I've taken the liberty of drafting up an agreement on discovery for the arbitration process."

Shaw made a low moaning sound, then cleared his throat. Tommy smiled inwardly, once again impressed by Abe, who pulled a set of papers, folded lengthwise, from an inside pocket of his overcoat. He handed out copies.

"Let me give you the highlights. Fifteen days for discovery. Three days for review, and one more day's leeway before I have to meet the petition filing deadline, after which no further discovery will be allowed. I suggest we hold the hearing in my office, where we have a suitably large conference room, as I expect we'll each want to hear from a fair number of witnesses. Will you be representing yourselves or will you have an attorney present?"

Shaw swallowed hard and appealed to Dengler, who mopped again at his face.

"Of course we'll have a lawyer," said Dengler. "And we need Connie to review these terms before we sign a thing."

"Connie Clough?" said Abe. "I'm frankly surprised you can afford him."

"Oh, we're not paying him. He's an old friend."

Abe frowned. *Connie Clough?* Tommy wrote.

"We don't have much time," said Abe. "You'll get back to us tomorrow? Excellent. Now, if there isn't anything else? No? Good. Note for the record that Principal Shaw and Superintendent Dengler both shook their heads to indicate they have nothing further. This meeting is concluded."

Abe retrieved the tape recorder and turned it off.

"We'll see you at the arbitration hearing, then, gentlemen."

Dengler rose, squeezed past Shaw, and went back to the window. He pushed it further open and leaned down to peer out, framed by the darkness of the night woods behind the school. In silence the other three men gathered up their things. Abe and Tommy put on their coats and went to the door. Tommy turned back. He felt the heft of his new briefcase and thought of Robert waiting at home. He spoke quietly.

"'The sum of all known value and respect, I add up in you, whoever you are.'"

Dengler turned from the window and cupped a hand to his ear. Tommy repeated himself, louder, and Dengler smiled.

"A fine sentiment, son, thank you."

Shaw shook his head at Dengler.

"You can thank Walt Whitman, Arnie. *Leaves of Grass.*"

Dengler appeared confused, and then bewildered.

"A classic," said Tommy. "I'm a fine English teacher, Mr. Dengler. My only agenda is to facilitate a love of literature."

He shifted his briefcase in front of him, held the handle with both hands.

"'I exist as I am—that is enough; If no other in the world be aware, I sit content.' Whitman again. The students—all of them—love that one."

He turned and walked out. Abe followed without another word.

At home, Tommy parked his VW Jetta. He scooped his briefcase out of the back seat and circled around behind the car to cross the short lawn into the screened breezeway. The streetlight at the edge of the gravel driveway had little effect on the starless night, and Tommy could sense the raw air that precedes an imminent snow. He was thankful that the TV crews from last week had turned their attention elsewhere. Inside the door to the kitchen he saw their tabby cat, Muriel, waiting for him as she always did. She opened her mouth, and he smiled as he imagined her scratchy meow, and then grew puzzled as she lowered her body and flattened her ears. Rapid steps approached him from behind. Two men rushed across the street, carrying themselves like soldiers. Swollen, shiny black parkas. Arms lifting as they hit the driveway. Guns, Tommy thought, but instead they were Maglites, as long as a policeman's baton. Before Tommy could even turn to run, he jammed his eyes closed against a sudden blinding light, then heard the fast friction of nylon as the second man closed in. Tommy instinctively whipped his head away. He flung up the briefcase as a shield. A Maglite slammed into his left cheekbone and ripped off his glasses, which raked across the soft skin just above the bridge of his nose. He lost the briefcase and hit the driveway hard, his right knee taking the brunt. He curled tight, face down in a fetal position, arms instinctively clutched around his head. The frozen gravel pierced his knees and elbows. The jolt of the first kick to his side broke apart his clenched posture, the second broke his ribs. And as he gulped for air that wouldn't come, as he heaved and squeaked with each attempt to breathe, he became aware of Robert screaming from the breezeway, and then there was a hand grasping his hair, yanking back his head, and the improbable smell of buttered popcorn and the feel of wet lips moving against his ear—"we know where you live, Sodomite"— and then the rush of retreating men. He pushed up onto all fours and frantically tried to gulp air; no air would come. Sparks of light shot through his peripheral vision. His shoulders quaked. Robert crouched beside him, saying something Tommy couldn't hear. A chill cascaded over him. He dragged miniscule breaths of whistling oxygen into his lungs, strangled and too shallow but carrying at least the promise of depth. Finally, a brutal shard of air cut a jagged path down his throat, and he instinctively sat up on his heels, lifted his head, and at last caught one desperate breath, and then another.

# 11

# Glory to the Fallen

Ludka laughed and set down her tumbler. Stanley Brozek had been sitting with her in front of the fireplace in their living room for only twenty minutes, and already she couldn't remember when she'd enjoyed herself quite so much, especially after the past week in which the news was crowded with what some were calling a modern-day witch hunt and others were calling an overdue purge. More than once last week Tommy and Robert had come over for respite, unable to bear the news teams outside their home. The cameras had been here, too, but Izaac had calmly set them straight on exactly where the property line began, way up the hill at the start of the long driveway. The distance, closed blinds, and covered access between the garage and the house meant a zoom lens was of very little use. Besides, even though Izaac had been largely out of the public eye for the past several years, he still commanded a great deal of respect, and most reporters had been treated well by him throughout his long career; they weren't that keen on invading his privacy, despite the story's importance. Still, one photo had appeared in the *Hampshire Gazette*, taken by a dauntless photographer who'd braved the wetland by night to get a shot of Izaac and Ludka sitting at the dining room table with Tommy. "Former AG Shelters Ousted Teacher" ran the headline. Now, as Ludka and Izaac visited with Brozek in front of the fire, the curtains and blinds hemmed them in.

"You are like head waiter," Ludka said over her shoulder, as Izaac retreated into the kitchen to refresh their drinks. To Stanley she said conspiratorially, "I can get used to pampering."

"You are used to pampering! Sixty years you're used to it!"

Ludka flapped a hand toward the kitchen and laughed. Stanley smiled. Ludka watched him admire the abstract Kantor hanging over the mantel.

"When we are dead, the Baldwin Museum will have best collection of Polish contemporary art in America."

"You should see the back coat closet," said Izaac as he carried in a tray and passed around the drinks. "Hasn't seen a coat in thirty years. We rotate a fair number of the pieces almost every month. Keeps our senses sharp."

Stanley stepped up onto the stone hearth next to Izaac, and peered more closely at the painting.

"We leave this one here more often than not, don't we, kochanie? Tadeusz Kantor, 1960, one of Ludka's favorites."

"We have also 1959 Kantor. More open, chaotic, but also flatter, good for summer light. And still with its darkness. Always we are drawn to darkness."

"The stuff I sell is mostly popular seascapes and impressionist knockoffs—all by decent enough painters but mostly just thrown-together stuff I know I can move." Stanley shrugged, and smiled over his shoulder at Ludka. "It's a living. But then I saw your book on Polish art, and now this . . ." He gestured toward the Kantor. "Now I'm thinking about a whole new direction."

Izaac talked more about the Kantor, and Ludka let the vodka tonic do its warming work. The men's banter fell into the background, and she settled more heavily into her wing chair. From behind, Stanley's stance was exactly like Oskar's, weight on his left leg, right leg forward and turned out like a dancer's, head slightly cocked. For one dizzying moment, as Izaac and Stanley fell silent and gazed together at the painting, Ludka felt time conflate. It seemed Oskar had been in her life all along, as she had been in his; he had written of her, sketched her, and inadvertently sent his grandson to close a circle that had yawned open for decades. Her throat began to ache, and it took a moment before she realized with some alarm that her cheekbones were warm and wet. She roughly swiped at them with the back of her wrist, straightened her spine, and furiously maneuvered herself to the edge of the chair, slopping the drink over her hand and onto her skirt. She rose, took a healthy swallow of vodka to bolster herself, and then tried to ignore the way the tumbler wobbled as she lowered it to the side table.

"Come and take art tour, then. We start upstairs."

"I'll do some more pampering," said Izaac. "Take your time." He disappeared into the kitchen.

Ludka hauled herself by the handrail up the dark, narrow staircase, placing both feet on one step before taking the next. She went up six and told Stanley to turn around.

"Best vantage for Musialowicz. *Glory to the Fallen*, from his Sacrum series. 2001."

Stanley made an appreciative sound, which endeared him to her further. The piece was more sculpture than painting, six feet tall, two-and-a-half feet wide, oil on assembled wood. At its center rose a narrow icon of charred wood with a knobby top for a head and a barely discernible visage carved into it. For the first year they owned it, Ludka would sit on the stairs and stare for so long she'd forget whether she'd been going up or going down and she'd have to call to Izaac to spot her so her stiff hips and sleeping feet wouldn't betray her. Now she glanced at it only on her way down, standing for brief moments as she landed on each stair.

Once a year they held the open house for the university's art students, and otherwise there was never much occasion for a tour, so showing Stanley around the upstairs gave Ludka renewed perspective; they owned a truly impressive collection: Jan Lebenstein, Aleksander Kobzdej, Teresa Pagowska, Jerzy Duda-Gracz, Wlodzimeirz Ksiazek.

"And how about the portrait?" Stanley stood in the bedroom door.

"It is nothing of value. The artist is unknown."

"I like the way she's checking over her shoulder, though. Is this the only thing you've got that isn't abstract? I mean, you've kind of got a thing for abstraction."

"Only she caught the fancy long ago and now she is like family, or sometimes like wallpaper."

When Ludka considered the portrait, she saw it for only a moment before she pictured the hidden Chopin; it was tricky to talk about when she gave tours. Most people didn't linger long, anxious instead to see what they thought of as the more valuable pieces, and Ludka always felt a complex combination of shame, fear, and excitement as they stood in front of her darkest secret, no one the wiser. Even now, as Stanley leaned closer, head and shoulders angled over the bureau, bulging stomach pressed against its edge, she felt these things, along with something resembling pride; she'd protected this masterpiece all these years, and here it was, hiding in plain sight.

"It's a lot smaller than most of your other stuff, and with such a deep frame. Funny."

Ludka wondered again if Oskar had written of the Chopin, and for one alarming moment she thought Stanley might reach out and pluck the painting from the wall. She noticed her heartbeat.

"She fits the space, that is all. Come. Eugeniusz Zak is next."

To her relief, Stanley retreated without further comment. She carefully closed the door behind him, felt the thunk of the thumb latch engage, and steered his attention to the end of the hall.

"Here is *Boy with a Landscape in the Background*. Every time, I catch breath. So you see, Stanley, not all abstract."

"I know this one. My grandfather had a print of it hanging in his kitchen. He said it reminded him of the Vistula, although I always thought the background was sky, not water."

Ludka immediately closed her eyes. She knew when she opened them she would never again see the Boy as she'd seen it all these years—a loss perhaps, or maybe a gain, but for now this uncommon moment of acute suspension between past and future, known and unknown, stasis and change. But even if she never looked again, she could not forestall time; already in her imagination she could see how Oskar would envision the water, not in place of the sky but beyond the painting's edge, and how the boy's defeated, exhausted posture might evoke for Oskar a sense of himself, back then. She opened her eyes. She smiled: not a loss then.

"Something smells good," said Stanley. "Like my grandmother's kitchen."

"Izaac will present classic Polish meal. Only we add green salad, but the rest will maybe be like your grandmother. Beetroot soup, kielbasa with pickled cucumbers, mushroom and sauerkraut pierogi. All but the kielbasa is made from scratch, even pickles. Izaac's retirement, you see?"

Stanley put a hand to his stomach.

"Grandmother never varied from her traditions, never even added salad. But after she died and Grandfather moved to California, he went cold turkey. Got completely onto a health kick, practically went veggie, the whole nine yards. He even got rid of Grandmother's stash, as we called it. They had an extra room in their tiny apartment—people would kill for that space in Chelsea—and it was always chock full of food, and I'm talking a lot of food. It was like a kiosk in there, cans and boxes stacked floor to ceiling on metal shelves. You could hardly move around."

Ludka imagined a woman standing quietly amidst the cans, steeling herself to walk back out into an untrustworthy world.

"So your grandmother was in war."

"I guess so, yeah. I don't know. They never talked about it. We always snuck in there and raided the jam."

He laughed as he recounted the way he and his brother would shovel fingers full of jam into their mouths before resealing the jar and moving on to the pickles. Ludka frowned. Stanley's face showed only the ghost of a mischievous boy's expression, not a trace of a man's reflective comprehension or compassion. Ludka turned abruptly for the stairs.

"Upstairs tour is over."

She clomped onto each stair, wishing she could move faster. Halfway down she stopped and pointed at the Musialowicz.

"Look."

The stair behind her creaked as Stanley shifted his weight.

Ludka stood for longer than she knew was comfortable. Stanley cleared his throat. She glared at the sculpture.

"Jar of jam could save life."

"What's that?" His voice was too loud in the narrow stairwell. Ludka continued down.

"I didn't hear you, Ludka."

She gripped the rail, stepped down onto the floor, and turned.

"Jar of jam." She frowned up at his bewildered face. "Could save life."

Stanley's lips fell open with a tiny smacking sound, and she gave him credit for appearing aggrieved. He passed a hand over his mouth and chin, then shook his head.

"I didn't know. How could I know? I was only a kid."

She moved away and he followed in silence.

The kitchen was full of rich aromas, heaping platters laid out on the counter by the pass-through, food enough to feed a family of eight. Izaac was washing the pots and pans, the sleeves of his turtleneck shoved back to his feeble biceps, frothy soap encasing his wrists.

"Izaac," said Stanley, "what can I do to help?"

Ludka was sorry Stanley had not said more, had not reflected out loud that as a grown man he should perhaps have known, or at least wondered, why his grandparents had been such hoarders. He seemed relieved to have skirted the subject as he moved to the dining room and pulled the platters from the pass-through to set them on the table. Not a mature man, then, and this was a disappointment. But of course she was not judging him fairly, this man who so closely resembled Oskar; poor Stanley didn't stand a chance, measured against the myth of a man forged from long memory.

They had just sat down and gotten through the bustle of passing platters and filling plates when they heard the mechanical whir of the rising garage door, which could only mean Tommy, and sure enough, he and Robert came into the back hall, ushering in an eddy of frigid air.

"You're just in time," called Izaac.

"We didn't realize you had company," said Robert.

His jet-black hair was uncharacteristically mussed, his ivory complexion even paler than usual. Tommy, his back to the room, began to unwind a bulky cashmere scarf that obscured most of his face. He started to take off his coat, but Robert stopped him and gently lifted the coat from his shoulders, bit by bit, then lowered it slowly until Tommy was free. Ludka clenched her jaw and pushed back from the table.

"What's trouble?" she said, just as Izaac said, "What is it, what is it?"

Tommy turned, and the first thing Ludka noticed was the mess of blood across his forehead. He wasn't wearing his glasses. He gingerly touched his cheek under his left eye, and just as Ludka saw the angry gash and the swelling flesh around it, Tommy stumbled, canted toward Robert, and began to collapse with a surprising grace. Robert rushed in and grabbed at Tommy, caught hold of the front of his sweater, flung his other arm around Tommy's back, and lowered him down to the floor, head and shoulders propped in Robert's narrow lap.

"I told you we should have gone to the hospital," said Robert. Tommy closed his eyes and nodded. Robert called out for 911, but Izaac was already on the phone in the kitchen, reciting their address. Tommy's sweater and T-shirt had pulled out from the front of his jeans, and the sight of his pale, taut belly, finely dusted with downy blond hair, stirred a burgeoning anger in Ludka, who pulled a shawl off the back of her wing chair and held it out to Robert; she wasn't steady enough to bend down herself, and this made her angrier.

"Where else are wounds? Who is responsible? Izaac, get a face-cloth. And warm water."

Izaac had already thought of this, too, and instantly appeared with a clean dishrag and a bowl of warm water. Suddenly Stanley was there beside them. He took the bowl and dishrag from Izaac and kneeled.

"I'm Stanley. Long story you don't need to hear now." He submerged the cloth into the water, dunked it in and out a few times, then loosely wrung it out and handed it to Tommy, who pressed it against the side of his face. Stanley took the shawl from Robert and draped it over Tommy's legs. Robert reached out and tucked Tommy's T-shirt back into the front of his jeans, and at that Ludka averted her eyes. Robert's own shirt—a white dress Calvin Klein he hadn't changed out of after a long day at the law firm—was smeared and stiff with brown blood. Robert pulled the shawl up to Tommy's ribs.

There was a sharp rap on the glass next to the back door, and Izaac hurried over, elbows jutting back. He started to pull open the door, but quickly realized he didn't see flashing lights. He peered past the curtain through the glass alongside the door.

"*Niech to szlag trafi!*" he muttered. He pushed the door tight. "Have you no decency? You are trespassing here. I'm calling the police."

"Paparazzi?" Tommy smiled weakly up at Robert.

"Channel 7," said Izaac. "Wendy Chen. Maybe a photographer, too."

"We're already losing our allure," said Tommy.

Robert shook his head and told Tommy to hush. A woman's muffled voice called back.

"We only want to know what happened to your grandson, Mr. Attorney General. Who attacked him? Is he okay?"

Ludka pushed past Izaac and yanked hard on the door. She felt a sharp pain in her left shoulder.

"Don't, kochanie, they'll force their way in."

She took the knob in both hands and slowly tugged at the door, opening it just a crack, not at all sure what she intended, knowing only that she wouldn't cower inside. She opened the door a bit wider and stepped between it and the storm door, then closed her eyes against the sudden onslaught of light and Wendy Chen's questions. Ludka pressed her right palm to the front of her left shoulder, covering the point of pain. Eyes closed, feeling the winter chill, tuning out the reporter, she simply stood there, jaw set, head slightly raised in what could have been construed as a haughty pose, pops of light from the photographer's flash penetrating her eyelids. On the eleven o'clock news and in the morning paper she'd look as if she were pledging allegiance, something that would secretly please Ludka and openly please the news editors, the symbolism of liberty and justice for all not lost on any of them. Chen's harangue began to slow as she grew unsure in the face of Ludka's silence. Behind Ludka, Izaac kept the door from drifting open in order to shield Tommy and Robert. Even with his heart hammering and thoughts racing, Izaac had the presence of mind to admire Ludka's stubborn protest. Leave it to his Ludka to cow the media with her unorthodox response.

Even with her eyes closed, Ludka sensed the bright light shift. The cameraman swung the camera around and angled it up the

hill to the road, where the ambulance had turned into the driveway. The siren abruptly quit midscream but the lights kept flashing. Ludka opened the storm door.

"You will all move aside now and get off property."

"Just tell us what happened, Professor. Is he okay?"

"He needs ambulance! What do you think?"

"Make way," said Izaac, stepping around the door. "Make way,
for god's sake."

The news crew vacated the stoop but not before they snagged
a few oblique shots of Tommy and Robert on the floor. Chen lowered her mic and held open the storm door as the EMTs came
through with their stretcher.

"Will you take him to Mercy?"

"Enough now." Izaac held up his hand and closed the door.


Ludka and Izaac got home just before eleven. All the lights had
been left on and the fire was out; they could feel the cool draft
from the open flue. They found that Stanley, who had urged them
to go ahead and he would see himself out, had cleared off the
dining room table, loaded the dishwasher, and wiped down the
kitchen counters.

"Mój Boże, but that's a welcome sight. Good man, Stanley."

Izaac took from the refrigerator a plate of sausage covered with
plastic wrap. He held out the plate toward Ludka, inquiring. She
shook her head. She rubbed her shoulder.

"Anymore I am too old for this, Izaac."

He set the plate on the counter, unwrapped the sausage,
selected one, and turned to consider her. Flyaway strands of pure
white hair had come loose from her usual swept-up style, forming

a haphazard halo. Aqua veins at her temples rose in sharp relief against her pale skin, and her gray-blue eyes were rimmed with red. He sometimes got unreasonably angry at her for appearing so old—only five years his senior, after all—but tonight he felt only an exhausted sort of love, and marveled not for the first time that he was still here, grateful to be with her after all these years, grateful for their independence. He took a bite of the sausage and assumed the position of pledging allegiance, mimicking her perfectly. She gave him a wan smile. He chewed and grinned.

They both fell silent. Ludka crossed the room, took his hand, and bit into the sausage. The spicy congealed fat coated the roof of her mouth, and for a moment she regretted her decision to eat it, but then the fat began to melt and the fennel seeds released their pungent licorice. She was suddenly ravenous and selected a whole sausage for herself. She leaned against the counter next to Izaac and settled into the relief that being home will bring after a long night in the emergency room.

"This violence is too familiar, kochanie, a harbinger. It's one thing to take over school boards, quite another to . . ." He backhanded the air with a vicious jab, shook his head, and then noticed with surprise he was still holding the sausage. "And it's certainly possible this goes beyond the school boards: town councils, state representatives, senators. This smacks of careful orchestration. Maybe they're in office right now!"

"But already Lolek would know this. You would know this! This is some hooligans only, a coincidence."

"Coincidence? You can't be serious. They called him a Sodomite, Ludka. Not any of the other derogations they might have chosen. What does that tell you?"

They fell silent again, Ludka trying not to think about a

harbinger, Izaac thinking with longing about synagogue, a bewildering notion after so many years of disbelief. They finished their sausages. Izaac licked his fingers and went to the sink to wash his hands.

"Those police officers were so respectful. The hospital staff, too. No different than they'd treat us. I was frankly a bit surprised."

Ludka twisted her engagement and wedding rings, both thin and loose after so many years of wear.

"Do you maybe wonder, Izaac?"

Izaac glanced over at her as he shook the water off his hands. He took the dishtowel off the oven handle.

"Do you maybe wonder if Tommy has done something we do not know? If there was merit at all in dismissal?"

Izaac froze, holding the dishtowel.

"No, I do not, Ludka, and neither should you. Tommy is a fine lad. Period. We know him."

"We are grandparents only. And gay man's life can be . . . there is sin."

Izaac frowned. "I hope you're not seriously listening to Father Skurski. Or any other damned Catholics for that matter. This is Tommy we're talking about."

"Damned Catholics saved your life, old man! Do not belittle us! This homosexual issue is a conflict in the church. You know this. It is no trifle. Many believe it is a sin."

"This homosexual issue? I'm going to pretend you didn't say that. Next you'll be quoting Leviticus! It's late. I'm going to bed."

Izaac walked out. Ludka covered the plate of sausages with the plastic and returned it to the fridge. It annoyed her when Izaac haughtily took the high road, as if he never had a doubt in his life, as if her own doubts were to be thoroughly dismissed without his usual scrutiny. He always walked away when he'd had enough, and more often than not she followed, despite the futility of pestering him. When Izaac was done, he was done, and no amount of cajoling could reengage him. She had to admit it was often a wise move; when she got wound up she could be brutally unreasonable. Still, she hurried out now, unwilling to let him have the last word. Izaac was kneeling, one knee on the hearth, a flowered throw pillow bunched between the stone and his knee. He reached carefully up into the fireplace to pull closed the damper. His cardigan hung loose on either side of his hips, brushing against the stone, and his spine poked a knobby ridge through the thin wool. The sight of the scrunched pillow protecting his bony knee took all the fight out of her. The damper swung shut with a thump and a sprinkling of creosote. Ludka climbed the stairs as Izaac went around to turn off the lights. On the fifth step, Ludka stopped. Gripping the handrail, she peered over her shoulder for a moment at the Musialowicz. At its base: the eye of providence, surrounded by golden rays of light. Always she was concerned about what she might not see.

It wasn't until she was under the covers, working her feet across each other to warm them, eyes closed and mind finally settling as she listened to the hum of Izaac's electric toothbrush, that she realized the bedroom door had been standing open. She was certain she had closed it behind Stanley. Her eyes flew open.

# 12

# At Mercy

Lolek drove the speed limit along the dark and nearly deserted Mass Pike, his plush town car too quiet and smooth for his mood. Sand and salt had been strewn across the road, creating wet patches that threw up a fine white mist that gradually and repeatedly coated the windshield.

He felt around on the passenger seat for his cell phone and put it on speaker. Marta's cell went straight to voice mail again, the tinny recording too loud in the car. He dialed their home phone and after six rings was about to hang up, but this time Marta answered, saying hello in a perfectly ordinary voice, as if it were the middle of the day and she was expecting a friend to phone.

"At least the ER doctor had the decency to call me back."

"I just got home, Lolek." She sounded tired. "I was about to call you, honestly. There was a lot going on. He'll be fine, though, he's okay."

"I had to hear it from Wendy Chen at Channel 7, for Christ's sake. She was already at the hospital, looking for a comment. What the hell happened? Abe called me earlier and said everything went as expected."

"Tommy thinks they might have followed him home from the meeting. Thank God they didn't have guns."

"But Abe said they kept it under wraps, that no one knew."

"Well somebody knew. Obviously!"

Lolek pressed the accelerator. He ran the wipers, flooded the windshield with fluid, and cleared off the salt.

"What about the media? I told Chen I'd get back to her."

Marta sighed loudly enough that she could have been sitting in the passenger seat.

"If you must know, she's not the only one camped outside emergency, waiting for the senate president to appear. I suppose that seals it for you. Get in your sound bite for the morning news."

"It's possible, you know, for me to care about our son and my job at the same time."

Marta didn't respond.

"How is he?"

"Terrified. Two broken ribs, a nasty laceration on his left cheek, another cut that narrowly missed his right eye, a concussion, and so far, thank God, no internal bleeding."

Now he was pushing eighty-five, and the scored white lines on the highway flashed past like an old film at the end of its reel. He eased up on the gas. Getting pulled over wouldn't help. When the car slowed to seventy-two, he engaged the cruise control.

"It's advantageous for Tommy if I address the media, Marta, you know that. Can you talk me through what you know?"

Marta was quiet for a moment and then she said, "I am not going to talk you through anything, not this time. I am not your chief of staff. Besides, Maria Rose is on her way here from the hospital. I have to go make up her bed."

"You called Maria Rose?"

"Tommy called her. He wanted his sister there."

"But not his father, apparently."

"He would have welcomed his father. He didn't want the senate president, or his entourage."

Lolek winced and rubbed his forehead, then smacked the steering wheel with the meat of his hands. He threw out his right arm and gestured angrily around at the empty car.

"There's no entourage here, Marta, it's just me. Just me, driving like a fucking maniac to get to the hospital to find out what's going on because my wife wouldn't return my calls!"

A semi gained on him from behind, and he flipped his rearview mirror to redirect the glaring headlights that flooded the car. The truck pulled out into the passing lane, and Lolek gripped the wheel more tightly to fight against the undertow of rushing air. Marta started to say something else, but the oncoming truck roared.

"Hang on a minute," he yelled. "I can't hear you."

With a slap of spray from the tires, the truck was past, and in the sudden darkness from the deserted highway behind him, in the truck's quieting wake, Lolek felt an immense sadness at the tone of the conversation with his wife. He imagined sitting at the kitchen table over cups of coffee, or maybe some Armagnac, hearing the whole story and talking late into the wee hours. He couldn't remember the last time they'd done that. He tapped the brake to disengage the cruise control and took the exit to 91 North.

"Marta? Honey?"

"Maria Rose just pulled in. Go to Mercy. I'll see you when you get back."

She clicked off. His fingers ached and he let his hands drop to his lap, loosely held the bottom of the wheel. The cell phone beeped to indicate the dropped call. He picked it up and punched in the shortcut for Aggie's number. She answered immediately.

"I'm about fifteen minutes from the hospital, Aggs. What's next?"


Tommy and Robert had the lights turned low in the hospital room, the TV off, and were grateful no one was in the other bed. Tommy's head had been pounding, but the Vicodin was finally taking hold, giving him a hopeful glimpse of a rest that might come. He touched the bandage covering his stitched left cheek, and Robert told him to leave it alone. A hematoma had spread beyond the borders of the bandage, filled his left eye, and leaked across to blend with the lesser bruise from the cut between his eyes, which the nurse had sealed with a Steri-Strip. Robert scooted his chair closer. He poured water into a paper cup from a mauve plastic pitcher on the nightstand and offered it to Tommy, who took a few sips and gave it back. Robert lowered his head to the bed and rested his forehead on the rough cotton sheet. He reached for Tommy's hand and held on. Tommy wanted to lean over to stroke Robert's hair, but pain from his ribs kicked him back. He held his breath against the pain, then closed his eyes and cautiously exhaled. Urgent energy had fueled him up to this point, but over the last hour it had finally started to wane; in its place was a growing dread.

"Robert?"

Tommy's voice broke. Robert sat up, immediately alert, a muscle pulsing in his taut jaw.

"What is it, Tom, should I get a nurse?"

"No, no, it's not that, I'm okay. It's just . . ."

He swallowed hard.

"It's just I can't stop wondering about those kids."

"What kids?"

"The superintendent said they didn't feel safe, that they were 'at risk.' He said they felt like I shut them out."

"Oh, Tom, don't let them get to you."

"But they are getting to me. They are. If those kids felt ostracized because of anything I did—"

The door opened. Lolek rushed in, bringing with him the smell of winter air and leather car seats and warm cashmere. In an instant, he took in the startled way Tommy and Robert had moved apart, and then, at the sight of Tommy sitting up in the bed, every bit of tension he'd been holding abruptly snapped loose and drained away in one grateful exhalation.

"Oh, Tommy, thank God."

Robert moved aside, and Lolek laid a tentative hand on Tommy's head and studied the wound beneath the Steri-Strip and his blood-filled eye.

"They did a number on you, didn't they? What the hell happened? What did they say about the concussion? Your mother said they were worried about bleeding. Christ. What kind of bastards would do such a thing?"

"Calm down, Dad, it's fine. I'm going to be fine."

Lolek took a step back, his chest and shoulders lifting as he took a deep breath. He looked around the room as if to get his bearings.

"Hi, Robert. How you holding up?"

He shook Robert's hand, then pulled off his overcoat, folded it carefully, and draped it over the back of the chair Robert had been sitting in. Robert and Tommy exchanged a glance.

"Can I get you some coffee, Senator? I was just about to go get some for myself."

Tommy asked for a bottle of cold water.

"The stuff in this pitcher tastes like plastic. It's giving me a headache."

"Ha ha," said Robert.

Lolek tried to decide whether Robert wanted an excuse to get away or was simply being kind, giving him some space to be alone with Tommy. He couldn't tell. Robert had always been perfectly pleasant, but wasn't what you'd call forthcoming. In truth, Lolek had learned more about Robert on the Web in the past week than he had in the six years Tommy and Robert had been together. He'd known Robert was a competent attorney, but he'd been surprised to see he'd argued a case in front of the state supreme court.

"Coffee would be great, Robert, thank you."

Robert closed the door behind him, and Lolek leaned over and grasped the back of the chair, working his hips left to right.

"You okay, Dad?"

Lolek straightened up and nodded.

"So what happened? What did the doctor say?"

Tommy told him about the meeting and the attack, and when he got to the part about being clubbed with the Maglite, Lolek had to sit down.

"Even while it was happening, I had the clear thought they expected to kill me. I don't know what would have happened if Robert hadn't interrupted them. The police wanted to do a composite when they got here, but the doctor wouldn't allow it because of the concussion, said there was no way could I sort through fifty sets of facial features. I'm sure they thought they'd blinded me with light, but I did see one of them. I think I could describe him—*maybe* if I saw him again, I'd recognize him, but it happened so fast I can't be sure."

While Tommy had been telling his story, Lolek had been taking mental notes, determining what to share with the media, what not to share. In his pocket, his cell phone had been vibrating every few minutes, but he studiously ignored it. While Lolek was brilliant at appearing completely attentive with his mind occupied backstage, and most people in the course of his day didn't notice, Tommy had always been sensitive to anything that smacked of inauthenticity. He was staring at Lolek right now, in fact, expectantly, as if he'd asked a question, which he very well might have done. Lolek was about to confess that his mind had wandered when Tommy sighed and closed his eyes.

"Did you already address them on the way in?"

"I came straight here, truly."

"Did you get the sound bite you came for?"

Lolek stood up and walked over to the door, peered out through the small reinforced window. He clasped his hands tightly behind his back, unaware that he was copying Izaac's posture. Across the hall, a man about his own age was being fitted with electrodes for an EKG.

"I'm right here, Tommy."

"Are you, Dad? Did you catch the bit where they called me a Sodomite? That's the one I'd recommend you use."

Lolek turned around, but Tommy's eyes were still closed.

"Good sound bites helped get you and your partner a whole lot of legal protections you wouldn't otherwise have, so don't give me that. I've championed every gay rights bill that's come across my desk and you know it."

"Husband."

"What's that?"

"Robert is my husband, Dad, not my partner. It's about time you knew."

Lolek stopped breathing. He frowned, his lips parted. Tommy opened his eyes but focused only on the ceiling. Lolek's eyes roved rapidly back and forth over Tommy's ruined face, from white bandage to bloody eye and back again.

"Your husband. You're married?"

"Almost a year."

Lolek took a deep breath and rubbed a finger hard over his lips, cleared some gummy spittle from the corners. Behind him he heard the thud of a soft kick on the door and there was Robert in the window. Lolek opened the door and Robert came in, a water bottle tucked under his arm, a cup of coffee in each hand.

Lolek felt a sudden pain in his jaw and realized how hard he was clenching his teeth. He massaged his jaw. Robert glanced from Tommy to Lolek and back to Tommy.

"Okay there, Tom?" Tommy nodded and closed his eyes again.

Lolek retrieved his coat, took the coffee from Robert, and, without another glance at either of them, walked out, carefully closing the door behind him. Across the hall, the man sat alone under fluorescent lights, electrodes snaking out the neck and sleeves of his johnny. Lolek strode down the hall and, just outside the waiting area, ducked into an oversized bathroom, locked the door behind him, and stood there, breathing audibly. Next to the toilet was a metal grab bar and a pull cord for summoning help. Lolek hung his coat on the back of the door. He tried to peel the sipping lid off the cup, but the whole thing popped off, sloshing hot coffee over his hand.

"For Christ's sake," he spat through clenched teeth.

He flung the lid into the open waste can and shook his hand over the low-slung sink. He took a drink of the coffee, grimaced, poured it down the drain, and filled the cup with cold water, which tasted like chlorine, damp paper, and cheap coffee. He crushed the cup and threw it hard into the garbage, then grabbed the sides of the sink and held on.

Lolek had learned a lot about Tommy and Robert over the past week, but not this news. He had hardly dared to consider what he might find by digging around in his son's life, but what he'd found was mostly pedestrian: season tickets to the Amherst Theatre Company, a rented cottage in Provincetown last summer, and apparently two weeks in Guatemala three years ago, volunteering with Habitat for Humanity. The most disturbing thing Lolek had learned was that he hadn't known about these ordinary things.

He turned on the hot water and let it run, pumped some liquid soap and washed his hands thoroughly, pumped some more and scrubbed a second time. His phone went off again and he let it go to voice mail. He left the water running while he dried his hands, then used the paper towels to shut off the faucets. He shrugged into his coat, put on his gloves, and stood there, holding the door handle. He closed his eyes, trying unsuccessfully to block out the image of a justice of the peace in some anonymous office, two friends standing in as witnesses. Or a wedding march, tuxedos, an intimate gathering sworn to secrecy.

How could he not have known his own son was married? How could Tommy have kept it from him, and for a whole year? Senator Zeilonka, champion of the successful effort to legalize same-sex marriage, son of a Massachusetts civil rights legend, favored MassEquality legislator for his perfect voting record . . .

"Damn him," he said sharply.

He yanked open the door and took the corridor that led from Tommy's room toward reception, telling himself that the last thing Tommy needed was his father going off on him. He punched the automatic door opener. Still, he didn't like to think of himself as a man who walked away. He stopped short in front of the open doors. Outside the waiting room, milling around on the sidewalk outside the broad glass entryway, a reporter saw him, and the whole group turned as one to catch a glimpse. What if one of them asked about Tommy's marriage? He held up a forefinger and mouthed "be right there." The automatic doors swung closed. He stripped off his gloves and shoved them into his overcoat pockets.

There was a lot he could finesse, but this? He covered his face with his hands, rubbed his eyes, and thought angrily about how helpful it would have been to showcase his own son's marriage over the past year. He patted the pockets of his overcoat and then reached in and searched through his suit for a tin of mints; the wretched taste of that coffee was nauseating.

A heavyset young man with woolly hair and a five-o'clock shadow materialized next to him. He wore navy scrubs, and purple rubber Crocs on his feet.

"Can I help you with something?"

"No, thank you, just catching my breath. My son is—"

The rising tears surprised him. He swallowed hard. He gazed beyond the man and focused on the opposite wall. A tiny hammer hung from a red fire alarm box. Lolek tentatively cleared his throat. If the man recognized Lolek, he was hiding it well, and Lolek was grateful for the private moment. He supposed hospital staff were trained to treat everyone equally.

"Is there a vending machine around, by chance?"

"Sure enough. Out into the waiting room, take a right around reception. Can't miss 'em."

Lolek sighed. The man followed Lolek's gaze and saw the reporters.

"On second thought, you know what? We've got our own stash. You're welcome to it. Come on through here."

Lolek smiled gratefully, and the man led him around the corner and through a door into a galley kitchen with a sink, industrial coffee machine, fridge, and vending machine lined up along one wall. A narrow counter ran the length of the other with open shelves above it. Three boxes of Dunkin' Donuts and a scattering of napkins lay on the counter.

"All yours."

Lolek thanked him and the man headed out. He stopped at the door and turned back.

"I hope you know you can count on us."

Lolek studied him, puzzled.

"You know, what they did to your son, to those other teachers. Unconscionable. Could just as easily have been nurses, any of us, really. People are scared. They think it's only the beginning. The tendency is to put your head down, you know? Just get by, get through, keep your mouth shut. But *you* tell us what to do? *You* lead the fight? We'll come out of the woodwork for you, Senator. Count on it."

Lolek didn't know if he could trust his voice. He nodded and offered the man his hand.

"Thank you, son, that means a lot."

"Least we can do. And we'll take good care of Tom, don't you worry about that. He's going to be just fine."

He walked out of the room. Lolek shook his head and smiled,

feeling fortified. From the vending machine he got a roll of peppermint Mentos and chewed one up, worked it around his mouth. He went out and made his way back to the hall, and glanced in the direction of Tommy's room. Going back was the right thing to do.

Tommy's room was darker than it had been. They'd pulled the curtain closed around them. Lolek was ashamed at his immediate relief, but he hesitated only momentarily before turning away. If a reporter asked about Tommy's marriage, he'd have to answer honestly; honest vulnerability in a politician was a rarity, and constituents were incredibly forgiving when politicians shared human failings like this one. It was the cover-ups that got them into trouble, the denial when denial was no longer plausible.

In front of the waiting room doors he paused, straightened the knot of his tie, buttoned his overcoat, and squared his shoulders. The doors eased open. He strode across the room, composing a serious expression suitable for the circumstances. The media teams surged forward, and someone held open the outside door. Lolek began to pull on his gloves, and as he crossed the threshold into the cold and waded into their midst, a thought accosted him as sharply as the shock of frigid air: Marta knew. Marta had known all along.

# 13
# The Warning Note

There was no question in Ludka's mind that Stanley had tampered with the Chopin. The average person wouldn't notice it, but Ludka had an eye for evenness and she lay there in bed, staring at the way the portrait hung imperceptibly off true. A nervous perspiration dampened her palms. Izaac was still puttering about in the bathroom, so she drew off the covers. She couldn't simply sit up and swing her legs to the floor anymore; she had to inch her entire body to the edge, then lower her legs while simultaneously pushing herself up with both arms. And then she had to sit for a moment, righting the world, before she could stand. She and Izaac both got out of bed this way, or off the daybed on the porch. They'd taken to calling it *the maneuver*.

She sidestepped her boots and hurried on bare feet over to the bureau, her silk long johns cooling quickly outside the covers. Carefully she lifted the small portrait off the wall, turned it around, and smiled with relief at the familiar sight of the thumb smudges on the back of the hidden canvas, the note about the buried provenance papers stapled to the frame. It had been a project to determine how to affix one stretched canvas behind the other while leaving enough room for the Chopin to breathe. She'd finally chosen a wooden frame with a deep rabbet that could accommodate both portraits; two hooks and eyes did the trick of holding the Chopin firmly in place. She'd been mistaken, then, about Stanley, and felt glad of it, for Oskar's sake. But her smile quickly morphed into a frown—the left hook was jammed halfway between opened and closed.

"What are you doing there, kochanie? I thought you were already in bed."

Ludka gave a start and nearly dropped the paintings. She quickly positioned her body as a shield so Izaac wouldn't see. She pushed home the hook into its eye.

"Only I remembered I meant tonight to inspect for the dust. Earlier on the tour it was an embarrassment."

Izaac snorted disbelievingly, sat on the bed, and took off his slippers. "This room hasn't seen dust in decades. Come to bed, you'll catch a chill."

Izaac was right about the chill. She set the nested paintings on the bureau and leaned them against the wall.

In bed, they lay on their backs, and Ludka rubbed her feet together. She stared wide-eyed at the portrait, wondering if it was possible for Stanley to have had the forethought to bring with him a used canvas, if he'd even gone so far as to bring a forgery! You could find images of the Chopin online, after all, thanks to the survival of black and white photographs.

"You look after your grandson," he'd said. "I can see myself out." The weasel.

"You can glare at it all you want, kochanie, but I promise the dust will still be there in the morning. Settle down now, and turn off that light."

He sounded sterner than he'd intended, but he was still irked by the way she'd talked about Tommy. And mój Boże but she was obsessed with that damned portrait! All the art they'd invested in, and this was the one that commanded her unflagging attention? He'd never understood it.

Ludka turned out the light but kept her eyes wide open. A shaft of moonlight cut across the floor, raced up the bureau, and landed on the upper corner of the portrait, casting a shadow that ballooned the frame to twice its size. Maybe she could sneak out of bed. Waiting until morning seemed an impossibility. Izaac rolled away from her and lifted the covers off her sore shoulder in the process, wafting in a bit of chill air. She adjusted the comforter, tucking it in more tightly. After a time, Izaac sighed heavily and lifted his head, turning it in her direction.

"Stop all that thinking." He dropped his head back on the pillow. "You could drown out a snow plow, for god's sake."

"Only I am lying here! Go to sleep, old man."

They lay together in tense silence.

As Izaac began to relax, he thought about the proficient way Robert had taken charge of the intake process at the ER; he'd provided Tommy's date of birth and social security number as if they were his own and handed over the insurance card, which covered them both. Robert's law firm was one of the first in the country to offer full coverage to domestic partners, something that conveyed a degree of legitimacy any judge or jury would recognize. Abe should be apprised. But what if Ludka was right? What if there was something they didn't know about Tommy? Damn her for planting doubts. He exhaled forcibly, as if he could expel his thoughts along with his breath.

"Sleep in other room if I am too much of bother!"

For one hopeful moment, Ludka thought he might comply. She lay there, rigid with waiting, feeling the beat of her riled-up heart. But Izaac just rolled toward her and fumbled around under the covers until he found her hand. He rubbed at her chilly fingers, then cupped his hand loosely around hers, his customary peace offering. With each of Izaac's breaths she caught the familiar whiff of peppermint toothpaste, a vestige of sausage, and something like crushed summer clover that was uniquely Izaac; for one aching moment, she wanted to whisper a confession, release herself from decades of deceit, but the moment passed as quickly as it had come. Telling him could only lead to relinquishing the painting, an idea which never failed to send her mind into a resistant scurry, for fear of losing the portrait itself, or revealing her secret, or something else entirely, she didn't know and didn't allow herself to consider. All she knew was that any thought of confession stirred a burgeoning anxiety that threatened to turn to outright panic, and so any flight of thought would do, as long as it outran her impulse to confess. So many times she had been tempted to tell him, but Izaac was a devotedly principled man who'd made a public career of being above reproach. In the early years, she'd been too ashamed to tell him, and the longer she waited the harder it became. Later, when he was running for reelection, it became impossible. Ludka didn't want to put him in a compromising position; if he knew she was harboring stolen art, he'd be forced to either collude or turn her over to the authorities. In either case, who would believe he could have been so easily deceived? Who would believe he hadn't been colluding? His career—not to mention her own—would have been over. This had been a helpful rationale, and she'd seized on it; she could never endanger Izaac.

Now she pressed his fingers before extricating her hand. She rolled away and breathed the cool, clear air. She closed her eyes. Nothing more to be done tonight.

Just as she was about to slip over into sleep, she startled awake at the sound of crunching snow. She lifted her head, her neck straining with the effort of listening. One more crunch and then nothing. She thumped Izaac on the shoulder.

"Something is there! In the snow."

"Mój Boże, Ludka! It's just the deer. They've gotten desperate and are browsing on the juniper. Now go to sleep."

She tried to relax, and even though she didn't hear another sound, she knew she wouldn't be able to settle down. She got up and told Izaac she was going downstairs.

She made her way down, stopping every second step to switch the nested paintings from one hand to the other, the hanging wire sharp inside the curl of her fingers. Halfway down she once again thought she heard something outside, but when she stopped to listen, there was only the hum of the refrigerator and then its sudden whine as it powered down. After that, silence. She held her breath. Nothing. Downstairs, she perched the frame on one of the ladder-back chairs in the dining room. She turned on all the lights, trying to make the room feel like it would at an ordinary hour. She adjusted her robe more snugly around her throat, tightened her belt, and turned up the thermostat. The furnace ticked and ignited immediately, then quickly began its steady drone. From the kitchen she retrieved a pair of white cotton gloves from a new twelve-pack, and from a drawer in the dining room sideboard she fetched a thin felt pad wrapped in plastic. She unwrapped the felt and smoothed it out on the dining room table, then carefully unfastened the Chopin's hooks and lifted it out onto the felt. She smiled with relief; nothing seemed amiss. As so often happened when she took the time to see the portrait, a feeling of calm descended.

"*Sukces*," she'd told Oskar in 1939 when she'd gone to his attic studio at the prearranged time. "The Mieroszewski is liberated. Chopin has been saved."

Oskar had pressed his hands together, pointed them at her, and smiled.

"It is Poland you are holding. Keep her safe."

Five days later, on the twenty-fifth day of the Nazi siege, when the terror bombing of Warsaw was incessantly fierce, a four-thousand-pound Satan had fallen from the body of a Heinkel twin-engine bomber and exploded on Swietojanska, blasting through the rear wall and blowing out the front windows of the empty Zeilonka apartment on Piwna. The next day, one day shy of Poland's surrender, Ludka had emerged from the bomb shelter and found the Chopin lying face up on the street in front of her apartment, miraculously unharmed but for one small dent and a coating of plaster dust. She could still see the young Chopin—pale countenance, sunken consumptive cheeks, and pronounced Adam's apple—lying on the ruined cobblestones, gazing up through the dust as if lost.

Now the pipes from the furnace clanked and shuddered as hot water rushed to the downstairs radiators, which set about releasing their pressure through sudden hisses of steam. In the bottom left corner of the canvas was the repaired dent that none but a conservator would notice, but which Ludka could see as clearly as the face of Chopin. After the siege, while the Nazis had made themselves at home in the surrendered city, it had been a challenge to find the hidden time to steam and press out the dent, but Ludka and Oskar had managed.

Ludka left the painting on the felt and went into the spacious study, which was buffered from the rest of the house by the stone chimney and the stairs. She sat at the scarred hardwood desk and woke up the laptop. She gathered the robe more closely around her neck and turned on the portable heater next to the desk.

*Sodomite*, she typed into the search engine. She'd expected the Wikipedia entry and competing dictionaries' definitions, as well as the references to Sodom and Gomorrah. She was surprised, though, to discover that someone had accused Cuba of "dumping its Sodomites into Florida" during the Carter administration, and that newly elected President Obama apparently had a Sodomite past, which was coming back to haunt him. She was also flabbergasted to see smiling American children holding colorful, vicious placards declaring God's hatred for people like Tommy. One boy, probably no more than seven, with blond lamb's-wool-tight curls, pale eyebrows, and deep-set, serious eyes that stared straight out of the photo, bothered her more than the others, perhaps because he had Tommy's coloring. She would have expected restlessness in a boy his age, or boredom, or fatigue from hoisting in his outstretched arms two poster boards nearly as tall as himself, but his countenance was chillingly determined, verging on angry. Still, there were bruise-colored bags beneath his eyes that didn't belong on such a young face, and Ludka wondered about his burdens. How naive she had allowed herself to become, sheltered in this eastern American university town. Somehow she had shielded herself from contemporary vitriol, from the kind of vile, unyielding beliefs she had dared to let herself believe she'd escaped long ago. She took a piece of scrap paper from the desk drawer and laid it out on the desk. She ran a hand over it as if she'd never before seen paper, hesitated, then reopened the drawer and grabbed a pencil. She quickly sketched the boy's face, flanked by the placards. She drew in the lettering and got lost in the work. When she was done, she sat for a long time, scrutinizing what she'd drawn. The last time she'd done such a sketch, she'd been breathing smoke and brick dust, documenting Warsaw's decimation. Abruptly she crumpled the sketch and threw it into the recycling bin beneath the desk.

A further online search indicated these children might be the exception, from some tiny and incestuous church in Kansas, and Ludka allowed herself to latch on to a slight feeling of relief, which amplified when she saw the usual sorts of churchy items on the Hampshire Redeemer Fellowship's website: Sunday school schedule, social service projects, gatherings and study groups, theology, sermons, community. Pastor Royce Leonard had a wise, compassionate face. While she printed out his long biography and statement of approach for later reading, she turned her attention to Stanley.

After five pages of irrelevant results, when she'd begun to wonder if Stanley wasn't who he said he was, she finally found the Fisherman's Wharf gallery about which he had bragged. The site was minimalist but appeared legitimate, complete with rotating photos of seascapes and the glass-fronted building with its modern, sea-foam-colored logo: Stanley Brozek | San Francisco. She dug a bit further, though, and was disturbed to discover he wasn't registered with the art dealers' associations of San Francisco, California, or America. Back on his website, the contact information was for e-mail only: no physical address, no directions, no phone number. Hours by appointment.

Ludka picked up the phone and dialed information. No listing anywhere in San Francisco. Ludka switched off the portable heater and moments later the furnace, too, kicked off. Even the refrigerator had finished its cycle, and in the advent of the sudden silence Ludka's body drained of a tension she'd not even known she was holding. She pressed her fingers into the hollow of her neck and closed her eyes. Perhaps she should go back to bed. Stanley had seemed kind, wringing out the rag for Tommy, cleaning up the kitchen. She was just about to call it a night when she caught sight of Stanley's name coupled with the word *shoplifting* in the search results. Dated last fall, it accompanied a small news item from the police blotter in the *Potrero Hill News*, a weekly online newspaper. He'd been questioned for allegedly taking two pairs of sunglasses from a Safeway supermarket. The paper quoted him as saying that the whole episode was a complete misunderstanding: "I'm wearing $345 Modos. Why would I need to steal from Safeway?"

Ludka sat back and dropped her hands in her lap. What kind of man spent $345 on sunglasses?

"Weasel," she muttered.

She couldn't find anything at all about Pawel Brozek. Last week she had spent some time searching and found nothing. Now she discovered a few things about Oskar's son—Stanley's father—who had made his name on Wall Street and didn't resemble Oskar in the least. He had died just last year, shortly after being indicted for fraud by the Securities and Exchange Commission. Members of his team had been found guilty. Surely if Oskar had been alive, he would have attended his son's funeral?

She was suddenly exhausted. She turned off the monitor and the desk lamp, and followed the light coming through the door from the living room. She parted the drapes over the French door to the screen porch, wondering if the deer were at the salt lick. The moon was high and bright, the yard bathed in snow-reflected light, and the deer were there, just as they'd been nearly every day at one point or another over the past week. One of them stood taller, having maybe sensed the movement of the curtain, but soon enough she relaxed her guard and pawed and nosed at the snow. Ludka thought about throwing on the floodlight, but just then the same deer faltered and pitched slowly forward onto her knees. Ludka threw a hand over her mouth, but then the deer lowered her back end and arranged herself for sleeping. The other two joined her in the same ungainly manner, settling close together to battle the cold. Ludka's face softened and she released a small sigh.

Just as she was about to turn away, she noticed that the door to the screen porch was ajar and one of the four chairs had been shoved back from the table. And on the table, dead center, was a fist-sized stone, anchoring what appeared to be an envelope. Ludka inhaled sharply and dropped the curtain. The refrigerator whined into life, and something wooden in the frame of the old house gave a sharp pop and groan. The deer wouldn't be there had someone been skulking outside, but Ludka still walked through the house and turned on the floodlights over the driveway. She spent a few tense minutes scanning the lighted areas and straining to hear any foreign sound. She double-checked the locks on all the doors, then fetched the cotton gloves from the dining room. She opened the door to the screen porch as quietly as she could, and was sorry that as soon as she stepped outside the deer snorted, scrambled to their feet, and bolted, white tails flung up as if in surrender. The porch was frigid. Ludka took the stone and envelope back into the dining room. She was aware of feeling some small, giddy pride that she had thought of the gloves; she wouldn't be responsible for disturbing what would shortly become evidence.

The envelope hadn't been sealed. Inside, neatly inked in thick black marker on a piece of folded copy paper, was a vulgar warning about Tommy.

# 14
# Night Visitor

What Meck first became aware of before he was fully awake, before he felt Jill shaking him or heard the steady knocking on his front door, was a high and persistent whining from Gracie, their typically silent greyhound. Meck flung himself to a sitting position, startling Jill, who apologized for scaring him.

"Someone's at the door," she said.

"What time is it?"

"Nearly ten-thirty."

Meck had been asleep less than half an hour. Across the brightly moonlit room, the dog was stretching cautiously forward through the doorway, long neck arched around the edge of the doorframe, peering down the stairs. The knocking was insistent, yet not terribly loud.

"Who's there, Gracie? Who is it, girl?"

Gracie scrabbled into the hallway and pelted down the stairs.

Meck got up. An accident? Gloria from next door? The knocking was odd: light, as if the person didn't want to alert the neighbors, as rapid as the drill of a small woodpecker. Then it stopped. A man's muffled voice seemed to be talking to the dog. Whit, maybe? The sudden rush of adrenaline and chill of the room turned to tension in his back and shoulders, and he shuddered involuntarily. He pulled a pair of jeans over his briefs, and a sea-blue Irish sweater over his T-shirt. Gracie had stopped whining, and he could hear her tail whacking the foot of the banister. Jill got up, but Meck told her to stay in bed, he'd take care of it. He shoved his feet into his leather slippers and headed downstairs. Gracie pressed her nose against the long oval window in the old oak door opposite the foot of the stairs. Eric Barton stood outside, blowing into his gloveless hands.

"Eric?"

Meck drew off the chain, threw open the deadbolt, and opened the door. Eric stamped his feet a few times and stepped inside, bringing in a rush of cold. Meck relocked the front door.

"What are you doing here, Eric? What's going on?"

Eric angrily shook his head.

"You tell me, Mr. Meck."

"Tell you what? Listen, come in. Don't worry about your boots."

Gracie trotted ahead of them into the kitchen. Eric unbuttoned his overcoat and stood somewhat awkwardly in front of the sink, looking as if he wasn't quite sure how he'd gotten there. He opened his mouth to speak, then shut it. He blew again into his hands. Meck gestured to a chair at the kitchen table, but Eric continued to stand. Gracie nosed Eric's hip and then leaned against him. He absentmindedly stroked her head.

"Did you do it yourself or farm it out?"

"What are you talking about, Eric?"

"They said there were two of them. Clean-cut. Who'd you get to go with you? I mean, I agreed to help, but I didn't sign up for this. A little information now and again is one thing, but this—"

"Eric!"

The effect of Meck's shout was as instantaneous as a slap—Eric shut up.

"Here, sit down, let me make us some coffee."

"Wait. You really don't know?"

Meck shook his head. He pulled out a chair and Eric sat. His overcoat bunched up around his neck and shoulders. He fussed with it and then stood up, took it off, and searched around for a place to put it. Meck took it from him and went back out into the hall and hung it in the closet tucked under the stairs. Jill came down the stairs, her blonde hair freshly brushed.

"You promised if I helped you I wouldn't be exposed," Eric called. "Who knew about tonight's review at the high school?"

Meck told Jill to head back up to bed. "It's just work," he whispered. "Nothing to concern you."

"Who's exposed?" she whispered back.

"No one. Go check on the kids."

"Shouldn't I at least make you some coffee?"

She leaned to peer past him into the kitchen, and Meck sternly held her shoulders.

"The kids. What did I just say?"

"You're right, Warren, I'm sorry."

He touched her cheek and she briefly closed her eyes. She tightened the belt on her robe and headed back up the stairs.

Meck sighed, regretting his unnecessarily stern tone; Eric's presence was unnerving. He smoothed his hair in the back, then in the front, and went into the kitchen, where Eric was pacing. Gracie was standing out of Eric's way, ears cocked, watching him carefully.

"Only a handful of us knew about the review," said Meck. "But what did you mean about helping me? Who promised you what?"

Eric opened his mouth to say something, frowned, and closed it. Despite the late hour and the drive he'd made from Boston, his suit was impeccable, his tie neatly knotted, but thick and random strands of his black hair had cracked free from the gel he'd used to slick it into place.

"Okay," he said, "now I'm confused. But that would explain why you were so overt when I saw you this morning—I figured you wouldn't admit you recognized me. Here's the thing—I've been helping your campaign with a little information now and then, that's all. Nothing major. But I didn't pass on information about the review. That seemed like too private a matter."

Meck's eyes widened. He turned away from Eric, put a hand over his mouth, and slowly walked over to the door.

"I'm sorry," said Eric. "I assumed you knew."

"No. No, I didn't know. When you say you've been helping my campaign, who exactly are you talking about? How long has this been going on?"

"About a month? Is there a problem?"

Meck crossed the floor and sank into a chair. Gracie followed and nosed up under his arm, which he pulled away, annoyed.

"But here's the thing," said Eric. "Somebody beat up the senator's son. Two 'clean-cut young men' they said. Put him in the hospital! It was all over the news."

Meck froze, then rested his hand on Gracie's neck.

"Beat him up? Is he . . . ?"

"He'll be fine."

"Thank God. It happened at the school? After the review?"

"In his driveway. He suspected he'd been followed. Did Whit Hammond know about the review?"

"Of course. Wait, Whit doesn't know about you, does he?"

"I thought so, but then again I thought you did, too."

Meck grew very still, then rubbed a sudden chill from the back of his neck.

"You can't be worried about Whit, Eric. Someone must have staked out Tommy's house. It could have been anyone. He's been all over the news. Listen, I want you to stop whatever it is you were doing. Immediately."

"Of course, sure. Am I in trouble?"

"I'd say if you kept doing whatever it is you've been doing, you could have derailed any hope of a future in politics, not to mention undermined our entire campaign. Who asked you to do this?"

Eric worked at one of the strands of hair, rubbing out the dried gel. He stared down at the floor.

"I think maybe it would be better if I didn't say."

"If I have someone on the campaign who's undermining our efforts, I'm sure you understand I want to confront them before they go too far. It wasn't Arnie Dengler, was it? Seems like something he'd blunder into. Or someone on one of our volunteer committees? The legislative team would make sense. What kind of information were you passing on?"

"Just whether the senator was aware of the bills, whether anyone in the office was talking about them, that sort of thing."

"You need to tell me who it is, Eric."

"I'll let them know we talked, I promise."

"I don't know what this person told you, Eric, but I'm in charge of this campaign. Nothing underhanded happens on my watch, okay? Tell them I said that."

"I want you to know, Mr. Meck, that I support your efforts. I'm a believer in the First Amendment and even though I don't go to your church . . . if there's anything else I can do . . . aboveboard, I mean."

"Here's what you can do. Put it behind you. Forget all about it. Work hard for the senator. Don't tell anyone—and I mean *anyone*—and don't ever—*ever*—do anything like it again, do you understand?"

Eric nodded soberly.

"I need to know I can count on you, Eric."

"You can, absolutely. And I'm awfully sorry. I've botched everything, haven't I?"

Meck got up and began to pace. He'd have to coordinate with Pastor Royce, come out strong in their condemnation of the assault, make it glaringly clear they would never condone such violence. He'd use Leviticus on tomorrow's show, try to allay any doubts. And then Pastor Royce could echo that at Wednesday's seeker service. Better yet, he'd see if the pastor could join him on the show tomorrow. Meck began to feel better, as he always did with a plan that included Pastor Royce. He stopped pacing.

"'Thou shalt not avenge,'" he said to Eric, "'nor bear any grudge against the children of thy people, but thou shalt love thy neighbor as thyself.' I'll use that tomorrow, and I'll call the senator myself and express my condolences and concerns. I think it's containable."

"What about the 'clean-cut young men'?" said Eric. "That part worries me. We're not talking about some gay-bashing rednecks out for a joyride."

"That is a concern, I admit. Let me ask around, see what I can find out. We certainly can't have any freelancers out there. I'll do what I can to forestall anyone's ideas about further violence."

Gracie wagged her tail and gazed at Eric. He ran his hand over her fawn-colored forehead and ears, then scratched her creamy, freckled neck. Eric sighed and looked around the kitchen as if seeing it for the first time. He smiled.

"What happened to that coffee?"

Meck put a hand to his brow and gave a short laugh.

"Never mind," said Eric. "Forget about it. I'll grab some at that all-night Starbucks out on the Pike."

"You're driving back? I assumed you'd be here in the district tomorrow."

"No, the senator's already here, and Aggie said we'd need more coverage in Boston. She wasn't sure if he'd be back tomorrow or not. Depends on his son."

"Why didn't you just call me? Or whoever you've been working with for that matter? Why drive all this way?"

"I was just kind of wondering that myself. I don't know, I was all wired up. And honestly?"

He drew himself up in his chair.

"I love your show, and I know how influential you are in the Christian community. And if your campaign succeeds, I assume you're going national. I thought maybe we could get reacquainted. Climbing the ladder, as you said. I guess after seeing you today I wanted to see you in person, make the connection."

He smiled sheepishly.

"And you thought showing up at my home late at night to accuse me of assault would be a good way to connect? I think what you really wanted was to see whether I would lie when you confronted me. No, I get that; I do. You had your doubts, that's understandable."

"The senator is a really good man, you know? We're doing some important work. Life-changing work. From all accounts his son

Tommy is a good guy, too. Even a good teacher. I do wonder if . . . I don't know, don't you ever wonder if you're doing the right thing?"

Meck nodded slowly. He turned when he heard shuffling behind him.

"Daddy?"

"Hey there, Sport. What are you doing up?"

Andrew stood in his pale blue footy pajamas, staring wide-eyed at Eric. Gracie trotted over and stood calmly beside him. She came up to his shoulder, and he put an arm around her neck, never taking his eyes off Eric.

"Who's this little guy?"

"My name is Andrew Meck. I'm pleased to meet you."

He held out his small hand and frowned at Eric. Eric laughed, and Meck smiled.

"That's right, Sport. But come on over here, where Eric can shake your hand."

Andrew buried his face in Gracie's neck. Gracie took a sideways step and craned her head around toward Andrew, who leaned on her too heavily.

"Come on over here. Join us."

Andrew shuffled over and leaned against Meck, staring again at Eric. Meck picked him up and then sat down and pulled him onto his lap.

"It's not that I wonder whether we're doing the right thing, Eric. We are absolutely doing the right thing. It's that we need to keep our focus, and that can be tough, especially in the face of someone as honorable as Lolek Zeilonka. You have to remember we're just trying to protect our kids."

He hefted Andrew into a more comfortable position.

"I'm sorry about Tommy Zeilonka, really I am. No one

deserves that. I'd love to see him get it together and go back into the classroom. But until he does, until they all do, our kids have to come first. Curtailing their speech in the classroom is only the first step down a slippery slope. Almost a dozen countries already classify some religious speech as a hate crime; people can't even quote the Biblical references about homosexuality. They call this 'tolerance' without a hint of irony. If we don't fight back, freedom of speech will be a thing of the past, and God knows that doesn't bode well for freedom of religion. I never lose sight of our grand vision, Eric. It's a vision I've kept in focus since I was a kid, listening to Pastor Royce's sermons in a tiny storefront church in a California strip mall. It's what keeps me resilient in the face of empathy, which often masquerades rather cleverly as doubt. We're restoring our Christian nation. Restoring it, step by step. If Lolek Zeilonka were on our side, he would do exactly what we're doing, make no mistake about that. We are not 'anti' either your senator or his son. We're pro-history. We're on the side of what's right and true."

Meck found he'd been punctuating his words again with a raised forefinger. He lowered his hand to Andrew's head and smoothed back his white-blond hair.

"What's right and true," murmured Eric. He rubbed Gracie's head with both hands. "You should run for office, Mr. Meck. Say something like that tomorrow on your radio show and that'll send just the right message to any freelancers. Listen, I'm sorry I barged in on you like this. I'd better hit the road if I'm going to get any sleep at all tonight. And sorry I—"

"Say nothing more, Eric. You're fine."

—

When Eric had gone, and Andrew was tucked back into bed, Meck used the kitchen phone to call Whit. It rang seven times before Whit answered.

"Eric Barton was just in my kitchen, Whit. No, sorry, it can't wait. Please, go downstairs into your office. We need to talk. Now."

# 15
# In the News

Frank Zeilonka walked into his brother's kitchen after quietly letting himself in through the back door. Lolek's car was out front. Frank wasn't surprised, given the situation with Tommy. He was surprised, though, that no one was up yet. Rough night, he supposed, and it was still early. But Marta was usually up by five, and more mornings than not she had coffee waiting for him. Somewhere along the line, he couldn't say exactly when, he had taken to stopping in on his way to the station, or sometimes on his way home if he was filling in for one of the guys on a night shift. He couldn't remember the last time he'd seen Lolek, and just the idea he was upstairs made Frank uneasy. Maybe he should have gone straight to Mercy to check in again on the kid. The coffee canister was cold from the refrigerator. He tucked the paper filter into the basket and scooped out enough coffee for a full pot. While it was brewing, he stepped out the front door and grabbed the newspaper off the stoop. As he pulled it out of its plastic bag, Frank peered out into the dark morning. His breath hung and then rose before him, drifting toward the road. Tommy's story led the news. The prominent photograph above the fold was Lolek emerging from the ER, a pained expression on his face, one glove on, the other hanging limp. Frank grinned at the second photograph, framed in a sidebar.

"Good one, Matka."

He shook open the paper and went back into the house just as Lolek lumbered down the stairs. Immediately Frank felt fine, happy to see his brother.

"How can anyone make Levis seem so formal?" said Frank. "Do you iron those things?"

Surprised, Lolek glanced at the back door, as if checking to see if Frank had broken the glass to get in. He hadn't seen his brother in months. Frank looked good, his dark tarnished copper hair cut short and neat, his thick biceps and muscular chest filling out a sheepskin-lined green sweatshirt, his fawn-colored Carhartt's relatively clean. He must be off today or he'd be in uniform. Only a slightly rounded belly betrayed his move from field to desk; when he'd taken over as fire chief in Huntsville, he'd sworn he wouldn't gain the requisite paunch. Lolek poured coffee into a mug and handed it to his brother. Frank wanted to get the cream out of the fridge, but hesitated. He sat at the round pine table.

"Got any cream?"

"Like I would know." Lolek opened the fridge.

"Senator's Son Attacked," read Frank. "Check out Matka! Professor stands sentinel, it says."

Lolek set the carton of cream in front of Frank and peered over his brother's shoulder at the paper. Instinctively and immediately he judged his own photograph effective. And then he saw his mother and was unexpectedly swept by a rush of gratitude and pride.

"What is she now, eighty-five? I hope I look that good at her age."

"You don't look that good now. You're like a middle-aged pony in winter."

Lolek smiled and ran a hand through his unkempt hair.

"It's like a still from some war epic," said Frank. "Closing scene, she's everyone's mother. Only need a battered flag waving in the foreground, maybe some swelling hymn. She's like a Polish Katherine Hepburn. What else have we got?"

He turned to page three. A photograph showed Frank leaving the hospital with their parents and Marta.

"I didn't know you were there," said Lolek.

"Why would they want this shot? You'd think we were the Kennedys. Of course I was there. I heard it on the scanner. I called Shelly over at police headquarters right away to let him know it was Tommy. He's all over it. Shelly's convinced a neighbor will have seen the attacker's car. He's probably still out there knocking on doors."

Lolek poured his own coffee and searched around in frustration for the sugar bowl. He should have thought to call Sheldon himself.

"It's here," said Frank, pushing the sugar across the table to Lolek.

Just as Lolek spooned out some sugar, the phone rang, and both brothers together glanced at the clock on the oven: 6:12. The second ring cut off abruptly, and they heard creaking from the master bedroom upstairs. Lolek picked up the kitchen extension and walked to stare out the back door.

"I'm on, Marta, what is it?"

Frank frowned at his brother's presumptuousness. Granted, his kid was in the hospital, but he'd bet Lolek would have picked up regardless. Lolek tended to command whatever space he was in.

"Wait, Dad, start from the beginning. What about the police?" He turned to Frank and mouthed, "It's Dad."

"I gathered."

After a few minutes, Marta came into the kitchen wearing long silk pajamas, navy with orange piping, and faded navy Keds with the backs squashed flat. Lolek frowned. She always dressed for company. Maybe she hadn't known Frank was here.

"I'll put in a call to Warren Meck today, Dad, at least see if he has any ideas. I do, I think he's honest. No, just instinct, something about him."

To Lolek's astonishment, as Marta walked sleepily past Frank, she paused to give him a quick kiss at the base of his right sideburn, then touched his shoulder ever so briefly. It wasn't the sort of kiss that sounded alarms in a long marriage—Lolek recognized it as merely friendly, sisterly—but it was also troubling, as casually routine as pouring a refill, which Marta now did for Frank. He suddenly wondered if Frank knew about Tommy's marriage. Last night when he'd gotten into bed, Marta had feigned sleep, and Lolek had let her. Now he stepped forward and held out his mug. Marta topped it off. He cradled the phone against his shoulder, moved between Marta and Frank, and stirred in some more sugar.

"I know, Dad, this takes it up a notch. You'll call Abe? We're heading over to Mercy as soon as we're done with our coffee." At this he turned inquiringly to Marta. She nodded. "Yes, I'll tell them. See if Abe can convince Tommy about the alarm system at the house. Tommy will listen to him. Better yet, have him tell Robert."

Marta sat down across from Frank. He turned the paper so she could see the front page and she reached for it. Lolek ended his call, and they looked at him expectantly. He leaned back against the counter, and his stomach cut uncomfortably into his waist-band. He crossed his arms and stood up straight.

"What are you doing here exactly?" he said to Frank.

"He's here," said Marta, "that's all. His godson, or have you forgotten?"

Lolek bent toward his right, trying to stretch out the tension in his left hip.

"What do either of you know about the Redeemer Fellowship?"

"You said police," said Frank. "Did something else happen?"

"Someone left a hate note on your parents' porch last night," said Marta. "A warning to think twice about defending . . . well, Tommy."

"'Your faggot grandson' is what they wrote." Lolek told Frank the story.

"Sheldon went over himself, which was nice of him. Said they had the place locked down like Fort Knox."

"They've got to be scared," said Marta.

Frank and Lolek both snorted at this. They exchanged a quick smile, and Lolek felt a sudden surge of fondness for his brother. He pulled out a chair and sat down.

"Excited, maybe," said Frank to Marta. "Nothing like a good cause to get a rise out of Dad. And Matka? Already it is adventure!" He held his hand over his heart.

Lolek laughed. Frank smiled down at his mug.

"I'm going up to get dressed," said Marta. "I'll phone the hospital and see what's going on. See what you two can do about some breakfast."

In her absence, the brothers sat and drank their coffee. After a minute, Frank retrieved the paper. He handed a section to Lolek. It was nice, Frank thought, sitting here with his brother. He was ashamed that he momentarily felt grateful for Tommy's situation, but it was such a rare thing, to get Lolek to himself.

"One of my guys at the station goes to that Redeemer church. He's reliable, a solid team member, works hard, smart. He never talks about it, isn't preachy or anything. Only thing is he never swears, never has a beer, not like the other kids I usually get. But he's quiet about it, doesn't keep anyone else from their fun. The men like him."

"Doesn't proselytize?"

"Well sure, at first, but nothing pushy, a couple years ago, right after he joined. He seemed almost apologetic, like maybe it had been assigned, like the Jehovahs. Maybe they have some kind of quota. They have another church on the Cape, I think. He and his family go there for vacation."

Immediately Lolek wondered if there were other branches around the state, if their locations were consistent with the districts that had fired teachers.

Marta came back into the room. She had brushed out her chestnut hair and put on a pair of boot-cut blue jeans and a lime-green angora sweater. Lolek got up and opened a bag of bagels on the counter and peered inside. He pulled cream cheese and a carton of eggs from the fridge.

"I spoke to Robert," said Marta. "They're letting Tommy go home this morning."

Lolek hadn't known his shoulders were tense. He smiled at Marta, who was looking with shining eyes at Frank. Frank smiled softly and nodded. Lolek turned back to the counter. He pulled a knife from its storage block and started slicing bagels. When he had three, he went to the fridge and stared into it.

"Do we have any lox?"

"Of course not."

Lolek carefully closed the door and set down the knife. He looked out the window over the sink. It had finally begun to get light. Some kind of wildlife had split a trail straight through the snow-covered yard.

"I've got to go get changed for the office," he said.

"I thought you weren't going in. Maria Rose is here."

"Have her call me when she gets up. Maybe we can meet up for lunch."

"But what about Tommy? I thought we'd help him get settled at home."

"Frank will be there. Won't you, Frank? Be there to help?"

Frank looked at Lolek like he wasn't quite sure what had just happened.

"If you need me. Of course."

"Well there you have it." Lolek left the room and speed-dialed Aggie's number.

# 16
# The Rape of Europa

"Today we watch film," said Ludka.

In the honors library, the students sat in oak armchairs around a large, polished conference table in the ornate room where they normally met. A huge crystal chandelier complemented the scale of the twenty-foot-high ceiling. Three wavy-glassed, twelve-over-twelve wood-framed windows punctuated the floor-to-ceiling bookcases. A lush maroon carpet muffled sound. A room with much history, Ludka always thought, a room in which she felt at home. She stood at one end of the table, fingertips lightly touching the surface, an incongruous TV and DVD player on a cart just behind her.

"I expect you all heard the news about Thomas Zeilonka. He is my grandson. Last night held little sleep for me and this morning . . . much fame."

She held up the newspaper and mimicked her own haughty pose. The class laughed.

"We wondered if you might cancel," said Will.

Ludka flapped her hand dismissively, although she had considered it.

"Already the bullies have disrupted too much. To cancel class is their victory. The one acquiescence is to teach by proxy of film to protect you from my muddled brain. Again, you will see that Mr. Stanley Brozek in the back there is our guest. He is trying for the free education and so far already he is succeeding."

More laughter. From where Stanley sat by the exit he lifted his hand and smiled.

"How's your grandson doing?" said Will. "Is he okay?"

Ludka could see Will's evident concern, and still it unsettled her, how quickly someone's personal trauma could be appropriated by others. Father Skurski had called on her first thing that morning, showing up unannounced at the house, and initially Ludka had been touched. But later, as he was leaving, when he told her he'd be praying for Tommy, she hadn't liked the subtle condescension in his tone and suspected he was rather enjoying himself, maybe even gathering material for his next sermon. For the first time since Tommy had explained to her and Izaac the nature of his relationship with Robert, six years ago now, Ludka had experienced what had to be a mere fraction of the judgment Tommy must routinely encounter. She had thought of the serious blond boy with the woolly curls, holding high his signs: *God Hates Fags* and *You're Going to Hell.*

How could she possibly tell Will whether Tommy was okay?

"This morning he is home, thank you."

"I guess they're organizing a protest rally," said Annika, cradling her tattooed arms by the elbows. "My brother's at the high school. He said it's not just for the school but for the whole district, in some public place, maybe even in Boston. The students all want him back."

The protest was news to Ludka, and she wanted to phone Izaac immediately. Sophie and Ashley, who sat together at the other end of the table, glanced at each other. Sophie nodded and Ashley bent her head to her cell phone and began to type. Sophie tentatively cleared her throat and fiddled with her cross, which now hung visibly outside her blouse and sweater. Will and Annika leaned forward to see beyond the row of students seated alongside them. Sophie dipped her head shyly and then lifted it again and addressed Annika.

"Some of the students are actually relieved," said Sophie. "My brother Brandon among them. No offense, Professor, but Mr. Zeilonka wasn't too tolerant of the Christian kids." She glanced at Will and dropped her gaze again. Ashley crossed her chunky arms.

"We'll just see how many people show up at the rally," said Will. "I'll put money on it the place is mobbed."

"And what will that prove?" said Sophie.

"Let us see," said Ludka. She made a show of digging into her bag. She pulled out the syllabus and held it up.

"As suspected, protest rally is not on the syllabus. *The Rape of Europa* is. Already who has seen this film?"

"Speaking of bullies," said Will. He surveyed the class. "Wait, no one else saw it? Nazis as art thieves? Seriously? They were the biggest art thieves of all time."

Ludka glanced at Stanley but couldn't read his expression. As previously arranged, he had met her here in the classroom while the rest of the students were arriving. Ludka had taken a hard look at the sunglasses he'd propped at the top of his forehead. She'd said nothing of her suspicions, only thanked him for cleaning the kitchen and tried to gauge his expression, which seemed to show nothing but concern for Tommy. After

the hubbub of last night's intruder, and before she woke Izaac
or called the police, Ludka had carefully locked the Chopin in
the back coat closet with the rest of the paintings, and taken
the subterfuge painting—the girl looking over her shoulder—
upstairs where it belonged. The climate-controlled closet con-
tained racks for any size canvas, Izaac's brainchild when their
collection had gotten too big. The painting would be secure
until she could find another hiding place, which she'd need to
do in the next three weeks, before Izaac pulled out the paintings for the student art tour.

Now, Will fingered the rings on his ear and held out a hand to
Ludka. "Enlighten these heathens, Professor."

She smiled and sat down, her fingers entwined in front of her
on the table.

"Not only did Nazis murder. Already they were also champion
art thieves, and on an industrial scale. World War II you think
concluded by atom bombs in Japan, but still today there is unfinished business. Adolf Hitler lost the war, yes?"

She glared around at them as they exchanged confused glances,
as if this were a trick question.

"Ask the Jews of Poland, my home country, who lost the
war. Before the war, more than three million Jews. My home
city, Warsaw, was the capital city of European Jewry. Today?
Somewhere between five and twenty thousand Jews only in whole
of Poland! Hitler is not rolling over in the grave."

"Have you been back, Professor? To Poland?"

Ludka twisted her rings and stared for a long moment at her
hands. Someone coughed nervously. Ludka shook her head.

"It is irrelevant. We focus on the art of the Holocaust. Why?
So we know the heart of the Nazi, and the resilient soul of a

people. Art created during the Holocaust, after Holocaust, and art as victim of Holocaust. Art still is missing, its provenance interrupted, masterpieces disappeared forever. Destroyed. Lost. Hidden. To steal art is to steal the soul of a people, to destroy culture."

Stanley lifted his briefcase onto his lap. He rested his arms across the top.

"In a couple weeks you will see a great collection of contemporary Polish art at my home. Mr. Brozek got private tour already last night."

"Wait till you see it," said Stanley.

"But why do I have modern collection? Why not great art from an earlier era? I will tell you why. I want Hitler rolling in his grave. *The Rape of Europa* will show he despised modern art—degenerate, he called it: Matisse, Picasso, Kandinsky, Van Gogh, all degenerate—and he destroyed it like he destroyed the people, through intentional system with vast bureaucratic support. Particularly he had hatred for Polish art. And Polish people, not only Jews, he directed killed without pity or mercy—Poles were in his mind same as Jews: subhuman. Thank God there are people who did what they could to protect Poland's cultural heritage, who today work still to recover art. Only I do my small part."

Ludka felt pain in her left wrist and realized she had been banging the table. *I did not steal*, she was thinking. *Only I liberated, and preserved!* She got up and turned to the TV, her face flushed. She wheeled the TV close to the table and felt a rising fury as she did.

"Enough speech. It is time to watch. Someone will pull blinds."

She jabbed the buttons on the TV and DVD player, and adjusted the volume.

"Mr. Brozek will turn out lights, yes?"

As the film began, she made her way through the flickering light to the back of the room. She would watch only until they began to show the destruction of Warsaw, and then she would have to leave. She had watched only once what the camera had captured as it silently panned the expanse of her leveled neighborhood, the sky a sudden shock of unencumbered space. She'd buried her memory of seeing that exact vista, which she'd witnessed while the choking dust and ash had still been settling heavily down, while the fires still burned. She had also been perplexed as modern tourists in the film strolled amidst the surreally colored buildings of her reconstructed neighborhood, known colloquially as Starówka: the cobbled streets, the wide, locked courtyard doors, the view of the Royal Castle from her own *ulica Piwna*. But this was one of many reasons she employed to explain to herself why she'd not been back—a reproduction, no matter how meticulously crafted, no matter how seemingly familiar, was an imitation nonetheless. She sat down next to Stanley, eyed him peripherally. His sunglasses were tight against his forehead, like a second set of eyes. He couldn't seem to get comfortable in his chair. As the narrator explained how Hitler had finally gained enough power to force his artistic tastes on Germany, Stanley leaned close to Ludka and told her he had already seen the film.

"I'm going to take off. Call you later?"

Ludka nodded. Stanley stood up. Ludka took hold of his wrist. Stanley smiled and bent down, his ear close to her mouth.

"Why does your gallery have no phone, Stanley?"

The shifting light from the TV roamed over his face as he drew back and squinted at her in bewilderment. Flames filled the screen as the narrator explained that thousands of purged artworks had simply been burned. Stanley flicked his eyes toward the TV, frowned, and rubbed a hand down over his mouth. He leaned close again.

"I'm embarrassed to say the phone company cut me off for non-payment. I've got someone working on it. In the meantime . . ."

He fished his cell phone out of his pocket and waggled it at her. He smiled, and she made an effort to smile back. She released his wrist. She glared at his sunglasses, nodded, and when he stepped away, she closed her eyes, blocking out the roiling blaze.

# 17

# Peaceably to Assemble

Despite the fine, icy snow that had fallen overnight, and the frigid wind that blasted across Boston Harbor and rushed through the meandering canyons of the building-flanked streets to tear out onto the Boston Common, the counterdemonstrators arrived just as Meck had prayed they would, en masse and on time, shortly before the rally's first scheduled presenter. The crowd had tripled in the last fifteen minutes. The initial group—roughly two hundred in support of the ousted teachers—was at first overjoyed about the sudden influx of newcomers, but soon became wary. Every one of the new additions wore or carried something red: hats, coats, scarves, ear muffs, extra-large T-shirts and aprons pulled over parkas, Halloween capes, choir robes, armbands, long skirts, jeans, high boots, umbrellas, flags, pom-poms. Throngs emerged from the Park Street T station and marched across the Common, up to the foot of Beacon Hill. Another crowd spilled out the exits from the underground parking area down near Charles Street and flowed up the wide plowed footpaths. A convoy of buses pulled to a stop and idled in a long line on Beacon Street in front of the State House, spitting out one passenger after another, all of whom proceeded quickly through the stone and iron gates and down the stairs onto the Common. The new group rapidly encircled the increasingly alarmed and now sorry-looking original crowd, which, later on the news, in video footage from Channel 7's helicopter, would resemble the ragged eye of a Katrina-force hurricane.

On the icy bottom step of the wide flight of stone stairs leading down from the State House to the Common, Meck stood out of foot traffic's way, the crowd fanning out below him. As people noticed him, they lifted their hands in greeting, and he nodded his thanks and waved back. There must have been five or six hundred people wearing red, and the mood was festive and noisy. Jill had brought the boys on one of the buses, deciding it was a good opportunity for a civics lesson. John ran repeatedly around a bench while Jill, nose and cheeks rosy with the cold, tried to settle him down. Ben stood apart with a group of his friends, and Andrew solemnly held Jill's hand, his eyes wide. They wore matching red ski hats. Young Brandon Braddock stood with members of his basketball team and his sister Sophie and her friend Ashley; the three of them had organized the buses. Red-faced and stamping his feet, Arnie Dengler was there with his wife, Helen. Scores of committee volunteers had also turned out. Meck couldn't stop smiling, but also couldn't stop scanning the crowd, wondering if anyone among them had assaulted Tommy Zeilonka and made a deal with Eric Barton.

The TV cameras rolled, and reporters affixed their microphones and recorders to the podium. Meck's own recorder was already in place. Four high school students, three girls and a boy, dress clothes sticking out below the hems of their bright ski jackets, stood a few paces behind the podium with their parents and a small group of other speakers, all of them waiting for the senate president and the former attorney general, who were just now making their way down the stairs, the golden dome of the State House behind them, blinding in the sharp, midafternoon sun. Despite the bitter cold, Lolek wasn't wearing a hat or gloves. Izaac, however, was bundled up in a gray overcoat, herringbone Harris Tweed with matching cap, midnight blue angora scarf, and black leather gloves. His eyes were leaking at the outer corners. Aggie, unfortunately, wore a red wool hip-length coat. Behind them trailed Eric Barton, and a handful of elected officials who wanted to be seen standing in solidarity behind the senate president. On nearly every step, the group halted when someone greeted either Lolek or Izaac or both, their progression as laborious as that of Governor Patrick entering the House of Representatives just last month to deliver his State of the Commonwealth address.

Meck checked his watch. Wouldn't be long now. Whit suddenly emerged from the crowd, stepped up next to him, and laid a hand on his shoulder.

"Sorry I'm late," he said.

Meck lifted his head toward the sky and smiled.

"I expect you're right on time."

Just then Meck caught the senator's eye, and Lolek stepped past Aggie, glanced at Whit, and shook Meck's gloved hand. The cameras rolled and clicked.

"Warren."

"Mr. President."

"Thank you for condemning the violence on your show last week. And please thank your pastor for me, too. It means a lot to my family that you both spoke out against the assault."

Meck inclined his head. Lolek gestured to the crowd.

"I hope your people heed your message today."

"I hope they do, too, Mr. President. I pray your son is doing well?"

"Yes, thank you."

Lolek released Meck's hand and moved past him. Aggie and Eric nodded cordially as they went by.

"Damn it," muttered Lolek as Aggie caught up to him. "We did it, didn't we? We underestimated him."

Aggie nodded, her face grim.

"Look who's skulking around in the crowd," she said.

Lolek followed her gaze. Carey Best, Gauch's top aide, who sported a woven red scarf over his black parka, was speaking to a hearty man with a white mane of hair.

"Who's he with?"

Aggie shrugged and shook her head.

As Lolek greeted the students behind the podium, the crowd stirred with new energy, sensing that the rally was about to begin. It was then Meck spotted Pastor Royce, talking with Carey Best. At yesterday's Sunday morning service, the pastor had spoken not of deception and dishonesty, as Meck thought he might in the wake of the assault and Eric's revelation, but of righteousness. Meck and Whit had both been impressed by his focus on the positive, by the way he'd turned to Job and held him up as a model of honesty; they hoped his sermon would be castigation enough for attacking the senator's son and approaching Eric—if, that is, the people responsible were in the congregation. Neither Meck, Whit, nor Pastor Royce had known for sure who might have been involved, although a week ago, the morning after Eric's visit, they'd tossed around a dozen unsupported theories; Arnie

Dengler had been high on the list. Pastor Royce had spoken to him, though, and believed him to be out of the running.

Now Pastor Royce lifted his hand in greeting, then wrapped his arms around himself and exaggerated a shiver. Meck smiled and waved back. Carey, who'd been extraordinarily helpful when Meck was preparing the legislation, saluted and grinned.

One of the high school girls stepped up to the bevy of microphones. Her purse strap was slung across her chest like an ammunition belt, and her straight blonde bangs blew up and back against the hem of her pale blue knitted hat. The crowd slowly fell silent, some taking longer than others to understand it was time to begin. She adjusted the microphone.

"Now," whispered Meck.

At the back of the crowd a man in a red plaid hunting jacket stepped up onto a park bench, lifted a gold trumpet and sounded a loud, high note, which swelled and grew and caused people inside their State House offices to pause and listen and wonder. The note faded and was then punctuated with a series of five blaring, staccato blasts: *tell-it-like-it-is*. On the fifth note, each and every person in red stood a little taller and struck the same pose: fingers closed into fists, wrists crossed in an X over their hearts. As one, the TV cameras swung around to the crowd. The inner group of protesters looked around uncertainly, wondering if this was something they were supposed to do, too, and a few of them hesitantly crossed and then uncrossed their wrists. Meck wanted to shout with gratitude and fling out his arms, but instead gave one sharp, satisfied nod and a quick pump of his fists where they hung by his sides. Whit pounded Meck's back and gave a low whistle. The hair on Meck's arms prickled. Lone photographers and reporters rushed around the perimeter to get to the trumpeter. Several cameras focused on Meck. Tomorrow's papers would capture his radiant smile,

Whit towering next to him, head inclined toward Meck. Both wore red scarves.

The people in red were utterly silent, while the others all began to murmur. Near the center of the crowd, a ruddy-faced woman, heavy with bulky winter clothing, began to call out in a loud but as yet indecipherable voice. She started to clamber up onto a stack of snow piled at the intersection of two wide paths, while her husband grabbed at her coat. She slapped his hand away. Next to him stood their daughter, arms wrapped tightly around her waist, head hanging low. Attaining the top, the woman unsteadily surveyed the crowd and tried to position her feet for a solid footing, stamping each one in turn. She pointed across the crowd at the trumpeter, who, despite the harangue of reporters peppering him with questions, stood silently on the bench with his wrists crossed, trumpet jutting out of one hand.

"Go ahead and blow your horn, you Jesus freak!" yelled the woman. "Like that will make a difference!"

She staggered suddenly and then regained her footing.

"Why can't you people just live and let live? Pack up your Christian hate and go home! Let us have our rally."

A few people began to shout out in agreement. Someone started a rhythmic clapping, which quickly caught on. The woman matched its meter, shouting "Pack up your hate, pack up your hate, pack up your hate!"

Meck watched with admiration and gratitude as the people in red maintained their silence and their positions, many turning to Pastor Royce, who beamed around at them, the wind tossing his hair this way and that. Many closest to the center had to break their pose to fend off the jostling. The woman's daughter suddenly lifted her head and barked one sharp word.

"Mom!"

The woman, startled, ceased her chanting, and as she met her daughter's disgusted gaze, her ruddy complexion flushed with deeper color. After a moment, she reached down, took the hand her husband had offered, and awkwardly made her way down to the ground.

At the podium, the girl who'd been waiting to speak looked behind her uncertainly. Lolek stepped forward and told her he would set the stage. She nodded with relief and moved away to stand with the other students. Lolek gazed out at the crowd.

"Good people," he said.

He waited a moment and then repeated himself, his hands cupped loosely together on the podium. The flat lapels of his black Brioni overcoat framed his white shirt and yellow tie. He stood calmly, smiled slightly, and repeated himself a third time. With sudden regret at a missed opportunity, he recalled the aide at Mercy: *We'll come out of the woodwork for you, Senator.* Lolek wouldn't make the same mistake twice. The crowd finally quieted.

"Good people, my name is Lolek Zeilonka. Welcome. If you know me at all, you probably know me as the Democratic senator from Hampshire County. Today, however, I stand before you not only as a senator, but also as a father. Thank you to so many of you who have reached out to support my wife, Marta, and me and the rest of our family as we come to terms with last week's brutal attack on my son Tommy. My wife is with him right now. His injuries prevented him from being here, but they both asked me to pass along their warmest regards and gratitude."

Tommy had wanted nothing more than to address the rally instead of his father. Abe had finally convinced him to listen to the doctors; plus, he'd said, strategically it was better right now to let others speak on his behalf.

Izaac was suddenly beside Lolek at the podium. He calmly placed a hand on Lolek's forearm, and Lolek understood he was to step aside. Another man as influential as Lolek might have been annoyed with this intrusion, but Lolek didn't think twice; he utterly trusted his father's political judgment. Without moving his mouth away from the microphone, he turned his head for a moment and held out an arm to the group behind him.

"With me here are students from Adams River Regional High School, representatives from the Gay and Lesbian Advocates and Defenders and Mass Equality, as well as a dozen of my esteemed colleagues from the state legislature. And here, of course, is my own father, Tommy's grandfather, the Honorable Izaac Rosenberg, former attorney general of this great commonwealth."

Lolek placed a hand on Izaac's back and ushered him to the center of the podium, then stepped back and stood next to Aggie. She cocked her head inquiringly, and he smiled.

"Watch this."

Izaac lifted a gloved hand against the applause. It had been some time since he had made a spontaneous speech. As a new immigrant, he had worked hard to perfect his English, and it had served him well throughout his long civil rights career. He'd officially withdrawn from public life two years ago when he turned seventy-eight, and the only appearance he'd made since then was to accept the Anti-Defamation League's lifetime achievement award, an honor that had touched him deeply. Today, he was glad to feel invigorated by the prospect of a speech, a feeling that helped quell his uneasiness about the zeal of this crowd. The people in red kept their wrists crossed. He wondered if the person who'd assaulted Tommy was out there, or the one who'd left the warning note on their porch. Unconsciously, he began to silently incant his name: *My name is Izaac Szymon Rosenberg, Izaac Szymon Rosenberg.*

"My friends."

He turned his head and cleared his throat into his fist, not because it was necessary, but because he'd long ago learned that a pause at the start of a speech had a way of drawing people closer.

"My friends. In my life . . . and a rather long life it has been . . ."

People chuckled as Izaac lifted his beetling eyebrows and smiled.

". . . I have never once witnessed such a gathering as this without a sense of pride and gratitude for the founding fathers of both our nation and our commonwealth. Thanks to their foresight, and their brilliant, enduring words, no one today can abridge 'the right of the people peaceably to assemble.'"

He lifted his hands toward the crowd and smiled again.

"And here we all are, two hundred and twenty years after the Bill of Rights was enacted, peaceably assembling. Isn't that incredible? This basic freedom, granted to each of us to ensure our voices are heard, guarantees that the spirit of the First Amendment not only survives, but thrives. And you know what? I love that!"

With the word *love*, he crossed his wrists and bumped his fists a few times against his chest.

"I trust you all know that this means *love* in American Sign Language?"

He paused and scanned the crowd. Some nodded, others appeared confused.

Whit bent down and whispered to Meck.

"He just co-opted our salute."

"Beautifully. Admirable move. I'm going to talk to him as soon as this is over. Invite him on the show. He'll be the consummate guest."

It had been Meck's idea to focus on loving the sinner. The inevitable public images of the former attorney general assuming the stance would provide Meck with the perfect entrée for explaining the crucial difference between objecting to sin and opposing the sinner.

"Well, I love"—Izaac bumped his chest again—"that our right peaceably to assemble remains true even if the majority of citizens would rather not hear what others have to profess. But I'll tell you something, friends. I have always wanted to hear what others have to profess. Even if—maybe especially if—I find their words offensive. Because listening to diverse voices—voices that are guaranteed a public forum by our Constitution—is inherently American. It is our right. It is our privilege. It is—dare I say it—our duty! I, for one, never take that for granted. As a young boy in Poland, this kind of freedom was impossible, an impossibility most of you have thankfully never known. I trust that each of you gathered here will respect the rights of your fellow citizens who are here assembled. And that you will listen with respect to these young people. With an open mind. Without interruption. I assume other forums will be organized at which we can hear countervailing opinions. I look forward to that."

Izaac held on to the sides of the podium. With one gloved forefinger, he wiped the outside corner of each eye.

Whit leaned down again toward Meck.

"You sure you want to give him a platform?"

"Think about it," said Meck in a low voice. "I agree with everything he just said. Everything! I start the interview by engaging in a discussion about the First Amendment, do what he's doing right here: establish common ground. Then I implore him to understand that our rights are being abridged, that our own kids simply want to voice their opinions."

Whit nodded thoughtfully.

"Brilliant. Appropriate his argument and use it to reason with him. I like it. Wonder if he'll agree to come on?"

"Look at him. He'll agree."

Izaac was smiling, his palms upturned, arms extended to the crowd. He turned and beckoned to the high school girl who'd stepped aside a moment ago.

"Now. I believe this young lady has something she'd like to say about my grandson."

# 18
# Revelations I

"Tommy can't sue, kochanie, at least not right away. The statute mandates arbitration."

Izaac and Ludka were sitting by the fire, which Izaac kept feeding. At the rally, he had gotten more chilled than he'd known, and he still couldn't quite shake the cold. Over a late dinner, he'd told Ludka everything, and she regretted having kept her unnecessary commitment to the faculty meeting, which Izaac had rightly questioned.

"What Tommy can do—if the arbitrator doesn't rule in his favor—is file a complaint with the Mass Commission Against Discrimination, and then after that he can file a civil action for damages or injunctive relief. I suspect he'll end up there; the board of ed determines the process for choosing the arbitrators, and now that they've shown their true colors . . ."

He gripped the chair's arms and slowly pushed himself up. He bent over the fireplace screen and poked at the burning wood, sending up sheets of fine sparks.

"At least it's the national group—the American Arbitration

Society—that provides the pool of arbitrators. They're an honest bunch. Of course I suppose expediency also demands they choose local people, so chances are high at least one of them will be sympathetic to the church, if that's who's behind this."

"Oh, it is church! I did some more digging on this Pastor Royce Leonard. He is up to his eyeballs with long activist history, always collaborating with senior brass at monolithic, so-called Christian organizations: Dobson, Robertson, Jarvis."

"Heavy hitters."

"His last church in Virginia has now more than forty thousand members. And suddenly to move to Hampshire five years ago only? This is no coincidence. And the other name always cropping up? Warren Meck. His mother was secretary to Jarvis most of her working life. But where do you think she got her start? As secretary to Royce Leonard! Be wary on that radio program, Izaac. It is Meck's heritage to be aligned against our Tommy. And they call themselves Christians."

She thumped the arms of her chair. Izaac smiled. Ludka started to speak, but Izaac held up a hand.

"I know you're serious, I know! But your belligerence can be so damned entertaining. I will be reasonable and fierce, how about that?"

He held up a hand, clawlike, and showed her his teeth. Ludka suppressed a smile. Izaac maneuvered the poker under the top log and gave it a shove.

"So tell me," he said cautiously, "how is what they say any different than what the Catholic Church says? You yourself said 'there is sin.' It's the same Bible."

"For one thing, you will not see the children of St. Hedwig's picketing with vulgar signs, or members of the congregation beating up an innocent young man."

"And that man who grabbed Tommy in church? What do you think he'd do if no one was watching?"

"He is the loose cannon, that one."

"Get your head out of the sand, Ludka. This is how it begins."

"Don't lecture me, old man."

She frowned and stared into the fire. Izaac fitted the poker back onto its stand and ran a hand roughly through his hair. He turned to face her and rubbed at his lower back with both hands.

"I have to tell you. Those counterprotesters were impressive, the whole sea of them. Utterly silent and still, even with people shouting in their faces from six inches away. Such discipline. I'm sure they'd call it faith, but it looked a lot like blind obedience. They frightened me. I was frightened."

He lowered himself slowly into his chair and drew together both sides of his open cardigan. Ludka felt her own fear rising. Tommy had seemed so panicked when Kulek had grabbed him in church. And what did she know about Kulek? Only that he routinely sat behind her on Sundays, that he was married, that he had a grown son who no longer attended mass at St. Hedwig's.

"Faith can be worse," said Izaac. "It trumps reason all too easily. Reason? Reason is impotent. They see what they see, believe what they believe, and that's that. Discrimination born of moral conviction is infectious. We know this. Don't be too tolerant of your church, kochanie. We're always so tolerant, but sometimes there are occasions for intolerance. And these folks are pretty confident, starting here. They'd have had an easier go of it in the big McCain states: Oklahoma or Wyoming or Idaho. I mean, Obama got sixty-two percent of our vote. Here in Hampshire County it was closer to eighty. I suppose if they win here, though, they can win anywhere. Maybe that's the point."

Ludka pulled a shawl off the back of the chair and onto her shoulders.

"They will not win. You said it yourself. This is America. Such things do not happen here."

They sat quietly, then, and stared into the fire, Ludka drawing courage from her resolute words, Izaac recalling an eerily similar sentiment that echoed down through the decades, haunting enough to trigger a chill, even by the blistering fire.

"Well, one thing's for sure," said Izaac, after a time. "They're not going to succeed tonight. I'm going to get ready for bed."

He yawned and pushed up out of the chair. He stretched his spine and rubbed again at his back.

"No more Stanley, then, eh?"

Ludka shook her head and thought of the Chopin secured away in the closet. She'd been surprised when Stanley had told her after class on Friday that he would go back to California on the weekend. He claimed she had renewed his inspiration for reviving his gallery. And maybe that's all it had been, in the end, a thought Ludka found surprisingly disappointing, and not a little disconcerting. Always she had relied on her intuition, on her keen powers of observation, and this time they had proven unreliable. She would have expected nothing but relief at his departure, but instead found herself feeling somewhat deflated. Izaac had been right that the pot needed to be stirred, and now that Stanley's appearance had stirred it, Ludka didn't want it to settle again. In all these years, she had never gotten this close to finding Oskar, and having his grandson nearby had transformed her hope from something chronic and ordinary into something fresh and remarkable. She'd even gone so far as to imagine an imminent reunion. But this angered her, too. How was it that someone who'd been absent so long could suddenly feel so newly lost?

"So he wasn't out to persecute you after all," said Izaac. "Just a young man missing his grandfather."

Ludka glared past Izaac at the fire, and he laughed. He whacked at the logs to break them apart so they'd burn out more quickly.

"Do you miss him, kochanie?"

"Why would I miss him? I hardly know him."

"I don't mean Stanley. I mean Oskar. Or should I call him Pawel now? But do you miss him? Do you miss Oskar?"

Ludka closed her eyes. *Always*, she thought.

"I remember him, you know," said Izaac. "From back then."

Ludka peered at him with surprise. She shook her head.

"Impossible."

"My Ludka, always so sure you know everything there is to know. I followed you. A few times. To his apartment building, to the ghetto, to the orphanage."

"You followed? You left the house? My god, Izaac! To the ghetto?"

She rose from her chair as fast as she could and shook a fist.

"There is no leaving house," she said in a low, warning tone. "How could you take such risk, all we do to protect you?"

"I was thirteen, Ludka. I'd been inside for three years. Even death would have been worth those walks. I wanted to go where you went, that's all. I wanted to feel normal again. It saved me."

With both hands Ludka clutched the shawl at her neck and darted glances all around, as if she feared someone might leap out.

"They will shoot you in head," she said in a fierce whisper. "They will set dogs on you! They will come for my parents! You must stay in house. You must!"

Izaac grew alarmed at her agitation. He spoke her name as calmly as he could, repeatedly, but she made no response. She took a few steps backward, as if she might be hoping for the protection of a wall at her back, and all at once her eyes locked onto something in the dining room. She froze. Izaac followed her gaze. She was staring at Stanislawsky's painting—*Irises by a Country Cottage*—as if she'd never seen it before.

"What is it, kochanie, what is it?"

He went to her. He put a tentative arm around her back. She flinched. He patted her clutched hands. She squinted at him in some confusion.

"You must not risk," she said in a small voice. "They will come for my Mama and Tata."

Izaac thought she might cry. He tightened his arm around her.

"Look at me. It's 2009. We're at home, in America."

She slumped against him and seemed to come to. Her breaths were quick and shallow. She searched his face and lightly touched his cheek. She couldn't steady her shaking hand and clutched again at her shawl.

"So vivid, Izaac. Like yesterday."

"What did you remember?"

She squinted in concentration, then slowly shook her head.

"Come. Why don't you go on up to bed? I'll tend to the fire."

"I must sit."

Izaac helped her into her chair and stood protectively by her side. She laid her fingers for a moment on her cheeks, and then pressed them against her lips. She closed her eyes and spoke through her fingers.

"It is like flashback, I think, these reveries. But nothing specific can I remember, just terror." She gazed searchingly at Izaac. "How is it we lived through such terror?"

Izaac shook his head.

"We just did. We just did."

"Why did you never tell me you followed me?"

Izaac ran a hand through his hair. He smiled.

"Maybe because I thought you'd react like this. No, no, that's a poor joke. Why didn't I tell you? I don't know, exactly. I suppose it was just my story, not yours. Sharing a thing can rob it of its power, and for so very long I had so little power. In a world of terrible secrets, I wanted one of my own. That's all. I haven't really thought of it in years."

Ludka took a deep breath and nodded slowly. She reached up and squeezed Izaac's hand. Something tugged at her mind. Something out of place. Everything around her felt reassuringly familiar: in front of her the hearth and the Kantor; to her right the back entryway and the door to the garage; to her left the curtains drawn across the French doors and the Musialowicz at the bottom of the stairs. It was probably nothing. Whoever had left that note on their porch had unsettled her more than she'd expected. The harassing phone calls had also continued. The police were now involved. She peered around the wing of the chair, behind her into the dining room. That was it: the Stanislawsky. It had not been there yesterday, she was certain. A Lebenstein had occupied that space. She envisioned the Chopin where she had stacked it in the closet. But where had the Stanislawsky been in relation? She couldn't recall.

"Already you rotated the art?"

"Just the Lebenstein. I couldn't take it another minute. All this with Tommy, I wanted something peaceful, something apolitical, without all that grim Lebenstein portent. I put up the *Irises* before you got home. It's a relief, don't you think?"

She scrutinized Izaac's face, trying to tell if he'd found the Chopin. But of course he would have said something.

"I am too wound up for sleep. I will sit longer, maybe make some tea, calm down. No, Izaac, you go on up. I am again myself. You are looking more worn out than I feel. I won't be long."

She gave him what she hoped was a reassuring smile. He nodded. He stepped back onto the hearth and took hold of the poker.

"The fire will die down," said Ludka. "I will take care of it."

Izaac hesitated and then replaced the poker.

"Don't forget—don't close up that flue unless the fire's out."

"In eighty-five years I have never put fire to bed before!"

Ordinarily Izaac would have laughed at this, but these episodes of dissociation disturbed him more and more. He was starting to feel reluctant to leave her alone.

"I think it's time to consult a doctor. No! No, I won't allow your protest this time. You don't see yourself. You go away completely. I don't know what might happen if I wasn't here, or if you were driving. Tomorrow we're calling to make an appointment."

Ludka knew Izaac was right. During a reverie, she lost time, in much the same way she might end up driving past her highway exit while occupied in deep thought. When she resurfaced, she knew only that she felt shaken and wrung out, that she'd been young again, during the war. Not once had she remembered the details. Perhaps a doctor could put the episodes to rest.

"I will call first thing."

Izaac's relief was evident.

"You shout out if you need me, won't you?"

She smiled and struck the pose: a half-hearted pledge of allegiance.

She waited until she heard him upstairs in the bedroom, and then in the bathroom. She listened hard for the hum of his toothbrush, but the distance was too great, or her hearing wasn't up to the task. Only when she expected he was engrossed in brushing did she get up. Her legs felt wobbly, but she took a few steps, paused, and judged herself capable. She retrieved the key from the toe of Izaac's old boot and fitted it into the coat closet's doorknob. She wished they had taken the trouble of installing a more vigorous lock. In the dim glow of the low wattage light she could tell immediately—the Chopin was gone.

"Izaac!"

Her cry was reactionary, instinctive, and she clapped a hand over her mouth as if she could call it back. She held her breath and listened for his steps, but heard nothing. She pawed through the rack, forcing herself to really see each painting, and then she searched again from the other direction, knowing it was futile; she'd felt it in her gut the instant she'd seen the Stanislawsky. Ludka gripped the door casing, her knees weak. But how had Stanley gotten into the house? The closet she could see, such a flimsy lock, but she'd believed their house was impenetrable. Since she'd seen Stanley last, the house had been empty only once, earlier today while Izaac had been in Boston and she'd been with the faculty. Then she remembered how her office door had been inexplicably open the morning Stanley had turned up. She closed her eyes and pressed her fingers over her mouth. He might toss the portrait into the trunk of a car, shove it into a backpack, maul it with gloveless hands. But surely he had taken it because he knew its value? Surely he would be cautious?

Oskar had held the painting so carefully, incrementally lowering the back of it over the steaming teakettle to relax the canvas before pressing out the dent. And all the while, shuddering up through the floorboards, vibrations from the passing German tanks.

Upstairs, Izaac flushed the toilet. Ludka realized that some small part of her had been hoping he would call out, or come back down to see if she was all right. Had he found her now, quaking as she was in the doorway of the unlocked closet, she wouldn't have had the wherewithal to lie. She turned off the closet light, the violated house growing quiet around her. She didn't call out to him again.

# Part II

# 19
# Tell It Like It Is

It hadn't taken long for progressive Americans, still understand-ably and deservedly giddy from the wildly successful opening act of what they assumed would be as history-making a presi-dency as Barack Obama's election, to grab hold of their laurels and, exhausted, sink into them like an armchair facing a cheery hearth, confident in the naive belief that Obama would carry not only the day but perhaps the next century, that at long last the pendulum of democracy had been halted in its arc, not only in that infinitesimal hesitation at its apex before it drops back, but finally retired, never to swing again.

Meck had anticipated these exhausted assumptions and watched with satisfaction as the majority of Obama supporters rolled down their sleeves and went back to their precampaign lives, figuring the people's work had been done; he couldn't have hoped for a better climate. The premature dismissals were a setback, certainly, as was last week's attack on Tommy Zeilonka, but the fundamentalist community across the nation was riled by their loss to Obama and far more ready to champion Meck's cause than he and Whit and Pastor Royce had dared to hope. Money was pouring in from all over the country, and the ACLU had already agreed to speak on their behalf at Zeilonka's arbitration hearing.

Meck was therefore in a buoyant mood the morning Izaac Rosenberg was to appear on *Tell It Like It Is,* but as airtime approached, his mood was rapidly deflating. He had arranged for Rosenberg to arrive thirty minutes early to acclimate him to the studio and give him the rundown. He was already twenty minutes late. For the fifth time, Meck went to the window in the suite's lobby and checked Main Street: finally! Rosenberg was picking his way across the slushy road, head lowered, one hand held out against possible traffic. Meck checked his watch and frowned. He stepped into the hallway, where the broadcast played quietly from a speaker they'd rigged outside the station's door. Chuck Little, who hosted the morning music program, went into his final wrap. Meck felt a building tension in his neck and massaged it as the old elevator inched its way up, a faltering bell announcing each floor. There was a long pause on two. Finally, the elevator doors slid open, and there at last was the former AG, hat in hand, smiling in such a way that Meck wondered if his tardiness had been a ploy. Meck gave him a tight smile, shook Izaac's hand, and ushered him as quickly as he could into the suite. By the time they entered the guest studio, Izaac had stripped off his coat and shoved his hat and scarf and gloves into a sleeve. Meck was surprised at how fragile he seemed without the bulk of his winter clothing, just a feeble old man, really, swimming in a corduroy sports coat with shiny, drooping elbows. He suddenly felt sorry for him.

Izaac noticed Meck's pitying expression. He thrust his over-coat at Meck as if Meck were a bellboy, then turned and settled himself in the guest chair, rolling up close to the counter. He put on the readied headphones, leaving one ear partially free, swung the microphone's boom into just the right position and, when Meck began to give him the rundown, raised his eyes to the clock and glowered.

"Unless I'm mistaken, Warren, you're on the air in ninety seconds. I might be old, but I'm also an old pro. I'll follow your lead."

Meck turned away, embarrassed, but also angry at the way Rosenberg had orchestrated this rushed beginning. He hung Izaac's coat behind the door and left the room, closing the door with controlled restraint. Izaac frowned and swiveled side to side in his chair. He'd intended all along to put Meck off balance, but now that he'd succeeded, he took no pleasure in it. Meck had been nothing but gracious in the conversations leading up to this program, and Izaac felt slightly chagrined at his sophomoric attempt to undermine his host's confidence. He resolved to be a gracious guest, and sat up a bit taller.

Inside the main studio, Meck had taken over from Chuck Little, and was laying out his notes in front of the sound board while the news aired. The board, computer monitors, and keyboards were all the color of putty, with worn spots and grungy stains from overuse, and the rest of the room was a dingy gray, with soundproof panels affixed to the walls and ceiling. The station was rudimentary, but Meck liked it that way—he was responsible for everything, the "chief cook and bottle washer," as his mother would have said. When he'd first arrived, he'd been bothered by the dismal environment, but not anymore. Once he had his headphones snug around his ears, everything faded away but the program itself.

Meck launched into his opening remarks. By the time he'd delivered his trademark *Tell It Like It Is* and given Rosenberg a long introduction, Meck was solidly back on his game, completely in his element. He adjusted the sound levels on his own mic and asked Izaac to repeat the gist of what he had said at the rally.

"We're off to a good start, Mr. Attorney General," he said when Izaac was through. "I couldn't agree with you more!"

Meck felt pleased that he'd succeeded in placing himself on exactly the common ground he'd hoped to establish, a perfect foundation upon which he knew his typical callers could build. He gave a broad outline of what the families of his Christian listeners were concerned about regarding their children's education, and asked listeners to call in and share their stories.

"Let's turn now to the phones—"

"Just one more thing, if I may," said Izaac. "Here's what concerns me."

Meck hesitated for what seemed to him an interminable amount of time for on-air silence but was no more than two seconds. His instinct urged him to steer away from Rosenberg in favor of the callers, but his intellect demanded magnanimity.

"Please. Tell it like it is."

"I'll tell it like *I* think it is. If only one teacher—my grandson, let's say—had been fired for what is commonly called but poorly defined by law as conduct unbecoming, my concern, and the concern of any arbiter, judge, or jury, would be to determine the probity of the accusations leveled against him. His termination would be based, presumably, on specific, identifiable behaviors. Are you with me so far?"

"I am indeed."

"Good. Now. How many teachers were fired throughout the commonwealth over the course of the last month? Eleven. And all within a few days of each other, all of them gay or lesbian. So now we're not just talking about the behavior of my grandson, we're talking about the behavior of a whole group of people, each of them in completely different circumstances. This leads me to question not the conduct of each individual within that group, but the motivation of those who've done the firing. It strains belief to think that almost a dozen teachers across the state have suddenly developed conduct that's unbecoming enough to warrant dismissal. It's one thing to accuse a person based on specific behavior, on observable actions. It's quite another once you start accusing someone based not on their behavior but on their personhood. Why then you're talking about bigotry. Then you're talking about accusing an entire class of people based on the idea that they're a certain kind of person. And this, Warren, is discrimination, pure and simple."

He sat back, away from the mic, and gestured to Meck with a small flourish, as if he were allowing him to pass first through a doorway. Meck smiled. Izaac hated to admit it even to himself, but he didn't entirely dislike the fact that Tommy's situation had led him here; getting out of the house for something like this was restorative. He hadn't realized when he'd withdrawn from public life how much he would miss being regularly asked for his opinion.

"For me," said Meck, "it doesn't strain belief to think that those who've done the firing have finally taken courage from each other and dared to blow the whistle on what has become a systemic problem within our public schools. This is not about discrimination against those teachers. It's about systemic discrimination against religious kids all over the state. These kids have been repeatedly coerced to accept a lifestyle that's anathema to everything they sincerely believe, and repeatedly rebuffed when they try to express their opposition to that lifestyle. If our kids aren't even allowed to quote from the Bible about the sin of homosexuality, how long do you think it will be before other religious speech is banned? It's a threat to our freedom of speech, pure and simple."

He'd framed their new rationale pretty well, he thought. Still, it irked him that the dismissals had cornered them into arguing against the discrimination angle.

"Listen, let's get our callers to weigh in on this. We've got first-time caller Sheila on the line, from Springfield. Sheila, you're on the air. Go ahead and tell it like it is."

"Oh, I'm so excited to be on, thank you! I just have to say I never miss a show. Thank God for you, Warren Meck, honestly, I mean that."

"Thank you, Sheila, I appreciate that. Do you have a question for the former attorney general or for me?"

"Well, if it's okay . . . I don't have a question, really, I just wanted to say something about those teachers?"

"Of course, please go ahead."

"I just want to say that I'm, well, I'm actually rejoicing about those teachers. I honestly think it's high time they got fired. I'm sorry, but that's what I think, and I'm not the only one. I don't see one thing wrong with lumping them together. I mean, they *are* a certain kind of person, aren't they? That's the whole point. What I can't believe is the way they've been allowed to come after our kids! You should see the propaganda my daughter brings home. All this about tolerating difference, who has two mommies and which two princes are getting married to each other and whatnot. It's disgusting. And who's tolerating my child? I don't see my child in any of that material."

"Let me ask you, Sheila," said Meck. "Do you believe in redemption? We're all sinners, right?"

"Absolutely."

"So tell me, why not give the homosexual teachers a chance to atone rather than casting them out? Why not help them instead of firing them?"

"They certainly need help, I do know that, but at the expense of my daughter? No thank you. They can repent on their own time. I've heard the idea about rounding them all up and letting them live together somewhere, on an island or something, and really, why not? They seem to want to be together anyway. But I don't know the solution, I just know I don't want them anywhere near my daughter. They've done enough damage. Like just a couple weeks ago my daughter told me her math teacher, Mister . . . well, I won't say his name, was talking about his husband. His husband, can you imagine? And she said it as if it was totally normal. She's only eight! You see how they got into her head? They have no business, no business at all! So, I have to say I've thanked God every day since he got fired."

Izaac pressed a fist against his mouth. Meck gave him a sympathetic smile. Izaac crossed his arms briefly over his chest, mimicking the rally salute, and then threw up his hands in a questioning gesture. He shook his head and leaned into the mic.

"Rounded up and put on an island," he said flatly. "That's my grandson you're talking about, Sheila, and you must understand that I feel as protective of him as you do of your daughter."

"I mean no disrespect, but my daughter's not brainwashing anyone, is she? She's not recruiting children into a degenerate lifestyle."

"Neither is my grandson; I can assure you. When I was at the attorney general's office, we were responsible for answering complaints from parents just like yourself, parents who felt their children were being discriminated against in school, so I've heard a lot of stories from a lot of parents about a lot of different types of bias. The most common harassment complaint we heard was about racial bias, but the second most common was from parents whose children were harassed about their perceived sexual orientation. You want to see vile? You should see what was done to some of those kids. Horrific, unimaginable things I can't repeat on the radio. It was my job to know if there was discrimination in Massachusetts schools. I took that job very seriously. I still have a lot of friends in my old office, and they tell me that in the last several years they've had only three complaints about religious discrimination in school. Three. It's not uncommon for the Civil Rights Division to get seven or eight hundred complaints in a year, so I think you can see that three complaints—all resolved amicably, by the way—certainly don't suggest there was a systemic problem significant enough to warrant the dismissal of eleven teachers across the state. I've been around the block a few times, and this situation smells like bigotry on a grand scale, and not, I'm afraid, against the Christian children, but against teachers like my grandson."

Izaac gave Meck a curt nod and pushed away from the mic. Meck did a station-ID break and launched a series of commercials. He took off his headphones and crossed around into the guest studio. Izaac pulled down his own headphones so they collared his neck.

"Things can get a little heated," said Meck.

"You have no idea, young man; trust me. I'm doing just fine."

"We could use an intellect like yours, Izaac. You should come over to what I'm sure you think of as the dark side. Work with me."

Izaac laughed, and Meck gave him the warm, expansive smile

that had endeared him to Lolek; Izaac was similarly swayed, disposed to like him, too.

"Really, Warren, tell me, what's a thinking man like yourself doing involved in this kind of witch hunt? It baffles me, truly."

Meck hadn't hesitated when Pastor Royce had asked him to lead the campaign. He'd been motivated in part by his son John's tiny ribcage, bruised nearly black from getting kicked by a group of older boys who routinely called him "Churchie" and "Jesus Freak." The school had downplayed the bias, calling the fights typical tussles between boys.

When Meck told Izaac about it, Izaac winced, picturing Tommy's battered face.

"I'm sorry about your boy, Warren. I know how you must feel."

"At least my wife and I have the ability to homeschool, but a lot of families can't afford it. I'm just trying to make things better for them."

Back in the main studio, Meck lined up a couple calls before the commercial break was over.

"Go ahead, Douglas, you're on the air. Tell it like it is."

"Good morning, Mr. Meck. Mr. Rosenberg, it's a real honor to get to speak to you. I never listen to this show. I only tuned in because I heard you were going to be on."

"Thank you, Douglas," said Izaac.

"Here's what I want to know. I mean, I totally agree with you about this being a bigoted campaign. It's about hatred, not about kids. It's about using those poor kids to advance an agenda of hate, pure and simple. I don't know how you can sleep at night, Mr. Meck, knowing you've ruined the lives of all those poor teachers, who didn't do a fu—oh, sorry—a darned thing wrong. You should be ashamed of yourself!"

"Did you have a question for us, Douglas?" asked Meck.

"Well, I guess that *is* my question: how can you sleep at night? I mean, really, the nerve of you to have on Tommy Zeilonka's grandfather, while that poor guy is home recovering from a brutal attack by your henchmen. You won't get away with it, I'm telling you. He's lucky his partner was home to intervene, or you people would be up for murder. Didn't you learn anything from Matthew Shepard, you fascist asshole?"

At that, Meck faded out the caller's volume and disconnected him. He tried to diffuse the negativity by talking about stirred passions, reiterating his condemnation of violence, and extolling his faith in the democratic process. As he talked, he was alarmed to see Izaac stand up and remove his headphones. Izaac raised a finger and mouthed to Meck he'd be right back. Meck loaded up the CD "Opposite Way" by Leeland, preparing to buy himself an interlude. He smoothed his bangs and tried to press them up under the headband, dislodging one ear cover. From the lobby, he heard shouting. Chuck Little was always telling Meck to lock the doors before he went on air, but Meck had never seen the point. He pushed up the volume slider. The gentle pulsing warble of the synthesizer, bold piano chords, and Leeland Mooring's silky upbeat voice buoyed Meck as he strode out into the lobby. Izaac was holding up both arms and patting the air, trying to calm the half-dozen men who dominated the small lobby with their agitated energy and bulky winter coats. Meck was always conscious of his small stature, but never so much as in this moment, facing these jeering men. His immediate thought was to dart back into the studio and call the police, and then he realized with some amount of shame that he was shielding himself behind Rosenberg, who stood his ground, baggy corduroy sleeves flouncing as he continued to pat the air. Meck stepped forward beside Rosenberg, who dropped his arms with a grateful sigh. Meck summoned forth his most explosive voice.

"Enough!"

The sound stormed the lobby, instantly shocking the men into silence, and it was then Meck realized he knew them. He frowned, confused.

"Danny? Clancy, Blair? What are you guys all doing here?"

Clancy, a muscular young man with close-cropped black hair, spoke from the back.

"What are you, now, Warren, getting soft on us? We were listening in the van, on our way over to the retirement home, you know, finishing up that library Pastor Royce asked us to do? Blair here said we should phone in, ask what's going on that you have this gentleman on, and I said let's swing over there and tell it like it is in person, remind him who's out there listening. You think we want to hear this homo defender going on about his faggot grandson?"

Clancy momentarily lowered his head.

"Sorry, I mean no offense, but give me a break, Warren."

Izaac gave a small start at "faggot grandson," exactly the expression used in the note left on their porch and in the harassing calls. He recovered himself, took a quiet breath, and calmly moved past the men to stand in front of Clancy.

"This homo defender, as you call me, is pleased to meet you. I'm Izaac Rosenberg. And, you are?"

Clancy pursed his lips and eyed Izaac's outstretched hand. Leeland's music filled the tense silence, and Meck took courage from hearing the singer's pride as he named himself "one of Yours, Lord."

Rosenberg bent forward and carefully took Clancy's hand in both his own. Clancy blushed, mumbled his name, and shook Rosenberg's hand.

"Warren," said Izaac, still holding Clancy's hand, "do you think we have a second chair in the studio for Clancy here? Would you like to be on the radio, son? Have a real conversation with this old man? I'm pretty sure we're back on the air momentarily."

Two of the men laughed quietly and exchanged glances.

"Come on, Clancy," said Blair, a man with sharply defined cheekbones and soft blond curls. "We've got to get over there to the home. We're already late."

"Are you kidding?" said Danny. "Get in there, Clancy, and tell it like it is for real! Now's your chance. You know what Pastor Royce told us to do . . ."

Clancy's warning glance silenced Danny. Meck wondered which of Pastor Royce's sermons Danny might have been about to misconstrue.

Izaac stepped away and went over to the guest studio. He held open the door. Clancy reddened further and turned to Meck.

"Just remember who's listening, Warren," he said. "Come on guys, let's go."

An hour later, Meck and Izaac stood together in the hallway, waiting for the elevator. Izaac clasped his hat and gloves in both hands behind his back.

"It's often the ones on your own side who treat you most poorly," said Izaac. "That never stopped surprising me. This man met me one time when we were in the midst of a heated and very public hearing about a piece of civil rights legislation I had drafted, a bill that clearly needed some work before it would pass, and when I offered him my hand by way of greeting, he spat on it, said exactly what the caller Douglas said to you today: 'How can you sleep at night?' People forget that democracy is about compromise."

Meck lowered his head and rubbed the back of his neck.

"They must be reading a different Bible than I am, I'll say that. It's certainly not the Bible Pastor Royce preaches from. I don't understand it. Such disrespect."

"There are as many Bibles as there are readers, Warren, and just as many versions of truth. You're young yet, you'll see."

Still rubbing his neck, Meck tilted his head and squinted at Izaac.

"Do you believe in God, Mr. Rosenberg?"

The elevator doors shuddered open. Izaac stepped in and turned to regard Meck.

"I do not. The question of God's existence was settled for me when I was only fourteen, in 1943, in Poland. You might imagine my reasons. My grandson, however—my faggot grandson, as your friends call him—does believe. He is Christian, baptized in the Catholic Church."

Izaac pushed the button for the ground floor.

"I'm no less baffled about you, by the way, but I do thank you for an interesting morning. Leaf through my grandson's Bible. I believe you'll find it's rather different than your own."

Meck inclined his head, and then the doors were closed.

# 20
# Ransom

"But you have to go, Dziadzio," said Tommy. "We'll be just fine. And you do know there are telephones and computers and fax machines in Warsaw, right? You won't miss a thing. Besides, Babcia needs you there."

On Friday night, to celebrate Ludka's unexpected invitation from the Jewish Historical Institute in Warsaw to attend a retrospective of her wartime sketches, Tommy, Robert, Izaac, Marta, and Frank were all crowded into Ludka and Izaac's kitchen, waiting for Lolek, a gathering Izaac had organized without Ludka's initial consent. Tommy and Robert were orchestrating the creation of gourmet pizzas, made from scratch right down to the dough. Everyone had at first been surprised and then relieved at the normalcy of their insistence that they cook dinner—Tommy and Robert had always loved to cook—and if it weren't for the drawn drapes throughout the house, the stitches on Tommy's cheek, the bruising around his eyes, which had turned a sickly yellow, and the way he kept pressing a hand to his ribs, it might have been any ordinary get-together.

Tommy raised his voice and called out the pass-through to Ludka, who was setting the dining room table.

"Right, Babcia? You need Dziadzio to go with you, don't you?"

"Dziadzio does as Dziadzio wishes, that is all. Need is irrelevant."

Izaac, who at Robert's instruction was sprinkling sautéed shitake mushrooms on one of the pizzas, shook his head and rolled his eyes, resulting in general laughter. Ludka opened the silverware drawer in the sideboard and counted out the knives and forks. Marta left the kitchen and joined her.

"What can I do?" said Marta.

Marta had on far more makeup than usual, and the beige foundation, creasing heavily along the lines in her forehead, did little to cover her pallor. Ludka patted her forearm and thanked her for the help.

"Napkins you can lay out."

"I don't want to miss arbitration," Izaac said firmly to Tommy. "Not even for this. Being there firsthand is a lot different than reading the transcripts after the fact. Maybe I'll be able to join Babcia after the hearing."

"It is one week only I will be there. Twenty-two hours one way. I don't think you'll be joining."

"Pizza's in the oven," said Robert.

"Perfect," said Tommy. "Come on everyone, out of the kitchen. Uncle Frank, can you bring the Sobieski? Robert's got the glasses."

"Shouldn't we wait for your father?" said Frank.

"Only if you want to be here all night," said Tommy.

Everyone followed Tommy into the living room. Marta laid down the last napkin and joined them, but Ludka stayed behind, continuing to lay out the silverware. Since she'd discovered Stanley's theft four days ago, four days that had passed excruciatingly slowly, she had kept almost frantically busy, trying to appear ordinary while anxiety clamored constantly for her attention. Her shoulder was still sore, and her chest felt intermittently constricted. More than once she'd been surprised to realize that the Act of Contrition was looping through her mind. Each time she became aware of it, she had abruptly stopped her thoughts. At some deep and unconscious level, she knew that hoarding the Chopin was an offense against God, not just a venial sin but undoubtedly a mortal one, laden as it was with decades of intentional deception, and she knew that to confess was her only salvation. Her conscious thought, however, was that confessing to anyone—Father Skurski, Shelly at the police station, her old colleagues at the Commission for Art Recovery, the FBI, even Izaac—still seemed dangerous and impossible. It was not a rational thought but a visceral one, and her recourse was to do what she had always done: rush away with other thoughts and soldier on. Yesterday, though, she'd come close to sending an anonymous tip through the FBI's website, thinking they could track down Stanley Brozek and rescue the Chopin. She stopped herself when she realized the FBI could likely trace the tip to her. Even if they couldn't, she expected Stanley would concoct some story. She called his cell phone repeatedly, obsessively checked her voice mail at work, at home, and on her cell phone. It's possible he was after a ransom. Or perhaps he had known of a reward—she repeatedly hunted online for some mention. She couldn't imagine what kind of collector would want to buy it on the black market. A Rembrandt she could see, or a Van Gogh or Cezanne, but a Mieroszewski? Hard to imagine.

And now there was yesterday's apologetic phone call from Director Mandelbaum at The Jewish Historical Institute, and the added whirlwind of complication about Warsaw. Even without this business with Stanley and with Tommy, she could think of plenty of reasons not to go—the travel alone would be far too taxing, her students were relying on her, her reveries could prove problematic—but at some largely unconscious level she knew they all boiled down to only one: fear. As the director had spoken to her in Polish, his accent rich with a lifetime untainted by foreign lands, a language that reverberated through her like a tolling church bell on a breezy November morning, her fear rose and billowed out and transformed itself into an anticipatory sense of something not unlike excitement. She didn't acquiesce to the trip because he had shared with her his seriousness of purpose about showcasing her important work, or because he flattered her and appealed to her sense of historical significance, but because he told her about the anonymous letter they'd received that revealed her identity as the artist. Several people besides Oskar—had they survived—knew about the sketches, but Ludka was convinced Oskar had written the letter. He would be there, she was certain. Before she'd finished the conversation with Mandelbaum, her own accent sounding watered down and unwieldy, she understood with a sudden clarity that everything she'd ever done had led her to this inevitability, and just like that, she was going home.

Tommy was suddenly standing beside her. She laid down another fork, and then a knife.

"You okay, Babcia?" he murmured. "You are the guest of honor, don't forget."

The white of Tommy's left eye was still pink, and the Steri-Strips were ragged at the edges, due off any day. The stitches should come out soon, too. He had to wear his glasses lower on his nose than usual, and the upward tilt of his head gave him a slightly arrogant air. He was smiling, but weariness haunted his eyes, and all at once she recognized the effort it was taking him to be there. She rallied herself and carefully set the rest of the silverware on the table. In an exaggeratedly animated fashion, Tommy offered Ludka his elbow, and she slipped her hand into the crook, careful not to bump against his ribs.

Ludka laid a hand on the back of her wing chair and faced her family. Frank and Robert had poured and passed the vodka shots, and Frank handed one now to Ludka and Tommy before moving in front of the fire to stand next to Marta. Quietly, he said something to her and she smiled. It had been years since Ludka had seen Frank with beard stubble, and this was several days old, dark copper red shot through with white. The fire was dizzyingly hot and the glass, chilled from the freezer, frigid enough to burn. She hoped the toast would be brief.

Just then, Lolek came into the back hallway and stomped his shoes.

"Am I too late? Sorry. The governor held me up."

"They are making unnecessary fuss," said Ludka. "But Frank brought Sobieski and so I am tolerant."

Lolek padded in his black dress socks into the kitchen. He came right back out with a shot glass and smiled around at everyone as he loosened his tie. He moved purposely to stand in front of Marta and Frank, and Frank stepped aside. Lolek clapped him on the back and held out his glass. Frank, holding the vodka bottle by the neck, set down his shot on the mantle, unscrewed the cap, and poured a full measure for Lolek, who raised his glass as if he were about to present the toast himself. He caught himself just in time and slowly lowered his arm, trying to appear as if he'd been merely waiting for the toast to be offered.

Izaac stepped up onto the hearth.

"There's a lot you don't know about your mother, your grandmother."

Ludka groaned.

"For this I must sit."

Gratefully, she put down the shot glass and sat in her wing chair. She rubbed her cold fingers, crossed her arms over her stomach, uncrossed them, and crossed them again.

"You're right, Matka," said Frank, "we might need fortification."

He threw back the shot.

Lolek laughed and followed suit, and while Izaac said "hey now, hey now," the rest of them, including Ludka, tossed back the vodka. There was general laughter, and Frank reached around to refill the glasses.

"If you need to get comfortable, then, by all means," said Izaac. He took a sip. "I think you'll want to hear this."

He patted at the air for them to sit down. Something in his tone made them comply with no further shenanigans. Tommy knelt on the floor next to Ludka and rested his forearm on the arm of her chair. Robert sat on the hearth and stretched out his lanky legs so his feet were touching Tommy's knees. Marta took Izaac's wing chair, Lolek and Frank continued to stand in front of the fire, and Izaac stood slightly above them on the hearth. Ludka touched her hair, feeling frail in comparison to even this tired bunch. She could hardly fathom she'd given birth to these two substantial men. She was grateful they blocked out some of the heat.

"You might wonder," said Izaac, "what business it is of the Jewish Historical Institute to want to put on a retrospective of sketches by a diehard Catholic. And even if you're not wondering, you know damned well I'm going to tell you anyway!"

He raised his eyebrows and smiled around at each of them.

"This show isn't really about art. Our Ludka didn't sketch for pleasure, or for practice. She was part of an effort organized by Emmanuel Ringelblum, a great man, a Jew who had the foresight in 1939 to understand he was living through a singular moment in history, a moment he knew should never be forgotten."

"And so begins lecture," said Ludka.

She forced a laugh, trying to diffuse her own mounting emotions. Her attempt sounded strained, even to her.

"Isn't it time they knew?" Izaac had asked yesterday, when he told her he'd organized this gathering, and she had protested. "What possible reason is there to keep silent any longer?"

Stupidly, still reeling from her conversation with Director Mandelbaum and worn down by Izaac's frustration and calm pride in her work, she'd capitulated, regretting it almost immediately. Once the stories were told, the questions would follow, and she didn't know if she could bear to think about the answers. There was only so much pot stirring she could handle.

"I'll keep the lecture brief, kochanie, both to keep you happy and to get the rest of you back to your Sobieski. Emmanuel Ringelblum was a social historian, a friend of my parents, may they all rest in peace."

The heat of the fire had gotten too much for him, and he moved to the edge of the hearth, away from the open firebox. Lolek stepped up and took his place.

"Ringelblum and a team of people he put together organized an archive of materials that detailed life in the ghetto. Our own Ludka—or Apolonia, as she was known to them—was an unusual member of the archival team, an anomaly: she wasn't a Jew, she was female, she was young, and she lived outside the ghetto walls.

But she was also known through her art circles to Gela Seksztajn—you know her, she painted that sullen boy we have in the study—and Gela's husband, Izrael, was part of Ringelblum's team. The only reason Gela's work is known today is because of what was preserved in the archives. And because Gela liked Ludka—she said her drawings were exemplary and necessary—Ringelblum asked her to contribute. She was one of a select few."

"So I sketched." Ludka stared into the fire. "It was not so much."

"It was crucial," said Izaac. "Crucial!"

Gela's face came to her vividly then, a face Ludka hadn't thought of for years, and she pressed her fingers over her mouth and closed her eyes. A bilious taste of vodka backed up in her throat and she swallowed hard. From the kitchen came a slightly rancid smell of old oil burning off the oven racks. Next to her, Tommy changed position so he was leaning gently against her calf.

"But you weren't in the ghetto, were you, Matka?" said Frank. "Why would you be?"

Ludka glanced at him, and then back at the fire. She shrugged, and gestured at Izaac to hurry up and be done.

"Ringelblum buried the archive inside the ghetto," said Izaac. "Two of the caches were found after the war, one in '47, one in 1950. It's taken them this long to figure out who did the sketches. And that's it. Next week she goes to Warsaw to finally be recognized for her work."

"Why didn't you just tell them it was you?" asked Tommy. "I mean, you must have known they'd found the archives?"

Ludka spoke sharply to Izaac in rapid Polish, telling him it was for these questions she did not want this gathering. Everyone looked at her in surprise. The Polish language had been a deliberate casualty of assimilation; none of them had learned more than a few common words and phrases.

She surveyed them, and patted Tommy's back.

"It is complicated."

"Well, it wasn't safe, was it," said Lolek matter-of-factly. He took off his tie and shoved it into his suit jacket pocket. He rubbed a hand across his forehead, his face doughier than usual. "The way I understand it, the war's still going on over there as far as anti-Semitism goes. Let's just say your Babcia wouldn't have been welcomed with open arms as the hero she really is, not in the fifties. And today only under the auspices of a place like the Institute."

"Do not use this word 'hero!'" Ludka thumped the arms of her chair. "Only I did what anyone would do."

"Kochanie—"

"Do not kochanie me, old man. Is there toast anytime soon or must we drink vodka lukewarm?"

Izaac peered down at his shot glass and shook his head nearly imperceptibly. More than once over the past several days he had asked her what was wrong, and each time she had claimed concern about her reveries, and Tommy, and then the return to Poland, how already she was too old for all this. But he suspected there was something more.

Now he lifted his head and raised his glass.

"Okay, then. Okay. To bearing witness. To remembrance. To our Ludka. *Na zdrowie!*"

"*Na zdrowie,*" everyone said, raising their glasses in Ludka's direction. She smiled and nodded as graciously as she could. The vodka had warmed slightly. She took only a sip. Tommy suddenly scrambled to his feet.

"The pizza!"

"Oh shit," said Robert. They both rushed into the kitchen.

"Saved it!" called Tommy. "Let's eat."

At the table, after the commotion of passing plates and the excla-
mations of delight about the pizza had died down, Lolek turned
first to Izaac and then to Ludka.

"I don't understand about the ghetto. Why would you have
been sketching in there?"

Ludka tore off a chunk of crust and began to chew. She wanted
nothing more than to push back her chair, calmly retreat to the
study, and close the door behind her. She might gaze upon Gela's
sullen boy or call in again to check her voice mail at work or sit
on the love seat and close her eyes until they'd all gone. She hadn't
talked with anyone about the ghetto since 1947, since her arrival
in America. When Izaac had arrived three years later, they had
deliberately—strategically—spoken of it once, at length over the
course of two grueling days, determined to say it all and then
leave it behind them. A couple of years back, Izaac had finally
broken his silence and given a long interview on camera for the
Shoah Foundation, an organization preserving stories of the
Holocaust from the rapidly diminishing pool of survivors. Ludka
had stayed at the university while they'd conducted the interview
here at home. Nothing Izaac said could convince her it might be
cathartic; there were things even Izaac did not know.

As Izaac helped himself to another slice of pizza, he glanced
warily at Ludka. She pretended she didn't notice. Let him think
she was lapsing into a reverie. Served him right, all this fuss.

"Matka?" said Lolek. "*Did* you sketch scenes from inside the
ghetto?"

She gave Lolek a curt nod and took another bite: roasted garlic, nutty goat cheese, crisp mushroom. She'd taken a larger bite than she should have. It felt dangerous in her mouth. One nostril wasn't clear, and she experienced a moment of panic and opened her mouth to breathe past the food. Embarrassed, she held up her napkin as she finished chewing with her mouth open. Her eyes watered.

Lolek started to ask her something further, but Tommy cut him off.

"Can't you see she doesn't want to talk about it? Leave her alone, Dad."

"Tommy," said Marta in a gentle but warning tone.

"No, Mom, I'm sorry, but this is supposed to be Babcia's celebration. Grilling her shouldn't be on the agenda."

"I wasn't grilling her, Tommy, I was merely asking a question."

Tommy got up, retrieved one of the empty serving trays, and took it into the kitchen. Lolek threw up his hands and sat back in his chair. He looked at Marta questioningly. She shook her head as if to say *not now*. Frank took another bite and studiously avoided any eye contact.

"Let me help, Tom," said Robert. He went into the kitchen. The oven door opened with a squeaky groan.

Ludka wouldn't mind leaving the table herself. She patted Lolek's arm.

"I did sketch inside ghetto, but it is long story, not so interesting, I think."

There was a period of somewhat awkward silence. From the kitchen came the sound of baking pans sliding on and off the metal oven racks, murmuring from Tommy and Robert.

"I think Tommy's right, though," said Lolek. He said it loudly, wanting Tommy to hear. "You should go, Dad. When will you have another chance? We can take care of things here. We'll keep you closely in the loop, I promise. There will be plenty left to do when you get back."

From the moment Ludka had told Izaac about the invitation, he had stubbornly refused to even consider the possibility of accompanying her, citing the importance of Tommy's arbitration hearing. But Ludka could tell he felt the same anxiety she did about going back to Warsaw, and Izaac was not one to flee from anxious feelings. Going back would be hard enough without his anxiety compounding her own, and she wasn't sure she should encourage him further. Still, it was hard to imagine being there without him. He was frowning down at his plate, then glanced at her almost apologetically, and she had a sinking feeling he was going to instigate more questions. He wiped his mouth and laid his napkin back on his lap.

"I'm nearly certain my parents worked with Ringelblum when they buried the archives. They were buried at sixty-eight Nowolipki, which was literally right in their backyard. *My* backyard, until . . . We lived on Dzielna, number sixty-seven, which opened back into the courtyard between Dzielna and Nowolipki. Both streets were walled inside the large ghetto. If you walked west on either street, you dead-ended at the wall, and the street just ran on beneath the bricks and continued on the other side, while you had no choice but to turn aside. Directly on the other side of the wall on Nowolipki was the Befehlsstelle, the German's office compound. My parents must have worried that the Nazis would hear them as they dug, it was that close. I have to say, I feel rather proud that perhaps my parents had a hand in preserving those archives."

He raised a slice of pizza to his mouth but paused before taking a bite.

"It might actually be nice to see them."

He nodded once, smiled slightly to himself, and Ludka realized he had decided to go. Now that he had, she couldn't imagine how she'd ever thought of going without him.

Frank cleared his throat.

"We never really did hear what happened to your parents, Dad."

He spoke offhandedly, as if it wouldn't matter to hear an answer, but his expression was somewhat hopeful, as if something he'd wondered about for a long time might finally be revealed.

"Your parents, either, Matka," said Frank.

"It was Nazis. What is more to know?"

She pressed her fingertips into her shoulder and the pain increased. She eased off and the pain receded to its original level.

"I expect," said Izaac, "that my parents went to the Umschlagplatz and got on a train to Treblinka, like three hundred and fifty thousand others from the ghetto. Unless they'd already died of typhus, or starved."

Frank let out his breath and set down his pizza. The phone rang.

"I'll grab that," called Tommy.

He said hello before either Izaac or Ludka could stop him from answering. They exchanged a look—they didn't want Tommy to have to endure any more harassing calls than he was already getting at home. Izaac had worked with the police and the phone company to set up traps on both their lines. He and Ludka now had a log on the fridge to track when the calls came in, to note down the specifics: gender and possible age of the caller, noticeable accents or speech impediments, background noise, what was said. They'd report the information to the phone company, which would hand the log and the related phone numbers over to the police, who would compile it with the data from Tommy and Robert's line and use it in their search for Tommy's attackers.

"I'm sorry about your parents, Dad," said Frank. Lolek and Marta both murmured their agreement.

"Yes," said Izaac. "Me, too. Thank you."

Tommy poked his head into the pass-through.

"Babcia? It's for you. That guy Stanley?"


In the study, holding the phone in a tremulous hand, Ludka stood staring at Gela Seksztajn's sullen boy, so perfectly rendered—so grim—and for the first time, she began to understand Izaac's impulse to replace the Lebenstein with Stanislawsky's *Irises*.

"So this is it," she said. "All of that about taking gallery in a new direction and worrying for your grandfather was excuse to scope out house."

"That about sums it up. Listen, I can give you some time. Say about two weeks? I'm not wholly unreasonable."

Ludka gripped the receiver. Her chest felt tight.

"You think I have this money? Under mattress, perhaps?"

"Of course not. That's what insurance is for. Report it stolen, get the money, give it to me, get your painting back. Simple."

They did have insurance, an excellent policy, but only for the paintings they legally owned. Provenance papers and qualified appraisals had been required.

"If I was museum, maybe, but I am person only. Nothing is this simple."

"Sure it is. Get me the money or I tell the authorities. I know it's not yours. The FBI thinks some Nazi has this painting. So do your friends over at the Commission for Art Recovery."

Ludka had to sit down. She sat poised on the edge of the love seat, as if she might have to hurriedly stand. Of course she had thought about the possibility of prosecution, but not for many years, and always it had been easy to trick herself into believing she was safe—only one other person knew about the Chopin, after all. She'd always assumed she could choose to unveil the painting in whatever manner she wished, the story hers to tell, perhaps even after she died, a codicil she imagined attaching to her will at the last possible moment. But Oskar had apparently grown careless. She laid a hand over her throat and closed her eyes. She lowered her voice to a near whisper.

"And if I don't care about reputation, or prosecution?"

The hair on her arms rose. She hadn't known she was going to say this. Stanley said nothing. From the dining room, laughter. Could it be as easy as this, then? After seventy years, could she simply surrender? When Stanley still didn't speak after a long moment, Ludka began to wonder if she might be gaining the upper hand; he clearly hadn't considered the possibility that she might just let him have it.

"Do whatever you have to do," Oskar had said to her before they'd all scattered, when it was finally clear that further hope was absurd. "Please. Just save yourself. Promise me. We'll find each other."

She had promised, but it bothered her that she couldn't remember if this was all she had said. There was just a vague memory of his rough cheek dashed against her own, the smell of char and oily hair and damp wool. And then he was gone. Two days later the Nazis imprisoned him at Pawiak.

"Tell me the truth, Stanley," said Ludka now. "Where is your grandfather?"

"I don't know where he is: Poland, New York, San Francisco? Like I said, he couldn't be bothered to tell us."

"Now I am starting to understand maybe why. You are weasel like your Wall Street father."

"Listen, Ludka, I'm not fucking around! I need you to get me the money. That's it. If you don't want to, I can always take a box cutter to the canvas, and find some easier mark. Like I said, simple."

Ludka closed her eyes against the image of this newly vulgar Stanley slashing a jagged tear through Mieroszewski's canvas. She pressed trembling fingers against her lips. Stanley laughed.

"You think I wouldn't, but I would, you see, no qualms at all. There are plenty of other paintings for the taking. I'll call again in a couple days—"

"Wait! I go to Warsaw on Monday, for one week."

Stanley was quiet again. She thought he had hung up.

"You know where he is, don't you? You're going there to see him."

She suddenly wondered if he was lying after all, if he knew Oskar was in Warsaw. But no, he hadn't sounded as if she'd caught him in a lie. He sounded like a petulant, maybe even envious, child.

"I do *not* know. I have been invited there for symposium. You can Google. It is at Jewish Historical Institute next Wednesday."

"Hold on."

She heard a shuffling, then two metallic thwacks, the clasps on Stanley's scarred briefcase. After a moment she heard the distinctive clacking of a laptop keyboard, and she imagined him seeing the sketch they were using to promote the symposium. It was one Ludka had forced out of her mind many years ago, one she'd had to close her eyes against when Izaac had pulled it up on the computer: a teenaged girl sitting on the street, her back against a stucco wall, stick legs splayed in front of her, a dead toddler lying slack across her lap.

Stanley muttered something and then he was back.

"Well, then, it's a good thing I'm a reasonable man and gave you two weeks to deliver. I've got your cell. Have it with you."

He hung up. Ludka eased herself back against the love seat, hearing the dead air. Then the phone clicked. And then nothing. She replaced the receiver. She felt like a husk of a person, sitting there, insubstantial enough to waft away on a light breeze. How would she ever make the long flight to Paris, the layover, the final leg to Warsaw? She wasn't even sure she could get back to the dining room. How could she even think about leaving while Stanley had the Chopin? She should have instructed him how to safely store the painting; she should have demanded proof it was intact. Isn't that what you were supposed to do, ask for a photograph with the current day's newspaper next to it? Perhaps there was someone she could quietly hire to help her cope, some kind of discreet negotiator or private investigator. After a moment, she checked the caller ID to see if Stanley had phoned from his cell, but the record said number unknown. One of the things the police had advised about tracking the harassing calls was to note any distinctive background noise. Before they'd suggested this, she never would have thought to listen that hard, but during her call with Stanley she'd paid attention. A few cars had started up, others had come to a stop and, throughout the call, the intermittent beeping of self-serve gas pumps. How this could possibly help narrow a search, Ludka couldn't imagine. Out in the dining room, things seem to have quieted. She had to get back. Slowly, she worked her way to the edge of the love seat and stood, feeling unsteady.

Back in the dining room, the conversation had turned to the attack on Tommy.

"Shelly tells me they still don't have any solid leads," said Frank, "but might have a witness who noticed an unfamiliar car?"

"Parked less than a quarter mile away," said Robert. "They're hoping to identify it. They're questioning everyone along that stretch of the road. Between that, and trying to track the phone calls, and Tommy's description of the guy who attacked him, we hope something might surface. Assuming there's a connection between the calls and the assault."

"Oh, there is connection!" said Ludka as she approached. "I have no doubt."

Everyone turned to her.

"No offense, kochanie, but I'm afraid your certainty means nothing in the eyes of the law."

She slipped into the kitchen. She pulled the phone log off the refrigerator and carried it into the corner where no one could see her from the pass-through. She logged in the details of Stanley's call.

# 21

# Preparations

Early the next morning, Saturday, Ludka stood before her open bureau drawer. She and Izaac were laying out on the bed the clothing they would take with them to Warsaw on Monday afternoon.

"I tell you, old man, I did not need this shrink before Warsaw. Already there was stress. At first she treated me like a child, and I told her 'If you have the psychological theory about me, I want to hear it!'"

"But you see how happy you made me, kochanie, going through with it? And now I'll be far better company."

He put his arms around her from behind. She smiled and slapped at his hands. He kissed the back of her head and went to the closet.

"She's a clinical psychologist, you said, or a psychiatrist?"

"The kind who wants only talk. I told her I do not want all this talking, and she said my reveries are a sign that talk is overdue. 'Post-traumatic stress disorder, delayed onset,' she called it. 'That is some delay,' I said."

"I hope she laughed?"

"I am apparently in the final developmental stage of life, according to Eric Erickson's theory, and I said 'thank goodness' and took it as small victory that this got a smile. But she says if there are things unresolved, or if I do not like what I see of my life, I could fall into despair and die a bitter old woman. Apparently, choices are only two: 'ego integrity' or 'despair.' I asked her which one would take less talk."

Izaac laughed.

"That poor woman has her work cut out for her. Can she help with the reveries?"

"Something is causing the flashbacks, and only until I talk will the reveries apparently subside. She wants already to see me every week."

"You'll go."

Ludka flapped a hand, but nodded.

"She did clear you for travel?"

"She did. She gave us tips to cope with the episodes, which she says will again most definitely come. You are to keep a close eye on me and call me back to the present if I drift. Or, if I am alone, she said play loud music or suck on a lemon. Also, I could hold an ice cube or sniff peppermint or recite out loud what is around me. Any of these should be interesting at symposium."

"And that's assuming you can tell when a reverie's coming on, which you can't."

"I have discovered this is not precisely true. Dr. Jaines harassed me with her questions long enough for me to see a pattern. First I begin to lose track of the moment, and then I grow still, like poured concrete starting to set, and then . . . whoosh."

She flung out her hands, then laid another skirt on the bed and stood back, fists on hips, gazing critically at the pile.

"When did we start to need so many clothes? It is one week only!"

She began to put things back into the closet and drawers. She glanced at Izaac's pile and was about to suggest he do the same, but then she took a closer look at what he had chosen: two pair of his favorite worn brown corduroys, his oldest cardigan, a tightly woven, zippered wool vest she had given him years ago, two soft cotton shirts, two narrow ties he'd always reserved for his toughest days in court, a small pillow he liked to clutch while sleeping, and his favorite soft pajamas. She was shocked to see on top of a small stack of socks a yarmulke, an item she hadn't even known he owned.

"So you are nervous to go as well?"

Izaac met her soft gaze, then sat on the edge of the bed, his shoulders rounded, hands clasped loosely in his lap.

"Terrified."

"There will be nothing we recognize," she said softly. "It will be as foreign as Prague or Grozny."

She wasn't sure she believed this, but it's what she'd been telling herself since the phone call with Mandelbaum. Izaac pressed his hands between his knees and shook his head.

"I wouldn't count on that, kochanie. They rebuilt Warsaw with scrupulous fidelity, apparently down to the smallest of details, using as much existing material as they could. And they rebuilt shortly after the war; those buildings are almost sixty-five years old."

"Is that what frightens you? That all will be the same, will bring back memories?"

Ludka resumed her packing. Izaac ran a hand roughly through his hair. He stared out the window into the woods, the morning light just beginning to soften the darkness.

"It's snowing," he said.

For a time, they were silent. Ludka knew it was only her imagination, but the portrait of the woman glancing back over her shoulder seemed diminished somehow, the canvas insubstantial, like a tired screen in an old porch door. Finally, Ludka stood back and surveyed with satisfaction her smaller pile of clothes. Izaac yawned, stood, and rubbed at his lower back.

"I'm not sure what frightens me. Maybe it's memories, maybe it's just that I'll feel too much, or that I'll remember something dreadful I hadn't even known I'd forgotten? I don't know, none of that feels quite right."

"We have to first survive the trip, which will be heroic feat. Maybe none of it will be an issue."

Izaac lifted his bag onto the bed. He started to pack. All at once he stopped.

"Huh."

Ludka was surprised to see his eyes were damp.

"What is it, Izaac?"

"I think I'm afraid I'll wish I'd gone back much sooner."

Ludka pressed a hand over her mouth. Nowhere inside her could she have retrieved that feeling, but now that Izaac had given it voice, she felt it rushing upon her. Her eyes sprang with tears. Quickly she gathered her favorite shawls from the bed and turned to put them into the small suitcase propped open on the chair near the bureau. They tumbled from her hands before she reached the suitcase and she let out a small "oh!" She stood there, holding on to the bureau, staring down at the disordered pile, thinking that bending and reaching to retrieve them would be impossible to manage.

"We would neither of us have been welcomed back, Izaac, you

know that. And don't also forget it was eighteen years ago only that Communists were ousted. It is different country."

Even as she was saying this, trying hard to rationalize away her rising grief, she knew it made no difference.

"But don't you wonder how going back might have changed things? I sometimes feel I left myself back there, you know? Left that boy behind. Does that sound crazy?"

"Dr. Jaines would not think so. I told her I had long ago locked the door on remembering, thrown away the key, and that so far it has worked like a charm. Do you know what she said? She said she is locksmith, and together we will grind a new key. When we get back, you can take my appointment, discover hidden child."

Immediately she regretted her choice of words, because of course Izaac had been just that, a hidden child who had lived inside from the time he was ten until he was nearly seventeen, with only a few stolen trips out into the city. Izaac didn't seem to have noticed what she'd said. He closed the cover of his suitcase and slid it to the edge of the bed. Very carefully he lifted a corner, testing its weight.

"Not too bad. I should be able to manage that."

He set the suitcase beside the door.


Later, while Izaac was on his way to Tommy and Robert's house for a breakfast meeting with Abe, Lolek, and Marta about the arbitration hearing scheduled for Tuesday morning, Ludka was online in the study, learning about private investigators. The upset over Stanley's deception was finally beginning to wear off. She was feeling somewhat vindicated that her instincts about him had not been wrong after all; knowing this provided her some courage. She had a gut feeling Stanley wasn't all that bright, and she'd started to wonder if this theft had been impulsive and somewhat thoughtless, if he had any idea what he was doing. She couldn't be certain of that, of course—there was the business with the sunglasses, and the questionable gallery, and the legacy of his father's fraud—but she had woken this morning filled with a fiery determination to outwit him. Perhaps a private investigator could even take care of things in her absence—safely retrieve the Chopin.

The work of private investigators seemed to focus heavily on cheating spouses. One firm boasted about their surveillance skills and provided video samples. Each clip showed shadowy, silent footage of a man and woman talking at a bar, embracing on the street, or sitting in the window of a restaurant or car, faces blurred out to protect their identities. The quality was poor, and the men and women were so appallingly ordinary that they appeared unreal, like bad actors in a low-budget soap opera. Ludka found herself rooting for the anonymous investigators and hoping these apparently cheating pairs would kiss or provide otherwise damning ammunition for the beleaguered spouses. After several clips, though, Ludka felt sullied, the surveillance not as thrilling and suspenseful as it might be in a movie, but voyeuristic and sad.

She chose a local company that had the most impressive website, peppered with words like *discreet, confidential,* and *private.* A pleasant woman with the raspy voice of a lifelong smoker answered the phone, took some basic information, and then connected Ludka to an investigator named Victor who, in polite and soothing tones, gave her the same assurances about confidentiality promised on their website.

"You tell no one? No disclosure you have to make to some authority?"

"I speak only to you, Ma'am, through whatever channels work best for you. Not even to anyone else here in the firm, unless you authorize it. Discretion is the heart of our business and we take your privacy very seriously. You can count on complete confidentiality."

Victor had a warm, pleasing voice and the easy confidence of a man you could trust, but his speech was too practiced, too canned. Ludka found herself wanting to say something to break through the veneer, to see what kind of man she was dealing with.

"So you say this person is missing?"

"Missing to me. I have his cell phone number, if that would help, and information on supposed art gallery in California."

"These would definitely help, yes. But let's back up a bit and talk about what you're trying to accomplish. We do everything above-board, nothing illegal, and that includes making certain that your own purpose is within the bounds of the law. He is a relative, perhaps? A child who has run away from home?"

"No, he is . . ." She almost said *weasel*. "He has taken from me something of value. I need to know where he is keeping it."

"I see. And what would you have us do when we locate him?"

Victor said this in a low, confidential voice, and Ludka hesitated, wondering what he might be insinuating. Was this the best approach, hiring someone to spy on Stanley? She left her desk and stood by the French doors. A light snow was still falling, and a small drift of it had filtered through the screen to a corner of the porch.

"What are options?"

"Well, we serve legal papers—subpoenas and that sort of thing—or conduct undercover discovery with the intention of determining where he's keeping your property. We could do surveillance to videotape or photograph him in possession of your property, which would provide crucial evidence in a criminal prosecution, if you're going that route. Or we could just turn over his location to law enforcement, and they could take over your case. It's entirely up to you."

"Could you get property back for me, just take it?"

"We can't steal it back, if that's what you mean. He'd have to give it to us of his own free will. Rarely happens, but it's not impossible. I've been known to be convincing."

"Do you look like police, wear a uniform? Maybe this would fool him?"

Victor sighed in a way that to someone else might have seemed unprofessional but to Ludka was a sign that he was capable of more than touting the company line. She began to think she might enlist his help.

"Exactly the kind of thing we can't do, although everyone asks. One thing we can do is try to befriend him. No law against that. He might slip up, reveal something."

While they talked about fees, Ludka wondered what she might tell Izaac about a withdrawal from their account—cash for Poland, perhaps. She told Victor she'd need some time to think it through.

Outside, the snow had let up, but the sky was still steely and threatening. On a whim, Ludka dialed Stanley's cell phone and was shocked when he picked up on the second ring, sounding wide awake. It wasn't quite eight o'clock, which meant it wasn't yet five in California. Stanley didn't strike her as an early riser.

"I can get money."

"Insurance come through like I said?"

"This is none of your business. What will be the arrangements? Will I ship money to California? How will I get painting?"

"Plenty of time for the details, Ludka."

She told Stanley to prove the painting was safe.

"You must convince me, or I cancel money."

Stanley made a small noise of displeasure, and then she heard the distinctive sound of silverware scraping across a plate and a quick shout in the background, like that of a short-order cook. And then came a sound she heard every morning at this time— three short blasts from the whistle of a train as it approached the university, followed by a long blare as it crossed the main drag on campus. Of course trains everywhere must sound similar, and so that proved nothing, but still she couldn't help but think he must be at Raymond's Riverside Diner, just down the road from the crossing.

"I don't have it with me," said Stanley.

"What do you mean? Who has it?"

"I couldn't leave it lying around, could I? It's perfectly safe, you don't need to worry about that."

"I should maybe just take your word, you think? No. You will send me photograph, with current newspaper."

"What is this, a made-for-TV movie? It's not that easy—"

"Says the man who thinks a million-dollar ransom is simple! You will send me photograph, that is all. You may text to cell phone. By 6:00 p.m."

"Impossible. I can't get to it until Monday at the earliest. I don't have access."

Ludka began to grow hopeful. Wouldn't this mean, then, that he had stored the painting in a safe-deposit box in a bank, or some short-term storage facility only opened during the week, someplace safe? But it could also be that he was on the road, days away from where it was hidden.

"Where are you, Stanley?"

"I'll text you a photo early next week. When can you get the money?"

"To this I don't have access until my return from Poland, so you must wait. I arrive home on eleven March."

She actually arrived two days earlier. When Stanley hung up, she immediately called Victor.

"I have big lead right now, but you must this minute start!"

Victor explained that he couldn't legally proceed without a signed contract or the required deposit, and while he was still explaining the process, Ludka hung up.

In the car, grateful that the snow had stopped, Ludka drove faster than the speed limit, something she hadn't done for years. She sat tall, eyes forward, neck as taut as if she had a bad crick, and gripped each side of the wheel at three and nine o'clock, the tension causing a tremor in her arms that went all the way to her shoulders. She realized with relief that her shoulder felt better. She took a breath and tried to relax her hands. Less than ten minutes later, she turned onto Riverside Road and slowed as she approached the diner. The parking area was packed. She wished she'd taken more notice of what Stanley had been driving—a small sedan, she knew, but what color or make she had no recollection. She went around back and pulled in alongside an enormous depository of plowed-up snow. As she was maneuvering her way out of the car, she realized she had forgotten her galoshes. With dismay, she surveyed the short expanse of treacherous ground that lay between her and the diner. The lot was dirt to begin with, and even though it had been repeatedly sanded and salted, the morning's light snow still mostly obscured the winter's worth of packed snow and ice that lay beneath. Too risky. Perhaps she could follow the scattered tire tracks back to the front entrance? Still sitting, she put both feet firmly on the ground, glad to feel the solid grit of salt and sand. Tentatively, she stood, keeping a hold on the seat back and the door. She shuffled to the side, closed the door, let go of the car, and pushed her right foot forward, then her left, and after a few tense moments she began to gain a confidence she tried immediately to squelch. At eighty-five, confidence was not always a virtue, and this was one of those times it could be downright dangerous. Another shuffling step, and then another, and then her foot began to slip forward of its own accord, and she caught herself with a shocking jolt before it could fly out from under her. Tingling adrenaline shot through her whole body, and she stood very still, arms held rigidly cocked for balance, four feet away from the car, an impossible distance from the diner, and it was in that moment, as she stood frozen in the parking lot, that she finally stopped to ask herself exactly what it was she planned to do. All the way over she had imagined confronting Stanley, making demands while he sat dumbly on a padded stool, an egg-filled fork halfway to his mouth that she would smack away before slapping again at his face, a bit of blood appearing on his teeth. But this was an image from some Hollywood picture, not from her own life, and she thought about how she'd told Victor that Stanley wasn't the brightest, and here she was, stupidly rushing forth. The whole of the last few days began to catch up with her. It was all she could do to stay standing. From the back wall of the diner, an industrial fan roared and spewed out kitchen exhaust: coffee grounds, friolator grease, and dishwasher steam laced with bleach. She surveyed the ground surrounding her. How could she possibly travel all the way to Warsaw when she couldn't even make it back to the car? She thought of the fallen shawls, and Izaac's yarmulke, and she drew in her arms and held them.

Two young women came around the corner, laughing, and then one of them called out to her.

"Do you need some help?"

Ludka automatically lifted an arm to wave off the offer, but stopped herself, and nodded grimly.

Back in the car, she called Victor, and he told her of course, he looked forward to meeting her, to come right over.

"In one hour I will be there."

She pulled the car around to the front of the diner and settled in to watch the front door.

# 22

# Preparing to Fight

Lolek sat uncomfortably between his father and Marta on a tall, caned chair at Tommy and Robert's kitchen island, the grit on his shoes from the sanded road grinding against the footrest. They had gathered to prepare for the arbitration hearing. The marbled gray counter—which Lolek had thought was granite but was apparently concrete—was cold under his hands. He was glad of the warm mug of coffee Robert had just handed him. Lolek hadn't been in Tommy's house since they'd first moved in a couple years ago; he was having trouble reconciling the fully adult furnishings with his notions about his son, which Lolek was starting to understand were outdated at best, or wholly and erroneously assumed at worst. In fact, now that he really thought about it, a memory of Tommy from years ago tended to color all his thoughts about his son, a singular image from Lolek's first campaign for statewide office: Tommy, at eleven, sitting at their kitchen table with ten-year-old Maria Rose, and with Frank and Marta, and his parents, and probably Aggie, although he couldn't be certain she'd joined him yet, folding letters and stuffing envelopes. Tommy had taken charge of routing the bundled letters into the correct bulk mail bins and preventing the supplies from overwhelming the table, and he kept them all entertained with stories about what they might do when they were "in the public eye," stories Lolek wished he could remember now. What he did remember was a specific moment in which Tommy had caught his eye, smiled warmly, and seemed so completely and utterly in his element that Lolek had allowed himself to imagine an entire political future with his son at his side. First Izaac, then Lolek, then Tommy: three generations, a new Massachusetts dynasty.

Now Tommy was scooping fresh coffee grounds into the steel coffee maker. His kitchen cabinets were bright white and glass-paned, the walls painted a soft mocha, and all the appliances were faced in spotless stainless steel, which Lolek knew from his Beacon Hill apartment were only stainless if you attended to them routinely with special cleansers, which Lolek did not. Among the photos neatly arranged on the surface of the refrigerator was one of Tommy and Robert at the edge of a calm surf on a vast, sandy beach, no one in sight behind them, the sky a brilliant blue. They each wore finely tailored suits the color of rich chocolate, the cuffs rolled messily up to just below their knees, their feet bare. They were holding hands, and laughing wildly, Tommy leaning forward as if about to clutch his stomach, Robert with his head thrown back, each of them holding a single calla lily. Lolek couldn't help but grin at their infectious, unfettered joy, but the smile faded immediately and he had to lower his head; he wondered who had been there to take the picture, and tried to keep himself from wondering if on another occasion Tommy would have put it in a drawer had he known Lolek was coming over, before the revelation last week, when Tommy confessed to being married.

Lolek's hip ached. He pushed off the tall chair and moved to the end of the island, his back to the fridge.

Robert opened the oven and pulled out a tray of parmesan-scallion scones, just as Abe Goodman came through the screened porch, knocking on the kitchen door as he entered.

"Your paparazzi's back," he said. "Just Channel 7, Wendy Chen. Asked me what our meeting was about, whether we might be planning a class action. I wish that were possible."

"It's not?" said Tommy.

"We don't have a large enough group, believe it or not, and we'd need to be suing a single entity, not a bunch of different schools."

Tommy went to the front windows in the dining room and peeked through the break in the curtains, which they'd kept drawn since the assault. The Channel 7 truck was parked across the road, its satellite dish rising into position. Wendy Chen talked with the woman operating the camera.

"They haven't been here all week," he said, coming back into the kitchen. "I wonder why today?"

"Saturday," said Lolek. "Slow news day."

"They thought they might find us out shoveling the walk?"

"Maybe they're getting B-roll, just in case," said Robert.

"With a satellite truck?" said Tommy. "More likely they're following the senator. Or maybe someone tipped them off about our meeting."

He stressed the word *someone*, and Lolek knew it was directed at him. He opened his palms questioningly, but Tommy didn't see him, or chose to ignore him. Marta shot him a look as if she didn't doubt that Lolek might have tipped them off, and he laid a hand over his heart and shook his head.

"It does look a little like *The Sopranos* out there," said Robert, "all those dark and important vehicles. Maybe they heard about the graffiti."

"I'm glad you were already able to paint over that," said Marta.

"What graffiti?" said Lolek.

"Don't scrutinize it," Tommy said to his mother. "It's really too cold to paint. I'm not convinced it won't bleed through, but we'll fix it up in the spring."

"I expect it's not the last time we'll have to paint," said Robert. He passed out small plates and napkins, and set a basket of scones on the island.

When no one answered Lolek about the graffiti, he found himself recoiling, retreating inside himself to calm his anger, and he realized just how often lately he'd had this feeling with his family, how quickly he'd begin to feel insignificant. He leaned on the counter with both fists, knuckles down, his wedding band clacking against the concrete. He could have sworn it was granite. When he took a hot scone, he grasped it so hard it split in two before he got it to his plate.

"I don't know why you still haven't installed a security system," he said. "You can't be too—"

"Because we just don't want to, Dad. Let's leave it at that."

"What I was going to say is you can't afford to be too naive. You and Robert have got to protect yourselves now. Things have changed."

"What's changed? What do you think is different?"

Tommy waved a hand over his bruised face and touched his tender ribs.

"This? This is nothing, Dad. This is nothing every gay man doesn't fear every day of his life."

Robert put a hand on Tommy's back and held it there. Lolek

wondered if Robert was warning Tommy to curb his tone or was instead offering a sign of support, an encouragement to say whatever he was going to say. Lolek told himself he shouldn't escalate the tension by responding, he should just turn to Abe to get the meeting underway. He took a breath and began to brush at the mess of crumbs he'd left on the counter, but when he saw the way his father was studiously chewing a bite of his scone, a sympathetic frown on his face, and Abe was busying himself with a stack of files, and Marta was eyeing the crumbs he had missed, Lolek knew he couldn't let himself be cowed by his own son, or allow the undercurrent of whatever Tommy was really trying to say go unaddressed.

"How can this be nothing, Tommy? It's not like you've had to deal with this kind of thing before."

Tommy let out a small sigh and shook his head. He looked at Abe and gestured toward the coffee maker, inquiring, and Abe thanked him and said yes. Tommy turned away to get a mug out of a cabinet, and Lolek began to feel smaller still, and again he knew the better thing to do was move past this moment, let all of them off the hook, and he made himself take a bite of the scone, which was crunchy, then tender, then exploding with the savory flavor of cheese and green onion. But Lolek was puzzled—truly puzzled—about what kind of fear Tommy might be talking about, what possible fear he might have experienced growing up in a liberal family in the even more liberal town of Hampshire, Massachusetts, and then in the heart of Cambridge for his graduate degree in arts education at Harvard. And hadn't Lolek done everything possible, hadn't he pushed past his own discomfort and—he had to admit—disappointment, and accepted Tommy's coming out with love and grace and support? Hadn't he devoted a large part of his career to gay rights—and at significant political risk—and welcomed Robert with open arms? Hadn't he always gone out of his way to make sure both of his kids were protected, especially Tommy?

"It's not that I don't know what gay men have to face, Tommy, you know that."

He spoke calmly, trying to sound merely concerned and interested.

"I can recite a lengthy list of hate crime victims, and I know what happened to each and every one: Jeremy Waggoner, Bill Clayton, Dano Fetty, Charlie Howard, Matthew Shepard of course, Scotty Joe Weaver, Brandon Teena. I could go on, believe me. But for you, until this assault . . . ?"

He raised his eyebrows and lifted his hands as if to ask *what*? He was afraid he hadn't succeeded with his tone, that he might have come across as preachy, or patronizing. Tommy gently scratched around the edges of the ragged Steri-Strip, and focused on anything other than Lolek. Robert stepped forward and handed around the basket of scones.

"It's really just a matter of degree, Senator."

Robert spoke reasonably and formally, as if addressing a judge, as if no tension had entered the room.

"In some strange way it's almost a relief this has happened. It's easy to convince yourself that all those second looks have nothing to do with physical violence—that all the taunts and shunning and mistrust aren't cousins to aggravated assault or getting fired from your job. We like to believe they're merely the folly of igno- rant people, that they're simply what you have to tolerate to be dif- ferent in this world. But we know better. We know we can't cater to bullies, and that's why we refuse to alarm our house; it would only be window dressing on a danger no alarm can keep out, a so-called 'security' system designed to convince us that inside we are safe, we can let down our guard. But we can never let down our guard. Does that make sense? It's why we're going to fight this thing as hard and as far as we can."

As if he'd just realized how lawyerly he sounded, Robert smiled sheepishly and ducked his head.

"That's it. I didn't mean to get into closing-remarks mode."

"Speaking of which," said Izaac. He held a fist over his mouth and cleared his throat. "Shall we get going?"

The words *taunting* and *shunning* resounded in Lolek's head, and he snuck a glance at Marta, but her expression told him nothing. He wondered when it had happened that they'd stopped presenting a united front, and when and where Tommy might have been bullied, whether any of it had taken place on his watch. He studied his son's battered face and felt ashamed that he had to wonder such a thing, that he truly had no idea. The family man in him began again to recoil, and he wasn't sure if it was his father's calm suggestion that they move on, or the fact that Robert had respectfully answered his question in a reasonable tone of voice and had addressed him as "Senator," but the politician in Lolek finally and thankfully stirred and took hold of the family man and shook him hard, reminding him that this was just another challenge he had to face, a challenge he could surely meet, that he was a powerful senator, after all, who'd been tasked with handling a crafty opponent. He had damn well better pull it together to figure out exactly how they were going to get justice for his son.

—

"Where does the teacher's union fit in here?" asked Marta. "Back when I was teaching they would have been all over this. Shouldn't they be involved?"

They'd all moved into the dining room, where there was more space at the table, and Lolek had deliberately let Robert and Abe sit at either head of the table, since they were leading the case. Lolek had chosen a seat next to Marta; he wanted her within reach in case an opportunity presented itself to soften the tension between them.

"We did consult with the MTA," said Robert, "but in the end they can only deal with contractual issues, not with statutory ones, and by law we can choose only one route or the other, either union or private counsel."

"That's why I called Abe from the outset," said Izaac. "Going the private route means we have more statutory options, most notably venturing beyond mere contractual issues into the arena of employment discrimination."

"And besides," said Tommy. "Who wouldn't rather work with Abe?"

Abe smiled and inclined his head toward Tommy.

"I talked it through with Joey Condon, too," said Lolek to Marta. "He's the MTA president, owes me a few, and he told me in confidence he thought hiring private counsel was a better choice in this instance. This way Tommy himself is the party to arbitration, rather than the MTA standing in on Tommy's behalf."

"And let's be clear," said Izaac. "Publicity is also a key component here, not only for Tommy, but for all those other teachers, and no matter what happens in arbitration, going the statutory route means the decision will be available to the public, and that means media exposure."

Lolek forced himself to appear neutral in response to this, despite feeling vindicated about his own approach to using the media. Maybe now Marta and Tommy would be reminded that Lolek did know how to use the press to advance a cause, that he wasn't solely motivated by egotistical or political reasons designed to keep himself in the public eye.

"But what if—God forbid—we come out on the losing side?" said Marta. "Won't the publicity just cause further damage?"

Lolek tore off a big piece of a scone and popped it into his mouth to help himself resist the urge to jump in with a response. Let his father make his case for him. And Izaac did. He explained that it was important to think about the bigger picture in all of this, and that the more media attention the issue received, the more the larger issue got brought into the public discourse.

"We could do worse than Wendy Chen," said Izaac. "That she's out there on a snowy Saturday means she cares about the issue. She's a fair-minded journalist, but she's also got a track record of giving minority groups the benefit of the doubt. If I'm not mistaken, her daughter—or maybe it's her niece—is lesbian."

"That's no guarantee," said Tommy.

"We have two days," said Izaac. "And I have only this meeting to help out before I get on a plane, so let's get busy. I've roughed out the complaint we'll submit to the Mass Commission Against Discrimination, so we'll be ready if arbitration doesn't go well. Tommy, where are you with urging your colleagues to do the same?"

"I've given them detailed information about filing a complaint, and I also took your advice and contacted as many of the others who were fired to urge them to get prepared, too. They're going to e-mail me their narratives and chronologies, and I'll share them around so we can each use them to build a case for conspiracy. I'm getting nothing but positive responses—these people want to fight."

"Excellent! The more complaints the commission receives on this issue, the more of a chance we've got. Abe, where are we on arbitration strategy?"

"First order of business is that the school didn't follow the law— Chapter 71 Section 42. They were required to give notice of their intent to dismiss ten days before they actually let Tommy go, and they were supposed to give him a full rationale and any accompanying documents so he would have an opportunity to contest. Any honest arbitrator should toss out the dismissal on those grounds alone, so there's some hope there, but Connie Clough is a tough cookie, and I suspect that right out of the gate he'll hammer on the idea of safety for those kids, claiming—I'm sorry to say, Tommy— that they had to remove Tommy immediately because their kids were at risk. It will be a bit of a hard sell since the regulatory code 603 CMR 26.00 does make it crystal clear that each school must have a notification, complaint, and dismissal procedure, and the way they fired Tommy clearly conflicts with Adams High's own written rules based on those regs. Still, I'm a bit worried about Pat Kinney, the arbitrator—he's not the most even-handed guy, and I've heard it said he skews hard toward the religious right. He should throw out the case and reinstate you on those grounds alone, so that could be room for appeal should it come to that."

"What about the LGBT kids?" said Robert. "Would it benefit our case to point out that the environment has to be safe for them, too? Surely we've got kids who will testify."

Abe scrunched up his face, thinking. "That's a tricky one. It could backfire on us, even though in principle it's right on. I say we keep that one in our back pocket. It would help to compile some bullying and suicide statistics on gay teens. Can you get those, Lolek?"

"My staff is already on it."

"Good. So. Clough will try to keep the entire focus on Tommy alone, which is what the arbitrator is also charged with doing; it's up to us to continually put Tommy's case into the larger context of this statewide witch hunt in order to keep Kinney's doubt alive about the school's—or should I say *church's*—motives. We can make a good case for discrimination—these schools are clearly in violation of the Fair Employment Practices law, which specifically prohibits discrimination based on sexual orientation. We have that damning recording from the meeting with Shaw and Dengler."

"About my so-called homosexual agenda," said Tommy.

"They do love that phrase," said Robert.

Abe smiled.

"What we have to do is make Tommy's specific situation hard to reconcile with the simultaneous dismissals around the state and the filing of all those bills. Where are you on those, Lolek?"

"We've managed to kill several of them already. The *moral piety* bill was relatively easy since it modified one of those obscure and ancient laws, the kind people like to scoff at, like no spitting on the sidewalk or no putting tomatoes in clam chowder. Committee members couldn't see dealing with the press on that one. I've been assured that the bill modifying Chapter 71 Section 39, which would have made it legal again to ask prospective teachers about their religious beliefs and political affiliations, will be sent to study committee. The constitutional issues involved are too squirrely, and of course once it's in study, it won't get out. There were a couple of others that were so blatant even Gauch couldn't get behind them. I have to tell you, though, the fight to table them wasn't simple—they got killed by only the slimmest majority. We've got our work cut out for us on the one we're most concerned has legs, House Bill 1298, which is the one I suspect they were championing all along. The others were probably filed primarily to divert our attention."

"That's the one that allows the board of ed to define sound moral character as it applies to teachers?" asked Izaac.

"That's right. They've titled it *An Act Further Protecting Our Schoolchildren.*"

"Smart," said Izaac. "That's pretty smart."

"On the surface it doesn't necessarily seem like a bad thing, does it?" said Marta.

"That's exactly right," said Lolek. "But as the bill is written, it's not demanding a *statutory* definition of sound moral character. It's demanding that the law would allow the board to define it in any way they want, whenever they want, which means the definition can be changed at any time, dependent on the current makeup of the board."

"You can see why people would want to support it," said Abe. "They'll only be thinking about themselves and their own values, how they'd want that flexibility, especially over time."

"So it's a blank slate," said Tommy.

"Exactly what Aggie said; you're absolutely right."

Lolek immediately wished he hadn't mentioned Aggie. It's not that Tommy didn't like her, just the opposite, but he suspected that in Tommy's mind, invoking her presence put Lolek more squarely in politician mode, which seemed to have become problematic, and he had liked the way this gathering was turning out;

he had started to feel like he was making progress with his son. As luck would have it, though, Tommy gave him a wry smile and said, "Me and Aggie, great minds," and Lolek began at last to relax.

"What do you think our chances are with 1298?" said Robert.

"Honestly, it's far too early to know. The hearing's scheduled for March eighteenth, Wednesday—seventeen calendar days to get ready. The public hearing isn't always important, but for this one, because of the media attention, it will be crucial. I've got my best staff liaising with the appropriate groups, and I know Aggie's going to call you and Robert, Tommy, to see who else we haven't thought of who we might enlist. I'll have her send you the bills, Abe."

He pulled out his phone and texted Aggie.

"Done. You should have them in your e-mail."

"Boy," said Abe. "I need an Aggie Roth."

"Who doesn't?" said Tommy, and Lolek wasn't sure if he meant it facetiously or not, but Tommy was smiling.

"One good thing about the arbitration hearing," said Abe, "is that the burden of proof is on the school, not on us, and I think we can make a darned good case for discrimination. They certainly weren't forthcoming about sharing complaints with Tommy, so how could he have possibly made any necessary changes?"

"And I would have!"

Robert laid a hand on Tommy's forearm.

"He's been heartsick about those Christian kids. It's killing him that he can't reach out to them."

"Then let's talk about those kids," said Abe.

He lifted a folder to show it to Robert, who sorted through a small stack of folders for his own copy.

"What we have to do," said Abe, "is go through these complaints one by one and determine how we're going to respond to them, if asked. They're likely to come down hard on the First Amendment, saying your behavior curtailed free speech. They might also try to make a case for free exercise of religion—you might not think it's relevant in the classroom but you'd be surprised. We're going to hear the phrase *against our sincere religious beliefs* over and over again, probably from the kids they'll get to testify. So, you'll have to be brutally honest with us about these complaints, Tommy. I want you to search your memory as hard as you can and look for anything you said that might have been misconstrued. We can't have any surprises in there."

Tommy nodded soberly.

"What about a curriculum expert?" he said. "Someone who can assess what I teach and prove it's balanced, which it is. I mean, I also teach T.S. Eliot! If *East Coker* isn't Christian, I don't know what is."

"Maybe have someone on call for that?" said Izaac. "In some ways it's beside the point, since you're still teaching the writers these folks object to."

"I agree," said Abe. "Tommy, if you can find someone? Great. We also have to go through that list again that you put together of supportive witnesses to see who will present themselves well, and make sure we're all well versed with the written evidence you collected about your success as a teacher. Lolek has provided some background data on—sorry, Tommy, I hate to say it, but you know it could come up—pedophilia, so I want each of you to familiarize yourself with the data and arguments."

Abe paused, and everyone fell silent. He put both hands on his head and smoothed back what little hair he had. He sighed.

"I'm sorry to say it, but I think we need to be prepared for a sexual harassment argument."

"You've got to be kidding me!" said Robert.

"But that's ludicrous," said Marta.

Tommy touched the tender skin around the edges of the Steri-Strip.

"Oh," said Lolek in a quiet voice. "Oh, I see. Jesus Christ, really?"

Abe and Izaac both nodded. Robert got an expression on his face like he'd just realized what they were implying. Lolek rubbed a hand hard across his forehead and closed his eyes.

"Will someone please explain this to me?" said Marta.

"It's the law about fair educational practice," said Lolek. "Chapter 151C."

Marta made an impatient gesture with her hand.

"Our problem," said Lolek, "could be in how sexual harassment is defined. It's got some serious wiggle room in it."

Robert was consulting his iPhone.

"Here we go," he said. "*The term sexual harassment means any sexual advances, requests for sexual favors and other verbal or physical conduct of a sexual nature, when* . . . and here it goes into specifics about whether kids would be rewarded or punished for submitting to or rejecting sexual advances and so on, and then we get to the tricky part. What they say here is that sexual harassment takes place when *Such advances, requests or conduct*—and I think it's that word *conduc*t that's the real problem—*have the purpose or effect of unreasonably interfering with an individual's education by creating an intimidating, hostile, humiliating or sexually offensive educational environment.*"

"Oh my god," said Tommy. "They told us when we met that they thought the kids were at risk. They said the kids felt unsafe, like they were targeted by my quote-unquote agenda."

He looked around at each of them, his eyes wide.

"We're not going to win this thing, are we?"

"No, no, no," said Abe, "don't think that for one minute, son. They're in the wrong here, not you. But this is why we need to review the specific complaints extremely carefully. We can't leave any smidgen of doubt about your intentions."

Tommy pushed his hands up under his glasses and rubbed his eyes.

"I can't even believe it. It's just poetry!"

"We're not really talking about poetry, Tom," Robert said quietly.

"I know that! For god's sake! Sorry. It's just . . . really? It's Whitman. It's Anderson."

Lolek yearned to reach out and touch his son in some small way, to smooth the worry from his expression and tell him everything would be okay, even though he wasn't at all sure it would be. He put his arm across the back of Marta's chair and touched her hair. She turned to him with surprise and he gave her a grave look. Her small, sad smile was enough to flood him with hope that whatever had brought on this chill between them could be dissolved, and that they could help each other support Tommy.

Izaac cleared his throat.

And then," he said quietly, as if to gently lead them out from under the shadow of defeat, "when we're done here today, we should all walk outside together—even you and Robert, Tommy—so Channel 7 shows us as a united force. And Tommy, I think if you want you can tell Wendy Chen off the record how you feel about the kids, and tell her when the hearing is over you'll give her an exclusive interview. Does that strategy make sense to you, Lolek?"

"It does make sense, yes, and that way you'll be able to control the timetable yourself. Whenever you're ready, Tommy. Whenever you and Abe and Robert think it might best serve your case."

Tommy nodded with understanding and agreement, and Lolek felt grateful for the connection. He gave Marta's shoulder a little shake, and she met his eyes. He saw her for what seemed like the first time in ages, and understood just how much he'd let his job consume him, how much he took her for granted. A heaviness had settled into her face, a softness had developed under her chin, and her chestnut hair had lost a bit of its old shine but none of its color, and he found himself wondering if she was dyeing it. He couldn't tell. Under his hand, her shoulder felt soft, and he massaged it for a moment, aware that his own hand and fingers had also grown thick. None of that mattered. What mattered is that they were still here together, thirty-six years later, taking care of their son.

"Your mother and I would be more than happy to stand by you in that interview, if you think it would help."

As soon as it was out of his mouth, he knew it was a mistake. But that's all he had been trying to say, truly it was, that he and Tommy's mother were here for Tommy all the way, that they would do whatever they could to take care of him, and he hadn't meant to imply at all what he could tell Tommy was now assuming, what he could see in Tommy's tightened jaw and averted eyes, what he saw pass between Tommy and Robert with one fleeting glance, that once again it was not Tommy's father they were dealing with but the calculating senate president, the egotistical politician who never engaged in anything without first considering his own agenda.

# 23
# Connie's Approach

Meck could hardly believe he'd just welcomed Connie Clough into his home. He still hadn't gotten accustomed to the idea of working with Connie, a nationally renowned constitutional law scholar and skilled litigator who was legendary in the Christian community because of his passion for religious freedom. He had flown in from Kansas City to prepare them for the arbitration hearing, and each time they met, Meck had to force himself not to succumb to idolatrous feelings in much the same way he'd had to with Pastor Royce when the pastor first recruited him. Connie physically loomed over Meck, but it was the size of his intellect that was truly towering. It helped that Connie was so down-to-earth; if you met him for the first time at a church social, you'd never know he was a legal giant.

"Perfect winter's day out there, Warren. Thank the good Lord for the men doing the plowing. Roads aren't too bad."

Gracie sniffed at Connie's boots, and Connie spoke to her in a low tone and roughed her up around her collar. When he stopped, she leaned against his thigh and stared up at him. He took off his oversized aviator glasses and waved them back and forth to clear the condensation. His eyes appeared smaller, more vulnerable without them. He held the glasses up to the hall light, and then put them back on. The flaxen wire rims matched his thinning hair and dominated his face, encircling his prominent cheeks almost completely. Meck thanked him for coming out on a Saturday, hung his coat in the closet under the stairs, and ushered him into the living room. Connie looked around pointedly, his eyes widening.

"I know, pretty outlandish," said Meck. "I went through a bit of a colonial phase."

His face grew warm and he frowned, berating himself for trivializing what was hardly a phase. What kind of shame must he feel that he not only anticipated a negative reaction from Connie but also tried to beat him to the punch by proactively judging himself outlandish? He took a breath and imagined he was in the studio, about to go on air.

"Truthfully, Connie, it's more than a phase. I love having the kind of furniture Sam Adams might have had. Consider this armchair. Late sixteen hundreds, solid oak, crafted by a joiner using the frame and panel method so the chair could weather swelling and shrinking from season to season. This one's notable for these intricately carved arches and lunettes. They called them *great chairs* not only because of their size but because they were reserved for heads of households or important guests. Please, try it. It's far more comfortable than you might imagine, although my own size is more suited to that little comb-back Windsor rocker."

Connie settled into the chair. He smiled and rubbed his hands back and forth along the wood.

"I feel as if I should be beckoning a servant to bring me some wine."

"That's ironic," said Jill, who had just walked in, ushering Ben and John in front of her while Andrew clung to her leg. "I was about to offer you coffee, Mr. Clough, how are you? No, no, please don't get up."

"Thank you, dear. I wonder if I could trouble you for a cup of black tea? With a little milk?"

"Certainly. Happy to oblige."

"Good wife you have there," said Connie after Jill left. "You must be proud."

Meck felt his face growing hot again, and he inclined his head to acknowledge the compliment.

"Thank you, I am. She does a great job."

The three boys stood uncertainly together in the middle of the room. Meck nodded once at Ben, prompting him to greet their visitor. Each boy wore a clean pair of khakis and a white button-down shirt under a navy-blue sweater. Their blond hair had been carefully combed and slicked, and Meck made a mental note to thank Jill for getting them ready. He was pleased at the mature way Ben approached Connie and offered his hand. Connie rose from the great chair to formally greet the boys. John, the eight-year-old, spun away from Connie as soon as they'd said hello, and skipped wildly over to the rocker. His skinny legs hung well above the floor, and he clung to the arms and pitched his torso forward, then back, getting the rocker going.

"It's not going to take flight, John. Just slow it down a bit."

John gave Meck a wide smile and let the rocker slow, then jutted his chin in and out to keep it moving more slowly. Connie sat back down in the great chair, and Meck took one end of the couch, his only concession to modernity, and even then it was Queen Anne style, designed to look like an antique. Andrew crawled up next to Meck and buried his head in Meck's armpit.

"I hope you don't mind, Connie, but I thought it might be a good experience for the boys to sit in. Since we've been home-schooling, Jill has put a heavy emphasis on social studies, even for young Andrew here. Right, Sport?" He smoothed a hand over Andrew's hair. Andrew nodded solemnly, never taking his eyes off Connie.

"I'm more than glad to have you boys here. One day when we have a whole team of Meck men setting our country's political agenda, we'll all remember this day."

Ben stood in front of Connie. He was small for his age, but confident enough to look Connie in the eye. He put his hands into his pants pockets and stood as if at attention.

"Mr. Clough, sir? I wanted to thank you for your work defending Bridget Mergens in front of the Supreme Court. Back when I was still in public school, they weren't going to let me form a Christian club, but they changed their minds when I showed them the Mergens decision. I couldn't believe they didn't already know about it."

Connie glanced at Meck in surprise, and Meck felt a surge of love for his son, who had asked him earlier if he might approach Connie. The day the school principal had refused Ben club privileges, Ben had come home not in tears but with a lip-trembling refusal to feel humiliated, and a stoic determination for justice. "The principal is just like those kids who kicked John," he'd said. Meck and Jill had steered him to the library to discover how he might fight back.

"How old are you, young man?" Connie asked now.

"Eleven, sir, nearly twelve."

"I'm impressed."

"Thank you, sir. I wrote a paper about the Mergens case last month."

"Well I'd like to see that, Ben, if you'd be willing to share."

Ben broke into a huge smile and nodded enthusiastically. Again Connie rubbed the great chair's smooth oak arms.

"That was some time ago," he said in a wistful tone.

"Yes, sir, 1990. Do you think what we're talking about today will draw on the Equal Access law the way you did? If the Christian kids are being discriminated against in the same way?"

"Excellent question, Ben. Let me turn it around and ask you— what do you think?"

Meck had to suppress a smile as Ben swept back his bangs with both hands, a gesture he had unconsciously copied from Pastor Royce. Meck realized with surprise that Ben was about the age Meck had been when he'd first met Pastor Royce. Meck had responded to the pastor in much the same way Ben was reacting to Connie.

"I guess I expect the law won't apply. It's only about extracurricular clubs, right?"

"Exactly right. This is more an issue of restricted speech and disrespect for religious beliefs within the classroom. The same moral principles apply, though, so you keep thinking along those lines. I'm glad you're here with us today, young man. I welcome your perspective."


When Whit, Ed Shaw, and Arnie Dengler arrived, they moved into a four-season sunroom and sat around a chestnut trestle table that could comfortably fit twelve. Jill came in with a pitcher of orange juice and a second cup of tea for Connie, then poured coffee all around. She laid small plates, juice glasses, and cloth napkins at each of their places and then brought out two serving platters, one with a stack of coffee cake squares, the other with frosted cinnamon rolls, all still warm from the oven. John immediately got to his knees on his chair and flung out an arm toward the cinnamon rolls, but a sharp look from his mother stopped him, and he sat back and folded his hands on the table, his tiny shoulders stiff with tension, like a leashed dog anticipating release.

"Is there anything else you need right now, Warren?" said Jill.

Meck shook his head.

"I'll leave you men to your business, then. Boys, you be respectful, and pay attention. I'll just be in the kitchen if anyone needs anything. Gracie-girl, you come along with me. There's a good girl."

The sound of a jazzy xylophone blasted the room. Whit murmured an apology, retrieved his phone, and stepped out. He came back while the cake and rolls were still being passed around.

"We have a problem. That was Pastor Royce. The Westboro Baptist Church people caught wind of the hearing. They're planning to picket."

"Oh, Judas Priest," said Dengler, closing his eyes as if he could block out the news. He pulled his handkerchief out of his back pocket and wiped his broad forehead. "The media will glom on to those people like nobody's business. We won't get a word in edgewise."

"How did they know where it is?" Ben glanced over at Meck to see if it was okay to have asked.

"Everyone in the Fellowship knows where it is, Ben," said Meck.

"Besides, it hardly matters. All they have to do is show up in town, and the media will find them. Either way, Arnie's right that the media will focus on them, and then everyone will think we're all totally . . . well—"

"Whackadoodle?" said Dengler.

John giggled, and Meck gave him a reprimanding look. John flopped back in his chair and cupped a hand over his mouth, his eyes shining merrily.

"Now Arnie," said Connie. "They may employ a different strategy, but they are Godly people."

"They're EGRs is what they are," said Dengler.

"Extra! Grace! Required!" said John, bopping his head with each syllable before clapping his hand back over his mouth.

"With friends like those . . ." muttered Dengler. "We've got to shut them down."

"Maybe, Connie," said Shaw, "you know someone in the Phelps family we can talk to?"

"I'm afraid this isn't a group you can reason with, Ed," said Whit. "There's no fighting them. We just have to be smart. We can use them to strategic advantage. They can help demonstrate our sanity. Pastor Royce said they're submitting an amicus brief, too."

First the early dismissals, then the assault, then the attempt to spy at the State House, then Danny, Clancy, and Blair muscling their way into the studio, and now this . . . Meck felt the campaign slipping from his grip. He closed his eyes, trying to avert the thought.

"I have to say," said Connie, "their briefs are well written. Completely useless, but well written. As much as I agree with them that we're doomed as a nation if we don't resurrect our Christian roots, how they think Bible passages and citations from biblical scholars will sway serious men of the law on matters of public policy is beyond me."

"Whackadoodle," said John. Dengler bellowed out a laugh. Meck and Whit exchanged a look, both suppressing smiles. Meck knew exactly what Whit was thinking—for an eight-year-old, John was remarkably quick-witted.

"How about I ask Pastor Royce to work up some talking points about the picketers?" said Whit. "Focus on free speech."

"Good idea," said Meck. "Hopefully he can work it into tomorrow's sermon. And dissuade any of our own people from protesting at the hearing. We don't need the bad press the Westboro folks will unleash."

"Let's get to the hearing itself, then, shall we?" said Connie. "I'll let you gentlemen work out the media bits on your own time."

Despite Connie's perfectly pleasant tone, Meck felt chastened. He wished he'd commandeered their agenda from the start instead of getting sidetracked by Westboro. He also wished he'd taken his usual seat at the head of the table instead of giving it to Connie. Sitting on the side meant he had to continually lean forward to see past Dengler's bulk, and he didn't much like that he was on a par with his kids, who'd never seen another man in his chair. He cleared his throat and let his resonant radio voice come forth. As soon as he began to speak in that tone, his boys sat up straighter, and every man's eyes were on him.

"Absolutely, Connie. We'll get through this as quickly as we can and let you get on with your weekend. Here's the lineup of witnesses. Arnie and Ed, of course, will both testify. We have four sets of parents, all good, well-spoken folks who are prepared to do whatever it takes. Their children will be there, too. We thought it would be important for the arbitrator to hear from them firsthand, and they're all good kids, they all know what's at stake. Pastor Royce spent a lot of time with the families, so I feel confident they're well-briefed. The pastor himself will testify, since he's counseled a lot of these kids, so he can speak to impact. I can do the same, if necessary."

"I almost forgot!" said Whit. "We did get Kinney as arbitrator. Pat Kinney."

"What luck!" said Dengler. "Thank the good Lord for small favors."

He laid a heavy arm over the back of Meck's chair. Meck frowned and leaned forward.

"Luck has nothing to do with it," said Meck. "Don't you remember that first meeting of Redeemer attorneys? Early 2004? You were there. Kinney being chosen to arbitrate this meeting began that day."

Connie put his hands over his ears.

"I didn't hear that, gentlemen."

John swiveled his head back and forth, and when no one responded to Connie, he raised his hand as if he were in school, and when Meck nodded, he repeated the part about luck having nothing to do with it. Dengler laughed, and John frowned at him.

"He's not laughing at you, John," said Meck, although he wasn't certain this was true. Ever since the visit from Eric, he'd been aware of keeping his distance from Arnie. Whit had said he didn't think Arnie was smart enough to have recruited Eric, and Pastor Royce had concurred. Still, Meck no longer trusted him.

"What Mr. Clough said, John, was just a figure of speech; he heard what I said, he was simply indicating that he didn't really want to know. Sometimes it's better to have a shield of ignorance. Do you know what I mean?"

John nodded uncertainly. Andrew, who'd been gravely chewing tiny bites of cinnamon roll since the meeting began, was trying in vain with his napkin to rub the icing off his fingers. He gave up, neatly folded the napkin, and pinned his wrists to the edge of the table, awkwardly holding up his fingers.

"Go on into the kitchen and see your mother, Sport. She'll get you cleaned up."

Andrew nodded and slid down off his chair, trying not to touch anything. He hesitated behind his chair, and Meck felt a sudden rush of love for this serious boy who wanted to do the right thing and push in his chair as he'd been taught, but wasn't sure he should with sticky fingers.

"Go ahead, Sport, you're okay."

Andrew looked full into Meck's eyes and gave him a small and grateful smile. He pushed in his chair and walked somberly out of the room.

"Just because we were assigned Kinney," said Meck, "doesn't mean we shouldn't be vigilant. He takes his job seriously and will work hard to be objective. Having him isn't any kind of guarantee—in fact, he'll probably go overboard to make sure he's unbiased. We have to do our jobs well. Our biggest coup to date is that we talked the ACLU into sending someone in person instead of just submitting a brief!"

"Afraid not," said Whit. "Zeilonka's people got to them. They're not coming."

"When did that happen?"

"This morning—e-mail. I figured you'd already seen it. They're pulling the brief, too, said something about 'compelling evidence' from the other side. Typical. I guess they weren't ready to go up against the senator."

"Wonder which verse of *Second Capitulations* they'll drag out to defend that decision?" said Dengler. John giggled again, and Ben joined him.

"That's okay," said Connie. "We're still in fine shape. Now, here's our basic legal argument. I don't think we'll have much trouble, to be honest, given the evidence and the fact that the law is on our side, but whatever we accomplish here today will influence every other hearing across the state, so we can't ever rest on our laurels, even if it seems like Kinney's going to rule in our favor, okay? We've got the First Amendment: free exercise of religion and speech. And their equivalents in the state Constitution, which essentially says the same thing. And here's our silver bullet: MGL Chapter 76 Section 5. I plan to hammer repeatedly on this one statute, because really it should be all we need. The law states in part *that no person shall be excluded from or discriminated against in admission to a public school of any town, or*—and this is the critical part—*in obtaining the advantages, privileges and courses of study of such public school on account of race, color, sex, religion, national origin, or sexual orientation.* We just need to prove our kids were discriminated against in such a way that they couldn't obtain the advantages they're due, and we've got plenty of evidence that this is the case. How can they learn in a hostile environment?"

"Sexual orientation," said Dengler with disgust. "Have you heard they're trying to add 'gender identity' now, too? It wasn't enough they got sexual orientation added to every last law on the books in '93? And people say there isn't a homosexual agenda. Judas Priest, it's more like an epidemic."

It annoyed Meck, the way Arnie said "Judas Priest," and he leaned farther forward to distance himself from Arnie's heavy arm, which was still slung across the back of Meck's chair. Meck lowered his head and rubbed his neck. He didn't like his boys being exposed to such cursing. He could easily see John bursting out with something at church one Sunday, not knowing what he was saying, and Ben had that unconscious habit of mimicking people. Meck would have to talk with them later. Now he peered over his shoulder at Dengler.

"Actually, Arnie, I think the fact that sexual orientation is included in the statute is helpful."

"I agree," said Shaw.

Dengler removed his arm and crossed both of them over his chest.

"We're not trying to discriminate against the homosexual kids," said Meck. "We're just trying to assert our equal rights under the same statute. Even the senator can't argue with that."

"This is an important distinction Warren makes," said Connie. "We need to keep the focus on equal opportunity and safe environment for our kids, and stay far away from any language that could be read as discriminating against Zeilonka because he's a homosexual. We can talk about the curriculum, of course, but we all need to steer clear of any mention—nothing about Zeilonka's agenda or lifestyle, not even a mention of the word *homosexual* if you can help it."

Shaw and Dengler exchanged a look.

"What is it?" said Meck.

"Criminy," said Dengler. "That's the whole point, isn't it? That he's a fag?"

Meck rubbed again at the back of his neck and sighed.

"You already talked about his lifestyle, didn't you?" It wasn't a question. "At the meeting."

"Well of course we did!" said Dengler. "We had to tell them what the parents and kids said, didn't we? No getting around it. But that's on them, not on us."

Shaw blanched.

"Except when you told Tommy you could help cure him, Arnie. I tried to stop him, Warren, honestly."

Meck gave Whit a sharp look.

"It's not as bad as you think," said Connie. "I've heard the tape."

"There's a tape?" said Meck.

He glared over his shoulder at Dengler and wondered again if he could be trusted.

"You were also terribly kind," Connie said to Dengler, "and I don't think Pat Kinney's going to fret too much about your language. I think we're actually in good shape. Between Chapter 76 Section 5 and the First Amendment, we have a solid case. And we also have one more ace up our sleeve should we need it, but I truly hope we don't. It would take us away from our focus on religious freedom and free speech, and that's the key here. But, if we get into trouble, we could go with sexual harassment. The legal definition of harassment is as broad as your great chair, Warren. We could argue that Tommy's choice of content is sexually suggestive, creating a hostile and offensive educational environment. It's obviously different from arguing that he shut down the Christian kids from speaking their piece, but it would do the trick if we think Kinney might rule against us and put him back into the classroom."

Quiet descended as they each thought through the ramifications of what Connie had just outlined. In light of Connie's calm confidence, Meck allowed himself a growing hope that they would win not only the Zeilonka case, but maybe the other ten as well.

He made eye contact with Whit and could tell he was feeling it, too; they could salvage this campaign.

"Five years ago," said Meck, directing his comments toward Whit, "we teamed up with the pastor and dreamed about making inroads. And here we are, on the cusp of . . . I'm starting to think we might actually win, Whit. And if we win Massachusetts"— Whit gave a low whistle—"it's a slam dunk for the nation."

John threw his arm into the air, fingers curled around an imaginary basketball, and flung it back down. His tiny hand slammed hard against the edge of the table, and Meck was instantly up and out of his seat, but John, who let out a yelp, gave his wrist a couple of quick shakes and then seemed to decide he was fine. He peered around at all of them, holding on to his hand, and broke into a big grin, but Meck, already halfway around the table, went to him anyway to make absolutely certain he wasn't badly hurt.

# Part III

# 24
# Starówka

After the Nazis had finally gotten their fill of Warsaw, when the last men of the *Verbrennungskommando* had shouldered their empty *Flammenwerfer 41s* and retreated in jackboots away from the oily flames they'd just thrown, the people of Warsaw began to return, the people who decided almost at once to do the unthinkable, what no one at all would have blamed them for not doing, what must have repeatedly seemed at best ill-advised, at worst impossible: resurrect their decimated city.

But resurrect it they did, and in such painstaking and excruciating detail that Ludka, holding tight to Izaac's trembling arm, had been standing open-mouthed and speechless for a long few minutes in the snowy center of Rynek Starego Miasta, in the heart of Starówka. If it hadn't been for one neon café sign touting modern beers—Carlsberg, Zywiec, Tyskie—and the intrepid tourists braving the cold to take photos with their phones of the famous buildings surrounding the square, it might have been 1934, when Ludka was ten, assisting her father as he created one of his popular snow sculptures. Once, she'd helped him build a small replica of Rynek Starego Miasta itself—a square within the square—large enough for children to walk through but small enough that adults could peer into it only from the outside. Eventually, the sculptures would erode and lose shape, and then the children would make them their own. Ludka wondered if she ever would have remembered such a thing had she not returned to Warsaw. It occurred to her then that her memories had seldom stretched back beyond September 1, 1939, when the Nazis had subsumed her childhood as thoroughly as they'd razed the city. Now she told Izaac about her father's snow sculptures.

"Your father created those? How could I not know that? I couldn't have been more than eight or nine, but I remember that row of people like it was yesterday. They were just over there; do you remember? Everyone holding hands, like Christmas carolers, or some kind of human barricade."

Ludka hadn't remembered, but remembered now it was the winter before the war, and one of her tedious tasks had been to bring her father bucket after bucket of snow; he couldn't seem to stop adding more people, Jews and Poles alike, anticipating, perhaps, that the sculpture wouldn't last more than a couple days before a gang of young men would bash through each pair of clasped hands. A year later, hauling snow had become a different job altogether—it was their primary source of water that first winter after the invasion.

Ludka's feet and ankles were still swollen from flying, and judging by the searing pain on the inside of her left anklebone, the skin from a throbbing blister must have sheared off. They'd been in Warsaw just long enough to get settled into the fifth-floor apartment on Plac Zambrowsky that Mandelbaum had secured for them, an airy space with heavy-beamed high ceilings and large windows facing the Royal Castle, and despite their utter exhaustion and the temptation of the king-sized sleigh bed, they had both felt the need to get out. Izaac had said they'd rest when they're dead, and Ludka had responded that that might be sooner than they'd expected after twenty-two hours on the road.

Arm in arm, they'd walked slowly up Swietojanska to the square, an unspoken and shared trepidation steering them away from the most direct route up Piwna, where the Zeilonka family apartment had been. The square was proving to be enough of a shock.

"The stones I had forgotten."

Ludka felt rather than saw Izaac nod. The snow wasn't heavy and in many places had been trampled or shoveled aside completely to reveal the intricately laid gray stones that paved the entire square. Streets throughout the Old Town, as they called it now, had been recobbled during the rebuilding; some stones were large and rounded, many small and square and worn smooth, nearly all of them salvaged from the rubble. Still clinging to Izaac's arm, Ludka turned in a slow circle, pulling him with her. Airport security hadn't allowed her to bring her spiked galoshes, and so she was relying on Izaac and her sensible boots to keep her steady. The golden light of the late afternoon sun swept across the north and east sides of the square, reflecting fiery light off the windows and heightening the colors of the plaster facades—salmon, putty, peach, cream, aqua. The buildings appeared unequivocally familiar.

"But how is this even possible, Izaac?"

Her voice sounded thin. She cleared her throat. Izaac squeezed her arm and said nothing. They were facing Strona Dekerta, the north side of the square, arguably the most beautiful of the four. But Ludka and Izaac both knew that Jan Dekert, while one of the most prominent Warsaw merchants of the late eighteenth century, had also been a vocal anti-Semite, and German by birth, the forefather, perhaps, to Ludka's neighbor Adolf Dekert, a man whom Ludka's mother had always said was aptly named. Izaac trembled again, and Ludka suggested they walk. The last time she had seen Strona Dekerta, the only thing that remained of the buildings had been their soot-smeared facades. The windows had been blown out, and the open casings looked like empty eye sockets in row upon row of stacked skulls. And through those openings there had been only sky. Miles and miles of sky in a place where previously no sky had been. Ludka raised her arm to point but paused, not sure where to even begin. She lowered it and covered her mouth with gloved fingers. She glanced at Izaac distractedly and swept her hand in an arc around the square.

"It is miracle."

Izaac wiped the outside corner of each of his eyes.

A short and stout elderly woman carrying bulging, pale blue plastic bags in each hand made her way diagonally across the square toward them, scrutinizing the trodden path. Her knotted head scarf, heavy wool coat and skirt, and thick hose were all in shades of brown and gray, and her ankle boots were not unlike Ludka's own. Without glancing up, the woman stepped aside and paused to let three giggling young women wearing stiletto-heeled boots totter past. All three held cigarettes, and the smoke hung low in the cold air. When they were safely away, the woman stepped back onto the path and resumed her careful procession. As she got closer, Izaac pulled Ludka aside to make room for her to pass, and greeted her.

"*Dzień dobry.*"

"*Dzień dobry.*" The woman spoke quietly and didn't meet their eyes. She gave a slight nod and trudged past, her flimsy bags rustling, an intimate odor of talcum and warm wool wafting behind her. Ludka was surprised to see poking from her scarf a tuft of bright crimson-colored hair. They watched her go, mesmerized, each of them thinking of their grandmothers before remembering that she might instead have been a former classmate. Before the week was out they would see many more like her, unapproachable old women with dyed hair, thick hose, and sensible shoes, and stern old men with crew cuts, overcoats, and scuffed-up boots, all of whom carried themselves cautiously and frowned suspiciously whenever Ludka or Izaac greeted them with American smiles.

A small and chilly gust of air blew through the square, bringing with it a smell of sausage, sauerkraut, and boiled dumplings.

"Good pierogi restaurant we must find, and then perhaps we should sleep."

"Even a poor pierogi would do me some good right now. Let's not do more than that. I'm asleep on my feet. Plus, you need to be rested for tomorrow."

Since boarding the plane at Logan only twenty-four hours earlier, Ludka had thought of little other than tomorrow's symposium. Mandelbaum had asked her to make a brief statement and be on hand to answer people's questions, and Ludka was grateful when he told her not to feel obligated to join the prearranged panel. Also, a reporter from *Gazeta Wyborcza* would be there and had requested an interview, which Ludka had declined. It was one thing to make a remark or two about her work, quite another to answer a string of probing questions. She had finally allowed herself to be curious about the condition of her sketches, which had been sealed and buried in one of the large milk cans Ringelblum had prayed wouldn't rust through. She couldn't recall everything she'd drawn and worried that seeing them might bring on an episode. Mostly, though, since boarding the plane, she had thought about Oskar. He would be there, she was convinced.

She searched for him now as she and Izaac walked out of the square and, in silent agreement, turned away from Swietojanska and took a right on Zapiecek, which would take them to Piwna. The sun no longer touched the tops of the buildings, and even though the sky was still bright, the street had grown dim, and the black iron lanterns hanging from many of the buildings had begun to glow. They passed the Galeria Zapiecek, but it wouldn't be until two days later that they would learn it was the best modern art gallery in Warsaw. And then there they were, standing in front of the wide, solid wooden gates at 28/30 Piwna, which they knew opened into a courtyard that led to the stairs to their old apartment.

"I guess I was inside so much, the gate doesn't feel that familiar. Does it to you, kochanie?"

Ludka nodded but all at once wasn't entirely certain what Izaac had asked. She started to say something but couldn't remember what it was she had intended. She felt her body go still and in a brief flash of clarity understood she was moving into a flashback. Just as quickly, the understanding was gone and then she was a young woman, rushing through the wooden gate, slamming it closed behind her and throwing the locks.

Izaac felt her stiffen and knew at once what was happening. He tightened his grip on her arm and bumped against her repeatedly, gently at first and then more strongly, saying her name urgently into her ear. He had a moment of panic, thinking she might collapse onto the street. He didn't know if he could bear her weight.

"Izaac, stop shaking me like rag doll!"

He released a big breath and a nervous laugh.

"I thought I was going to lose you there. But it worked! Your therapist was right!"

"I was running from something. No, from someone."

In the same way a dream can prove elusive, Ludka found herself nearly grasping a particular memory, but not quite. She thought her Mama and Tata were there, in their apartment, and something else was there, too, something different, not Izaac, not another person, although maybe there was another person, she couldn't be sure. Was it a dog? It was! A dog!

"Ludka? Kochanie? Are you still with me?"

She nodded. Her heart was thumping wildly, though, and a hollow fear had spread inside her chest. *Danger, Ludka, uwaga!* The dog had been a German shepherd. Straight-backed and all black but with expressive butterscotch eyebrows over warm brown eyes. He had been . . . What had he been doing there? She had felt sorry for him, that was it. So terribly sorry, the way he was straining against that tight leash . . . She shivered and closed her eyes. Somewhere in the distance she thought she heard a piano, and a group of drunk young men cavorted behind them, one of them singing loudly, the rest of them laughing and shoving each other. One of them bumped against Izaac and slurred an apology.

"Hooligans!" Ludka said, her heart still thumping madly.

She shook a fist, but feebly, and knew how ridiculous she must appear. Even her voice felt weak.

"Did you remember something, kochanie?"

She felt certain it was better not to think of the dog, and she latched her gaze onto the cobblestones, long rectangles with smoothed edges in shades of dusty rose and gray. Imagine if they'd been able to put every stone back in its exact place.

"No, Izaac. I remember nothing."

"Are you back with me now?"

She nodded. He smiled.

"That was a close one. Do you want to go back to the apartment?"

"I am fine. Food first, then we go back."

She clung to him. Izaac looked up and down the street for a place to eat.

"Well, what do you know," he said. "Do you remember? Up there on the gold building across from our apartment. The eye of providence. See it there?"

"I had forgotten."

"Me, too. Astonishing. It's as familiar as the back of my hand. I stared out at that thing all the time. Your mother had told me it was the eye of God watching over us, and even then I remember thinking he wasn't doing the best job of it. Still, I prayed and prayed and prayed. I wonder, kochanie, if you would indulge me for a minute? If you're okay?"

She nodded that she was fine, and again she steered her mind away from the dog. Izaac gently freed his arm from hers, and removed his gloves and hat.

"Hold these?"

He pulled from his pocket the yarmulke, and held it tentatively in both hands. He appeared shy, almost embarrassed, and Ludka hugged his hat and gloves and reminded herself what year it was, that Izaac was free to do what he was about to do.

"I haven't done this for so long. I feel a little stupid."

He backed up against the wall near the gate and gazed up at the eye of providence.

"Being here, though, seeing all of this, is worth an offering of thanks, don't you think?"

"And it is God you will thank, after all this time?"

She hadn't meant to sound accusatory. She stepped aside and averted her eyes to give him some privacy as he reached up to put on the yarmulke. She could see him out of the corner of her eye. He patted at it awkwardly, his head bent low, chin thrust forward. He could have done with some bobby pins. He straightened, took another look around, gave her an embarrassed smile, closed his eyes, and began to murmur.

"*Baruch atah Adonai, eloheinu melekh ha'olam . . .*"

When he finished, he opened his eyes. They were teary.

"The first time I tried to follow you when you went to meet Oskar, I didn't get beyond the sidewalk. I was terrified. I almost rushed back in, but instead I prayed on this very spot. Of course I didn't have a head covering, so I pretended I was picking through my hair for lice and kept my palms over my head. I expect I recited the same prayer."

Ludka felt a bit sick, thinking how exposed he had been, how one false move . . .

"What does it mean, this prayer?"

"In essence it means thank you. The best translation is probably something like *Blessed is God, who has granted us life, sustained us, and enabled us to reach this occasion.* And here we are, Ludka, can you believe it? I don't credit any god, however, so don't get any ideas. This is nostalgia talking, that's all."

He palmed the yarmulke and discreetly slid it off the side of his head. Ludka sent up her own little prayer of thanks, not only that they had lived to return together, but also that she had not slipped into a terrible memory that might have marred this first night. Again she took hold of Izaac. She'd never held on to him this tightly, for this long.

Partway down Piwna, she realized with disbelief that she'd walked right past the entrance to St. John's on Swietojanska on their way to the square. She had been baptized at St. John's, and taken her first communion there, and it was in the hallways of its chilly crypt that she had first met Oskar during those initial hushed meetings of Żegota, when at fifteen she had still believed it was possible to defeat the Nazis.

"Please we will just make tiny detour. Through alley here back to Swietojanska so I can see St. John's."

"Didn't they firebomb it—after the uprising?"

Ludka stopped and waggled her foot, trying to pull her blistered ankle away from the side of her boot, but as soon as she returned her foot to the ground, the pain returned.

"Everything they burned."

They moved slowly. For Ludka, each step was a misery, but she forced herself not to think about it; they were in Starówka, walking on cobblestones, on their way to St. John's! All around them the people spoke Polish. A chilly wind blew up from the Vistula, bringing with it a familiar smell of icy mud and something that hinted of the spring rains to come. Ludka's thoughts flashed happily on Oskar's vision of Eugeniusz Zak's *Boy*, sitting by the river; she imagined the boy rising and stretching languidly and turning away from the water to climb freely onto the bridge to scamper home. All through the alley she patted the walls, as if she still couldn't quite accept that they were standing.

Back on Swietojanska, a keyboard player was braving the cold in fingerless gloves, a tin box opened for donations on the side-walk in front of him. He met Ludka's eyes and nodded before ducking his head to monitor his fingers as he raced into a heavy chord pattern. It built in speed and intensity and volume and was then joined by a wild trilling with his right hand that all at once made Ludka want to throw out her arms in celebration. She turned to Izaac with an openmouthed smile that ended in a laugh. He smiled back and gave her arm a little shake, as if to say he knew exactly how she felt because he could feel it, too.

"Of course it's Chopin," he said. "Has to be."

And in a rush her sudden high spirits were dashed and it all came back to her—Stanley, the Chopin, the assault on Tommy—everything she'd been able to put behind her during the long flight, everything that hadn't seemed to matter quite as much once they'd taxied out of the gate and turned the plane toward the east, because what could you do from thirty-five thousand feet above the earth, what could you affect from an ocean away? For one terrible moment she thought she might collapse.

"We need to get you something to eat, kochanie. What about the church?"

He stepped away from her. She swayed, then caught herself. Izaac dropped a two złoty coin into the pianist's box, and the pianist lifted his head and said "*Dzięki*."

"*Proszę*."

Izaac joined Ludka across the street, where she stood in front of the church.

"But St. John's is Gothic Revival, not this brick . . ." she said.

Izaac clasped his hands behind his back and leaned forward to read a brass plaque bolted next to the door.

"Bazylika Archikatedralna święty Jana. Apparently they rebuilt it the way it was in the fourteenth century. But it's the same church all right."

"It is most certainly not same church."

She stared up at it, vexed by the garish illuminated facade of staggered brick pillars that formed a tall triangle, high at its apex the cross. Gone were the vast arches, the ornate turrets, and the statues of saints watching over the city.

"Maybe the inside's the same, kochanie. Should we go in?"

She wondered if the crucifix had been saved, if there'd been a miracle like the one at St. Hedwig's that Frank had described to her nearly twenty years ago now, when that arsonist had burned so much of their church, but the crucifix remained unscathed. She briefly closed her eyes and imagined St. John's as she had known it, and then she winced as she pictured it in flames. She couldn't bear the thought of finding it utterly altered. She shook her head, but Izaac had already tried the door and, finding it open, walked in and held it for her. She shook her head again, but Izaac was peering into the church, and so she stepped inside.

The hush was total in the deserted church, the only sound that of Izaac's shuffling steps as he moved beyond the vestibule entry and into the dimly lit nave. In one swift glance Ludka took in enough to know that everything had changed, and she dipped her fingers into the holy water, made the sign of the cross, and forced herself to think of this as simply an unknown, foreign church and not an imposter standing on ashes. A spider's web of brick supports ran up the white plaster walls and crisscrossed the vast white ceiling. A checkerboard marble floor paved the way to the sanctuary, and the small, unfamiliar crucifix, isolated on a pedestal off to the side, gleamed with shiny gold.

Ludka swayed again, still not sure of her land legs after so much time in the air. She held on to the end of a dark-stained pew and took her weight off her throbbing ankle. A moment later, she was glad for the pew's support, because there above the priest's chair was a reproduction of the Black Madonna of Częstochowa, exactly like the one at St. Hedwig's, and at her old St. John's. Ludka gazed at it gratefully, the holy water still damp on her forehead, and wondered if this was the very painting she'd known as a girl? She began then to see other familiar items—the priest's chair, the chandeliers, a marble statue of St. John the Baptist—and a burble of unexpected laughter burst forth, because once again the Black Madonna had lived up to her legend and saved the church from annihilation by fire. Izaac, startled by Ludka's laughter, hurried back.

She tried to tell him not to worry, but couldn't get out the words. She could feel the laughter coming on, the hysterical kind that originates from tension and exhaustion, a laughter that has to run its course. Still hanging on to the pew, she laid the other hand on Izaac's chest and met his eyes. She tried to shush herself, but that set her off again. She made a clumsy effort to genuflect, moved into the pew and sank down onto the seat and began to rock with laughter. Izaac stood uncertainly, but her laughter was infectious, and he began to chuckle, asking "What is it? What is it?" But Ludka could only shake her head and wipe away her tears as her laughter ricocheted throughout the cavernous church. Finally, Izaac sat beside her, and his own laughter overtook him, infusing Ludka's with new life. Wave after wave rolled through them, and Ludka clutched at her tightened stomach, and Izaac threw back his head and hooted and slapped his thighs, and all at once Ludka thought she might be sobbing, but it was so much like the laughing, she couldn't be sure, until Izaac turned to her and he was crying, too, both of them crying and crying.

# 25
# The Jewish Historical Institute

The next afternoon, standing in front of the Jewish Historical Institute's polished wood doors, Ludka's mouth was completely dry, and her palms grew damp inside her leather gloves. She had slept well but woken early because of the time change; now, at home, it would be almost 11:00 p.m. Even though she'd taken a nap earlier in the day, she felt mildly disoriented, as if she had a slight hangover, and her limbs felt too heavy to manage. She had doctored her ankle with ointment and bandages Izaac had gone to fetch that morning, and the sharp throbbing had subsided. One edge of the tape pinched, though, and she hoped she wouldn't develop a new hot spot. A chime not unlike a fork hitting a wine glass sounded from her shoulder bag.

"What the hell is that?" said Izaac.

"This is text sound, I think?"

"From Tommy? More good news?"

Earlier in the day, Izaac had gotten a detailed e-mail from

Abe, letting them know the arbitration hearing had gone better than expected, but had been extended into a second day. Connie Clough and the school seemed to be steering clear of sexual harassment. The media, however, was having a field day thanks to the Westboro Baptist Church picketers. Judging by the clips Abe had forwarded, Channel 7 was the only station airing reasonable reports.

Ludka took off her gloves, shoved them into the bag, and found her phone. On the screen was a photograph of the Chopin with a *San Francisco Chronicle* next to it. The message said "Happy now?" The photo was too small, of course, to see at a glance either the date on the paper or the condition of the painting, and she wondered when she might slip away to inspect it more closely. Had he gone back to San Francisco after all? Or gotten the paper locally? She muted the phone and slipped it back into her bag.

"Phone company," she said. "I have told and told them not to text when bill is ready and still they persist."

Her heart hammered so hard in her ears that she was sure Izaac would hear it.

"I am wishing now we had stayed home."

"Come, kochanie. You'll be okay. Let's see how those sketches have held up."

The next several minutes were a blur of preparation in Ezra Mandelbaum's office, as he took their coats and walked them through the program and the staging. The names of the panelists flew from Ludka's mind as soon as she'd heard them, and later, during the program, she'd have to be prompted when it was her turn to speak, since she'd barely heard Mandelbaum's instructions. She drank a glass of water and was grateful when a student intern brought her a bottle. She tucked it into her bag, and then they were climbing the wide marble stairs to the exhibition hall. In his lovely Polish, Mandelbaum explained to them that most of the permanent exhibition was on view, that they'd used one side of the hall to display a large portion of her sketches, while the rest were shown in a glossy book they'd printed for the occasion. Mandelbaum, a portly man with a trim white beard, wiped a hand across his sweating brow, and Ludka realized he was as nervous as she was.

"Had we known about you sooner, we would of course have consulted with you, and if you're willing, we would like to work with you to produce an updated edition. We of course will give you a copy of the one we have."

She lifted her hand in a noncommittal gesture, exhausted just thinking about a project of that magnitude. She hauled herself up the stairs by the wrought iron rail, Izaac just behind her. It hadn't occurred to her that the Institute might be concerned about her intentions, might be worried she would demand to keep the sketches for herself, a thought that hadn't even crossed her mind. Now that it had, she did wonder how she'd feel when she saw them, whether she'd want to take them home. And then they were at the top of the stairs, the exhibition hall open before them.

Izaac gripped Ludka's elbow and thanked Mandelbaum, who told them to make themselves at home and enjoy the exhibition, that the formal program would start in half an hour. Izaac steered Ludka away from the stairs and backed them up against a wall. In front of them a wide entryway opened into the exhibition area, and above the packed, milling crowd soared a twelve-foot-high black-and-white photograph of a long-bearded and serious old

Jew wearing a short-brimmed Greek fisherman's cap and holding a book to his chest, hand loosely curled around the spine. But for the book and his slight smile, he might have stepped out of Roslan's *Prelude, 1939*, and for the first time Ludka realized that the Institute's permanent collection might feel far more like home than Warsaw itself. The portion of the crowd visible through the entryway seemed mostly elderly, with a few middle-aged couples mixed in and only a handful of students. Ludka sought out all the old men, wondering in what condition she'd find Oskar. Mandelbaum had shown them the anonymous typed letter that had alerted the Institute to her identity; if Oskar had, in fact, written it, he had apparently recognized her work in the poster advertising the symposium. She wiped her palms on the sides of her long gray skirt. Izaac shook her elbow. High on the wall hung another photograph, mural-sized and sepia-toned: two vast hills of pulverized ruins separated by a narrow valley and a bumpy, dusty jeep track that ran the valley's length. The only building still intact, far in the distance, was the tower and steeple of the Catholic Archdiocese. This photo was a still from the scene Ludka had watched only that once in *The Rape of Europa*. Her mouth went dry again, as if she had been breathing brick dust and smoke. She groped in her bag for the tin of strong peppermints.

"I do not think I can do this, Izaac."

"I'm not so sure I can either, kochanie. I'm not so sure."

Ludka opened the peppermint tin, popped one in her mouth, and gave one to Izaac. She wondered if Oskar would be bald, stooped, using a cane or a walker. All she could picture was Stanley as he'd appeared that day in her office. She frowned.

The exhibition area was crowded enough that it was nearly impossible to move without touching someone, but the noise was muted as people spoke quietly, or not at all. Hanging high on the walls for unobstructed viewing were more enlarged photographs. Ludka glanced at them only long enough to register a penetrating dread. Izaac studied them for signs of his parents. Throughout the hall, freestanding display boards showed pieces of their history.

"What's the story with the puppet's head?" asked Izaac.

Ludka followed his gaze, let out a little "oh," and pressed a hand over her mouth.

"*Kostucha*, we called them."

"As in the Grim Reaper?"

"During resistance, we stuck Kostucha's head on a pole, put a hat on it, and poked him above the street barricades to draw fire, while we crouched and scampered like rats to the other side of the street. It became like sport to Nazis. Never did we have enough hats."

"But the Grim Reaper doesn't prevent death, he ushers it in."

Ludka looked on him with pity.

"Not always, Izaac, did Kostucha succeed."

A waiter interrupted with a tray of drinks, and Ludka unthinkingly took a glass of white wine. She winced as the tepid sour taste mixed with the peppermint.

"Is it me only, Izaac, who thinks it is like leafing through an old yearbook, all of this? Or an old family photo album. Do you understand? How surreal?"

"Probably more so for you than for me."

Ludka wondered how many of the other old people in the room felt the same way, as if they were seeing not the preserved history of a people and a genocide, but their own scrapbooks.

Two college-aged women looked closely at a set of vulgar posters depicting Jewish caricatures crawling with typhus-infested lice.

"Żydzi Wszy," one of them read. "Jews! Lice! Who could have possibly taken these seriously?"

Izaac raised his eyebrows in disbelief, but Ludka thought of her initially dismissive reaction to the Westboro picketers, her visceral relief at learning they were small in number. Now she imagined Tommy trying to get past the picketers to attend his arbitration hearing, the boy with lamb's-wool hair berating him with vulgar placards, and for the first time since the assault, she wasn't able to deflect the terrible question that had been loitering at the periphery of her mind: What, exactly, had arisen in their midst? She tightened her grip on her shoulder bag.

"There it is," said Izaac.

Inside a waist-high Plexiglas box, lovingly displayed as if it were a family heirloom, rested one of the rusty milk cans that had housed the Ringelblum archives. They walked over, and Izaac stood solemnly, hands clasped loosely together. He wiped the outside corner of each eye. Ludka remembered the can's original dull lead color, now obscured by dark brown rust. Without thinking, she took another swallow of wine, and grimaced as it went down. She searched around for somewhere to set the glass, and that's when she saw him. Not Oskar in the flesh, but Oskar as she had sketched him, full-bodied, staring straight at her, hands pressed protectively over the small chest of a big-eyed young boy who leaned back against him. The first boy they'd saved—Aaron, she remembered with surprise. Suddenly Izaac's arm was around her waist, and he asked if she needed to sit down. She took a deep breath and shook her head. She held out the wine glass.

"Take this."

While Izaac looked for a place to get rid of the glass, Ludka clutched the strap of her bag and walked slowly over to her drawing of Oskar, the gateway to the rest of her work. She caught only glimpses of the exhibit as people came and went, but it was enough. There were her parents, folding the blankets for distribution. Ten-year-old Izaac read at the kitchen table, a heavily curtained window behind him. Manny Ringelblum bent over a worktable littered with papers, Gela Seksztajn and her husband, Izrael, by his side. A scrawny dog lifted his nose toward a tiny boy no older than six, who held a loaf of bread like an American football and reared back to launch it over the ghetto wall. A young nurse crouched in the back of an ambulance, and held tight to a laundry bin. Because Ludka had stowed him there herself, she knew a skeletal, sedated, ten-year-old Izaac lay in the bottom of the bin, under laundry they'd made to appear soiled. Typhus terrified the Nazis, so the nurses typically went unmolested, although the word *typical* had lost its credence; many nurses, of course, had been lost.

The paper had yellowed, and some of the drawings had splotches of stain from water or mold or both, but all were largely intact. Ludka held on to the display with her left hand and found that with her right she was gripping her thumb and fingers as if holding a pencil, as if it hadn't been more than sixty years since she'd regularly sketched. She hurriedly let go. The drawing of Oskar wasn't quite right, and in a rush she remembered how much trouble she'd had with the thickness of his hair, how later she had grabbed it in both hands and given it a frustrated tug.

"*Odstawić*, Polly, leave off!" Oskar had said, grabbing her wrists.

But in the sketch, his hair was the only thing not right, and she touched the glass as if she could reach through it and hold a palm against his cheek. She searched the gallery again. There were so many people!

At last the milling around was over, and everyone filed out of the exhibition area and filled the rows of chairs. Ludka stood in front of her reserved chair in the front row and scanned the crowd, randomly at first and then methodically, row by row. Izaac urged her to sit, but she ignored him and started again, from the back, scrutinizing each man in every row, and then those who were standing two deep in the back and along the sides. She could not believe he'd be unrecognizable, and it was impossible he wouldn't see her standing alone there in the front. Finally, she could delay no longer and she sat, the entire crowd at her back. When Izaac took her hand after a moment, she realized she'd been slumping, her eyes closed. She straightened and hitched up her shoulders, swallowing hard and trying to appear alert as Mandelbaum took the podium.

It wouldn't be until the following week when she was home, when she watched the symposium on the Institute's website, that she would realize just how special it had been. The scholars were thorough and respectful, putting her work into the larger context of Holocaust art, praising both her talent and her courage, and expressing their gratitude that she had been found so they could thank her in person. One young woman, a professor at the University of Warsaw who ran a slide show of Ludka's sketches during her entire lecture, cried openly when she was through and seized Ludka's hands and leaned down to kiss her on both cheeks, one of the few things Ludka remembered. She would be relieved to see that her long professional experience had carried her through without embarrassment, despite her rusty Polish, and that she'd even managed to be gracious.

But sitting at the Institute as the symposium wore on, trying not to glance back over the crowd, trying to appear attentive, all

Ludka could think about was what it might mean that Oskar had not come. Izaac nudged her.

"It's time, kochanie. You must go up. Do you need me to help you?"

She shook her head but held tightly to his hand as she stood. She swayed for a moment, then let go and stepped to the podium where Mandelbaum had made room for her. She grabbed hold of the podium and could at last survey the crowd. Oskar was not there. Mandelbaum seemed to be presenting her with something, and then there was an outburst of applause, and the crowd rose to its feet, and people clapped harder and harder, and she thought they would never stop. In the video, she would see herself frowning, tears spilling down her cheeks, lips pursed, eyes darting around like a cornered animal, Mandelbaum applauding beside her, smiling broadly through his own tears. With one hand she held on to the podium, with the other she clutched the glossy book Mandelbaum had presented to her along with a fresh new sketchbook, "for happier times," he said.

And then they were back in the exhibition hall, and many people wanted to take Ludka's hands or kiss her or share their own stories, while others milled around in her vicinity, staring at her peripherally but not daring to approach. Izaac flagged down a waiter who came over with a tray of fried pierogi.

"Give us a moment, please," Izaac said to the waiting people. "Here, kochanie, eat these." He handed her three pierogi, and all at once she realized how weak she felt and gratefully she ate them, all of them filled with aromatic mushrooms and cheese. From her bag, she took the bottle of water and drank half, offering the rest to Izaac, who also drank greedily. And then, across the room, she glimpsed a familiar boy in a large photograph.

"There's that street busker with his violin. I knew I had seen him! Alexander Roslan painted that same boy, that exact expression. I must have seen him on the street. Look at that raised bow!"

She put a hand to her throat, and for the first time since they'd arrived at the Institute, she smiled, and that was when she saw him, contemplating the same photograph, his back to her, head slightly cocked, right leg turned out like a dancer's. His tightly cinched, worn trousers hung as if made for a much larger man. He was bald. For a moment she thinks she has made a mistake. Surely this is some other man, some other man who will turn, his face a stranger's, but then he does turn—Oskar does—and looks directly at her.

"What is it?" says Izaac. "Where are you going?"

As fast as she dares she makes her way toward him. He pushes into the crowd, away from her—but he did see her, didn't he?—and she loses sight of him, and wonders again if her mind is playing tricks, if she is imagining all of it, having an episode. But there he goes, skirting a young couple. He checks back over his shoulder, finds her. She lifts a hand, then clutches at her bag as it begins to slip. Something's wrong with his hip, she thinks—a vestige of what they did to him at Pawiak? She has to touch people to alert them she wants to pass. They smile and address her, their voices muffled as if trapped inside a display case, and she nods absently. Now he has an open passage to the door—that's it, she will lose him—and then, abruptly, he stops. His shoulders fall as if in defeat. He rubs a hand back and forth over his bald head. He turns, and waits. She's alarmed by his eyes—dusky bags entrenched beneath them—the eyes of a depressive, an insomniac, a man unaccustomed to smiling. And he does not smile now. He tugs at a limp silk ascot and, like a leery child in the presence of an unfamiliar dog, doesn't take his eyes off her. Vaguely, she senses a woman's voice addressing her, a presence beside her. She excuses herself, waits for an elderly couple to pass, and then she is standing before him.

"Hello, Polly," he says.

She throws a hand over her mouth and tears spring forth. Oskar averts his gaze. Ludka slowly lowers her hand. She makes a fist and shakes it at him, then grips his bony elbow to keep from swaying. She speaks to him in Polish.

"I knew you would come. It was you, the letter to Mandelbaum? I knew it. But listen, Oskar." She lowers her voice, suddenly aware that Izaac is watching from a respectful distance. "Immediately I must tell you, you must listen carefully. You have to forgive me, Oskar, *wybacz mi!*" And in a torrent of broken words that don't string sensibly together, that fall all over themselves to get out, she explains about Stanley, and Victor, and how she had kept it safe for so long, and how she had waited outside the diner, and how the weasel had never come out—

"Polly! Polly. Kochanie Polly."

Again she presses her fingers to her lips, and they stand there assessing each other. Oskar finally smiles. She laughs and touches his cheek. Her bag jolts off her shoulder, and Oskar deftly catches it before it slams into the crook of her elbow. He frees it from her, sets it on the floor, and takes her hands. "Still full of the drama," he says. "How wonderful."

He pulls her hands to his chest and presses them there and slowly shakes his head, then gives one satisfied nod, as if his work were done, and all the tension Ludka has been holding simply drains away, and for the first time in a long time she feels calm, and grounded, and steady on her feet.

# 26

# Arbitration

The glass wall at Meck's back was making him uneasy. Behind him, across an open, busy hallway, a cluster of gray cubicles housed a group of paralegals and an assistant who kept them stocked with fresh coffee and water and anything else Abe Goodman requested. Goodman had been a gracious host at yesterday's arbitration hearing. Today it was Connie's turn to present the school's case against Tommy Zeilonka, and Meck's confidence wasn't what he'd like it to be, given Pat Kinney's presence in the arbiter's seat. Goodman had presented a compelling case yesterday, and Pat hadn't given him the sort of drubbing Meck had expected. Assuming the students and parents stayed on script today, Meck thought they'd provide Pat with enough ammunition to uphold Tommy's dismissal, but so far Meck couldn't tell which way Pat was leaning.

The parents and students were arriving now, and Meck rose and greeted each as they entered and showed them to their seats around the edge of the room; the polished conference table was reserved for the attorneys and selected representatives from each side. Goodman, Tommy, and his friend Robert conferred on the other side of the table; Tommy's mother, his two colleagues who had also been fired, and some of the students and their parents who had testified yesterday on his behalf sat behind Tommy along a wall of windows. His cheeks sported bright, rouge spots in an otherwise pallid face, as if he'd had to smack himself to bring up some color. Meck felt sorry for him. Tommy turned toward the window and despite a discouraging hand from his mother, spun fully around in his chair and stepped over to a section of the glass wall that didn't have chairs in front of it. The Westboro picketers must have arrived. Meck made his way around the table and stood five feet from Tommy. Seeing the two of them from behind, one might mistake them for brothers: same height, slight frames, similar blond hair.

Three stories below, half a dozen picketers—one young man, three middle-aged women, and a boy and a girl no older than ten—circled on the sidewalk. The boy noticed them watching at the window and stepped out of the circle. He stared at Tommy and held high his signs: *God Hates Fag Teachers* and *Fag Teachers Corrupt Kids*. Meck winced and glanced over at Tommy, who briefly closed his eyes.

"Shame on them," said Meck.

Tommy glanced at him, surprised.

"I don't condone their behavior," said Meck. "I want you to know that."

Tommy dismissively turned his attention back to the picketers. "They're entitled."

"True enough. Even so."

Tommy pushed his fingers up under his glasses and rubbed his eyes. He and Robert had assumed Meck would want a repeat performance of the Boston rally outside of this hearing, and Tommy had wanted to organize a counterprotest to outnumber the picketers. Izaac, however, in his e-mail from Warsaw, had wisely advised otherwise. "Warren will want as much distance from these people as he can get," he had written. "Trust me on this one. Wait for the Education Committee's public hearing at the State House—that's when we'll pull out all the stops." As it turned out, outnumbering them wouldn't have been difficult. There were already twice as many reporters as picketers.

The boy leaned his signs against a trash receptacle, disappeared from view, and came back with a new one. He held it high over his head as if trying to get as close to Tommy as he could: *God Hates You.* A cameraman followed the boy's gaze and got shots of Tommy quickly stepping away from the window, while Meck calmly stood his ground. Meck thought fleetingly about crossing his wrists over his chest in the now-heralded salute, but he didn't believe God hated anyone. He stepped away.

"Tell me something," said Tommy. "If you don't condone their behavior, how can you condone your own? Those picketers out there didn't plot to strip me of my job, and don't say you did it for the kids. I'm committed to those kids, but you've made them your pawns. That's something *I* don't condone."

Meck rubbed the back of his neck. When he spoke, his voice came out too loud.

"These children . . ."

Robert, who'd been conferring with Abe, heard Meck and joined Tommy. Meck swallowed and tempered his tone.

"These children are not here for me. They're here because they feel like they've been discriminated against, silenced. They believe in the First Amendment, as do I."

Before Tommy could respond, a burst of laughter out in the hall distracted him. A man with a mane of white hair clapped Pat Kinney on the shoulder and, still laughing, spoke to Kinney, who nodded rapidly before holding open the door.

"Who's that?" Tommy asked.

"Royce Leonard, our pastor at the Fellowship."

Tommy frowned.

"Kinney seems to know him."

"I do believe they're acquainted, yes. Let me introduce you."

"We'll pass, thanks," said Robert.

But Meck had already waved him over. The pastor smelled like wood smoke, as if he'd spent a cozy morning reading by the fire. He used both hands to warmly shake Robert's. He did the same with Tommy, and encouraged them to call him Royce. Meck didn't know how anyone couldn't like the pastor. Merely being in his presence made Meck feel like a better man. The pastor held on to Tommy's hand.

"I'm so very sorry about what happened to you, Tommy. Are you healing up all right?"

Tommy was struck by his kind eyes, the absence of malice. He wanted not to trust the pastor's expression, to label it false; that he couldn't angered him.

"I am healing, thank you."

Pastor Royce shook his head.

"Terrible thing, that. Just terrible. I hope you'll come and visit our church, fellas. See for yourself we're not like our misguided brethren out there. Wednesdays are best—those are our seeker services. Curious newcomers plus the regular contingent. You might be surprised at how welcoming we are."

Robert spoke up.

"My husband already has one unwelcoming church, Pastor. Please don't pretend we'd be welcome at yours."

Meck tried not to wince when Robert said "husband." Before Pastor Royce could respond, Kinney addressed the room.

"Okay, people, let's get started."

In the hubbub of the settling crowd, Pastor Royce laid one hand on Robert's shoulder, the other on Tommy's, then leaned away and opened his arms as if to encompass everyone sitting on their side of the room.

"Each and every one of you are most welcome. Really, you are! I hope you'll come. Good to meet you both."

He looked from one to the other, gave a single nod, then turned away and held out an arm to usher Meck back to their seats.

"Bastards," said Robert. "We should show up. Give them a little thrill."

Kinney, an angular man with short, tidy hair, called out again and then sat down with a flourish at the head of the table, as if accommodating a judge's robe instead of a simple blue suit.

"Be mindful of our time today, gentlemen. I want to finish by three."

Meck frowned. Pat was cutting short their time. For the benefit of those new to the hearing, Kinney went through the ground rules, asked for but received no questions, and turned to Abe.

"I promised you fifteen minutes this morning, Abe. Mind you don't exceed it."

Abe inclined his head.

"I'd like to call on Superintendent Arnie Dengler."

"Oh heck," said Dengler. "Again?"

Meck shot him a look and Dengler threw up his hands.

"Okay, okay. Go ahead, Abe, shoot."

"Just a couple more questions, Arnie. Here's what I'm wondering. At what point in the process of deciding to let my client go did you and Ed discuss Chapter 71 Section 42, or 603 CMR 26.00? No need to scowl, it's not a trick question."

Dengler took out his handkerchief and mopped his brow. He appealed to Shaw for help.

"Eddie might recall better than I do—"

"Ed will have his chance, but now I'm asking you. Did you specifically discuss the law? How about the dismissal rules from the Adams High handbook?"

Connie, who sat to Dengler's right, whispered to Dengler.

"What I mostly remember," said Dengler, ". . . you have to understand we were under some serious pressure from these good people." He indicated the parents and kids sitting behind him, then leaned forward and peered past Connie to address himself to Kinney. "And for good reason! Wait till you hear their stories, Pat! So, no, I guess I don't remember, not precisely, anyway, talking about those issues."

"They're not issues, Arnie, they're the law. You're telling me they didn't come up?"

"No, by golly, that's not what I'm telling you. I'm saying I don't well remember. Eddie, help me out here?"

Abe told Shaw to go ahead.

"I remember we said there are times when the children's safety comes first, and we felt it was one of those times. We believed we had to act fast."

"But what of the law specifically, Ed? Did you discuss it? Were you even aware of it?"

Shaw rubbed at the skin under his eyes and sighed. He appealed to Kinney, who nodded for him to go ahead.

"I'm the principal, Abe. Of course I'm aware of it."

"And you discounted it."

"We put the kids—the children, first."

Abe opened a folder. He handed a paper to Shaw and asked him to read it out loud. Shaw scanned it.

"Is this really necessary? He wants me to read the statute and regs."

"If you don't, I will," said Abe. "I want the exact language in the record."

"I'm familiar with the language," Kinney said sharply. "And you already spent a good part of yesterday driving home this point. I get it. They didn't follow procedure. Now move on."

Abe nodded once at Kinney. Some of the tension drained from Meck's neck and shoulders.

"Just one more thing," said Abe.

He made a beckoning gesture toward the cubicles across the hall. The assistant immediately came to the door.

"George, can you turn on the sound? And when I say the word, hit *play*. I've got something queued up."

Meck sat taller in his chair and scanned his memory for anything detrimental that might have been said on his program. Ed and Arnie had been guests last week, but Meck couldn't remember any admissions about skirting the law, although Arnie's typical blustering certainly hadn't been professional or admirable. Meck had spent the whole show alternately feeling nervous about what Arnie might say next, and hopeful that he'd trip up and reveal an impropriety; he still wasn't convinced Arnie didn't have anything to do with at least recruiting Eric. He certainly hadn't assaulted Tommy himself, but maybe he'd persuaded someone else? Meck wasn't sure he could trust his own judgment when it came to Arnie.

Now Arnie's voice filled the hearing room but not from a recording of *Tell It Like It Is*. Arnie was saying he could help Tommy, that he knew Tommy had gotten trapped in the sin of homosexual behavior, and it quickly became evident the tape was from the review meeting to contest Tommy's dismissal. People on both sides of the room winced or shook their heads or closed their eyes. Arnie avoided meeting anyone's eyes. Thankfully, Kinney held up a hand and told Abe to turn it off. Abe nodded to the assistant, and the room went quiet. Meck smiled inwardly when the last voice they heard on the tape was Shaw's, sounding sincere, telling Abe they were as concerned as he was.

"This was already introduced," said Kinney. "I feel compelled to remind you that you're not trying to sway a jury here, Abe. You're just relating the facts to me. And this, I've already heard."

"I do understand that, Pat; I just think it's important that everyone here has a chance to listen firsthand so they know how focused Arnie and Ed have been on my client's sexuality, a focus which is expressly forbidden under the Fair Employment Protection law. And it's no coincidence that every other teacher who got fired just days after they dismissed my client is also gay or lesbian, yet every one of those cases has been framed exactly like this one: as an issue of religious discrimination and equal access to education. Don't you find that even remotely suspicious?" He addressed the families. "It's a smokescreen, people. My client was fired for being gay, pure and simple, and that is against the law, as I made abundantly clear yesterday. Chapter 151B, Pat, to be specific."

Kinney's tone was conciliatory.

"You did make it clear, Abe, don't worry. I know the law and I'll make sure the chapter's in the record."

Pastor Royce leaned close to Meck and spoke quietly into his ear while Abe made his closing statement.

"I'm getting nervous, Warren."

"I am, too, but it's early yet. The kids will be great. *You'll* be great. And even if Pat rules against us, we can learn from our mistakes and do a better job at the other teachers' hearings. If Pat rules in our favor, though, Goodman's still clearly going to appeal. You watch—he's going to try to goad our kids into making discriminatory statements, which could give him fuel to bring a case to the Mass Commission Against Discrimination. He's probably thinking he can prove discrimination, which might very well be true. I wouldn't be surprised, either, if he advises Tommy to file a civil action against the school, trying to secure damages as well as reinstatement."

Pastor Royce whistled low under his breath.

"Man's got both oars in the water, is that what I hear you saying? This thing is far from over?"

"I'm saying Goodman is an expert oarsman. Even in a storm."


Connie efficiently presented their case, without fanfare, making it clear that under MGL Chapter 76 Section 5 the children had experienced discrimination that had thwarted their ability to participate equally in Tommy's classroom. As planned, Connie spoke only briefly; the kids' testimonies were the main attraction. First up was Brandon Braddock. As he passed in front of Meck to take his seat at the table next to Kinney, he smiled and whispered, "even when the rain falls."

"Tell it like it is," said Meck.

After a brief introduction, Connie asked Brandon to share in his own words his experience of being a student in Mr. Zeilonka's AP English class. Brandon, wearing a suit and tie, sat up straight and clasped his hands together on the table in front of him. He directed his comments to Kinney and avoided looking directly at Tommy.

When Tommy had reviewed the list of students who would testify, he'd been particularly distraught about Brandon.

"Dammit. I love that kid!" he'd told Abe. "He's one of my best students. No way have I discriminated against Brandon. He's never given any indication there was anything wrong."

Now Brandon was telling Kinney the class had been difficult for him.

"I mean, when we had to read *Find Me*—that's by Carl Anderson—it was hard, you know? I could barely get through it because it was so . . . well, it goes against everything I believe in." He glanced over at Pastor Royce. "Against my sincere religious beliefs."

"Oh, here we go," Robert whispered to Tommy.

"But I wanted to keep my grades up, you know? I need that AP credit. I want to get into a good college."

"So you felt you had no choice?" asked Connie.

"That's right, I had no choice."

Abe spoke up.

"Mr. Zeilonka remembers that you were enthusiastic about that book, Brandon. He remembers you telling him you loved it."

Brandon lowered his head and shook it.

"What's that, son?" said Abe.

"What else was I going to tell him, you know? I try to be polite."

"I understand you're a terrific student. Mr. Zeilonka says you're one of his best."

Brandon started to pick at his thumbnail.

"You earn top marks if I'm not mistaken and even, as I understand it, asked for extra credit assignments on *Find Me*. Why would you do that if you found it so objectionable?"

"Overcompensating?" said Brandon.

The other students laughed, and Brandon flashed them an anxious grin.

"The truth is, sir, I felt as if having to study *Find Me* was a test. You know, from God. To see how I would react in the presence of Satan."

"They got to him," Tommy whispered to Robert. "This isn't the Brandon I know."

"Isn't 'Satan' a bit melodramatic?" asked Abe.

Brandon shook his head with the utmost seriousness.

"Not at all, sir. Not in my culture."

"What culture is that, son? America? Massachusetts? Adams High? The basketball team, for goodness' sake?"

Brandon sat up taller.

"Christianity is my culture, sir. The only one that matters. It's where I learned, like, my sincere religious beliefs."

"Now that's the second time you've used that particular phrase. Were you coached to say that, son?"

Brandon's gaze slowly shifted over to Pastor Royce.

"No, sir."

"Do you know what I mean when I say *coached*?"

"I'm captain of my varsity basketball team, Mr. Goodman."

"Then you listen to your coach, do you? Follow his instructions?"

"Yes, sir."

"And are you following instructions right now, Brandon? Did someone tell you to say that? Your pastor, maybe?"

"Shame this isn't a court of law," said Connie. "I'd sure love to object to leading the witness here."

Kinney cautioned Abe, and Abe nodded.

"Did anyone sit down with you, Brandon, to let you know how this arbitration hearing would go?"

"Sure they did, of course."

"Who helped you?"

Brandon glanced over at Meck, who nodded.

"Mr. Clough."

"*Only* Mr. Clough?"

"No, sir."

"Please speak up, son."

"No, sir! Pastor Royce and Mr. Meck helped us, too."

"Us?"

"All us kids." Brandon lifted a hand to indicate the others.

"And what did Mr. Clough and Mr. Meck and your pastor recommend?"

Brandon licked his lips. His Adam's apple rose and fell, and his eyes strayed again to Pastor Royce, then to Connie, and finally to Meck. Meck smiled encouragingly. This was the moment that would make or break Brandon's testimony, that would set the example for the students next on the docket. Meck's tight neck muscles were giving him a headache.

"That I speak from the heart, sir. That I tell the truth. And the truth is, I didn't believe I could speak freely in Mr. Zeilonka's class."

Pastor Royce elbowed Meck collegially, and they exchanged relieved expressions.

"Do you understand, son, that one of the laws we've been discussing—MGL Chapter 76 Section 5—is about whether discrimination excludes you from, and I'm quoting here, *the advantages, privileges and courses of study* of your public school?"

"Yes sir, I do."

"You're a straight A student, aren't you, son?"

"Yes, sir."

"Including the A you received last year from Mr. Zeilonka, and the A average you hold in his current class?"

"That's right."

"Do you think your track record is the sign of a student who has been excluded from advantages or privileges or courses of study?"

Brandon looked confused.

"This, Pat," said Abe, "is what the law demands you to consider. If young Brandon here had really been discriminated against to the point of exclusion, his studies would have suffered. But he is a fully engaged and successful student, as are the other kids who are here to testify. You won't find a bad report card among them. In fact, they're all A students."

Meck clenched his teeth. He whispered to Pastor Royce.

"We should have anticipated they'd frame it that way. We should have brought in some kids who'd dropped out or turned to homeschooling."

Pastor Royce nodded sympathetically and whispered back.

"Shame on us for assuming the underachievers wouldn't be well-spoken."

Connie spoke up as if he'd heard them.

"Have all your friends done as well in Mr. Zeilonka's classes, Brandon?"

"Not all of them, sir. A couple kids opted out altogether, and some kids didn't complete the assignments if they had, you know, *different* content. My sister Sophie warned me to stay away, but, you know, it's hard, because he's the only one teaching AP. And two of our best players—"

"*Different* content?" asked Abe.

Brandon picked again at his thumbnail. He seemed to be waiting for Connie to step in and say something. When he didn't, Brandon said quietly, "About homosexuals."

"You need to speak up, son."

"I said homosexuals! Are different."

"And what did your sister say?" asked Abe.

"My sister?"

"You said Sophie warned you not to take Mr. Zeilonka's class."

"Oh, yeah, I just told her it was hard."

"Hard in what way?"

"Because he's homosexual," he murmured.

"Again, son, I need you to speak up."

"I said because he's homosexual! I mean, he kept me after school and told me what I wrote about *Find Me* was . . . wasn't right. I just wrote what I sincerely believe, that the protagonist was an abomination. Mr. Zeilonka told me that was wrong. *I* was wrong."

Tommy pressed his fingers over his mouth, closed his eyes, and shook his head.

"This is a nightmare," he whispered to Robert. "He's like a different kid."

"My understanding," said Abe, "is that Mr. Zeilonka encouraged you to try to do better with that particular essay, that it wasn't on a par with your previous work. In fact, I believe he suggested that if you wanted your opinion about the protagonist to be taken seriously, you had to be more thorough in your reasoning. He tells me he suggested you revise the piece from a Christian perspective, and bolster your arguments with Biblical citations.

And I believe you took his advice, didn't you? What grade did you get on that essay, Brandon?"

Brandon snaked a finger under his collar and pulled it away from his neck. Abe allowed the silence to build. For the first time, Brandon glanced directly at Tommy. Tommy smiled sympathetically as if to apologize for the way Brandon was being put on the spot. Blood rushed to Brandon's face, and he lowered his head. Meck tightened his fists, willing the boy to remain calm.

"Two of my friends got, like, taken out of school last year by their parents. Our best point guard and one of our starting forwards. Because of him. Because I guess he has an agenda, you know? It freaks people out. We could have been state champs if it wasn't for him! We were so close to winning, but without those two guys we couldn't pull it off, and it's his fault, because he had to go and try to recruit kids by making us read all that disgusting stuff, and the parents don't like it, do they? Why should we have to face his homosexual agenda every day in school, Mr. Kinney? That's all I'm trying to say. Those picketers out there aren't wrong. I mean, Pastor Royce told us men aren't supposed to lie with other men, right?"

Meck could sense Pastor Royce tensing beside him. Brandon continued, his voice getting increasingly high and whiny.

"Pastor Royce showed us—it's right there in Leviticus, in black and white, and in Paul's letter to the Romans, so if Pastor Royce and God both say it's an abomination, then it's an abomination! God says the homosexuals will get punished for what they do. So there you have it—they're getting punished. Hey, if Pastor Royce hates the gays, then I—"

"Now, now," said Pastor Royce, rising abruptly. He held out his arms as if addressing his congregation. Abe threw up a hand against him.

"Let the boy be heard, Pastor. Isn't this what you say you want, for your kids to be heard? Are you speaking from the heart now, Brandon? Are you telling us your truth?"

"Yes sir, you bet I am!"

"No need to badger the child!" said Pastor Royce. "You aren't going to allow this, are you, Pat?"

A clammy sweat became apparent in Meck's armpits. Pastor Royce's face flushed red.

"That's okay," said Abe. "I think Brandon has made himself clear."

Pastor Royce angrily swept back his hair and sank into his chair, kicking up an all-too-human waft of oniony sweat that Meck wished he hadn't noticed. Pastor Royce closed his eyes.

"For the record, everyone," said Abe, "Brandon received an A-minus on his essay."

Meck lowered his suddenly heavy head. Brandon had been their best witness.

# 27

# Oskar

O skar sat at the head of his battered worktable, and Ludka sat on a bench on the side, as close to him as possible, a solid wall at her back, his fifth-floor studio opening out in front of her, industrial-sized windows warm and bright with crisp morning sun. With both hands she held on to a mug of milky tea.

"Ludka."

Oskar said her name as if it were a foreign word he couldn't quite pronounce.

"Pawel," she said.

He smiled, and with a hint of the old Humphrey Bogart swagger called her Polly. Then, as if he had a train to catch, he took a rushed sip of his tea and pushed back from the table. He'd been speaking in perfect, nearly unaccented English, showing off, she thought amusedly.

"First things first. I have a little present for you."

Time had diminished Oskar's height and bulk, and with a hitch in his stride he moved slowly but with evident purpose to a heavy oak sideboard. A hip replacement some years ago, he told her, but he sounded evasive, and she didn't dare ask about his time at Pawiak. He'd also complained of arthritis in his fingers, a hindrance he vigorously ignored each day in order to do his work, which was strewn and stacked all over the studio: wood and metal sculptures; torn paper, strips of tin, and thick oil affixed to canvas. What little hair he had—now white—remained only in a fringe just above his ears and around the base of his skull. Age spots dotted his sun-browned scalp. She couldn't tear herself away from studying him; he was more fully himself than her imagination had ever led her to expect, and so she felt shockingly at ease, as if she had seen him just last week.

He opened a drawer and took out a package loosely wrapped in a scrap of cotton, a torn T-shirt by the looks of it. He carried it to her as if whatever lay within couldn't possibly be good enough. She smiled at the sloppy cloth.

"So much trouble you went to."

Back then he would have laughed. Now, as he tried unsuccessfully to arrange his face into a smile, Ludka's easy feeling began to slip. She wanted to ask what had happened to him—he seemed almost fearful of her—but then she touched the package and knew at once what it was and looked at him urgently. He nodded, and sat.

"You have not opened it then?"

"Oh no, of course I opened it. But this is more dramatic, don't you think?"

His words sounded hollow, rehearsed. She threw out a string of questions, and Oskar leaned away and held up a hand as if to ward off a blow.

"Good grief, Polly, just open it. Here."

With an abrupt gesture he pulled off the wrapping, and there was the tin box she'd last seen in 1939. The tarnished lid opened easily to reveal the burlap-wrapped vodka bottle. The burlap shed coarse threads as Ludka hurriedly unwound it. Oskar had of course already broken the wax seal. Ludka tried but didn't have the strength to pull out the cork, so Oskar used his teeth.

"Be careful with the paper. It's seen better days."

"Please, you will do this."

Her hands shook, and she wrapped them again around her mug. Oskar upended the bottle and with a knobby forefinger worked at tightening the rolled paper so it could pass through the narrow neck.

"Two years ago, after I'd gotten involved with the artists here at the university, I arranged a commission to dig for it. Ogród Saski has been restored like so much else around here, and it was shockingly easy to find the roots of that old tree. And there it was, right where I'd left it. I couldn't believe it. I told them it was something else, though, one of Xawery Dunikowski's drawings from Auschwitz. I did have one; now it's at Królikarnia. They have his whole collection."

He set the bottle aside, shoved away the box and burlap, and gave her the paper. She pulled it open. It trembled in her hands like a newly hatched butterfly. She scanned the names until she saw the one that should have been last on the list—Laura Ciechomska—but penned below it, in faded, bloated ink, written in Polish in Oskar's hand, was a final entry: *Transferred for safekeeping to Ludka Zeilonka, 28/30 ul. Piwna, Warszawa, Polska, Września, 1939.* Ludka frowned, confused.

"But when did you write this? How could you know my—"

"I knew everyone's names, Polly. Did you really think we wouldn't thoroughly check you out when you first joined Żegota?"

Ludka let go, and the paper furled into a loose scroll. She stared at him in disbelief. He avoided her gaze and ran a hand back and forth over his head. The bench felt suddenly too close, and she pushed her back against the wall. Oskar sighed and rubbed at the loose skin under his eyes. He closed them and forcefully massaged his lips and jaw, as if to arrest whatever words he might be tempted to say. He sat back, his hands lying limp on the table, and that's when she noticed the first joint of his right pinky was missing. In a practiced gesture, he casually covered his right hand with his left. Without thinking, Ludka abruptly said, "Pawiak?" and when he winced, she knew it was true, even though he shook his head and said, "skill saw."

"All this time, Oskar—"

"I kept expecting life would get simpler, but it never did." Again his words sounded rehearsed. "And then you had your first baby, you had Izaac, you seemed happy."

She lifted her hands as if she might cover her face but seemed to forget what she'd intended—her fingers collapsed into loose fists, which fell to her lap where they lay like wary sparrows. Outside, across the street, a young woman leaned from her fifth-floor window and shook out a small throw rug. The roiling dust mingled in the air with the woman's icy breath. Oskar lowered his head into his hands. Ludka spoke in a measured tone.

"Always people have asked why I am Zeilonka and not Rosenberg, sometimes with an undercurrent of suspicion that maybe I did not want Jewish name, and always I claimed professional reasons, that to change it would be detrimental. But Zeilonka was for you. On the off chance . . . So many times I thought you must be . . . I never stopped searching, Oskar. Never! But you . . . *fifty-eight years ago* was my first baby!"

Her fists were tight now, her voice high and terse.

"I didn't think you'd want to see me, Polly. Not after what I did—"

"Not want to see you?"

She thumped her fists on the table, and it was Oskar's turn to appear confused. He searched her eyes, frowned, then let out a long breath and shook his head, slowly and methodically, as if trying to ratchet back time.

"Żegota did not rest while you were in Pawiak, Oskar—*I* did not rest—until a guard accepted our bribe. I waited in your attic. All week I waited. Waited and waited. And then Milosz said he'd seen you. In Krakow."

Oskar lowered his head and held it in both hands as if trying to staunch a migraine. A thick vein popped out on his temple, and he inhaled deeply through his mouth.

"I didn't know," he said. "A bribe?"

"How else did you think? That they would release you for no reason?"

He muttered to himself as if he were alone in the room, his words indecipherable. Abruptly, he smacked both hands on his head, startling Ludka, and then he straightened up, screwed his eyes shut, and nodded, as if resigning himself to something only he understood. A chill crawled up the back of Ludka's neck and advanced like a regiment of lice across her scalp. She touched her hair with both hands.

"I never knew," said Oskar. "I didn't know."

He broke the brittle threads off one edge of the burlap and rubbed them into a ragged dust. The skin on his neck hung slack, stippled as if plucked, raw from shaving. He cleared his throat and gazed into the distance, as if searching for words.

"For me . . . for me I had my first and only baby fifty-*nine* years ago. I thought it was the virtuous thing to do, marrying his mother. You see? But I don't know, Polly. I just don't know. 'For this we survived?' my wife, Basia, used to say. She blamed me for ruining our son, and I blamed her for blaming me."

Ludka had the distinct impression he was telling her the truth, but not the whole truth. *Jar of jam,* she thought, with a surge of compassion for Basia.

"I suppose it's what I deserved. My son spent his life doing despicable things, then shot himself in the head. Thank god Basia didn't live to see that. And now there's my grandson, another fucking waste."

Ludka recoiled at his sudden vulgarity, so much like Stanley's, and in that instant she wanted nothing more than to be on the plane with Izaac, the door irrevocably locked, the flight attendants instructing them to buckle up. Oskar wrinkled his nose as if he smelled something foul and rubbed again at his eyes. He pushed back from the table.

"I'll make us some more tea."

The woman across the way was back at the window with another rug, and as she shook it out, she burst into laughter and said something over her shoulder. Oskar busied himself at a hotplate on top of the oak sideboard, and, for just a moment, Ludka saw him as that young man who had held the damaged canvas over the steaming kettle, while the tanks shuddered past in the street. "Voilà!" he had said, when he was done. They stepped back to view the results. "Only we will ever notice," she had told him, even though she knew, and suspected he did, too, that a practiced eye could easily pick out the damage. He'd lifted her off her feet then, and she'd wrapped her legs around his hips.

Now she wanted to go to him and take his face in her hands and kiss away the angry sorrow from each eye, ask him what was truly going on, what he wasn't telling her. An inadvertent whimper escaped her throat—*all this time he'd known where she was!*—as she imagined that young man on a trolley in New York. She would have run after his outstretched hand, pulling herself up to his side, while behind them, mouth open in disbelief, Izaac would have stood where she'd left him, Lolek squalling in his arms.

She furiously maneuvered herself along the bench to get out. She stepped unsteadily into the studio and stopped in front of an unfinished portrait, mixed media, Cubist-inspired. She leaned toward it and laid a hand over her throat. The disembodied features were small and flaccid, bitter and weary, as if they could hardly bear to have made an appearance. Heavy bags dragged down the familiar, averted eyes. Ludka cradled her elbows, rubbed her arms. The kettle began to shriek and then abruptly wound down.

"I'll bet Stanley told you I wasn't an artist," said Oskar. "He doesn't know one damn thing. Home Depot's trash was full of material, not to mention the scraps from all those kitchens."

Oskar spoke far too fast, with an unsettling, freshly manufactured cheer that must have taken heroic energy to dredge up.

"I never stopped working. I just never shared it with anyone. For years I kept a little place down on East Fourth Street, then in San Francisco a friend let me use a corner of his loft. And now! Now I find myself represented by Galeria Zapiecek, the best gallery in Warsaw. Not that it was my doing, understand—a friend arranged all of it without my knowledge."

"If self-portrait is any indication, I am not surprised you are in best gallery. Is this the only one you've done?"

"No." He rubbed the stump of his missing finger, then filled the teapot. "But it's the only honest one."

A dull metal strip, lead maybe, barricaded the mouth, and dirty cheesecloth covered the ears. Ludka had an impulse to heave it out the window. Oskar handed her a mug of tea, too heavy now, she thought. She concentrated on gripping the handle so it wouldn't tip. Oskar studied the self-portrait.

"I'm sorry for my language earlier. My grandson brings out the worst in me, I'm afraid. I should have done far more for that boy. Breaking and entering is his bread and butter, not to mention fraud, so I'm not at all surprised he's trying blackmail. I'm sorry I wasn't more careful with my papers, though. I should have brought them with me."

"Like drawings of me?"

Oskar said nothing.

"Stanley presented a drawing of me as the old woman I am. I thought you had the keen imagination."

"Chicago. That lecture you did at the Art Institute."

"You were there?"

"I took photos, worked from those. I should have said hello."

"You should have said hello," Ludka said disdainfully. The mug had begun to tip, and she righted it before the tea spilled over.

Again as if Oskar were alone, he muttered something Ludka didn't catch. His eyes shone with a sudden excitement, and he reached out to take her hand, then hesitated and drew back.

"I know where to find Stanley, and I know how to get through to him. I can get your Mieroszewski. It's the least I can do."

*Your Mieroszewski.* Ludka flashed him a look, as the consequences of his *little present* finally dawned on her. She thrust the mug at him and didn't hear him swear when the hot tea slopped

over his hand. She hastened to the table and unrolled the provenance papers.

"Yes, Polly, it's all perfectly legal. Remember Wojno at the
university? I consulted with him about adding your name.
'Extraordinary circumstances,' he told me. That was the last time
I saw him. Treblinka, I heard." He fell silent for a moment, and
then spoke gently.

"But you see, Polly? The Chopin belongs to you."

Weakness tackled her at the knees, she sank into Oskar's chair,
and for the first time Oskar laughed his old laugh.

"This solves everything, don't you see?"

She did see, and she waited eagerly for the relief she knew
she should feel. A spark of panic took hold instead. A fiery heat
rushed into her face, and the room began to waver. She locked her
gaze onto Oskar's self-portrait, and after a moment she frowned,
wondering why he'd need to barricade his mouth, what words
he couldn't say. But maybe the lead strip was about something
he *shouldn't have said,* something from his past—from *their* past.
An idea began to take shape in her mind, an unclear notion that
she couldn't quite grasp but that nevertheless amplified her anxiety, and just as the idea was about to come clear, it vanished. She
closed her eyes with relief.

Later, though, when she was once more safely ensconced at
home, the idea would materialize again, this time fully formed
and glaringly clear, at which point she would fervently wish that
Oskar had simply stayed missing.

# Part IV

# 28
# Brothers

Late in the afternoon on the day Ludka and Izaac returned from Warsaw, Lolek was in his office when Aggie called out to him from the other room.

"Hey Senator, look who just came in from the cold!"

In a more normal tone she said, "I haven't seen you in a dog's age, Frank. How the hell are you?"

When Lolek got to the door, his brother Frank, decked out in dress uniform with white chief's hat in hand, was giving Aggie a one-armed hug. When he let go, she stepped back, put her hands on her hips, and looked him up and down.

"You certainly have come up in the world. Nice to see all those gold stripes on your sleeves."

Frank grinned. "I'm actually dying to take this thing off. I need a stiff drink. I don't know how you can walk around all day on all this marble. My feet are killing me. Not to mention all the glad-handing. Makes me want to be back on the truck."

"I expect your brother can oblige you with that drink, can't you, Mr. President? I'm on my way out, so we're officially closed."

Lolek smiled and shook Frank's hand.

"I thought I might see you. Lot of dress blues walking around this place today. How was the public safety hearing?"

"You know how it goes. It's over, thank God."

"Come on in. Scotch? Neat?"

Frank smiled. He undid the top button of his crisp white shirt and loosened his tie. Lolek admired the gold-buttoned, double-breasted jacket. It enhanced Frank's already commanding presence, which along with his solid, calm demeanor, meant emergencies felt less catastrophic with him in charge; Frank had made a wise career choice, and Lolek found himself feeling proud of his kid brother. Frank took off his jacket and hung it over the back of a chair. He laid his hat on the conference table.

"I just had a call from Dad," said Frank. "He and Matka are home from their trip."

"They okay?"

Frank nodded. Lolek handed Frank his Scotch. They touched glasses and drank.

"But they came home to a freezing house and a busted dining room window. Brick. Another hate note about Tommy, this one more threatening. No one seems to have entered the house, but I'm worried. I alerted Shelly and got one of our bomb guys over there to check things out, just in case. Someone's clearly targeting Dad. I talked to him, and of course he says they've weathered worse and they're just glad to be home—they're exhausted; it took them almost twenty-four hours—but I spoke to your wife, and she suggested they stay over at your place tonight. They also have that student art tour on Friday, but Matka won't hear of putting it off. I'm just not sure it's the best idea to have a bunch of strangers traipsing through their house right now. I was hoping you could check in on them, try to talk sense."

Lolek sat down behind his desk.

"You spoke to my wife?"

Frank went over to the cold fireplace and squatted down to poke in his head.

"When's the last time you cleaned this flue?"

"1873. What do you think! It's fine."

"I just thought Marta could go over there and check on them, since you and I are here. She's probably getting there about now."

Frank stood and stared at the logs piled on the fire grate. The brothers fell silent and sipped their drinks.

When Lolek had first decided to run for office, he never anticipated he'd end up viewing everyone—including his brother—with such suspicion. Everything seemed like posturing, everything had the trappings of calculation. Had Marta's familiar way of greeting Frank that morning in their kitchen been *deliberately* sisterly? Even as Lolek became aware that this memory had been niggling him, he forced the thought from his mind; his brother was as honest as a summer day was long. Lolek wasn't so sure about Marta.

"I'll check in on them, Frank. Did Shelly say anything about his progress? Have they IDed that car?"

"No one saw it clearly enough. But I guess Tommy was finally able to give them details for a composite, so Shelly's working that angle. And he's still hoping for some traction on the phone calls. I feel bad for Tommy and Robert though, having to listen to them. Must wear them down. At least Dad and Matka got a break from all that."

"Dad say how their trip was?"

"Overwhelming, I guess. Can you imagine? But of course all he wanted to do was hear about Tommy. Hey, what's the word on appealing the arbitration decision?"

"Abe filed for it the next morning, last Thursday—he was ready for it. In the end he thinks the Christian kids got through to Kinney, and then the pastor cemented things by letting Kinney know how many other kids had come to him with similar stories. Still, I don't think Abe will have any trouble securing an appeal. Turns out Kinney's old law firm is largely comprised of Redeemer Fellowship members. He should have recused himself. That said, Abe's preparing for the next step, too. Even if Tommy wins on appeal, they want to file a discrimination complaint—they're working on that now. Abe's pulled together the attorneys for the other teachers so they can orchestrate their filings. I'm sure he'll also end up filing for damages and injunctive relief in a civil suit, but that has to wait until ninety days have passed since filing the complaint."

"Long haul, isn't it? Tommy getting any money at all from the school?"

"Not a penny, but I think Robert does pretty well. Tommy says they're okay financially. Did you know, by the way, that they're married?"

Lolek watched his brother through narrowed eyes. Frank froze, his glass halfway to his mouth. He turned to Lolek with genuine surprise.

"Married?"

"Married. Over a year ago. Tommy sprang it on me when he was in the hospital."

Frank began to laugh.

"Good for them! That's the way to go: sneak off and get it done, don't breathe a word to anyone."

He raised his glass.

"Jesus, Frank, don't you think they should have told us? Marta knows, I'm sure of it."

"No way does Marta know. She would have told you. You didn't talk to her about it?"

Lolek drank down the rest of his Scotch. His face began to feel warm.

"I've hardly seen her. I thought she was keeping it from me."

"She wouldn't do that."

"And how would you know that exactly?"

Frank stared into his empty glass, then waggled it.

"Got any more?"

Lolek gestured with his own glass to a cabinet on the far side of the conference table, and Frank helped himself. Lolek could see why Marta might be attracted to Frank, why any woman would. Nearly eight years had passed since Frank's wife died, and Lolek had given up on encouraging him to try dating. Thinking now about Marta and Frank together made him feel surprisingly more tired than disturbed. He found himself wondering, almost idly, as if it had nothing to do with him, if he and Marta might divorce.

"How do things look for next week's Education Committee hearing on that bill?" said Frank.

"Hard to tell since we don't know what Warren Meck and his pastor have planned, but I do know Aggie has pulled out all the stops, so no matter what happens with the actual bill, we're going to get a lot of important news coverage. This bill would never fly if the Education Committee wasn't mostly composed of members in districts that seem to have been infiltrated by the likes of Meck. There's a reason the statute doesn't already define *sound moral character*—to give that power to the board of education is asking for trouble."

"But isn't that dangerous for them, too? Couldn't a liberal board define it in a way that excludes them?"

"Yes, indeed, but they seem to have successfully stacked the current board with friends, and they've clearly planted their flag in Massachusetts. Apparently the church at the old Regent is one of eight or nine branches throughout the state! They've moved in their supporters from all over the place. They expect to stay, and grow. They've targeted us, Frank. We never saw them coming."

"What do you need me to do? When is it, a week from today?"

"A week from Wednesday, March eighteenth. Nine o'clock in A-1. I didn't even think about you being there. It's not really your area."

"Of course I'm going to be there. Aggie must have written out some talking points. Let me have a copy. I'll testify."

Lolek took a drink and squinted at Frank over the top of his glass.

"You don't need to do that, Frank. We have plenty of people lined up."

"You don't want me there?"

"I just don't know why you would be."

"Because it's family, Lolek."

"*My* family, Frank. Not yours."

Frank lowered his head, then lifted it fast. His expression wasn't angry as Lolek might have expected, but pitying. Anger Lolek would have welcomed, because then they might have had it out, but pity was something else entirely; pity gave Frank the upper hand. Lolek shifted in his chair, trying to stretch out his hip. Frank quietly set his empty glass on the conference table, then pulled on and methodically buttoned his coat. He fastened the top button of his shirt and cinched his tie.

"Don't be like that, Frank, come on. It's just that—I don't know, this business with Tommy is getting to me. And then to find out he got married? What kind of kid gets married without telling his father?"

Frank picked up his hat. He fingered the metal fire department emblem affixed above the brim.

"Are you really asking?"

*Was* he asking? Didn't he already know? Lolek swallowed the last of his Scotch.

Frank carefully put on his hat. He palmed the back of it into place, then tugged down on the brim. At the door he stopped walking but didn't turn around.

"Call your wife, Lolek. She misses you. We all do."

Frank walked out.

"What's that supposed to mean? I'm right here! Didn't we just have a nice drink?"

The door to the outer office opened, then closed.

"Son of a bitch!"

Lolek cocked his arm and disappointed himself when he didn't throw the glass. It felt heavy in his hand. What bothered him was not that Frank had prompted his outburst, or demanded he call Marta, or looked on him with pity. What bothered him wasn't even that Frank had turned his back and walked out. What bothered Lolek was how he had allowed himself to get things so damned wrong with Tommy, how for years—*years*—he had successfully soldiered forth in the fight for equality without ever noticing that his vulnerable son was standing on the front lines. Carefully, Lolek set down the trembling glass. He rubbed a hand hard across his brow. He straightened his back.

"Aggie?"

But of course she had gone. A hiss of steam escaped from the ancient radiator near her desk in the outer office. And then silence.

# 29
# The Art Tour

When Will knocked on Ludka's office door to see if he could catch a ride to her house for the art tour, Ludka had been sitting at her desk for nearly fifteen minutes, staring at her sketch of Oskar and Aaron, that first boy they'd rescued. Director Mandelbaum had seemed relieved she'd wanted only the one sketch, and had made arrangements to ship it to her office, where it had been waiting when she first got back to work, three days ago now. The other thing that had been waiting was a brown paper package from Stanley. The department's assistant said he had dropped it off and asked that it be locked in her office, "a surprise for when she returns." So, Ludka had thought, the weasel had been in town all along.

On their last full day in Warsaw, Ludka and Izaac had gone with Oskar to the Galeria Zapiecek to see his work, and Oskar had taken her aside.

"You can fire that private investigator. Stanley will return your Mieroszewski."

When she peered at him inquisitively, he lowered his head. In a flat and tired voice, he said, "I threatened him, Polly. I know things about Stanley I should have reported to the police a long time ago; it seems I'm rather good at deluding myself."

He had looked at her then with such sorrow and such disdain for himself that she hadn't dared press him for details.

Now she tucked the Chopin—packaged with surprising care by Stanley—inside the canvas tote bag she used when she had to bring home more papers than could fit in her satchel. Izaac would not question her about the bag's contents, and the art tour gave her exactly the chaos she needed to return it unnoticed to the bedroom.

She called to Will to come in and remembered too late to put away the sketch. Will saw it at once.

"That looks like the guy who's been coming to our class."

Ludka said nothing and carefully placed the drawing in the gray archival box she'd brought in for safe storage. Will, cheeks flushed, shoved his hands in the pockets of his pea coat. He glanced at her, then lowered his head.

"I know you're Apolonia."

She drew back in her chair.

"I'm sorry, Professor. I was just curious. I saw the video from last week. From Warsaw."

Ludka sighed and gave a small nod. She reopened the archival box and turned it around so Will could see.

"This is Stanley's grandfather. An old . . . friend. Together we were in war."

"Is that one of the Jewish kids you rescued? They say you saved almost as many as Oskar Schindler."

"About that I do not know."

"But *they* know! You should be recognized by Yad Vashem.

You're one of the Righteous Among the Nations. I'll nominate you myself!"

Ludka looked at him sharply.

"Who is it who knows?"

"The Institute. In Warsaw. New blog post."

He took his cell phone from his pocket, tapped its screen a few times, then turned it around and held it out to her. Ludka stared beyond it at her sketch. Oskar must have gone to them again, told them about the role they'd played in Żegota. She splayed her fingers on the desk and pressed hard, anchoring herself. Will hesitantly pulled back his phone and asked if she was okay.

"I didn't mean to upset you."

Ludka took a deep breath. She spoke quietly.

"You lock the door, young man."

Will glanced in confusion at the open door.

"Against the remembering, I mean. You lock the door."

She fitted the lid on the archival box and laid it aside on her desk.

"But this says you did so much good for so many kids. Why wouldn't you want to remember that?"

When she and Oskar had found Aaron, he was in shock, kneeling on the stone street, holding his slaughtered father's hand. Nearby, his bloodied mother and sister lay twisted. Aaron had been half a block away, waiting on line for bread.

"Because neighbors would kill you for doing this good. You have no choice but to learn to forget. Forgetting means you survive."

Abruptly, Ludka stood, her heart banging. She fished in her bag and popped a peppermint into her mouth.

"No more of this now. We must go. Please hand me my cape."

Will did as he was asked.

—

At home, Ludka introduced Will to Izaac, who was in the kitchen wearing an apron. There was still a half hour to go before the rest of the class arrived, and Will happily set about taking trays from the pass-through to put out on the table. Ludka went upstairs, ostensibly to change but really to secure the Chopin. Anticipating this moment had tethered her to reality this past week; without it she might have disappeared into a fog of disorientation that had nothing to do with jet lag. Having been in Warsaw, home had taken on an oddly surreal quality, as if experiencing it for the first time even while it felt utterly familiar. She had never foreseen, either, that finding Oskar would ultimately feel like a loss, but after sixty-four years of searching, sixty-four years of hope and despair and more hope, she felt not only the relieved happiness she'd experienced in Warsaw—and there had been happiness, this was true—but also a stark void that the living Oskar could never fill. Knowing now how he had aged and where he lived and what had transpired in the intervening years, having the ability to clearly picture him in his cinched trousers at work in his studio or walking the newly familiar streets of Warsaw, and hearing him speak in an English nearly devoid of accent had stripped her of all she had imagined about him for all that time. In her bedroom now, as she carefully unwrapped the Chopin, she could not remember even one of the many rooms she had imagined him in over the years; all she could see was the cluttered studio, the disturbing self-portrait, and the woman across the way shaking out her rugs.

The Chopin was unchanged. Ludka sat on the edge of the bed, laid the portrait gently in her lap, and, despite a rising clamor from downstairs that announced someone's early arrival, allowed herself a moment before she had to fit the hooks into their respective eyes. She had expected to feel elation at this moment, along with the familiar sense of calm security, but instead she felt slightly ridiculous, and bone tired. She forced herself to scrutinize the painting's condition, then tried to see the portrait through fresh eyes, as if for the first time, to see it as the valuable masterpiece it was. After a moment she realized with alarm that she was stroking the dent with her bare fingers. She jerked back as if burned. Carefully she reached beneath the frame for the hooks, maneuvered her way into standing, and restored the Chopin to its hiding place. She took off her shawl, a nod to her excuse about needing to change her clothes, then felt too exposed. She pulled on a silk scarf.

When she got downstairs, Izaac called out from the kitchen.

"Look who's here, kochanie!"

Tommy, grinning, emerged from the kitchen. Ludka threw up both hands with delight.

"Miss me, Babcia?"

He gave her a kiss on both cheeks.

"I thought this year you would sit out!" she said. "Already you have too much going on."

"What would the art tour be without me and my hors d'oeuvres? It's tradition! Robert's on his way, too. We'll spend the night as usual, hear about your trip. Come on, try these."

He took her by the arm and hustled her into the kitchen. Atop the stove, lined up in rows on a baking tray, small puff pastries steamed. Tommy lifted one onto a napkin and blew on it as if about to feed a small child. Ludka lightly smacked his hand and took it from him. The whole thing fit easily into her mouth.

"Perfection!" she said.

She reached for another, and it was his turn to swat her. She laughed and lifted a hand to his chin. He let her inspect him. His eye was clear, the yellowness of the bruise nearly unnoticeable, the scar on his cheek faint.

"The Steri-Strip came off yesterday. Looks pretty good, don't you think?"

He put a hand to his ribs.

"This is the only thing that still hurts, and only when I laugh too hard, or cough."

Ludka patted his cheek and smiled. The phone rang. Izaac answered. After a moment he sighed, hung up, and made a notation on the log. The muscles flexed in Tommy's jaw. He lowered his head and spoke to Will through the pass-through.

"Hey, you want the exclusive upstairs tour before the masses get here?"

"That'd be great," said Will.

When they had gone, Izaac spoke quietly to Ludka.

"Shelly called. He's suggesting twenty-four-hour surveillance on both our houses. Tommy and Robert had a brick, too, poor lads. And more graffiti. We're not the only ones being targeted, either. Tommy just told me that the other two teachers who were fired have been vandalized."

A week ago Ludka could have dismissed her rising apprehension, but now what flooded her mind was a conflation of slogans: *Żydzi Wszy* and *God Hates Faggots*.

"I can't stop thinking about all those people in red," said Izaac.

"It's that pastor behind all of this, Izaac. And that Meck. Where did these people come from?"

"Warren Meck wouldn't incite violence, kochanie, I'm pretty sure. You didn't see how shaken he was at the studio that day. He sounded like you, actually, not understanding how they could call themselves Christian."

"What did you tell Shelly?"

"I told him by all means, we want the protection. He's sending someone over tomorrow to meet with us."

Ludka jumped when the doorbell rang. The students were beginning to arrive.

As he did for every art tour, Izaac had emptied the coat closet of paintings. Because they didn't have enough wall space, he had years ago added picture rails to the windows and French doors in the dining and living rooms, as well as in the study. Ludka had found a set of brass hooks and chains from the Victorian era that they used to hang the paintings. The effect downstairs, then, was as of a gallery; the setting sun provided a backdrop for those specially hung pieces. When all the students had arrived, Ludka stepped up onto the hearth and called them to attention. They filled the living and dining rooms, most of them with mouths full and drinks in hand.

"Your assignment," Ludka said, to groans, "is to choose the piece of art that stirs in you many questions. The answers you must find yourself and share with me in an informal paper."

"When is it due?" asked Sophie.

"It is due when you are done. Before semester's end, of course, but this one is for your fun alone. Do not fuss about presentation, I am interested only in your thoughts and observations. Now look around, upstairs and down, eat and drink, and if you need anything do not tell me, tell Izaac in kitchen."

The students laughed, and Ludka stepped down off the hearth.

In the kitchen doorway, Will began talking with Tommy and Robert. As Ludka drew nearer to them, her heart gave a little start when Tommy fed one of his puff pastries to Will, who briefly closed his lips on Tommy's fingers.

"We're spending the night," said Tommy provocatively.

The three of them laughed, and Ludka, struck anew by her naiveté, averted both her gaze and her thoughts. Sophie and Ashley had overheard, too; they wrinkled their noses as if they'd smelled something foul, and turned away. Ludka wasn't surprised to see them gravitate to the Jerzy Duda-Gracz in the dining room. Izaac had hung the oil painting in front of the newly repaired dining room window, the one that had been victim to the brick. The large square oil painting depicted Pope John Paul II at the feet of a portrait of the Black Madonna of Częstochowa. Behind both, a sepia-toned city in ruins, a steeple the only thing undamaged. Ludka hurried over to hear what Sophie and Ashley were saying. When she got there, they fell silent, and Ludka thought of them in class that day—the distasteful way Sophie had said "homosexuals," and the way Ashley had then sidled up to Sophie. Ludka wondered if they'd been at the rally, wearing red, if they were capable of throwing bricks. Ludka rearranged her scarf to better cover the back of her neck.

"Please, I am curious to know what you are thinking. This is *Polish Motif: All Hers*. Jerzy Duda-Gracz."

Ashley glanced sheepishly at Sophie, and Sophie's hand strayed to her gold cross.

"We were just saying," said Sophie, "that it's weird the way the Pope is sort of lying down. Disrespectful, like. And why is the baby Jesus black? And Mary. The whole thing is kind of weird and spooky."

"These are perhaps the questions you must answer then, yes? If you would like to work together, you may."

"Well, that's not fair," said Will jauntily, appearing at Ludka's side. To Sophie and Ashley, he said, "I suppose you're thinking this is blasphemous?"

"It might be," said Sophie. "That's what we have to find out."

"Of course Jesus was dark," said Will. "He was a Jew from the Middle East. Wait, you're surprised? You think Jesus really *is* some handsome white hippie born in Texas? Seriously, what do they teach you at that church?"

Will's tone was jovial, but Sophie narrowed her eyes. Her nostrils flared.

"Come on, Ashley, let's look around."

Ludka didn't know if her increasingly suspicious imagination had conjured it, or if Sophie had in fact muttered "faggot" as they walked away. Ludka darted a glance at Will, who didn't seem to have heard a thing.

"You, young man, are provocateur."

Will grinned and shrugged.

"So I'm told."

More than half an hour later, Sophie and Ashley were back at the Duda-Gracz. Ashley stood in front of the painting as Sophie pulled it away from the window and poked her head and shoulders around behind. From across the room Ludka threw out a hand as if she could stop her, but Sophie was being careful not to touch the painting's surface. Ludka left them alone.


Later that night, after staying up late with Tommy and Robert, Ludka had finally fallen into a restless sleep when the smoke detector began to shriek. She bolted upright just as Tommy charged into the room, shouting "Babcia! Dziadzio! Get up, we have to get out!"

Izaac was already on his feet. Tommy rushed back out and pounded down the stairs. The hall light poured harshly into the bedroom. Ludka hastily pulled on her boots, a flush of adrenaline coursing into her limbs. Her silk long johns cooled outside of the covers, and she grabbed a wool shawl and tied it snugly around her neck. She clapped her hands over her ears. The deafening blasts were now screeching intermittently from all over the house.

"Come on," Izaac was shouting. "Come on!"

Halfway down the stairs she smelled the smoke, and it was only then she understood that the house really was on fire. She wheeled around. She rushed back up the stairs and into the bedroom, Izaac shouting behind her. With astonishing speed, she pulled down the nested portraits. A rough edge of the hanging wire ripped across her left palm. She nearly collided with Izaac at the top of the stairs. He had begun to cough.

"What the hell are you doing?" he yelled.

He shoved her in front of him, and she went as fast as she could, the portraits banging hard against her left leg. Light flooded the downstairs. Tommy was shouting something she couldn't hear, waving them toward the back entrance hall. Robert, head turned away from the flames, eyes squinting against the smoke, directed a gushing fire extinguisher at the dining room window, at the Duda-Gracz. The curtains on either side of it were in flames, and as the foam slapped across the Black Madonna of Częstochowa, Ludka cried out and tried to rush forth, but Izaac grabbed her arm. He tugged at the paintings, shouting at her to let go. Ludka yanked them away, and that was when reality began to slip. She hefted the paintings to her chest and clutched them in both arms. She froze. In the room with them she saw a gray-green uniform, visor cap, jackboots, and a black German shepherd with butterscotch eyebrows. Ludka whimpered and backed away with jerky steps. She began to cough. The dog strained at his leash, trying to get to . . . who was it? Tommy. No.

"Tata!" she yelled. "Mama!"

A gloved hand released the leash and the dog lunged. Ludka slammed her eyes shut, and that was when Izaac slapped her. Her eyes flew open, and even though Izaac's face was inches from her own, his hair wild, sweat coursing down his ashen cheeks, she didn't know him. She was having trouble breathing. Izaac tugged again.

"For God's sake, Ludka, let go!"

Her eyes burned. Someone was shouting at her to get on the floor. Where was the dog? Something bumped the back of her knees, and she crumpled, but a strong hand guided her down. The paintings slammed onto the rug, face first. Her left hand smashed into the canvas. It surprised her to see blood. Had the dog bitten her? Where was Tata? Where was Mama? But there was . . . Izaac. Izaac was crawling toward the back entrance. He stopped and turned back, shouting at her to go faster. She dragged the paintings across the rug. The wire bit painfully into her wounded palm. She seized it with her other hand and awkwardly hauled the paintings underneath her, over to her right side. The wire caught on her hanging wool shawl but then tore free. Someone— her grandson, she thought with confusion—was shouting in her ear. He had a hand under her left arm and was trying to push her forward. She crawled as best she could, awkwardly lugging . . . what? The Chopin. She yanked the hooks from their eyes, then grappled again for the hanging wire and held on. At the back door, Izaac collapsed. Tommy dashed over to him. At the sight of Izaac slumped on the floor, Ludka's mind snapped clear. The smoke roiled. Robert thrashed at the curtains. The alarm blared. With inhuman strength, Ludka rose to her feet, still gripping the Chopin. Mieroszewski's thumbprints wavered through her watering eyes. Her own blood smeared the back of the canvas. In the split second before she called out to Izaac and Tommy, before she hastened toward them through the smoke, before she shouted to Robert to get himself to safety, Ludka tugged her shawl over her nose and mouth, cast up a prayer to the Black Madonna of Częstochowa, and let the painting go.

# 30
# Revelations II

Ludka still couldn't open her eyes. For what felt like half a century she'd repeatedly wakened, then fallen directly back into a fretful sleep. Each time she woke, she failed to pry open her eyes. This time, though, she came fully awake. When she lifted her hands to her face, she discovered a bandage wrapped around her left hand and a nasal cannula pushed into her nose. Her throat felt raw, her chest hurt when she inhaled, and every joint and muscle ached, especially her wrists and knees. Her eyelids were crusted with gummy crud, which she picked and rubbed away. At last she could see, through painful tearing eyes. Izaac, also on oxygen, the plastic tubing running from his nose over his ears and to the next bed, watched her from a visitor's chair pulled close to her bed, his bloodshot eyes rheumy. His old cardigan covered a hospital johnny and a white blanket covered his legs. Ludka's eyes widened as she began to remember the fire. Her neck and shoulders tensed as she tried in vain to sit up. Izaac quickly reached for her hand. His voice was hoarse.

"Everyone's fine, kochanie, relax. The fire is out. It's okay. Everything's okay!"

Ludka slumped into the pillow, her heart thumping fast in her ears. At least the dim lighting was easy on her eyes. She groaned.

"I know," said Izaac. He tenderly squeezed her right hand in both of his. "It feels worse than it is—the doctor says we're both just a little banged up, but otherwise fine. Our bloodwork came back squeaky clean, so no harm done. Here, let me raise the head of the bed."

He pushed a button on the gurney and raised Ludka to a near-sitting position. Just leaning forward while he arranged the pillow behind her took Herculean effort. She had only vague memories of being treated in the ER. Izaac gave her a cup of water, which cooled and soothed her throat.

"Again . . ." Ludka coughed lightly. "Again we survived."

Izaac smiled weakly.

"Thank god for Robert and Tommy. Robert put out the fire before the truck arrived. I guess you passed out shortly after I did. The paramedics got there moments later, or so Tommy tells me. Robert raced home—they were convinced their own house had been hit, too, which it hadn't, thank god. I sent Tommy home a little later. He's convinced it was arson, that it's all his fault."

Frank, smelling like smoke, stepped through the open door into the room. His unkempt coppery hair lay plastered to his forehead, the sweat now dried. He still wore his khaki-colored turnout gear; the neon yellow reflective bands flashed too brightly in the dim room. He took off the heavy jacket and lowered it to the floor, pulled off the protective throat tab, and plucked his navy T-shirt away from his skin to let in some air.

"Glad you're awake, Matka." He cleared his throat. "How are you feeling?"

Frank's muscular presence filled the room with a solid, capable energy that Ludka could hardly imagine she herself had ever possessed, and a sudden gratitude and overwhelming love for her handsome, competent son infused her; she didn't trust herself to speak, so she brushed off his question with a flap of her hand, which brought a wry smile to his lips.

"Listen, I wanted to let you know you don't have to worry about a thing. Robert acted fast, so the smoke damage is minimal. You'll be able to reenter the premises . . . sorry, still on duty, I guess. You'll be able to go home as soon as they release you, which will probably be tomorrow morning at the latest. I arranged to get a cleaning team in there. The only thing I told them not to touch is the paintings. I assumed you'd want to handle those yourself. I left them all exactly where they were, except the one we found on the living room floor, which I guess sustained some damage. You should get in touch with your insurance company right away."

Ludka nodded absently, her brow furrowed. A painting on the floor? She pressed the palm of her bandaged hand and remembered the wire, the blood, and all that ridiculous dragging. What in heaven's name had she been thinking? But Frank had said one painting only? She had an irrational thought of Stanley dressed like a firefighter, creeping into the smoky house.

"Damage?" she said.

"That's what I was told. I didn't see it."

Ludka slowly exhaled, as weak and weary as she'd ever been. She lay propped against the thin pillow, astonished by this tempting new feeling welling up inside her, this growing inclination toward resignation. The Chopin would be there, or it wouldn't. She pressed her fingers over her lips.

"I prayed to her, Frank," she said. "Did you see her? The Black Madonna of Częstochowa?"

Frank nodded somberly and ran a hand roughly through his hair. She was, in fact, the first thing he had seen when he arrived at the house. As he had approached the painting, he'd experienced a long episode of déjà vu and upon emerging from it remembered the arson at Saint Hedwig's, how his mother had told him that the Black Madonna had saved the church, exactly as the legend had prophesied. Now he thought he should get a reproduction for himself, hang it in his home.

"Listen, I'm afraid Tommy was right. That fire was set, and none too subtly. Someone cut right through the screen and opened the window—the guy who replaced that glass must have left it unlocked. It appears they put a lighter or a match to the curtains. The Black Madonna fared the worst, I'm afraid, since it was right at the point of origin. The fire investigator already came in and got what he needed. I asked him to report to Shelly. Whoever did it never entered the house, but they did leave fingerprints on the windowsill, inside and out. Could be just the work guy, they'll check that out."

Ludka had been listening, first with a nagging sense of suspicion and then, as more of the evening came back into focus, with abrupt and chilling clarity.

"It was not the work guy. It was girls from my class. They go to the Regent—the Redeemer church. One of them was snooping around behind Duda-Gracz during the art tour."

"Are you sure?" asked Frank.

Ludka raised her eyebrows and nodded.

"They heard Tommy say he was spending the night with us."

"Mój Boże!" said Izaac.

Frank crouched down and retrieved his cell phone from one of his jacket pockets.

"Shelly," he said, "I've got a lead. Matka, what are their names?"

Ludka could not remember Ashley's last name but gave him Sophie's. Frank explained the situation to Shelly. He tugged again at his T-shirt and smiled at his parents with bright eyes.

"I know," he said into the phone. "This could be important. If Matka's right, those girls could be our ticket!"

He finished the call and retrieved his heavy turnout jacket from the floor.

"Shelly's on it," he said. "Now we just have to get a good crowd at the public hearing on Wednesday, help Lolek defeat that bill. Wouldn't it be great if we caught the people responsible for all this by then?"

Frank quickly ran a hand through his hair, grinning like a boy. Ludka flashed on a memory of that same grin, when ten-year-old Frank watched as the mallard he'd freed from a six-pack ring slapped her way across the wetland and took flight. Now he buttoned his jacket almost sheepishly, took a breath, straightened his spine, and put on his professional face.

"Listen, I want you both to be aware of something. You might find yourself reacting strangely now that the fire is out and the danger has passed. It's not uncommon at all to experience intense or unpredictable emotions, flashbacks to the incident itself, sensitivity to loud noises or smoky smells. All of this is normal. If, in a month from now, you're still experiencing any of these symptoms, let me know; longevity might indicate posttraumatic stress disorder, and for that it's good to get some help."

Ludka, thinking about Dr. Jaines, refrained from catching Izaac's eye, so she wouldn't laugh inappropriately.

"Thank you, Frank," said Izaac. "We're no strangers to PTSD."

"Of course," said Frank. "I should have thought—"

"Nonsense," said Ludka. "You are right to warn us."

Frank retrieved his protective throat tab from the floor and held it in both hands.

"Okay, I have to go. I want to check in on Tommy and Robert. Is there anything you need from the house? No? You're sure? If you change your mind, give Lolek or Marta a call. They're coming in a little later—Lolek's on his way from Boston. Want this door closed?"

Izaac nodded. When Frank had gone, the two of them simultaneously exhaled. Izaac rearranged the blanket over his legs, took her hand again, and leaned his head against the back of the chair.

"I'm going to that public hearing at the State House on Wednesday."

"If you are better only, Izaac."

"No. No matter what, I am going. The fire might be out . . ." His voice trailed off.

"But danger has not passed."

Izaac rolled his head back and forth against the chair.

"I'd say it's just begun."

At the art tour, Sophie had been wearing a pale blue cardigan, and with rising fury Ludka thought of it now—its innocent girlish simplicity, the shiny gold cross. Had Sophie known precisely why she was unlocking that window? Had she meant to kill them all, or had someone duped her into thinking a scare would advance whatever misguided mission the church was peddling?

"Mój Boże, kochanie, let go!"

Izaac wrenched his hand from hers.

"Already I was thinking of Sophie, whether she is real student or imposter."

Izaac raised his thorny eyebrows.

"Before last night I would have said you were being ridiculous. Now . . ."

Ludka mined her memory for the kinds of details she might work into a sketch: the lift of Sophie's shoulder as she pushed behind the painting; the folds of Ashley's chubby back; the way the Duda-Gracz continued to sway long after they'd moved on.

"I, too, will go to this hearing, Izaac. There are a few things I'd like to say."

Izaac smiled, then closed his eyes. They sat quietly then, listening to the gentle murmur of oxygen and the muffled beeps and conversation from the nurses' station. After a moment, Izaac sighed. He bent forward, chest to his knees, and before Ludka had time to be alarmed, he straightened up and, to her astonishment, lifted the Chopin onto his lap. Her mouth fell open. Izaac held up a stern hand, and Ludka touched her throat.

"Tommy brought it in. He seemed to think you might need it. Now before you say a word, I have something to show you."

He fumbled in his cardigan pocket, carelessly bumping the painting, and withdrew a closed fist. He weighed whatever he was concealing, as if he might change his mind, and then with a sigh gave it over to Ludka. The metal disc—an antique watch case—felt cold and too heavy in her palm, even before she saw the engraved name: *Rosenberg*. She drew in a quick breath, and the oxygen hissed.

"Open it," said Izaac.

With shaking hands, she thumbed open the clasp. Inside the cracked leather interior lay a pitted silver pocket watch, its face yellowed, the time incorrect. Engraved on the back was Izaac's father's name: *Abram Tomasz Rosenberg*. Ludka's heart paused for a long, long moment, then resumed with a gallop.

"So you see, kochanie," said Izaac, giving the Chopin a little shake, "you are not the only one."

Ludka could hear the hooks tapping against the back of the Chopin's frame. Was that a new dent, just above Chopin's right shoulder? She reached out a beckoning hand, but Izaac didn't notice. He let the painting fall back into his lap. Ludka hadn't the energy to protest. She shut the silent watch in its case, reverently stroked the silver, then laid it on the bed. Izaac took it.

"My father habitually carried this in his coat pocket. On the day you smuggled me from the ghetto, I stole it. So stupid—I must have thought I could use it as a bribe if I got caught. I'm surprised you didn't hear the ticking, even from under all that soiled laundry. Even half-sedated, it's all I could hear. I haven't wound it since."

Ludka's mouth went dry. A vein bulged in the center of Izaac's forehead. He absentmindedly flipped open and snapped closed the case, as if it were an old habit. Ludka worked her tongue around in her mouth, but it didn't much help.

"And all this time you have—" Her voice broke.

"Carried it. Yes, Lukda, I have carried it. All these years. Like you."

He sounded as weary as she felt. She swallowed, wincing at her sore throat. He placed the Chopin on the bed. He held closed his cardigan.

Ludka caught a whiff of smoke and became aware that she was clasping the Chopin to her chest, face out so her arms pressed fully against the front of the canvas. She quickly loosened her hold. Seeing it upside down disconcerted her. Had the paint always held so many cracks? They assailed Chopin's young face like an eruption of spidery veins. She closed her eyes against the memory of dragging it across the living room floor. Soon she would arrange to have it sent to the National Gallery of Warsaw. No, not soon. Monday. She laid it carefully on the bed, where it rested against her knee like a discarded sketch pad. She and Izaac both jumped when someone yanked open the door, apologized quickly, and closed it again. Izaac laughed nervously, but to Ludka his laughter came as if from inside a wardrobe on the other side of the room, where she knew Izaac was now hiding, even as she also saw him sitting beside her. As if viewing a movie, she watched, strangely devoid of emotion, as two Waffen-SS soldiers and a German shepherd burst into the kitchen of her Piwna apartment. She saw herself standing like a mannequin next to her similarly still parents, her hand clutching a fistful of sketches she'd failed to hide in time. The soldier with the dog circled the room, while the other jabbed a pistol at them, shouting something in German only her father, whose hands were up in a posture of surrender, could understand. The one word she could decipher was Żegota; someone had betrayed them. She backed slowly away until she hit the kitchen wall, slid down it until she was sitting, and dropped the sketches, which skidded across the floor. The dog, tail tucked between his legs, kept glancing up with worried eyes at the soldier holding his leash, as if the dog was there against his will. For a moment, in the part of her mind that sat in the hospital, Ludka felt sorry for the dog, and hoped he would not obey the order she now understood would come next. But the dog did obey, and when the soldier unclasped the leash, Ludka knew what the dog would do, and he did. But before he clamped down a second time, and locked his jaws in the fatal bite, Ludka found herself fully back in the hospital, Izaac's face inches from her own. This time she remembered everything.

When the dog had finished with her father, as her father lay bleeding out on the floor, Ludka's mother charged the nearest soldier. She did not die in slow motion, groaning and writhing like a Hollywood star shot down. She died efficiently instead, in an instant, collapsing all at once like a marionette cut loose, a single bullet in her head.

For an unbearably long, unknown amount of time after the soldiers had ransacked the apartment and seized damning evidence of Żegota's work, after they'd searched the wardrobe and found nothing, because Izaac had slipped through the hidden panel into the wall, Ludka had been forced to sit at the kitchen table, her parents' bodies within reach. The soldier with the dog had taken a fancy to her sketches and demanded a portrait. He sat facing her in her father's chair, his dog sitting dutifully by his side. Ludka dutifully drew them both. She did not at first remember that she'd been crying, but now, telling Izaac, the memory returned, the way she'd had to continually wipe her eyes to see clearly as she sketched. The dog had watched her, repeatedly cocking his head, those butterscotch eyebrows knitted in concern. When she was done, when she handed over the portrait to the soldier, the dog stood, shook himself, and began to wag. He walked over to her, his eyes soft, his tail still waving, and before she knew what she was doing, she had offered him her open hand. He licked it, tentatively at first, then more methodically: palm, fingers, thumb.

"He licked away tears, too, Izaac."

She touched both cheeks with trembling fingers. She gazed at Izaac in bewilderment.

"And you did not stop him, kochanie, and that's okay."

Ludka was crying in earnest now. She had done more than not stop the dog; she had welcomed him. He had been kind at precisely the moment you needed kindness—*she* needed kindness—and remembering him now—that murderous, gentle dog, his soothing tongue, the depth of his soft fur—something cracked open inside Ludka and sorrow swept in. And with the sorrow hurtled another, more recent memory: the idea that had eluded her in Oskar's studio, about why Oskar had barricaded his mouth, about what Oskar shouldn't have said. He told her that he hadn't known Żegota bribed a guard to get him out of Pawiak, and that he didn't think she'd want to see him after what he had . . . How then, had he secured his release? Ludka's breath stalled. Her face grew suddenly hot.

As the Nazis had departed, leaving her inconceivably alive, the soldier holding the dog had paused on the threshold. In butchered Polish, he said something over and over, trying to get her to understand. The one word she had clearly understood was Pawiak, a warning, she'd thought. But now, propped crying in a hospital bed, Izaac holding her hand, Oskar's self-portrait as clear in her memory as the Chopin in her lap, she remembered with horror what else the soldier had stressed—a name. A name she hadn't then recognized. A traitorous name: *Pawel Brozek.*

# 31
# The Sermon

Meck left his technician in charge of recording Pastor Royce's sermon and hustled down from the Regent's old projectionist's room to join Jill and the boys in the congregation. Each Sunday for the past five years, when he walked down the aisle and settled into a worn red velvet seat, he often felt as eager as a boy on movie night; sometimes he imagined he could even smell popcorn. Today, though, his mind was on only one thing as he took his seat between Jill and Whit in the forward center section, their combined families occupying nearly the entire row. Meck's flagging confidence had been shored up by last week's surprising arbitration win, but Friday night's fire at Izaac Rosenberg's had toppled it. He spoke tersely to Whit.

"In the end it doesn't matter who did it, does it? The perception now is that our campaign is about arson, and assault and hatred. How do we recover from that, Whit? I mean, I knew we'd have to deal with a fringe response at some point, I just didn't think it would happen so soon, or be so extreme. I can't believe it would be one of us who set that fire, can you? Who would—"

He cut himself off, and shook his head. A muscle pulsed in Whit's jaw. Jill smiled at Meck sympathetically, and for the flash of an instant he felt fine. He smiled gratefully, took her hand, and gazed beyond her at their boys. John, as usual, was bouncing around in his seat, while Andrew, who leaned against his mother, frowned up at the stage. Ben had his back to them, talking with a friend in the row behind them. Meck turned his attention to the crowd, wondering about each person he saw. To Whit he said, "This whole thing is starting to feel planned."

Pastor Royce, in jeans and an untucked navy blue shirt with the sleeves rolled up, walked steadily across the stage. When Meck had been Ben's age, Pastor Royce had had jet-black hair and a slim build, but the calm and confident way he crossed the stage was exactly the same. The crowd began to hush. A simple wooden podium stood at center stage. Projected onto the old movie screen behind the podium was an array of crisscrossed beams of light that periodically pulsed new shades of purple and blue. The pastor held on to the podium, his over-the-ear wire-thin microphone barely visible against his cheek. He patiently scanned the congregation, side to side and up into the balcony, and when silence reigned, he waited a few more moments before spreading out his arms and beaming out a smile.

"Good morning, Redeemers!"

The crowd burst into returned greetings, and Meck felt buoyed by the swell of collective anticipation.

"Thanks to the miracle of modern technology, I also extend a warm good morning to those of you joining us from our county fellowships across the state. Good morning, Berkshires! Good morning, Franklin, Hampden, and Worcester! Hello, Middlesex, Norfolk, Plymouth, and Bristol! And I'm thrilled to announce today that our newest fellowship in Essex County is joining us for the first time, meaning that as of now we have fellowships in ten out of fourteen counties. And counting! Let's give a rousing Redeemer welcome to our brothers and sisters from Essex!"

Meck and Whit exchanged smiles as they applauded and stamped their feet, and suddenly Meck felt full up, unconcerned. Whatever happened, he wasn't alone.

"Now," said Pastor Royce, sounding more serious.

He shook back his hair and gripped the sides of the podium.

"We have some solemn business to discuss today."

On the screen behind him two words appeared: *Religious Liberty.*

"I know you're all aware of the homosexual teachers who were fired from their jobs less than two months ago, an action I understand many of you have welcomed. One of those teachers, our senator's son, Tommy Zeilonka, was violently assaulted a month ago. He and the other teachers who were fired have also suffered harassment and vandalism. And then, just two nights past, Thomas Zeilonka was spending the night with his grandparents—I'm sure you know his grandfather, Izaac Rosenberg, our former attorney general, who was a guest on *Tell It Like It Is* not long ago? So Tommy Zeilonka was spending the night with his grandparents, and . . . someone attempted to burn down their house."

He held up both hands to quiet the rising murmur.

"No one was seriously hurt, and the house, I'm told, had only minor damage. In addition to assault, harassment, vandalism, and arson, our community has also attracted the attention of the Westboro Baptist Church, and I'm sure you saw on the news the picketing they did at Tommy Zeilonka's arbitration hearing, which I myself, and some of you, attended in defense of our children. What manner of disturbance, you might rightly ask, has come into our community? And what does the Bible have to offer us during this time? We will explore Paul's letter to the Romans, and see."

Meck found that his tension had drained away, as it had on so many other occasions throughout his life when Pastor Royce had commandeered the stage and addressed Meck's pressing issues. He relaxed into his seat, then had to shift his position a few times to avoid a bulging spring, which threatened to poke through.

"There are those among us," said the pastor, "who call what's happening now a culture war, a war for the very heart and soul of our nation. I would not disagree. We are certainly being sorely tested. But war employs hatred as a weapon, and as a Christian, hatred is not allowed. Jesus won't allow it, which we know from what is written in John. *A new commandment I give unto you,* Jesus said, *That ye love one another; as I have loved you.*"

Pastor Royce crossed his wrists over his chest and smiled as the verse appeared on the screen behind him. Most of the congregation echoed his gesture, and Meck smiled inwardly, remembering the Boston rally. Pastor Royce stepped out from behind the podium and threw out his arms.

"'*As I have loved you!*' When we love one another we are the word made flesh, made manifest, made evident. But in the climate of our current culture war, if you disagree with someone, you're apt to be called *a hater.*" He held up his fists. "The people at the Westboro Baptist Church believe that *God* is a hater. That God hates homosexuals, in this case. But hate has no place in Christianity, my friends, does it? No, it does not! So the idea of hate has arisen in our community, and some would think we are haters. The other idea that has arisen in our community is a concept I find much more insidious, at least as it's being defined today. I'm speaking about *tolerance*. There was a time when tolerance meant what it means. I turn now to that other great book, *The American Heritage Dictionary*, to show you what it means. I'll let you read this for yourself."

He strode to far stage left and turned toward the screen, where the definition appeared: *The capacity for or the practice of recognizing and respecting the beliefs or practices of others.*

"The key word here is *respect*, my friends. Tolerance used to mean we treated each other respectfully, no matter how much we disagreed. But today we hear the word tolerance and it seems to mean something else entirely. It seems to mean that anything goes. Anything at all! That every idea is equally as valid as another. Well you know what I say to that?"

He stepped to the very edge of the stage and cupped his hands behind his ears.

"Do you know what I say?"

Meck's son John stretched high out of his seat and, with a few other people, called out "Poppycock!" Pastor Royce laughed and went back to the podium.

"Poppycock, that's right. This newly defined tolerance is the reason we've run into trouble here in our beloved state. This newly defined tolerance is the reason we now face a threat to the words you saw earlier on the screen that you thought by now I'd forgotten."

The congregation murmured protests, and laughed. *Religious Liberty* appeared again on the screen.

"What I'm about to say, what I'm about to quote from the Bible, is something I'm afraid I won't be able to say for much longer if we don't put our collective might into this culture war, because already there are vast forces at work trying to silence me and you and our children and grandchildren and great grandchildren. We've seen this already in our public schools. We've seen this in the liberal media when we're painted as haters. But this is not a war against Christians alone. This is *America* under siege. This is our First Amendment under siege. This is our liberty under siege."

He wiped the back of a wrist across his brow. He reached beneath the podium and took a long drink of water from a clear plastic bottle. He faced them and took a deep breath. He spoke quietly, urgently.

"I am here to tell you we are not going down without a fight. We are *not*. Please turn to your Bible now and read with me from Paul's letter to the Romans, chapter one, verses twenty-four to twenty-eight. If we don't win this culture war, it will not be long before we cannot even quote this passage aloud. Make no mistake . . . I am not exaggerating. God's word—in the name of this newly defined tolerance—will be silenced."

Meck turned to Jill for their Bible. John was staring at them expectantly, and when Jill nodded, he happily snatched a Bible from the rack in front of him. With evident excitement he began to riffle through the pages. Meck leaned across Jill.

"Not so rough, John. And share with your brother."

John nodded rapidly and threw an elbow into Ben's bicep. Ben punched him on the thigh and both boys laughed, although Meck could tell it took an effort for John not to grab his leg where Ben had hit him. Meck and Jill simultaneously told them to cool it. Andrew looked beseechingly at Meck.

"Come on over here, Sport. You can sit with me, away from the danger zone."

Andrew politely squeezed past Jill's knees and crawled up into Meck's lap. Pastor Royce began to read.

"*Wherefore,* Paul says to the Romans, *God also gave them up to uncleanness through the lusts of their own hearts, to dishonor their own bodies between themselves: Who changed the truth of God into a lie, and worshipped and served the creature more than the Creator, who is blessed forever. Amen. For this cause God gave them up unto vile affections: for even their women did change the natural use into that which is against nature: And likewise also the men, leaving the natural use of the woman, burned in their lust one toward another; men with men working that which is unseemly, and receiving in themselves that recompense of their error which was meet. And even as they did not like to retain God in their knowledge, God gave them over to a reprobate mind, to do those things which are not convenient . . .*"

Meck glanced over at Ben and John to see what they were making of what Pastor Royce was saying, and for once felt relieved that they didn't seem to be paying attention. He wondered what Andrew could understand at five years old, and made a mental note to talk with Jill about how they should approach the subject when Andrew asked his inevitable questions. They'd have to keep the focus on changing the truth of God into a lie.

As if Pastor Royce had read Meck's thoughts, he said, "I hope you can see as clearly as I can how the people we are battling have turned away from God, have '*changed the truth of God into a lie.*' What we are witnessing in our community is the result of these people receiving the '*recompense of their error.*' The teachers who have been silencing our children and proselytizing about their own degrading passions as if they were natural have turned their backs on God. And what has God done? God has let them go their own way without him, and now they are reaping their recompense."

Meck frowned. He turned to Whit in confusion.

"It sounds almost like he's condoning the violence," he whispered.

Whit skeptically raised an eyebrow.

"And lest you think I'm applauding these recent acts of violence," said the pastor, "I want to clarify."

Whit gave Meck a look as if to say *you see?* Meck smiled as if he should have known better. Still, he couldn't shake his uneasy feeling. Pastor Royce went on.

"I understand the violence. I do. I understand the violence because I understand that God has told us here in Romans 1:27 that if we turn away from Him, there will be dire consequences, and the homosexuals who have turned away from Him must face those consequences. I also understand that we who believe that homosexual behavior is sinful grow weary of tolerating—in the original, noble definition of this word—we grow weary of tolerating the sinners. We grow weary when the sinners are influencing our children. When they're silencing our children. When they're berating our children for speaking from the heart. When they're telling our children that sinful living is normal, that the Bible is not the word of God, that freedom of speech is only free for some, and that religion is not to be tolerated."

Meck slowly became aware of Andrew squirming, and repeatedly whispering "Daddy?" Meck relaxed his hold. Neither Whit nor Jill seemed concerned about Pastor Royce's tone, about what he seemed to be insinuating, but Meck found himself thinking about Eric's refusal to name the person who'd approached him for information. Arnie Dengler wasn't clever enough to have enlisted

Eric's help, but Pastor Royce was. Meck massaged the back of his prickling neck. He was reading too far between the lines. Had to be.

"But we are a forgiving and a kind church," said the pastor, "a church that walks in the footsteps of Jesus, and I know there are some among us who have homosexual desires, and many more among us who have people in their families whom they deeply love who consider themselves homosexual. And so I say to you now, show patience and compassion, as we have learned from Paul in First Corinthians, chapter six, verse eleven, when he says, *'And such were some of you'*—sinners, he means—*'Such were some of you: but ye are washed, but ye are sanctified, but ye are justified in the name of the Lord Jesus, and by the Spirit of our God.'* So show patience and compassion, and welcome to our church our homosexual brothers and sisters, and help them to be washed and sanctified and justified. Help them to get back with the Lord, help them to celebrate the end of their depravity, then breathe a sigh of relief for the preservation of our freedom to speak out about our beliefs, our freedom to practice our religion. This is our preferred method for winning the culture war, Redeemers, this is it, to do our best to bring our homosexual brothers and sisters back from their depravity, away from their due penalties, back to the Lord."

Meck softened. This sounded more like the Pastor Royce he knew.

"I know that some of you are thinking that patience in this case could be dangerous to our children, and to you I would say this: I understand. I understand. When it comes to protecting our children, we must do what needs to be done. As we well know from Ecclesiastes 3:1, *'To every thing there is a season, and a time to every purpose under the heaven.'"*

The passage from Ecclesiastes showed on the screen, then faded back into *Religious Liberty*. Meck frowned, once again confused. Was it only his newly wary imagination, or had others also heard a hidden meaning in Pastor Royce's emphasis on *do what needs to be done*? No one around Meck seemed concerned. Pastor Royce walked far stage right, then stretched out an arm toward the screen.

"We must protect our religious liberty, my friends, whatever it takes. Solemn business. Challenging times. Now go in peace and do God's work, Redeemers. *Do God's work*! Amen."

As vigorous applause burst forth from the congregation, as people called out *amen*, Meck once again became aware that his son was calling out to him, but this time Andrew also pushed hard against Meck's chest.

"You're crushing me, Daddy, let go."

Meck immediately relaxed his arms. Andrew flashed him an annoyed look and climbed down.

"I'm sorry, Sport, I wasn't paying attention. I was trying to hear Pastor Royce. Did I hurt you?"

Andrew, his hands on Meck's knees, considered this, then shook his head and shyly smiled. Meck smoothed a hand over Andrew's hair. On either side of them, Whit and Jill continued to applaud. All Meck could hear was *whatever it takes*.


Afterward, in the lobby, Meck stood with Whit, while their wives and kids converged on the refreshments table.

"I can see why you're saying that," said Whit, "but don't forget he also came right out and said he wasn't applauding the acts of violence, that our preferred method is patience and compassion. Hang on, here he comes."

Pastor Royce was making his way toward them through the crowded foyer. When he saw Meck watching him, he donned a comically frantic expression and mimicked doing the breast-stroke to cut through the crowd. Meck smiled.

"What do you think, fellas?" said Pastor Royce. "Too much political talk, not enough Bible?"

"No, no," said Whit, "it was just right. You struck the right tone of urgency and patience. Nice touch, too, with Corinthians."

"I don't know. I think I was too wishy-washy about the violence."

"Honestly?" said Meck. "I did think you could have come out more strongly in your condemnation."

His heart picked up speed; he'd sounded more stern than he had intended, and Pastor Royce looked at him sharply. Whit rushed in to thwart the rising tension.

"You've been going apace, Pastor, it's understandable."

Pastor Royce dropped his hands and clasped them over his belly.

"I guess I am a little weary these days. You don't think those Westboro folks are behind all this, do you?" Then, as if thinking better of what he'd just said, he shook his head. "No, they do make a point about their protests being nonviolent."

"Doesn't mean their message doesn't encourage others to do their dirty work," said Whit.

Pastor Royce patted his belly.

"Come on now, you two, it's Sunday. Day of rest. How about some refreshments to see you on your way? And listen. I'm sorry if I let you fellas down."

"Not at all," said Whit.

Meck smiled thinly, and followed Pastor Royce to the refreshments table.

—

As Meck and Jill and the boys left the church, St. Hedwig's was also getting out, and Meck saw Senator Zeilonka coming down the stairs with an elderly white-haired woman on his arm. She wore a black cape with a wide alpaca shawl in shades of gold and brown drawn over her shoulders. As Meck neared the church, the senator called out and asked if he might have a word. Meck told Jill to go on ahead with the boys, that he would catch up. A chill wind had picked up, and the senator's already unkempt hair got further mussed. He didn't seem to notice. The woman's cape billowed out, and with her free hand she gathered the shawl closed against her throat. Frowning, she assessed him. Meck took off his right glove and shook the senator's hand, which was warm despite the icy air and the fact he wore no gloves.

"Warren, this is my mother, Professor Emeritus Ludka Zeilonka."

Ludka let go of Lolek's arm and reluctantly offered her gloved hand to Meck. She wasn't surprised at his flaccid handshake, at his assumption that she'd be fragile; she confidently grasped his hand and was rewarded when he widened his eyes in surprise, and tightened his grip.

"So you are the man who gave my husband a run for his money on radio. The man who is glad my grandson has been fired."

Meck made a little bow.

"I wouldn't say glad, Professor. I'm sorry it had to come to that. I was horrified when he was attacked. And I was sorry to hear about the fire. On the news it said you were both fine—I hope this is true?"

"I would not say *fine*, young man. So far we have a battered grandson, the bricks through the windows, incessant harassment on phone, vandalism, trespassing, threatening notes, picketers, and arson. All started when your cronies fired my grandson. How is this *fine*?"

She threw up her hands, then clutched again at the neck of her cape. With some difficulty she pulled up her shawl to form a hood. Meck wondered if anger or the cold or both caused her to tremble. The wind wouldn't quit. Meck flipped up his coat collar and fastened the top button. The air rang with shouts and laughter from the kids playing King of the Mountain in the parking lot, and despite the chilly air, people talked together on St. Hedwig's steps.

"I assure you, Professor, no one I know had anything to do with the violence."

"That's what I wanted to talk to you about," said Lolek. "Did you know the police are questioning two young women who go to your church?"

Meck put a hand over his mouth.

"Sophie Braddock and Ashley Grimes, do you know them?"

Meck lowered his hand. He pressed it against his suddenly hollow stomach. He didn't remember seeing either of them at the service, but of course the crowd was so large he could easily have missed them.

"I do know them."

"They enabled the arsonist," said Ludka. "Already they were at my home just two nights ago, for student tour of Polish art. And later that night? Fire!"

"Do you know anything about it?" said Lolek.

The senator's jaw was tight, his eyes watchful, suspicious. Meck was troubled to find himself thinking about Pastor Royce, about

the way he had said *do God's work*. He told them the truth, that
he knew nothing.

"Are you sure, though, that it's Sophie and Ashley? I can't imagine them doing something like this."

"Then you are a naive young man," said Ludka.

"Okay, Matka, okay," said the senator.

"Do not shush me, Lolek."

Lolek sighed.

"The police do think they facilitated entry for someone else,"
he said.

The first person Meck thought of was Brandon and his friends
from the team. Sophie and her brother were close. But while Meck
had been surprised to see Brandon's anger at the arbitration hearing, he didn't think him capable of arson. Really, though, how well
did he know him?

"It might be good," said Lolek, "for you to proactively talk to
the police. I imagine your fellowship will come under some heavy
scrutiny, and I expect you know most of the players. My friend
Shelly's in charge over there. Tell him I sent you."

The senator scrawled a phone number on the back of a business
card and handed it to Meck.

"Of course, Senator, I'll call him as soon as I get home."

"For what it's worth, Warren, there are some who threw out
your name as a suspect"—the way he said it made Meck think the
senator himself might have been one of those people, and clearly,
judging by the way she was watching him, the professor seemed to
have no doubt he was involved—"but my father spoke up on your
behalf. I don't know what transpired between you two during that
radio show, but he thinks you can be trusted."

Meck flashed on the dignity with which Rosenberg had taken

Clancy's hand and invited him into the guest studio. He winced, remembering his own fear in the face of that small mob.

"Your father—your husband," Meck said, inclining his head to Ludka, "is an admirable man, and he's right. I can be trusted, I promise you. Believe me when I tell you I'm as concerned as you are. There's no room in my circle for such things."

"Watch out for the confidence, young man," said Ludka. "When you fired my grandson, you unleashed your circle."

She heard herself use the word *unleashed* and swayed on her feet. She took Lolek's arm again, and he turned to her with concern.

"Okay then, Matka?" She nodded. To Meck he said, "She got out of the hospital only yesterday."

He gazed beyond Meck, then, and seemed to be considering whether or not to say what he was thinking. He momentarily closed his eyes, and when he opened them, he looked directly at Meck.

"If I've learned one thing in all my years in politics, Warren, it's this."

He waited for a group of people to pass by.

"You don't always notice what's right in front of you. People will surprise you. You think of trust as a virtue, but it can also be a naiveté."

Under Lolek's searching gaze Meck withered. Meck swallowed hard and shivered again—the senator must know about Eric, and if he knew about Eric, it made sense he would believe Meck was up to no good. But then the senator's face fell, and he appeared exhausted, his mind far away on something else entirely.

"I expect," Meck said tentatively, "in a position like yours it would be hard to trust anyone."

The senator seemed to drag his thoughts back to the moment.

"Take a look around, Warren. I find it hard to believe this recent violence is random. Someone is orchestrating it. Someone who believes in fear as a motivating force. Someone people trust, and blindly follow."

*I know,* Meck thought. He closed his eyes against the realization that for some time now—and not just since this morning's dubious sermon—he'd been trying not to admit to himself precisely what the senator was telling him. But the senator was right—there had been far too much violence for it to be random, and there was only one person in the campaign who could command such blind obedience. He opened his eyes to quell the thought. Both the senator and his mother were watching him pointedly, and Meck abruptly understood that they suspected Meck himself. He tensed and took a deep breath through flared nostrils to calm himself so his voice didn't thunder.

"It's not me, if that's what you're thinking."

The senator and his mother both narrowed their eyes, and for an uncomfortably long moment they appraised him.

"Come, Lolek," said Ludka. "He is pawn only."

Meck winced. His whole body flushed with an uncomfortable heat, and his hands and feet broke with sweat. How dare this woman call him a pawn?

"You know nothing at all about me, Professor."

He hadn't tempered his most thunderous voice, and both the senator and his mother visibly recoiled. From St. Hedwig's steps, a slew of heads swiveled toward Meck. He lowered his gaze and repeated, more quietly, "You know nothing about me."

"I know you work for that pastor," said Ludka. Her eyes shifted beyond Meck to the Regent. "That is all I need to know."

Meck looked back at the church, where people were still exiting. Outside the door, Pastor Royce put a hand on Arnie Dengler's shoulder and leaned in close to speak to him.

"You'll call the police, then, Warren?" said Lolek.

Meck inclined his head, not trusting himself to speak.

"See you Wednesday at the Education Committee's public hearing, I presume?" Again, Meck nodded.

"Better get there early if you want a seat," said Lolek. "A-1 gets crowded pretty damned fast."

With that, the senator and his mother walked away. Meck flexed his fingers, damp inside his leather gloves, and tried to curb the shameful mental image of hitting the old woman in the back with a piece of hurled ice. He didn't remember ever having felt this angry, but he wasn't so angry that he didn't have the presence of mind to realize she wasn't the proper target. He had to find out what was going on so he could bring his campaign back to heel. Reluctantly, he turned and headed back to the Fellowship. The front doors were now closed. Pastor Royce and Arnie Dengler were nowhere in sight.

# 32
# The Chorus

Three days later, Meck sat in Representative Gauch's State House office with Whit and Pastor Royce, preparing to testify later that morning at the Education Committee's public hearing, scheduled for 11:00 a.m. in Room A-1. Pastor Royce's seldom-worn suit had fitted him nicely a year ago, but now the jacket was tight across the shoulders and hung open like decorative curtains on either side of his bulging stomach. He was still breathing heavily from the walk to the fourth floor.

On Sunday, when Meck had found him alone in the green room, the pastor had assured him that he was just as surprised as Meck to hear about Sophie and Ashley.

"There must have been plenty of other kids at the art function that night," he had said. "I can't believe it would be them."

"But something isn't right," Meck said. "This thing is starting to seem orchestrated. You have to be more careful about what you say. You said it yourself today—you've been too wishy-washy about condemning the violence. People parse your words, you know that."

Pastor Royce was quiet as he pulled on his hooded parka. He sighed.

"Look, Warren, I'm doing the best I can. I'm sorry if you feel I've let you down."

He zipped his parka and pulled on a pair of fleece gloves.

"I've frankly started to wonder lately if I should step aside, if I'm getting too old for this. What you're seeing, Warren, is a tired-out man, a man who's not at the top of his game. I hope you can understand that. Can we just get through next week's State House hearing and then pull up and assess where we're at?"

Pastor Royce put a hand on Meck's back and steered him toward the green room's exit. The pastor had sounded so unlike himself that Meck, bewildered, had simply fallen in next to him and let himself be led out.

Now, crowded into Representative Gauch's office, Meck could see the fatigue on Pastor Royce's face, the sag of his jowls, the heavy folds of his upper eyelids. With sudden alarm he wondered if the pastor was ill, if that's what had been going on. On Sunday, Jill had suggested that Meck start reaching out to other national leaders so he didn't risk his chance of moving up to the next level; he had angrily dismissed her. Now he wondered if she'd been prescient. Adrenaline coursed through his chest and back. His palms grew clammy.

"Don't forget," said Gauch, "that today we have to pull out all the stops. Our job here is to convince this committee that it's crucial for the board of ed to define sound moral character when it comes to certifying our teachers, that a legally vague definition is no longer acceptable. And the best way to do that is to show the committee what *unsound* moral character looks like. I know my office heard from Arnie Dengler yesterday, and he's planning to bring photographs. Any idea what he's got?"

Meck and Whit exchanged a look, and Pastor Royce laughed.

"It's Arnie," said the pastor. "Only the Lord knows what he's up to."

"I'm feeling fairly confident," said Gauch, "but not enough to tell you 1298 will pass. We need at least nine votes and I'm only certain of seven."

Meck checked his watch.

"We have a couple of hours—there must be two fence-sitters we can coax over to our side. Who should we talk to?"

The door flew open and Carey Best stepped in. He greeted them quickly.

"I don't know how I missed this, but they're setting up for a press conference at the foot of the Grand Staircase. It wasn't on the calendar when I checked, close-of-business yesterday. Zeilonka must have snuck it on there this morning. I'm sorry, Chief."

Gauch quickly stood and buttoned his suit coat. Meck and Whit did the same. Pastor Royce stood more slowly. He tried in vain to button his jacket. Gauch tossed his reading glasses on the desk.

"Get Jensen, Peabody, and Creedon out there, Carey. At least we can be available for counterpoint comments. Who's here?"

"I only saw Wendy Chen, but you can bet if she's here, everyone will be here. There's already quite a crowd assembling near the stairs. I'll get out there as soon as I can."

"At least the Westboro people have gone home," said Meck. "We won't have that distraction."

Carey hurried from the office.

"Warren," said Gauch, "your fence-sitters will probably turn up at the press conference. You might want to try to catch them before they head over. Reps Sweeney and Nicholas. Both are right here in this suite."

"We're on it," said Meck.

One floor below, in Lolek's office, Wendy Chen and the Channel 7 news crew had just arrived for an exclusive interview with Tommy and Robert, who sat side by side on one of the rosy brocade-covered couches. Two LED lights had been raised and directed at them from adjacent angles, and the woman who'd adjusted the LEDs dabbed light foundation on their faces, explaining that it dulled any shine.

"Can we get some mascara to go with that?" asked Tommy.

Aggie, who was leaning back against the front of Lolek's desk, barked out a laugh, just as Robert lightly backhanded Tommy's chest.

"We could tease your hair, too, if you like," said Aggie, pushing at her own.

"Always already with the jokes," said Ludka, smiling at Tommy. She sat between Izaac and Marta at the conference table while Frank and Lolek stood nearby. Izaac took her hand, something he'd been doing often since the fire.

"Our boys," he whispered.

He was gazing at Lolek and Frank, who did make a formidable pair: Frank strong and trustworthy in his dress blues, Lolek powerful and determined in his tailored gray suit. Sitting here in Lolek's majestic office, in the seat of the state's government, surrounded by her family, Ludka let herself relax a bit for the first time since the fire. She and Izaac had talked extensively since then, finally sharing again what they'd shared all those years ago when they'd first been together in this country—stories of the war, this time fully told. Oskar's betrayal of her parents—and of Żegota— had gutted her. She'd deleted his e-mails unread. Countless times she'd gone over what had transpired in his studio, how distraught he'd been to learn Żegota had bribed a guard to free him, how so much of what he'd said had felt rehearsed. Now she understood the answer to her question about what had happened to his life— his terrible guilt had taken its toll, but she was nowhere near ready to declare it payment enough.

"Are we all set then?" asked Wendy Chen.

Tommy took Robert's hand and lifted it in Wendy Chen's direction, then checked his lapel mic. Wendy Chen sat on the opposite couch. She addressed the woman holding the camera.

"Focus on them alone, and after we'll get a couple of shots of me sitting here, okay?" To Tommy and Robert, she said, "We're not live, so no worries. Editing is our friend."

She smiled, took a breath, signaled to start the camera rolling, then asked her first question. The three of them talked easily for a few minutes about the assault, the harassment, and the fire. What Ludka noticed most was the absence of emotion in Tommy's and Robert's responses, how quickly these violent things had become commonplace. Izaac had remarked on this phenomenon just yesterday, when she finally allowed him to tell her about the interview he'd done with the Shoah Foundation for their Holocaust survivor archives.

"It struck me," Izaac had said, "how someone watching me would think I was a cold fish, I was so dispassionate. But really, over time everything becomes ordinary, doesn't it? It's just what happened in my life, nothing more."

Ludka had missed Wendy Chen's last question, but the energy of the interview had grown chilly. Marta tensed beside her, and Aggie nervously bumped her clasped hands against her mouth.

"I'm sorry, Wendy," said Robert, "but that question isn't relevant."

"But surely it's not a surprise to you. Many of the Christian parents are concerned that Tommy may have molested their kids. Here's your chance to tell your side of the story."

"The way you've framed the question," said Robert, "assumes that the stories the parents are telling are valid, and worthy of our defense. They're not valid stories. They're misplaced, mythical fears. All parents are concerned about protecting their kids from predators, and they're right to be concerned. But they're not right to be concerned about Tommy."

"I want to introduce them to great literature," said Tommy. "That's all. Not gay literature. Not straight literature. Not Christian or atheist literature. Just literature. You know, beautifully written, moving books that turn kids into lifelong readers."

Lolek was suddenly behind Marta, his hands on her shoulders. She leaned her head against him.

"You're a news journalist, Wendy," Robert said firmly, "so I know you appreciate fact-finding to get to the truth. Let me make your job a little easier. Want to know who's more apt to molest children? I'll give you a hint—it's not Tommy. Read the research that proves it. I'll send you these citations: Finkelhor and Araji; Groth and Birnbaum; Jenny, et al; Freund, et al; Groth and Gary; Dr. Nathanial McConaghy. Please, do your homework."

Wendy Chen indicated she would do just that.

"One more question. You lost in arbitration, which means the arbitrator believed there was good cause not to reinstate you. Of the other ten gay teachers who were also fired, only one of them has been reinstated. It doesn't look good for you, you have to admit. How do you account for this?"

Tommy and Robert glanced at each other, determining who should answer. Tommy leaned away from Robert, smiled, and jerked a thumb at him.

"He's the attorney."

"And like a good attorney," said Robert, "I'll address only what I know and refrain from speculating on what I don't know. In Tommy's case, we're appealing the arbitration decision because the arbitrator should have recused himself. His former law firm is comprised almost solely of people who attend the Hampshire Redeemer Fellowship, and the Fellowship is behind this antigay campaign. They're behind the legislation we're here at the State House today to combat."

"So you're saying the arbitrator was biased."

"That's right."

"And what of the other nine? Surely nine independent arbitrators can't all be biased. You have to admit that's a stretch."

"We'll find out more during the appeals processes."

Tommy pushed his hands between his knees and hunched his shoulders forward.

"I'm not a lawyer, but I do have one . . . observation, I guess you would call it. The one teacher who was reinstated is the *only* one who doesn't live in a district that houses a branch of the Redeemer Fellowship."

This seemed to be news to Wendy Chen. She leaned forward.

"Are you saying what I think you're saying? That the arbitration system was rigged?"

"I'm saying I think that's an excellent question worth exploring."

Wendy Chen, her eyes shining, sat back and shook her head as if to say *wow*. Aggie stepped forward.

"Sorry to interrupt, but we really need to get downstairs for the press conference."

Wendy Chen checked her watch and immediately told the camerawoman to get the B-roll so they could head out. She thanked Tommy and Robert and told them she hoped to have the interview ready for the news at noon and would most likely have clips on the evening news as well. Tommy grabbed Robert's hand again and lifted it up.

"Our own personal paparazzi, at last!"

The press conference held no surprises for Meck, which gave him confidence; he'd done his homework and felt well-prepared for the hearing. The usual suspects spoke—Senator Zeilonka, Izaac, Tommy and his friend Robert, and a couple of Tommy's students. The crowd they'd gathered was impressive, though, and Meck had raced down to A-1 and laid out on one of the pew-like benches his overcoat, Pastor Royce's parka, and Whit's jacket. He wasn't the only one who'd had the idea; nearly every seat was already saved.

The crowd jammed the expansive marble foyer at the foot of the Grand Staircase and spilled back into Memorial Hall. Every major TV station was there, and out of the dozen or more reporters milling around, Meck recognized the State House reporter and journalists from the *Boston Globe,* the *Boston Herald,* and the *Hampshire Gazette*. Meck, Whit, and Pastor Royce had decided against calling a press conference because they knew the media would attend the hearing and they wanted the focus to be on people's testimony. Committees typically heard the arguments in favor of legislation first, so Meck's wager had been that the media would get their footage and leave before the other side even got to testify. Now he hoped he hadn't miscalculated. It's possible the media would take what they got at the press conference and not even attend the hearing, although he couldn't believe they'd all skip out. Gauch was talking with the State House reporter, and Pastor Royce was holding court with the reporter from the *Hampshire Gazette*. Pastor Royce seemed to have regained his energy. Meck was just about to suggest to Whit that they split up and try to get in a word with the two major city papers, when Senator Zeilonka stepped back up to the podium. He said nothing. High above and behind him up the stairs, the colorful stained glass window over the stairway's broad landing shone brightly with light from the Great Hall beyond. After a moment, people noticed he was there and the noise began to subside. The senator took a step back, went up a couple stairs, and made a beckoning gesture up to the third-floor horseshoe of balconies. Meck noticed Aggie Roth talking with Tommy and Robert, who stood with Izaac and his wife. Meck felt a momentary shame, remembering how he'd wanted to throw something at the professor. Behind the senator, a wave of tuxedo-clad men came down the stairs, and quickly covered the entire staircase. Meck saw Tommy's mouth drop open and he pressed his hands to his chest, then grabbed hold of Robert's arm and shook it, as if trying to compel Robert to jump up and down. Tommy said something to Aggie, and she inclined her head toward the senator. Tommy shook his head in disbelief then called out to his father, who smiled. Meck turned to Whit, who sighed heavily and briefly closed his eyes.

"The Boston Gay Men's Chorus," said Whit.

"Smart," said Meck. "They've succeeded at framing this whole thing around discrimination. Pastor Royce never should have permitted those dismissals."

Arnie Dengler was suddenly next to them, asking if he'd properly heard Whit. Whit nodded.

"Oh, criminy," said Arnie. His voice was too loud in the quieting crowd and people glared. Meck took a step away from him, closer to Whit.

One man, the conductor, Meck assumed, stepped out of the front row of the chorus and shook the senator's hand. The senator left the podium, and Eric Barton came forward and wheeled it away. Another man in a tuxedo wheeled in a portable electronic keyboard, and a second man walked in with a snare drum secured to a shoulder harness. When they'd taken up their positions, the conductor faced the chorus, raised his arms, and the crowd grew quieter still. Finally, the conductor nodded to the drummer, who started a quiet and intermittent drumroll that stirred Meck's heart even before he recognized the song. The flinty snare evoked echoes of the drum and fife corps from revolutionary days, and what better place to hear it than in this august building? The conductor nodded to the pianist, who began a quiet prelude, and then with a gentle lift of his arms, the conductor called forth the men. The vast chorus sang so softly at first that Meck wasn't certain they'd truly begun, and then he recognized the traditional song. In unison the men sang.

*We shall overcome, we shall overcome,*

*We shall overcome someday.*

Dengler stepped closer and said with disgust, "Every one of them, a faggot."

Without even turning his head, Meck said, "For once in your life, Arnie, give it a rest."

More people quietly joined the crowd. People on the third floor hung over the balcony's iron railing and peered down on the singers. The door to the treasurer's office opened, and the staff sidled out, their arms self-consciously crossed. Memorial Hall at Meck's back filled with tourists and staffers and legislators alike, and Meck imagined John Eliot stepping down out of Henry Walker's mural to see who was stealing the show.

In six-part harmony, the chorus came quietly down from the refrain, ending in unison. Just as quietly, the restrained piano and drum began again. Within seconds the conductor had given them permission to let loose, and they did. The pounding drum and piano invited the chorus into the next verse, and the conductor threw himself onto his toes and marched his arms and asked for a rousing volume that the men met full voice, singing,

*We are not afraid, we are not afraid,*
*We are not afraid today.*

Meck, who had closed his eyes, who felt the thrum of his own humming deep in his chest, whose throat ached, thought he'd never heard anything quite so beautiful. He searched for Pastor Royce in the crowd and found him studying the chorus, arms crossed necessarily high on his chest, his stomach straining to be free of his dress shirt. Meck had hoped to exchange a look of shared wonder, of acknowledgment that this had been a brilliant move on Zeilonka's part, of disappointment that they hadn't thought to do the same with the Christian Chorale, the exact same thing, with the same timeless song. But Meck caught Pastor Royce in an unguarded moment, and his disgusted, compassionless expression sent a shard of horrified understanding straight into Meck's heart. His suspicions about the origins of the violence—which he thought he had quelled—instantly flared up, took hold, and turned into a steady flame of certainty. Numerous moments from the past several weeks rushed to mind: in the studio, the way Clancy had silenced Danny when he'd started to explain what Pastor Royce had told them to do; in the arbitration hearing, when Pastor Royce had stood up to keep Brandon from saying anything more about how much the pastor hated the gays; during Sunday's sermon, which Meck now knew had been scripted for two sets of listeners, one of which was meant to read between the lines. Meck swallowed back a sudden threatening bile and blindly reached out for something to hold on to so he wouldn't double over. Whit grabbed his arm.

"What is it, Warren? What's wrong?"

"I think Pastor Royce . . . I think . . ."

But what if Meck was wrong? He shook his head and gave Whit what he hoped would seem like an embarrassed smile.

"I got a little dizzy there. Not enough breakfast, I guess. I'm fine."

Something pressed against Meck's leg, and there was his son Andrew, gazing up at him. Meck hoisted Andrew into his arms and hugged him, his own heart thumping fast against his small son's chest. Jill was beside him now, with John and Ben. Their presence steadied him, and Meck knew he'd have to confront Pastor Royce, and if his suspicions were accurate, report his transgressions to the national leaders. It was the right thing to do. It would also decimate their campaign. Andrew squirmed against him. Meck set him down. The chorus began another verse, and once again they sang in hushed tones, the drumroll airy, skittering: *Truth will make us free someday.*

Meck stood a little taller. He would talk with Whit. Maybe together they would renounce Pastor Royce, and go as a team to

Washington. The national leaders wouldn't be able to blame them for the campaign's failure; they'd make sure of that. But then a troubling new thought occurred to Meck. His arms got heavy. He smelled the acidic aftermath of bile on his breath. Maybe inciting the violence hadn't been Pastor Royce's idea. Maybe he was following orders as part of the grander national plan, in which case Meck had to rethink absolutely everything, in which case maybe that old professor had been right. Maybe Meck was merely a pawn.

# 33

# The Public Hearing

L olek ushered Ludka and Izaac through one of the two public
entrances at the back of the wood-paneled hearing room and
steered them to a pew-like bench on the left side of the room,
already mobbed with like-minded people. The carpeted, utilitar-
ian, windowless room was a far cry from the Victorian majesty
of Lolek's office or the marble grandeur of the Grand Staircase,
but the anticipatory excitement Ludka had felt all morning hadn't
diminished. Since the fire, only five days ago, and since her terrible but cathartic recollection, Ludka had been both exhausted and
agitated. The fire had sobered her into finally acknowledging the
full and frightening extent of what they were dealing with, and
the security team that now patrolled their property and guarded
Tommy and Robert's house was there to remind her, should she
forget. But today's turnout, both here and at the press conference,
gave her a guarded hope; such widespread public resistance so
early in the fight surely meant that they could readily rout this
infestation of so-called Christian crusaders.

Members of the Boston Gay Men's Chorus stood three deep

against the back wall. Ludka was surprised to see Will there, too, with Annika and two other students from her class. Will waved. A group of men and women wearing hospital scrubs lingered against the wall to her left, trying to hold their meager space on the floor as the media set up all around them. Frank, his chief's hat under his arm, was talking with the heavyset woolly-haired nurse who had cared for Tommy. High school students besieged Tommy when he came in, and Ludka thought he might be fighting back tears of gratitude. Had Alexander Roslan painted this scene there would have been ample eye contact, even joy; he might have titled it *Resolve, 2009.*

He would also, of course, have captured the equally evident resolve of the people on the other side of the room. The students over there gave Tommy sideways glances. Izaac greeted Warren Meck with a lift of his hand, but Ludka shifted her gaze without acknowledging him. Another man sat with Meck, along with a woman who must be Meck's wife. A serious young boy sat on her lap. The pastor looked a little the worse for wear. His snowy hair needed a good brushing.

The pew-shaped bench Ludka sat on was ancient oak with taut leather riveted onto the back and had been set at an angle to form one side of the large semicircle of benches that faced the wooden dais up front. The dais itself spanned the length of the wide room and it, too, was curved so that committee members could see each other without effort. Committee members were arriving haphazardly, without fanfare, through the two private entrances behind the dais. They slid brass nameplates into wooden slots in front of their seats. Between the benches and the dais stood a plain wood table with three armchairs set to face the committee. People clustered around the table, signing up to testify.

Izaac sat on Ludka's right and on her left sat Tommy, then Robert, then Marta. Five in one bench was a snug fit, and Ludka was immediately too warm. She took off her silk scarf and stuffed it into her bag, which sat on the floor in front of her feet.

"There's never any good air in these rooms," said Izaac. "It's only going to get hotter."

Lolek leaned in from the aisle, and asked who would testify. Ludka hesitated. In the hospital, in the aftermath of the shock from the fire, she had felt so determined to speak out, but this morning's turnout made her wonder if her participation was necessary. If even half of all these people got up to offer brief comments, it would still take most of the day. Already the cushion beneath her felt too thin.

"Matka?" said Lolek. "You testifying?"

She shook her head. Before Izaac could say anything, she held up a hand between them.

"Already there are enough voices, Izaac. No one needs to also hear ridiculous old woman."

"And there you have it, kochanie, the trouble with democracy."

Lolek stood up to confer with Aggie, and she went up front to sign them in. Lolek leaned back in over the bench.

"I'll be in and out. There are two other hearings I need to attend to. And listen. This hearing is important, but if things don't go our way, it's not the end of the world, truly. It's only the beginning. We still have second and third readings in the House, and then the bill has to make it through three hearings in the Senate as well. There's plenty of time to kill this bill. I personally appointed Senator Sullivan who chairs the Senate Committee on Bills in the Third Reading, so I'm confident if the bill gets that far we can put a stop to it then. The important thing is that today we've already made a great splash in the news, and that's to our advantage."

Izaac spoke up.

"Lolek's right. This is only the beginning. We still have a discrimination case we can win, so don't forget that avenue's open to us."

Lolek glanced behind him at the media pool.

"The full contingent is here—that's a great sign. Tommy, you and Robert were terrific with Wendy Chen. Don't hesitate to talk to any reporter who approaches you, okay?" He checked his watch. "I'll be back."

Lolek slowly straightened, his hip tight, and strode as best he could from the room. Aggie came back and handed each of them the text of H. 1298. She crouched at the end of the bench, and they all leaned toward her to listen while she told them what to expect from the hearing, and what protocol demanded from their testimony. As she was reminding them to spell out for the committee that they should vote *ought not to pass*, Tommy made a small noise of surprise.

"Oh my god!" he said. He grabbed for Ludka's and Robert's hands. "It's him. It's one of the guys who attacked me."

Ludka followed Tommy's gaze to the front of the room where a clean-cut young man was handing papers to Carey Best, who stood sentinel at Representative Gauch's shoulder.

"Who?" said Aggie.

"That guy holding the black parka, right in the middle there."

"Are you sure?" asked Robert.

"Positive. It's him."

The man said something, and Carey threw back his head and laughed.

"Okay, listen," said Aggie. "You have got to be two hundred percent sure. He seems pretty chummy with Gauch's top aide, and he's no slouch."

As she was talking, she was working her thumbs over her cell phone, sending a text to Lolek. The last of the committee members were settling into their seats.

"They blasted that flashlight in your eyes, though, Tom," said Robert. "How can you be sure?"

"They might have *thought* they blinded me, but I'm telling you—I'm four hundred percent sure. I recognized him right away. He's the guy who called me a Sodomite."

"Wait!" said Ludka. "I know this one. He is Danny, son of that Kulek who accosted you in church."

Lolek showed up with a State Police officer, and everyone crowded out into the aisle. By the time Ludka got into the circle, Lolek was saying, "It's pretty simple. We have him arrested. As long as you're sure, Tommy."

Tommy nodded.

"That's your cue, Gordy," Lolek said to the trooper. "Go get him. His name's Danny Kulek."

"You want me to go quietly, Senator? I can cuff him outside the hearing room, away from the cameras."

Lolek started to answer, and was glad when he caught himself. He turned to Tommy.

"Your call, son. Whatever you think is best."

Tommy considered.

"I think it's probably better if everyone sees what we're up against. What do you think, Dad?"

Lolek nodded. Gordy made his way to the front of the room. Committee members seemed to think he was just going to pass behind them, through to the private exits. They greeted him by name. He stopped next to Danny. Gauch looked up in surprise.

"Danny Kulek?" said Gordy.

"The one and only," said Carey, reaching over the dais to clap Danny on the shoulder.

Danny smiled, and nodded.

"Danny Kulek, you're under arrest for the aggravated assault and battery of Thomas Zeilonka on February 16, 2009. You have the right to remain silent."

As one, the media came to life and surged forward. TV cameras rose and perched on shoulders. Lights flashed on. Still cameras whirred and clicked. Fuzzy booms extended. The hearing room erupted with noisy speculation. Gauch was on his feet, telling the trooper there must be some mistake.

"He'd never be involved in something like this. I know his father."

Danny's face darkened. He scanned the crowd. Finding Tommy, he narrowed his eyes but said nothing. Tommy didn't shy away. Gauch saw the exchange and went pale.

"You have the right to an attorney," said the officer. "If you cannot afford . . ."

"I can afford a damned attorney," Danny snapped.

". . . one will be appointed to you. Do you understand these rights as I've told them to you?"

Handcuffed now, Danny nodded.

"You need to answer me verbally, Mr. Kulek."

Danny squared his shoulders and lifted his chin.

"I hear you loud and clear, officer. I understand."

The policeman escorted him from the room through the private legislators' entrance and closed the door on the cameras.

Reporters rushed out the back doors. Gauch, grim-faced, slammed down a gavel and called for a brief recess.

On the other side of the hearing room, Meck sat with Jill, who had Andrew in her lap. On Meck's right sat Whit and Pastor Royce. Ben and John had asked to stand against the wall so they could see better, and they both looked serious in their blue suits. Meck and Whit and Pastor Royce had decided to discourage people from again wearing red; the State House was no place for such a show. Meck was dying to take off his own suit jacket. The room was suffused with too much body heat. On the way in Meck had sought out Eric Barton and asked him directly if he'd dealt with Pastor Royce. Eric, looking stricken, had said nothing. Meck had turned away without another word. He hadn't yet confronted the pastor. He'd decided it might be best to get through the hearing and talk with Whit about it back at home before making a plan. His heart was hammering, though, and his body trembled with tension. And then he had watched with astonishment as the police arrested Danny.

Meck could no longer stand the heat. He stripped off his suit coat. Without thinking, he handed it over to Jill, who received it without complaint. He leaned past Whit and spoke quietly but angrily to Pastor Royce.

"How many other sycophants did you get to do your dirty work?"

"Whoa," said Whit. He held out an arm as if Meck was his passenger in a skidding car. "What's going on, Warren?"

Pastor Royce sighed heavily, not looking at either of them. On the other side of the room the media returned, and settled down when a shaken Representative Gauch reentered and prepared to begin the proceedings.

"What's going on, Whit, is that he's the one who's been orchestrating all this violence. Tell us otherwise, Pastor?"

Pastor Royce dragged his hands down over his face a few times, rubbing at his eyes. He sighed again and then turned to face them.

"But we're winning, Warren, aren't we?"

Meck slumped back in his seat, not realizing until that moment that he'd still been hoping he was wrong.

"Wait, wait, wait," said Whit. "What are you talking about? Pastor Royce, tell me this isn't true."

"Don't you see, fellas, we *have* to win, whatever it takes. If we win Massachusetts . . ."

Whit turned to Meck with a horrified expression; thank God Whit hadn't known either.

"It's a slam dunk for the nation," Whit whispered. "Oh my God."

"Warren, Whit, take it easy now. Let's just get through this hearing, shall we, and we'll talk it all through? The way we always do? There's more than one way to win a campaign."

"*Are* we winning, Pastor Royce?" Meck leaned toward him again. "Did you *ever* believe that 'all who take up the sword will perish by the sword'? Did you forget Jesus's commandment to love one another? Do you think you're somehow exempt?"

Meck had no idea what would happen from here on out. If Pastor Royce were to atone for his sins, could Meck forgive him and continue in their work? Could he do this work at all if it turned out the violence was condoned, or even overlooked, at the national level? He might blow the whistle on Pastor Royce and find himself cast out instead of celebrated, the victim of a national cover-up. His whole life he had worked to be exactly where he was right now. What else could he possibly do? As an answer to that question presented itself, a wave of vertigo washed over him, and he thought he might pass out. He could simply go along. Pretend he knew nothing. Finish up the campaign. Maybe even win it. He pressed a hand over his eyes and then tugged at his tie. He felt a hand on his back and turned to see Andrew staring at him with concern. Meck couldn't even muster up a reassuring smile.

"Ladies and gentlemen," said Gauch, "thank you for attending this hearing of the Joint Committee on Education."

Meck and Whit locked eyes. Whit kept shaking his head. Pastor Royce sat with his eyes closed, his hands lying limp in his lap.

"Sorry for the chaotic start," said Gauch. His face bore a sheen of perspiration. "My senate co-chair sends her regrets today. She's needed elsewhere in the building. We have a full house today and a lot of people who wish to testify, so I'm going to ask you to keep your comments to a minimum—three minutes max. We have your written testimony, so don't feel like you must repeat what's written—we know how to read. I'll call people up in groups of three in the order in which you signed up. We will not be taking any official breaks, so you'll need to take care of yourselves as you see fit. There are restrooms and vending machines just down the hall.

"As is our custom, we'll hear first from those who support H. 1298."

He consulted the signup sheet.

"First up we have Warren Meck, Whit Hammond, and Pastor Royce Leonard."

Meck wished he was far away from here, maybe at the station, about to go on the air. Pastor Royce made to stand and Meck hissed at him.

"You're not saying a thing. Stay right where you are."

Pastor Royce lifted his hands in surrender as Meck and Whit got up. As they approached the table, Meck said, "Mr. Chairman, Royce Leonard will not be testifying today after all."

A murmur arose around the room. Meck hated how petty he sounded, and how bitter he felt, refusing to say *Pastor*. He could feel Whit watching him.

Gauch consulted his sheet.

"Arnold Dengler, then?"

Meck groaned inwardly. Dengler, holding a stack of nine-by-twelve glossies, joined them. Too late, Meck realized with embarrassment that Jill was still holding his suit jacket. Decorum was important in this building. A trickle of sweat ran from his left armpit down his side. He smoothed his bangs.

"Mr. Chairman, members of the committee, my name is Warren Meck and I live in Hampshire."

A hush fell over the room, and every member of the committee looked up, surprised by the depth and power of the large voice coming from such a small man. Meck's hands trembled and he clasped them together in front of him on the table. He'd never been as grateful as he was in that moment for all the ways live radio had prepared him to think on his feet.

"I'm grateful for the opportunity to speak first this morning because I'd like to set a collegial tone. I think it's safe to say that everyone in this room can agree on one thing—we all believe our children should be taught by teachers who possess sound moral characters. Most of you on the committee know that Whit Hammond here and I were two of the chief architects of this bill, and that Chairman Gauch was kind enough to file it on our behalf. I want to be clear with everyone here about our intentions.

We believe this bill will help to identify potential problems before they begin, during a teacher's certification phase. If the board has clearly defined what constitutes a sound moral character, the certification process can be tailored to weed out the unsavory elements before they ever get near a classroom."

Even as he was saying this, he began to question his own logic. Wouldn't he have unhesitatingly held up Pastor Royce as a role model for sound moral character? And over the past five and a half weeks, since Whit had broken the news about the dismissals, hadn't Pastor Royce repeatedly and blatantly lied to them? The room seemed to slow down around him, and he suddenly wanted nothing more than to be home with Jill and the boys, the campaign a distant memory. He shuddered as he thought of what the pastor had done, not only to Meck and Whit and the campaign, but to himself as well. Psalms 101:7 said, *He that worketh deceit shall not dwell within my house: he that telleth lies shall not tarry in my sight.* He swallowed hard, knowing he had to press on. With or without Pastor Royce, Meck was still in charge of this campaign. He meant to see it through. Chairman Gauch was watching him expectantly. Meck squared his shoulders.

"The law as it stands now," he said, "demands but nowhere defines the terminology *sound moral character,* and we believe this vagueness is partially responsible for the lax behavior we've seen on the part of teachers throughout our public schools. Let's face it, the current process to determine a prospective teacher's character is to get their self-selected references. I think we all know that anyone can find at least two people to say something good about them. In recent years we've seen an increase in prosecutions for pedophilia, for instance, and we know enough about pedophiles by now to know that many of them are gregarious and engaging people who can even make good teachers. Except, of course, for the despicable things they do behind closed doors. These people can get good character references because they're skilled at keeping their true identities secret. We'd like to weed them out before they ever get near a student. A surprising number of our teachers have also been found to have problems with drugs, alcohol, and gambling. My written testimony contains specific statistics that I trust you can read for yourselves. Recently, as I'm sure you know, teachers in our commonwealth have been discriminating against Christian children, and within the last two months principals and superintendents have seen fit to fire eleven teachers for this religious discrimination. I don't need to tell you that this discrimination is unconstitutional. What House Bill 1298 will do is fill a gap that's been in the law for far too long. By allowing the good people on the board of education to define sound moral character, and put into place a certification process that will weed out every bad seed, our children will be safer and happier in our public schools. I leave you with the words of one of our founding fathers, James Madison, who reminds us that 'We have staked the whole of our political institutions on the capacity of mankind to govern themselves according to the Ten Commandments of God.' This founder's vision of sound moral character has been lost, and 1298 is one small attempt to find it again, in the important realm of our children's education. I strongly urge you to vote in favor of House Bill 1298."

Meck sat back in his chair, amazed at how composed he had sounded. As Whit began to testify, Meck thought again about the two of them going alone together to Washington. Pastor Royce's time was clearly coming to an end. Perhaps a schism had begun in this very room mere moments ago, when Meck had chosen to strip the pastor of his title; didn't new leaders always emerge from a divide? Connie Clough had said it himself when he addressed Meck's boys, suggesting that one day a whole team of Meck men might set America's political agenda. Maybe, Meck thought, glancing around to find Andrew, John, and Ben, and feeling himself gearing up, that day began right now.

Arnie Dengler stood up when Whit was finished with his testimony. Gauch told him he didn't have to stand, and Dengler said he preferred to. Gauch gave him an impatient look, which Dengler seemed not to notice.

"What I want to point out," said Dengler, "is that the flip side of sound moral character is unsound moral character."

He held up the stack of photographs as if raising the paten during the Eucharist.

"I'm not a man to mince words, so I'm just going to *tell it like it is.*"

Meck winced at Dengler's imitation of Meck's radio voice. Dengler chuckled, but Meck refused to acknowledge him. Dengler cleared his throat.

"Simply put, I do not want these people teaching our children."

He held up one photograph in each hand and moved them slowly around for the committee, and then the public, to see. He held them longest as he faced the media. Then he passed the photos to the committee member closest to him.

"Take a good long look," he said, "and tell me you're okay with these people teaching your kids."

He held out more and more photographs. Nearly naked men with oiled torsos wore wild feathered head pieces. A team of hefty shirtless men harnessed like carriage horses, bits tight in their mouths, pulled a two-wheeled cart carrying a muscular young man wielding a whip. Huge men with blond wigs and falsies teetered on high-heeled boots, their tight skirts high above their thighs. Bare-breasted fat women sported shaved heads, tattoos, and facial hair.

Across the room, Ludka grimaced, then pressed her fingers over her mouth, but forced herself not to look away, thinking about Nazi propaganda. Next to her, Tommy's leg shot up and down like a piston. Izaac watched calmly, as if he'd seen it all before. In her peripheral vision, Ludka caught sight of a tuxedo. Numerous members of the chorus were moving to various places around the room. Excited, she nudged Izaac. They exchanged a bright-eyed look of anticipation.

"You see the filth I'm talking about?" said Dengler. "How many of these homosexuals are teaching your children?"

Senator Curtis, a gray-haired woman in a rose-colored suit and pearls, whom Lolek had told them was a friend, interrupted.

"Mr. Dengler, have you ever been to Mardi Gras?"

Dengler froze, a set of photos held out before him.

"It's a simple question, Mr. Dengler. Are you familiar with Mardi Gras?"

Dengler lowered his arms.

"You mean the crazy voodoo shenanigans they get up to in New Orleans every year, all those beads and masks and headdresses?"

He smiled around at the crowd to see who might be with him at finding Mardi Gras crazy.

"Sure, I know about Mardi Gras."

"Did you know, Mr. Dengler, that Mardi Gras has its roots in Christian tradition? That's right. It takes place on the Tuesday before Ash Wednesday, a final celebration before the Lenten season. I can see that surprises you. From the looks of these photographs, I assume they're all taken from the Gay Pride march we have here in Boston every year, isn't that right? That's what I thought. And do you know the history of Gay Pride, Mr. Dengler? It's a celebration of difference, and a public stance against the very kind of discrimination you're practicing here. And just like Mardi Gras, it's deliberately *carnivalesque*. I, myself have marched in the parade, alongside Mayor Menino. That's all, Mr. Dengler; you may proceed."

Tommy's leg went still. He smiled at Ludka with shining eyes.

"You have marched in this parade?" she asked.

Tommy nodded.

"I always wear a cape! I can't get Robert to go, though."

Robert leaned forward and whispered to Ludka.

"It's far too queer for my taste," he said. "I mean, I'm a lawyer!"

Ludka smiled uncertainly.

Dengler cleared his throat, clearly derailed by the senator's line of questioning. He handed the rest of the photographs to the committee, and as he returned to the table, a voice called out from the back of the room.

"I'm a pediatrician, and I'm gay."

Everyone turned to see who had spoken. Ludka couldn't tell who it might have been. Another voice, this time from the other side of the room, called out, "I'm a certified public accountant, and I'm gay." This time Ludka saw the man, one of the singers, a balding man in his seventies with reading glasses hanging from a beaded chain around his neck. And with that the singers proceeded with another type of chorus, one after another calling out their professions at breakneck speed: development director, postmaster, artistic director, tax attorney, investment advisor, graphic

designer, property manager, realtor, architect, psychiatrist, foren-
sic biologist, chiropractor, short-order cook, botanist, veterinary
technician, landscape manager, minister, dentist, climate change
specialist, UPS driver, state senator. Representative Gauch hammered his gavel, but the men didn't stop. The nurse Ludka had
recognized stepped forth and declared himself. Will and Annika
stood up as one and smiled at her as they said in unison, "I am an
artist, and I am gay."

When Ludka had finally been cleared for entry to work with
Żegota, her first official meeting had begun with code names.
Many of those in attendance, including Oskar, had been active
for some time, but new members numbered around twenty, all
of whom needed names. When they'd each quietly chosen their
own, the whole group, old and new, announced themselves one by
one. Now, sitting in this hot room, her throat aching, the hair on
her arms standing on end, hearing the individual resolve of what
added up to an impressive and heartening collective resistance,
Ludka felt exactly as she had in the damp and chilly bowels of St.
John's crypt, declaring to Żegota that her name was Apolonia.

Despite the suffocatingly warm room, she shivered. She had
witnessed enough during the war to know that Oskar had never
meant to betray her parents, that he had honestly believed he
could withstand the tortures of Pawiak. Divulging their names
had not brought an end to his torment, rather it had signaled the
beginning of the guilt-riddled life he had ended up living. *There
but for the grace of God*, Ludka thought. She reached for Izaac's
hand, and held on.

Now Chairman Gauch—repeatedly yelling "Order! Order!"—
was standing, but so were a good number of other people. Izaac
suddenly squeezed Ludka's hand, and she followed his gaze to the

other side of the room, where two muscular men stood against the wall, their arms crossed.

"Those are the other men I told you about, from the radio station that day. Danny Kulek's cronies. Clancy is that one, and Blair, I think is the other one."

One of the chorus members was returning to his place in the back of the room. As he passed in front of the men, Clancy threw out his foot and simultaneously slammed the singer across the back, throwing him against the edge of the nearest bench. Ludka heard the crack of contact as the man's body caromed off the bench and smashed onto the floor.

Gauch hammered his gavel. Senator Curtis rushed out one of the private exits. Members of the chorus went to the man's aid, while others whipped out their cell phones. Clancy and Blair pushed their way to the nearest exit. Reporters and their teams broke like an impeded river into two branches that flooded the front and back aisles of the room as they raced to get closer to the scene. Senator Curtis reentered the room with two state troopers, and people began to shout and point to where Clancy and Blair struggled to get through the door. One of the troopers went after him, while the other checked the fallen singer and used his shoulder radio to call for an ambulance. And then he turned to the room and called for calm.

# 34

# Testimony

The hearing droned on without further incident. One after another people testified, and the temperature rose, and members of the crowd wandered restlessly in and out of the room. At one point Ludka, whose sitting bones ached, whose head hurt from dehydration, and whose astonishment at the hateful testimony had finally given way to a determined understanding and anger, had fallen asleep. She'd been jolted awake when her head bobbed up hard. Izaac looked on her with sympathy and asked Tommy to go fetch them all some water.

Finally, the list of those testifying in favor of the bill had been exhausted, and Tommy and Robert, and Izaac, Marta, and Frank had all just spoken, testimony that moved Ludka in much the same way the chorus had. Lolek had come in earlier, just as they were about to testify, but the chairman had held up a hand to stop them when he saw Lolek.

"The chairman recognizes the good senator from Hampshire, President Zeilonka. As I've mentioned before, our custom is to

allow elected officials to speak at will, given their other responsi-
bilities in the building. Mr. President?"

"Thank you, Mr. Chairman, but I defer to those already standing to testify. It's far more important that you hear from my
family than it is to hear from me. I'm happy to wait until they're
done."

Lolek had been rewarded with smiles from both Tommy and
Marta, and now they smiled again as they returned to their seats.
Lolek went alone to the front of the room. He unbuttoned his suit
coat and sat down. Ludka couldn't get over how broad he was,
how heavy he'd become, how even now his hair was the same
unkempt mess it had been when he was born. Every member of
the committee had their eyes on him.

"Mr. Chairman, members of the committee, my name is Lolek
Zeilonka and I am the state senator representing Hampshire
County. I'm here to strongly urge you to vote against House Bill
1298, and I'll tell you precisely why. The folks here on my right who
have testified in favor of this bill have stressed the protection of
their children and their children's right to free speech and religion.
They have suggested that only by allowing the board of education
to define sound moral character will the problem of bad teachers be resolved. They have further suggested that modeling the
definition on Christian principles and the Ten Commandments
would be the perfect place to start."

Ludka and Izaac simultaneously reached for each other's
hands. "Our boy," Izaac mouthed. Ludka's throat grew tight.

"I believe, however," said Lolek, "that we need look no further
than the people who are behind this bill to understand what's
wrong with it. If you see who filed the bill, and the legislators
who signed on, you'll notice that every one of them is somehow

affiliated with the Hampshire Redeemer Fellowship or one of its nine branches around the state."

"Ten!" someone called out.

"Ten branches around the state," said Lolek. "Now. On the face of this there's nothing wrong with that. In fact, there's a case to be made that this kind of show is laudable, a perfect example of democracy in action. There's only one problem. Every one of them is homophobic. It's a free country, you might say. People are entitled to their opinions, and that's true. But some of them have been motivated by their homophobia to break our laws. Some of them are directly responsible for the violence you've both witnessed and heard about today. All you have to do is listen to Pastor Royce Leonard's sermon from this past Sunday to understand he's been encouraging violence. He's smart, though. He never comes right out and condones the violence. But I have it on good authority, from someone who's close to him, that it will be worth our effort to investigate him in relation to the assault on my son, the property damage in our district, and the arson at the house I grew up in, committed while my parents and my son and his husband were sleeping inside."

The crowd erupted with protests and speculation. Pastor Royce glared over at Meck, who stared straight ahead, his jaw muscle flexing. Pastor Royce bent down to retrieve his coat and slid out of the bench.

"Not true, not true," he said loudly. For a moment he stood awkwardly, as if trying to decide whether to stay or go, and then he pushed into a tight spot next to Ben and John, who stood against the wall. Meck called out to them.

"Come away from there, boys."

Whit slid out of the bench to let the boys sit next to their father, and then slid back in.

Ludka, who'd been listening carefully to Lolek, thinking of Sophie and Ashley and the fire, did not at first register the fact that Lolek had referred to Robert as Tommy's husband. When she did, she turned first to Izaac, who was glaring at the pastor, and then to Tommy, who met her scrutiny with a sheepish expression.

"I should have told you, Babcia," he whispered. "We should have told all of you."

Ludka imagined Tommy and Robert standing on the altar at St. Hedwig's, Father Skurski performing the ceremony, and to her surprise, perhaps because of her utter exhaustion, perhaps because she desperately loved these two young men, she began to laugh. Tommy looked at her with astonishment and smiled uncertainly, then fully. Izaac told her to hush. The bench shook with her repressed laughter. Lolek glanced around before continuing.

"What does this have to do with our board of education defining sound moral values? I'll tell you. The majority of members currently sitting on the board are also members of the Hampshire Redeemer Fellowship, encouraged to lobby the governor for those appointments by none other than Pastor Royce Leonard. So I ask you, members of the committee. Are these the sorts of people you want defining sound moral character?"

Ludka's mouth was suddenly dry, and her heart began to hammer as she realized that she wanted to testify after all.

"I'll leave you with that thought, and ask you again: give this bill your vote of *ought not to pass* and nip this discrimination in the bud, before it becomes institutionalized. And lest you think I'm overreacting to a few bad apples, allow me to share with you this quote, delivered just three years ago by the Nigerian ambassador to the United Nations, Joseph Ayalogu. He said, and I quote, 'The notion that executions for offences such as homosexuality and lesbianism are excessive is judgmental rather than objective. What may be seen by some as disproportional penalty in such serious offences and odious conduct may be seen by others as appropriate and just punishment.'

"This, ladies and gentlemen of the committee, is what happens when homophobia is allowed to take hold. Again, do not let this bill out of committee. Thank you."

Ludka stood up. Izaac, alarmed, asked her if she was okay.

"Żydzi Wszy!" she cried, shaking her fist. "Jews! Lice!"

Every head in the room turned. Chairman Gauch gave a look as if to say "oh no, not again." Ludka, holding tight to the back of the bench in front of her, shooed Izaac, telling him she wanted to get out.

"You're not on the list, kochanie."

To Gauch she said, "I must give the testimony."

Gauch peered in confusion at his list, and Lolek approached him and spoke to him quietly. Ludka swayed at the end of the bench, holding on to Izaac.

"The chair recognizes Professor Zeilonka."

Lolek hurried back and offered Ludka his arm. She took it. Together they made their way to the table. Lolek pulled out a chair. Ludka's knees, still bruised from her frantic crawl across the living room floor, protested as she lowered herself into the hard chair. Now that she was here, she wondered what she might say.

"State your name," Lolek said quietly as he sat down beside her.

Ludka frowned.

"All day I have been listening, Lolek."

Lolek held up a hand by way of apology and sat back in his chair. Ludka sat as tall as she could, greeted the committee and stated her name.

"Already you all think I am ridiculous old woman, shouting out about Jews and lice. You are right that I am old."

At this, people laughed.

"Already I am oldest person in this room, followed only by your former attorney general, my husband, Izaac Rosenberg. And this means that I have seen more than any of you. I do not call out this Żydzi Wszy—which is Polish for Jews and lice—for no reason. I call it out because for seventy years I have tried to forget this terrible stereotype, this derogation plastered on posters all over Warsaw, where I lived during Holocaust. My husband is a Jew, and his father, like my grandson, was fired from his teaching job because of who he was, not because of how he taught. Nazi decree was to blame. In war, I was rescuer of Jews, including your attorney general. Now must I become rescuer of gays, of my grandson and his . . . husband? Do not make me do this. I am old woman only, with far better things to do."

Again, people laughed.

"But this I will do if it needs to be done. I admit that I did not want to see the truth of this homophobia. I did not want to believe that such things can happen in America. But then my grandson was attacked. My house set on fire. And I am not glad for that beautiful singer today who got hurt, and I pray he recovers swiftly—but I am glad that you have all been witness. It is the wake-up call to all of you. This is not trifle! The Holocaust did not begin with the gassing of the Jews at camps. The Holocaust began here."

She struggled back to her feet. She pressed her hand over her heart, and turned a circle so everyone could see.

"The Holocaust began in hearts of people. As soon as you go and say 'that Jew,' it has begun. That is where it starts. That is the beginning. Today I hear the vulgar terms, so many of them, used to describe my grandson, and I think Żydzi Wszy, I think it has begun. Today I ask you, what is equivalent of *Mein Kampf*? This book Hitler wrote was explicit—*explicit!* —about what he would do to Jews. No one then could believe such nonsense. Today you can read same terrifying plans on web, directed at my Tommy and my Robert, and all those others who testified today with the courage. Do not overlook what is obvious. This bill, this flimsy piece of paper, carries mighty words. I am telling you, this is where it begins. You must not pass this bill. That is all."

Her heart hammering, Ludka reached blindly for Lolek, who quickly stood and took her arm. Later, she wouldn't remember walking back to the bench, or shaking Will's hand as she passed by, or retaking her place, or hearing what Izaac and Tommy and Robert said by way of thanks.

When Ludka finally settled down, when her heart was back to normal, the nurses had gone up to testify, and she was holding Izaac's hand. She let go and bent over to retrieve her bag. Inside the bag she pulled out her scarf and immediately found what she needed. With the exception of pushing past it for some other item, she hadn't touched the new sketchbook since Director Mandelbaum had presented it to her, *for happier times*, he had said. She retrieved a pencil. She opened the cover to the first unsullied page. Next to her, Izaac watched from the corner of his eye, holding his breath. He thought of the crumpled sketch he'd found in the recycling bin, of the blond boy from the Westboro Baptist Church. He'd smoothed it out and tucked it into Ludka's book on American collectors of Polish art, thinking he'd know when the time was right to retrieve it.

Ludka stared at the blank page. She closed her eyes. She smelled

Izaac's warm corduroy jacket, her own stale breath, and a waft of saccharine aftershave followed by someone's sharp body odor. She could sketch the broken window and the brick, the threatening note under the rock, the angry graffiti on Tommy's house. She could draw the blazing curtains and the Black Madonna, and Izaac crumpled on the floor. She could draw her own sliced hand, and the smeared blood on the back of the Chopin. She could sketch Warren Meck and the man who'd fired Tommy, and the bedraggled pastor as he'd stood outside his church, and the singer being hit. She could sketch Tommy wilting into Robert's arms, or Kulek holding him fast, or the Steri-Strip across his brow. She remembered how in the hospital she'd thought through a sketch of Sophie and Ashley with the Duda-Gracz, and that's when she knew to begin at the beginning, to capture that moment in front of the Roslan she had nearly forgotten, that moment when Ashley laid her hand on Sophie's shoulder, when the two of them had instinctively joined forces. In an instant she saw the blank page filled, Roslan's *Prelude, 1939* in the background, Will kneeling at the street busker's feet. And in the foreground, seen from behind as she sat on the tufted black leather bench, shawl wrapped tightly around her shoulders, Ludka herself, bearing witness to it all. Ludka opened her eyes, touched the pencil to the page, and began.

# Acknowledgments

A writer is never alone, and many people have supported me as I have written this novel. Every word has been buoyed by your support, and I am continuously, deeply grateful.

I'm indebted to the generosity of the Elizabeth George Foundation—their research grant came at a time when I sorely needed a boost, and the novel is immeasurably better because of the primary research I was able to conduct. The United States Holocaust Memorial Museum in Washington, DC, has an incredible archive, and I spent two weeks there, watching interviews of Polish Holocaust survivors, collected and preserved by the USC Shoah Foundation, as well as poring through countless collections of Holocaust art. I also spent a month in Poland, in Warsaw—on Ulica Piwna in Ludka and Izaac's old Stare Miasto neighborhood. There I spent time at the Jewish Historical Institute, which contains the Underground Archive of the Warsaw Ghetto, also known as the Ringelblum Archive—I was thrilled beyond measure to stand among the items preserved by the brave men and women who worked with

Emmanuel Ringelblum to ensure that the story of the Warsaw Ghetto would never be forgotten.

I am grateful on a daily basis for the Antioch University MFA in Creative Writing Program—for the amazing education I received, the lifelong friends I developed, and the extended, diverse community to which I will always happily belong.

Special thanks go to the team at She Writes Press and SparkPoint Studio, for blazing a trail that I'm proud and honored to walk upon. Thanks also to the She Writes Press community of authors—trailblazers, all!

I appreciate Edite Kroll, who stepped in as my literary agent at a crucial moment, Susan T. Landry for her keen editorial eye, Jim Tierney for telling me what life as an attorney general would really be like for Izaac Rosenberg, and Urszula Humienik-Dworakowska, who dusted off my poor Polish translations (remaining errors are mine).

For the most important gift one can give a writer—the gift of time—I thank the AIM/Hatchfund and the Maine Arts Commission, and this long list of wonderful folks, who came forward to support me when I needed them most: Charlotte Agell, John Bak, Collista Bejjani, Tony Belisle, Paula Berardinelli, Suzy Laurendeau Bigelow, Charlie Borden, Joanne Bourbeau, Dan Bouvier, Shaktima Brien, David Brightman, Ebba Brooks, Brenda Buchanan, Pat Chanterelle, Michael Culliton, Peggy Cunniff, Jim Dwyer, Ellen Fenner, Mike Flanigan, Mary Lee Fowler, Elizabeth Garber, Mark Geffen, Jennifer Genest, Dave Georgis, Lowell Gerber, Caryn Ginsberg, Darlene Goetzman, Che Green, Cheryl Hamilton, Lisa Hammer, Nancy Harding, James Hayman, Graham Haynes, Kara Holmquist, Tara Ison, Rene Jalbert, Alec Koumjian, Kelly Kraemer, Scott Kraft, Lily King, Emily

Laurendeau, Bob and Amy Ledwell, Ellen Leone, Christine Little, Carter Luke, Sibyl Masquelier, Katherine Mayfield, Maureen McLellan, Rich McLellan, Julie Morris, Laurie Monty, Shawn Monty, Barbara Nicolazzo, Joel Olicker, Larry Paulhus, Steve Pogson, Ric Plaisance, William Rogers, Vicki Ross, Laura Saba, Irving Sager, Tony Sager, Christine Salem, Kathy Savesky, Suzanne Strempek Shea, Lee Smith, Steven Snelling, Cortney Stanley, Sherry Blake Stanley, Barb and John Stolz, Andrea Tate, Lise Thorup, Joyce Tischler, Hillary Twining, Jane Vella, Brit Vitalius, Stephen Wallace, Zoe Weil, and Emily Weiss.

Second only to time is the gift of solitary space in which to write, and I am indebted to Margaret Broucek and Tracy St. Pierre for their lovely cabin, Tony Sager for year after year in Wellfleet (my all-time favorite place to write), Natasha Yakovlev for #37 (where breakthroughs happen), and Bert Troughton for "The Shed," where I most happily and gratefully spend my every day.

For early reading and keen observations that improved the manuscript, thanks go to Margaret Broucek, Susan Dempsey, Sue Digeser and her book group (you finally get to read the ending), Catherine Gentile, Silke Georgi, Andrew Gouse, Kathy Johnson, Mary Plouffe, Pat Reilly, Ken Shapiro, and Bert Troughton.

Mary Plouffe, an admirable writer, has been a stalwart writing companion, special "psychological advisor" and dear friend. Ken Shapiro gave crucial support, accompanied me through the streets of Warsaw, and never fails to challenge me in scintillating and witty conversation. Jim Lapierre came through at a critical time, and never tired of hearing me talk about the book—his long friendship and endless enthusiasm for my dreams sustains me. Kathy Johnson, lifelong friend, has championed me and this project from its inception, and is as excited as I am to get it out into the world. My sister, Susan Dempsey, is dearer to me than I can say—she has been there for me every step of the way. Matthew Goodman, my dear old friend who has inspired me since the early 1980s with his own impressive writing, is one of my most trusted readers. If Matty says it's good, I trust it's good. Natasha Yakovlev—dearest companion of my days—has read and reread this book in many incarnations, and has been my most steadfast champion; the novel and I are both much improved for her friendship. My mother, Margi Dempsey, and my late father, Chuck Dempsey, taught me to read and adore books, and always encouraged me to follow my heart, no matter where it might take me—I am a writer thanks to them.

Of special note are my dearest Antioch writing companions and friends—Dawna Kemper, Mary Rechner, and Christa Mastrangelo Joyce. For more than ten years we have diligently communicated every single month, supporting each other through absolutely everything, and each of them read this manuscript countless times over the past seven or eight years. I have them to thank for a breakthrough with Warren Meck; "Give him a wife and kids," they said, and they were right. I am the writer I am in large part thanks to them.

Finally, I dedicate this book to Bert Troughton, who knows all there is to know and loves me still. My writing life has forced her to repeatedly stretch far beyond her own comfort zone, and I am eternally grateful for her willingness to accompany me on this journey. You are my one good thing, Sweetie.

# About the Author

© Greta Rybus

N ew England native Joan Dempsey received an MFA and teaching certificate in creative writing from Antioch University, Los Angeles. Her writing has been published in the *Adirondack Review, Alligator Juniper, Obsidian: Literature of the African Diaspora,* and *Plenitude Magazine,* and aired on National Public Radio. Dempsey was the recipient of a significant research grant from the Elizabeth George Foundation for her work on *This Is How It Begins.* She lives in Maine with her partner, Bert Troughton, and their family of animals. Find her online at www. joandempsey.com.

# Reader's Guide

## Questions for Discussion

1. At the heart of *This Is How It Begins* lies the theme of empathy—the ability to share someone else's feelings. At what key moments in the novel do you see empathy in action, either from the characters themselves, or in the way the author portrays the characters? Why are these moments so important?

2. As you read, when did you yourself feel empathy? Who did you feel it for, and why? Were you at all surprised by your feelings?

3. Warren Meck and Izaac Rosenberg demonstrate mutual respect for one another. What is it that allows them each to feel such respect, despite their differences?

4. In the final chapter, Ludka testifies before the legislative committee, and one of the things she says is "The Holocaust began in hearts of people. As soon as you go and say 'that Jew,' it has begun. That is where it starts.

That is the beginning." Name-calling dehumanization, bullying, ridicule, and slurs are all early behaviors that, if left unchecked, can develop into discrimination, bias-motivated violence, and—ultimately—genocide. Where in the novel do you see these behaviors? From whom?

5. Violent assaults, including arson, play an important role in this novel. What happened as a result of those actions? What do you think those perpetrating the violence hoped to gain? Did they or didn't they succeed?

6. In the final chapter, Ludka decides to testify, and also to sketch, to bear witness once again to the rise of hatred, as she did during WWII. What prompted her decision—what does testifying and sketching indicate about how Ludka has changed?

7. The author takes care not to directly compare the discrimination in her story with the Holocaust. Why do you think she made that choice?

8. Meck and Ludka both face crushing blows when they discover they've been betrayed by the people closest to them—Pastor Royce, and Oskar, respectively. How are these betrayals important to the plot?

9. Think about the myriad artworks in the novel—at the Baldwin Museum, in Ludka and Izaac's home, at the State House, at the Jewish Historical Institute, and in Oskar's studio. Why do you think art is so central? What role does art play?

10. What secrets are the characters keeping from each other,

and what motivates them to keep those secrets? What happens when each secret is revealed? What might have been different in the lives of the characters had each secret been revealed earlier?

11. Why do you think Ludka hoarded the Chopin portrait over all those years? And why do you think Izaac secreted his father's watch? Why didn't they tell each other about these items? What do these objects represent?

12. Warren Meck wants to ensure that Christian kids can speak about their sincerely held religious beliefs, and those supporting Tommy and the other teachers who were fired want to ensure that this religious speech does not contribute to homophobia or incite discrimination against the LGBTQ community. Do you think these two competing rights can peacefully coexist in our American democracy? How might we achieve this?

13. The two sides in this novel—the progressive left and the conservative Christian right—*each* contain a political spectrum that ranges from liberal to conservative. How does the author show each of these spectrums on both sides? What do you make of this?

14. Participatory democracy is on full display in this novel. Think about all the ways in which the characters engage politically. How effective or ineffective do you think they are? What does this tell you about democracy in general?

15. What does how fathers are portrayed in the novel—in both minor and major roles—say about fatherhood?

# Books I Found Helpful

## On Art

Blatter, Janet and Sybil Milton, *Art of the Holocaust,* The Rutledge Press, New York, 1981

Czapliński, Czesław, *Polish Art Collections in America,* Fundacja Dobrej Książki, 2005

Edsel, Robert M., *The Monuments Men: Allied Heroes, Nazi Thieves, and the Greatest Treasure Hunt in History,* Center Street, New York, Boston, Nashville, 2009

## On the Christian Culture War

Alexander-Moegerle, Gil, *James Dobson's War on America,* Prometheus Books, Amherst, NY, 1997

Gilgoff, Dan, *The Jesus Machine: How James Dobson, Focus on the Family, and Evangelical America Are Winning the Culture War,* St. Martin's Griffin, New York, 2008

Goldberg, Michelle, *Kingdom Coming: The Rise of Christian Nationalism,* W.W. Norton & Company, New York and London, 2006

Harris, Sam, *The End of Faith: Religion, Terror, and the Future of Reason,* W.W. Norton & Company, New York and London, 2005

Hedges, Chris, *American Fascists: The Christian Right and the War on America,* Free Press, New York, London, Toronto, Sydney, 2006

O'Reilly, Bill, *Culture Warrior*, Broadway Books, New York, 2006

Sheldon, Rev. Louis P., *The Agenda: The Homosexual Plan to Change America*, FrontLine, Lake Mary, FL, 2005

## On Human Nature

Block, Gay and Malka Drucker, *Rescuers: Portraits of Moral Courage in the Holocaust*, Holmes & Meier Publishers, Inc., New York and London, 1992

Fogelman, Eva, *Conscience & Courage: Rescuers of Jews During the Holocaust*, Anchor Books, New York, 1994

Tec, Nechama, *When Light Pierced the Darkness: Christian Rescue of Jews in Nazi-Occupied Poland*, Oxford University Press, New York and Oxford, 1986

Zimbardo, Philip, *The Lucifer Effect: Understanding How Good People Turn Evil*, Random House Trade Paperbacks, New York, 2007

## On Warsaw During WWII

Ackerman, Diane, *The Zookeeper's Wife: A War Story*, W.W. Norton & Company, Inc., New York, 2007

Grynberg, Michał, Ed., Philip Boehm, translator, *Words to Outlive Us: Eyewitness Accounts from the Warsaw Ghetto*, Picador, New York, 2003

Gutman, Israel, *Resistance: The Warsaw Ghetto Uprising*, Houghton Mifflin Company, Boston and New York, 1994

Ringelblum, Emmanuel, edited by Jacob Sloan, *Notes from the Warsaw Ghetto*, iBooks, Inc., New York, 2006

Tomaszewski, Irene and Tecia Werbowski, *Żegota: The Council for Aid to Jews in Occupied Poland 1942–45,* Price-Patterson Ltd., Montreal, Quebec, Canada, 1999

# SELECTED TITLES FROM SHE WRITES PRESS

She Writes Press is an independent publishing company
founded to serve women writers everywhere.
Visit us at www.shewritespress.com.

*In a Silent Way* by Mary Jo Hetzel $16.95, 978-1-63152-135-5
When Jeanna Kendall—a young white teacher at a progressive urban school—becomes involved with a community activist group, she finds herself grappling with issues of racism, sexism, and oppression of various shades in both her professional and personal life.

*Again and Again* by Ellen Bravo $16.95, 978-1-63152-939-9
When the man who raped her roommate in college becomes a Senate candidate, women's rights leader Deborah Borenstein must make a choice—one that could determine control of the Senate, the course of a friendship, and the fate of a marriage.

*Peregrine Island* by Diane B. Saxton $16.95, 978-1-63152-151-5
The Peregrine family's lives are turned upside-down one summer when so-called "art experts" appear on the doorstep of their Connecticut island home to appraise a favorite heirloom paint-ing—and incriminating papers are discovered behind the painting in question.

*Shelter Us* by Laura Diamond $16.95, 978-1-63152-970-2
Lawyer-turned-stay-at-home-mom Sarah Shaw is still struggling to find a steady happiness after the death of her infant daughter when she meets a young homeless mother and toddler she can't get out of her mind—and becomes determined to rescue them.

*The Rooms Are Filled* by Jessica Null Vealitzek $16.95, 978-1-938314-58-2
The coming-of-age story of two outcasts—a nine-year-old boy who just lost his father, and a closeted young woman—brought together by circumstance.

*What is Found, What is Lost* by Anne Leigh Parrish
$16.95, 978-1-938314-95-7
After her husband passes away, a series of family crises forces Freddie, a woman raised on religion, to confront long-held questions about her faith.